Thea swallowed and surveyed the room for a glass of water. Her gaze went from St. James, to the table and chair, to the bed.

Hmm . . . there seemed to be something missing. And it wasn't the water.

As he stood, her attention drifted back to the bed. "Where do you plan to sleep?"

"In that bed."

Her brow furrowed as she slid a glance to him. "And where will I sleep?"

"With me, of course." His matter-of-fact delivery did nothing to quell the sudden jump of her pulse as he casually untied his cravat. "I can hardly trust you alone. But fear not, there will be no improper advances. You will be beneath the coverlet. I will be on top of it with a bolster pillow wedged between us. I presume that would be preferable to being tied to that chair?"

"*Tied to the—*" Her mouth snapped shut as she stared at the length of black silk he absently tossed onto the table. If she required further proof that he found her conversation utterly boring and saw her as little more than a nuisance, she certainly had it. "How magnanimous of you."

Also by Vivienne Lorret

The Liars' Club
IT HAD TO BE A DUKE
THE TROUBLE WITH INVENTING A VISCOUNT

The Mating Habits of Scoundrels Series
LORD HOLT TAKES A BRIDE
MY KIND OF EARL • THE WRONG MARQUESS
HOW TO STEAL A SCOUNDREL'S HEART
NEVER SEDUCE A DUKE

The Misadventures in Matchmaking Series
HOW TO FORGET A DUKE
TEN KISSES TO SCANDAL • THE ROGUE TO RUIN

The Season's Original Series
"The Duke's Christmas Wish" (in
ALL I WANT FOR CHRISTMAS IS A DUKE
and A CHRISTMAS TO REMEMBER)
THE DEBUTANTE IS MINE • THIS EARL IS ON FIRE
WHEN A MARQUESS LOVES A WOMAN
JUST ANOTHER VISCOUNT IN LOVE (novella)

The Rakes of Fallow Hall Series
THE ELUSIVE LORD EVERHART
THE DEVILISH MR. DANVERS
THE MADDENING LORD MONTWOOD

The Wallflower Wedding Series
TEMPTING MR. WEATHERSTONE (novella)
DARING MISS DANVERS
WINNING MISS WAKEFIELD
FINDING MISS MCFARLAND

This MUCH Is *True*

THE LIARS' CLUB

VIVIENNE LORRET

AVON

An Imprint of HarperCollinsPublishers

THIS MUCH IS TRUE. Copyright © 2025 by Vivienne Lorret. All rights reserved. Printed in the United States of America. No part of this book may be used or reproduced in any manner whatsoever without written permission except in the case of brief quotations embodied in critical articles and reviews. For information, address HarperCollins Publishers, 195 Broadway, New York, NY 10007.

First Avon Books mass market printing: June 2025

Print Edition ISBN: 978-0-06-335250-6
Digital Edition ISBN: 978-0-06-335251-3

Cover design by Amy Halperin
Cover illustration by Judy York
Cover images © iStock/Getty Images

FIRST EDITION

25 26 27 28 29 BVGM 10 9 8 7 6 5 4 3 2 1

For my readers.

Thank you.

As soon as you trust yourself, you will know how to live.

—Johann Wolfgang von Goethe

This MUCH Is True

Chapter One

༄༅

ALTHEA HARTLEY DIDN'T need a miracle. Only the desperate *needed* a miracle. And she wasn't desperate.

Well . . . not entirely.

Regardless, it wasn't as though she were asking for a biblical, survive the next plague sort of miracle. Just a smallish, rainy morning in London sort. Half a miracle, really.

Pausing just outside the shop front of her favorite stationers, she dragged in a stalwart breath that left no room for doubt. This would do the trick. It had to.

When her thready exhale collected in a brief, tenuous fog before a biting April breeze carried it away, she refused to acknowledge it. Instead, she reached out and opened the door.

A bell jingled overhead as a waft of achingly familiar scents filled her nostrils. The mélange of sweet paper, rich leather, sharp ink and a hint of pipe tobacco had never failed her. She'd always been able to depend upon the divine fragrance to make her scalp tingle in a frisson of anticipation, the sensation sprinting down her arms and to the tips of her fingers as if with some ancient calling. The same calling that had inspired the first Egyptians, Greeks and Romans to chisel away at rock—the need to tell a story.

That need ran through her veins, too. It had been with her all her life.

At least, until recently. Now it seemed that all the words

that used to flow as freely as the blood in her veins had dried up. Much like her heart.

But she wasn't going to think about that.

All that mattered was that she'd returned to London for another Season and everything would be different this time.

Squaring her shoulders, she took two resolute steps into the shop, ready for her miracle.

Let the tingling begin!

Yet, as the beveled glass door closed behind her and the bell offered a discordant *plink*, all she felt was a cold plop of rain falling from the brim of her bonnet to the tip of her nose.

Then again, it was still morning and far too early to give up hope. Besides, perhaps the Office of Celestial Intervention had yet to open. After all, who knew if Heaven was on London time? Therefore, she was willing to give her miracle a few more minutes.

Fife's Feathered Quill was a little shop. Unlike other stationers, Mr. Fife was not a bookseller as well. His specialty, he often said, was paper and ink. Simple as that.

The narrow space was flanked by walls of towering walnut shelves filled with an array of boxes of assorted sizes that housed every type of paper, ink and writing implement imaginable. Along the far wall, which was a mere seven steps from the door, was a glass display case of tortoiseshell pens, feathered quills with scroll-etched nibs, and embossed silver letter knives.

She'd found the cozy shop purely by accident during her first Season, two years ago. One day, after leaving her modiste, she'd taken a wrong turn down a winding alley. Well, several wrong turns actually. Countess Broadbent—an old family friend who was her sponsor and chaperone—had been quite vexed with her at the time and accused her of having the directional wherewithal of dandelion fluff.

Sadly, she wasn't incorrect.

Be that as it may, Thea often considered her own tendency to end up not quite in the location she'd set out for as an opportunity for happenstance. As everyone knew, happenstance was the gateway to creativity.

That day it had led her here. And, she'd hoped, one step closer to realizing her dream of writing a play for the London stage.

The reminder sent a twinge to the center of her chest.

She chose to ignore it. And why shouldn't she? In the past year she'd become exceptional at ignoring whatever plagued her.

Surely, taking such pains to spare her family and acquaintances from a veritable tidal wave of misery ought to earn her some favor in the heavens.

She cast an expectant look up to the tin ceiling. But the tick-tocking from the pendulum clock in the corner continued on without even a snick of a miracle. Honestly, had the celestial being assigned to dole out favors to the deserving fallen asleep at his post?

Wake up, you dolt!

The entire purpose of coming back to London to endure a third Season of idle chitchat with dullards and popinjays was to reclaim what she'd lost. Her last hope was to find it here. And yet, her creative spark still wasn't sparking.

Her heavy sigh filled the empty shop as she trudged toward the back.

Stopping at the glass case, she glanced down to a selection of ornate silver letter knives. Dimly, she wondered if she were to drive the point through the layers of wool, cambric and bone stays between her breasts, would the blade simply sail through the empty husk that used to be her heart? Or was there a kernel of something that remained of her old self that might still bleed?

She also wondered if she was being a trifle melodramatic.

Hmm . . . perhaps. But as the youngest child in a family reared on daily performances of Shakespeare, she could hardly have turned out any other way. Therefore, she blamed her parents.

Besides, how else was she supposed to feel after dragging the corpse of her crushed soul behind her for nearly a year? Her inner Greek Chorus agreed with a solemn nod.

"Why, Miss Hartley, as I live and breathe."

Thea looked up from the knives to find the old shopkeeper emerge from the back room. A bird's nest of wiry silver brows arched over a pair of wizened gray-eyes at the sight of her.

She held out her hand in warm welcome and he clasped it. "Mr. Fife. How good it is to see you again. You are well, I trust?"

"Better now at the sight of my best customer." He patted her hand before he released her, his face creasing like parchment with his smile. "Though, I daresay this is quite the surprise. When you'd disappeared last spring, I thought you'd lost your heart to some dashing gentleman and married. Perhaps to that playwright who accompanied you a time or two?"

Thea swallowed, her throat tight. "No."

"Ah. Then you've returned to take a crack at another Season. Good on you," he said with an encouraging nod. If he noticed a twitch from the corpse on the tiled floor behind her, he was good enough not to mention it. "You're just in time, too, for I received a new shipment of pocket ledgers yesterday."

His brows lifted in expectation. He knew this news had always thrilled her in the past.

Ever since she was a little girl, pockets had been sewn into her day dresses. This practice had begun shortly after her nurse confiscated the stub of a pencil and scrap of foolscap stashed in her stockings one Sunday morning before church services. The nurse declared that only when the vicar began carrying odds and ends on his person could Thea do the same.

Naturally, this brought on a slew of questions. So, in the middle of service, she'd asked what the vicar had beneath his robes.

Even though her parents weren't the sort to become embarrassed—and in truth her father always had a merry chuckle every time someone mentioned the vicar's robes—it was enough to prompt the addition of hidden pockets to all her dresses. That way she'd always had a small ledger on hand whenever inspiration struck.

"Shall I put your usual order together?" Mr. Fife asked.

"Thank you, yes. That would be lovely."

Perhaps if she continued to pretend that everything was as it should be, inspiration might strike again.

As the shopkeeper turned away to assemble her parcel, she glanced once more toward the ceiling. *I'm still waiting.*

She'd had no trouble finding worthy ideas during her first Season. Of course, she'd had to cajole the ever-proper Lady Broadbent into asking their modiste to add pockets to her ball gowns. But she'd succeeded and was prepared for every tingle of creativity.

Her second Season had begun in the same fashion until . . . Well, she didn't want to think about that.

For this third Season, she'd only pressed for two of her gowns to have pockets. Though, she wasn't sure why she'd bothered at all. Moths were more likely to fly out of the plackets than ideas.

There she'd be, midwaltz in a grand ballroom as a flurry of gray winged insects would cloud around her. Then everyone would watch on in horror as the moths—doing what those fools naturally did—would fly to the flicker of candlelit chandeliers and incinerate themselves in acrid puffs of smoke.

Dimly, she wondered if she'd been a moth in a former life. It would explain so much.

"Here we are," Mr. Fife said as he turned back to her, setting the paper-wrapped parcel between them. Twin birds' nests waggled in eager anticipation as he chafed his hands together. "Any new stories to share, hmm?"

This had always been a game of theirs. She would tell him about a play she was developing—which was usually inspired by real episodes of the *ton* behaving outrageously—and he would try to guess the parties involved.

Like her, he enjoyed observing people. For him, it was more for entertainment. For her, she enjoyed the puzzle of it, fascinated to uncover the mystery of what lay beneath the surface of the façade that individuals presented to the rest of society.

Shakespeare had been a master of that. So was London's current famed playwright, Sir Kellum Archer. Who, for a time, had been the center of her world. She'd even allowed herself to believe . . .

Thea let the thought fade away, unfinished as a blank page.

"Regrettably, no," she said to Mr. Fife with a sad shake of her head. She couldn't admit aloud that she'd been unable to write a word since last year. But when his eyes softened as if he could see through to the truth of the matter, she hastily added, "I haven't been to any soirees yet. In fact, you are the very first notable person I've seen since my arrival."

He was kind enough to pretend to believe her. Patting her hand once more, he said, "Next time, then."

"Next time," she promised.

It wasn't a lie. Not entirely.

He began to walk her to the door, those magnificent brows knitting together in concentration. Then he stopped suddenly and held up a finger. "It just so happens that I might have a story for you."

Willing to accept breadcrumbs of creativity at this point, she faced him.

He glanced over his shoulder as if he feared the quills might pop out of their boxes to eavesdrop, then leaned in to whisper. "The other day a gentleman stumbled inside this very shop, his face pale as a turnip. Without a word, he went to the window and peered out as if he thought someone were following him. And when I greeted him, he nearly jumped out of his fancy buckled shoes. To ease the stranger's mind, I thought to make a quip. So, I said, 'Fear not. I'm hardly a highwayman.' And do you know what he did next?"

She shook her head.

"Shrieked like a kitchen maid over a mouse, then was out the door before the bell could ring." Mr. Fife grinned and hooked his thumbs beneath his lapels. "Well, what do you think? Quite the character, I'd say."

"Indeed," she said and did her best to appear captivated, pasting on a smile.

But oh, how she'd wanted to feel that familiar thrill, that tingle dancing over her scalp and down her spine. She'd wanted her fingertips to itch for the coarse texture of a pencil in her grasp as she filled a ledger with ideas for a new play.

Instead she felt numb, as if every page inside her were covered in a film of wax that no amount of lead or ink could penetrate.

There would be no miracle today. Not even half of one.

Bidding farewell, Thea left the shop. With her, she carried a parcel of six pocket ledgers, three pencils, and the corpse of her withered soul.

To make matters worse, it was raining in earnest and she had no umbrella.

Lady Broadbent wasn't going to be happy with the state of her pelisse. Not to mention, Thea had left the countess in the tea shop around the corner, promising that her jaunt into Fife's wouldn't take more than a minute.

Ducking her head, Thea scuttled down the narrow alley. But with her focus on navigating the larger puddles collecting in the uneven dips of cobblestones, she didn't see the obstacle in her path. Not until her shoulder collided with a solid mass. Hard.

She must have run into an outcropping of the brick wall. A chimney, perhaps. The impact was so jarring, she could have sworn she heard her bones breaking like glass. The force of the collision even spun her around like a one-winged whirligig shaken from a tree . . . and directly into a thick cloud of tobacco smoke.

She coughed, waving a hand in front of her face as a prickle of uncertainty niggled at her.

Before she'd left on her errand, Lady Broadbent had made a point of explaining that the tobacconist was in the opposite direction of the tea shop.

Cupping a hand over the lip of her bonnet, Thea looked up to the dripping sign hanging from a wrought iron bracket. Painted on the wood was a red pipe.

Her inner Greek chorus, which delighted in reminding her of all her failings, chimed in with a derisive *And thus, she had gone the wrong way. Yet again.*

Drat! Turning on her heel, she headed back the way she'd come.

As soon as she reached the mouth of the alley, she paused to look for the tea shop. But just as she peered across the street, her gaze snagged on something. Or someone, rather.

Standing on the pavement beneath a rain-slicked awning was none other than Sir Kellum Archer—the famed playwright, the toast of London, and the man who'd gleefully ripped out her soul and crushed it beneath the heel of his shoe like the butt of a cheroot.

She blinked. It had to be a mistake. He was rumored to

be in Paris, writing his next masterpiece. That was the only reason she'd taken the chance to return to London. So why was he here?

Then she saw the reason.

A woman. A beautiful blonde woman in a red walking costume, tailored to her hourglass figure. The sway of her hips must have been audible, like the beat of a drum, because he turned to watch her approach.

His mouth spread in the same grin that Thea had once thought was reserved only for her. Then the woman threaded her arm through his. A gesture of ownership. And he did nothing to disprove the claim as he gazed adoringly down to her upturned face.

For the woman's sake, Thea hoped she had no other aspirations than to be a sycophant. Kellum could be kind when he was being adored. But Heaven help the woman if she admitted to having dreams of her own.

You, a playwright? An organ grinder's monkey is more entertaining than anything you've written thus far.

Go back to your unremarkable family in your wretched little hamlet, child. Forget about the London stage, just as it forgets all those who lack the talent to leave their mark. You are not even worthy of a footnote.

The memory lodged in Thea's throat, the words like shards of glass, too painful to swallow.

Through the interlacing of carriages passing to and fro, she saw him lift an arm to hail a nearby hackney. The dingy yellow conveyance stopped on the street between them, blocking her view.

It wasn't until Thea saw a folded white handkerchief materialize before her that she realized she was no longer alone on the pavement. Not only that, but she was beneath someone's umbrella. Someone who stood just beyond the frame of her bonnet. A man, likely, considering the size of the black-gloved hand proffering the handkerchief.

"If I may," he said from at least a head above her.

She didn't recognize the low scratch of his voice. A stranger, then. After all, he must have been or else he'd have addressed her by name.

A shiver tightened her scalp, slipping beneath the damp collar of her pelisse. Clearly, she'd been standing in the cold rain for far too long. And, peculiarly, the strong scent of wine surrounded her. But she supposed that was better than the odors that the London streets usually offered.

Accepting the handkerchief, she dabbed at her cheeks and the tip of her nose without turning her head far enough to meet his gaze. An introduction at such a time would only be more embarrassing for her.

"Thank you." When she finished, she held out the slightly used square of linen.

"A token." That large hand gestured with a dismissive wave. "However, if you require further assistance . . ."

Even without looking at him, she sensed that his gaze was also on the hackney that spurred into motion, the wheels crunching against wet cobblestones. "Not unless you have a festering head of cabbage to hurl or a few rotten tomatoes in your pocket."

"In my other coat."

The corner of her mouth twitched at his quick response. "Pity that. Though, I'd actually prefer a henchman for hire or an army of marauders. You wouldn't happen to have them at your disposal, would you?"

"Left them at my flat, I'm afraid."

"Must be terribly crowded."

"You've no idea."

His droll reply had her grinning in earnest. It was her first genuine smile in weeks. Months, even.

She drew in a breath that didn't feel quite as weighted with gloom. "Thank you for coming to my aid. It was a kindness that I will not"—she turned to this stranger, only to find that she was standing alone, the rain collecting on her skin—"forget."

Just as she was about to survey the foot traffic for a glimpse of him, a black-lacquered carriage stopped in front of her. A liveried tiger bounded down from the springboard to open the door and lower the step.

"Honestly, Miss Hartley. I was about to send the hounds," Lady Broadbent chided from the confines, her regal face pinched with disapproval beneath an artful chignon of dove gray hair. "Come along before you catch your death."

Thea moved toward the open door, the rain misting on her face as she searched both directions for a tall figure. But the man wasn't there. Among the few head-bent and hurried pedestrians, none were carrying an umbrella.

Disappointed, she stepped into the carriage. Settling on the bench, she stared down at the handkerchief and the saturated parcel of ledgers in her grasp. Then she smiled again.

For the first time in nearly a year, an idea filled her head with thoughts of a new character. A character so clear in her mind that she might actually be able to open a fresh ledger and write.

He could be anyone, she thought. *Even a highwayman.*

Chapter Two

WHEN JASPER TRUEBLOOD, Viscount St. James, didn't want to be seen, he wasn't. Which likely accounted for the reason Miss Hartley had barreled into him as she'd left the stationers, and the fact that he now smelled like a drunkard on a three-day soak.

His uncle wouldn't be pleased that his prized port had become a piss puddle in a London alley. Then again, even if Jasper had delivered the wine on a velvet ceremonial pillow with a dozen litter bearers to scatter rose petals at the feet of the Earl of Redcliffe, it would not have been enough.

So he put it out of his mind for the moment. Instead, he stared after Miss Hartley's retreating carriage from the shadows.

When he'd spotted her standing on the pavement, he hadn't meant to approach. And surely, if she'd recognized him, she wouldn't have wanted him to either. He wasn't the sort of man with whom debutantes desired an acquaintance.

Even so, there had been something that compelled him to stand by her side. Something that caused him to engage with her as he never did with those in society.

Had it been seeing her face with her complexion so pale as to make raindrops appear almost silver on her skin? The cloud of mist that had hovered in front of her parted lips, their faded pink hue like that of a watercolor disappearing into a canvas? Or the way her dark lashes were so thick they appeared dusted with soot as the dew clung to them?

But no. It had been her eyes, he decided.

Haunted, bewitching, pale blue eyes. They were to blame for him speaking without thought and forgetting to disguise his voice—things he couldn't afford to do. Ever.

His gaze strayed across the street to the vacant space beneath the awning once more. What or who had Miss Hartley seen that had so troubled her?

The answer was unclear.

Besides, whatever had distressed her was none of his concern. At present, ensuring the welfare of his aunt and two cousins, in addition to managing his army of marauders, was all he could deal with while keeping his sanity.

Absently hearing the magpie chatter of maids from the window above him, he reacted on instinct, adjusting the position of his umbrella to redirect the putrid shower from a chamber pot.

As he stepped away from the alcove—successfully avoiding smelling like a drunkard *and* a piss pot—he wondered where the same carefully honed instincts had been when he'd first seen Miss Hartley dashing through the rain. He'd just stood there, stock-still like the addlepated nitwit most of society thought he was.

A frustrated growl rumbled in his throat.

Shoving the encounter aside, he turned in the direction of his flat, calculating the fastest route. A hackney would expedite matters, but he couldn't spare the coin. Therefore, he would walk to Marylebone, change out of this jug-bitten frock coat, then find a way to replace the port before he saw his uncle.

At the beginning of each month, Redcliffe tasked Jasper with fetching a specific vintage of port from the vintner. Even though his uncle paid for the port and was wealthy enough to have it carted to him by way of golden chariot,

he preferred to have his nephew deliver it. Like a supplicant. In turn, he would inspect the bottle with a gem cut-
ter's precision to see if his late sister's only child deserved
a monthly allowance.

Just thinking about it, anger coursed through him, his
long stride eating up the rain-slick pavement as water
leached through the worn soles of his boots.

Jasper hated that he had to go to his uncle like a beggar.
Hated every time he saw that gleam of malicious triumph
in those coal black eyes when he was forced to ask for what
should rightfully be his. Hated that he had to continue this
charade until—

Turning the corner, he stopped short as he spotted a disaster about to unfold.

An old woman leaving the tea shop, stoop-shouldered
beneath a shawl shrouded over her head against the rain,
stepped into the path of a speeding hack. Seeing it an instant too late, she squawked in alarm.

With no time to waste, he darted forward and pulled the
woman onto the pavement, immediately turning himself to
absorb the splash from the wheel hitting a puddle.

"Good gracious! That cab came out of nowhere. You
saved my—" She broke off as she craned her neck to look
up at him. Recognition sharpened her steel gray eyes and
whatever gratitude she might have uttered fell silent. Instead, she pursed her lips as if tasting something sour. "St.
James."

Jasper was used to the reaction.

This time, he had no trouble remembering to disguise
his voice. Constricting his throat, he ensured that his usual
deep timbre came out shallow and airy. And as the rain
dripped down from the brim of his hat to blur the lenses
of his spectacles, he inclined his head. "Lady Abernathy."

The wet wool of his coat tightened over his shoulders
as he bent to retrieve his fallen umbrella, then held it over

her as she primly adjusted the threadbare shawl around her shoulders.

"I was just on my way to the milliner," the dowager viscountess said, her tone defensive, chin wrinkling as she held it high. "I sent my maid ahead for a new hat after the one I was wearing fell to pieces in the rain. Worthless bit of rubbish."

He wasn't sure how to respond, or whether she was talking about the hat or the maid. So he stayed silent. It was always better if he stayed silent.

Then she spared him a sideways glance and offered him the wing of her elbow. "Well, don't just stand there like a big ape."

Any other man might have taken offense, but he'd heard much worse in his twenty-four years. Not only that, but when he saw the tremor in her arm as she held it out, he knew how difficult it must have been for someone as proud as she to ask for assistance, especially from the likes of him.

He responded by shifting the umbrella to his other fist before escorting her across the cobblestones. Though, with him well over six feet and with her barely taller than his biceps, it took some maneuvering to keep the umbrella over her head and not stab himself in the throat. Not only that, but for every one of his steps, she needed four. And for every four of hers, the number of harried curricles and carriages on the street increased, drivers railing curses down on their heads as they swerved past. If that wasn't enough, a veritable river of water and refuse blocked their path to the pavement.

He looked to the right, wondering if they could circumvent it. That was when he caught sight of a coach barreling down on them.

The driver saw them but didn't slow. In fact, there was a hard set to his jaw and in the gimlet eyes shadowed beneath the dripping felt brim of his hat, as if he saw any pedestrian in his path as a challenge to his manhood.

This left Jasper only one option.

"Apologies, my lady," he said, then reached behind her, cupped his hands beneath both of her elbows and lifted her off her feet.

A strangled yawp rose from her throat. Her legs paddled in the air for the two seconds it took him to step over the puddle and set her down.

It wasn't the most delicate or gentlemanly way to treat an elderly woman. But it was either that or be mowed down. And at least he'd managed to avoid being sprayed with any more rank—

Before he could finish the thought, the coach veered closer. The front wheel splashed through the gutter, sending a wave of putrid water in an upward arc . . . that promptly gushed down Jasper's back.

Lady Abernathy turned, her expression livid, her lips parting to rail at him.

Fine, he thought, resigned. It wasn't as if his morning could get any worse.

Then something slithered off the brim of his hat, slopped to his shoulder and then slid down his sleeve. Dimly, he glanced down at the misshapen lump and determined that it was a rat. Or rather, half a rat because the tail end wasn't—

A slurping sound interrupted his thought. Then the rat's other half slid off his hat and plopped to the pavement.

Bloody hell.

And somehow, through all that, he still managed to hold the umbrella over Lady Abernathy's head. But that didn't mean he was expecting a modicum of gratitude.

Clenching his jaw, he looked at her, ready for her castigations.

Instead, her mouth pinched closed and she turned, issuing an impatient sigh. Apparently, *she* was in a hurry and didn't want to be detained by the man who'd just saved her life. Twice.

The insanity of this entire morning nearly made him laugh.

"My lady! My lady!" cried a mousy young woman scurrying toward them on the slick pavement. The maidservant held fast to the dripping straw bonnet on her head, her other hand carrying a hatbox, the side battering against her leg with every other step. "I beg you would forgive me, but the milliner bade me to wait while she drew up a bill of accounts, believing the last two must have been misdirected, and I wasn't certain if—"

"Cease your prattling, stupid girl. Can you not see that it's raining? Well, get me into the coach."

The maid nodded vehemently, color rising to her cheeks.

In her scramble to assist, she lost her bonnet and almost upended the hatbox until Jasper intervened. Without a word, he handed the umbrella to the maid. Taking up the hatbox and the fallen bonnet, he strode to the waiting carriage.

Like his own, it was a small conveyance that had seen better days. Though, as he handed the women inside the worn and musty interior, he felt his brow furrow.

Viscount Abernathy, her ladyship's son, was quite flush in the pocket. He kept a mistress in jewels, silks, furs and a Mayfair townhouse. So why was his mother wearing a threadbare shawl and struggling to pay for a simple hat?

The obvious answer infuriated him.

Women were, all too often, left at the mercy of a male relative who did not look after their best interests. Men who did not shield or protect them. Who thoughtlessly discarded them like rubbish . . . or worse. And if a woman in the winter of her life, no matter how proud or disagreeable, could not depend upon her indolent, spoiled progeny to see to her welfare, then who?

Feeling Lady Abernathy's scrutiny on him, he knew she was likely worried that he might spread word about her strained finances. He'd learned long ago that it was best to appear less than astute in such circumstances.

It wasn't a difficult act to perform. He'd been pretending to be an addlepated clod for years. So, in keeping with his usual performances, he boggled the umbrella that the maid returned to him. Considering his size—*big ape* and all—it was always easy to look clumsy. He even went so far as to turn the contraption inside out.

When he heard the dowager viscountess sigh as she shook her head, he knew he'd performed well. Setting his hand on the door, he was just about to close it when—

"Is my nephew bothering you, Beatrice?"

Jasper stiffened. The imperious sound of his uncle's voice lashed across every nerve along his spine. Apparently, his theatrics had gained the notice of an unintended party.

And he thought this morning couldn't get any worse.

Seeing the earl approach, Lady Abernathy's wizened countenance lifted in a smile. "Redcliffe. Such a lovely surprise. What brings you out on such a dreary morning?"

"My solicitor is nearby," he said, bowing over the hand she proffered. Releasing it, he stepped back and posed with his own hand on the head of his walking stick as his ever-nervous secretary, Mr. Entwistle, held an umbrella over his lordship's head. "And fortunate, too, for I witnessed my nephew making a nuisance of himself. Pray, accept my humble apologies in his stead."

"No need to apologize. St. James was kind enough to"—her lips puckered sourly as if she held a lemon wedge between her teeth—"assist me across the street."

"The fact that you survived the episode so well speaks to your unflappability, *and* all of it without a hair out of place on your beautiful head."

"You flatter me, sir. Though you must take credit, for I am certain that any display of chivalry he had learned was by your example."

Redcliffe's fingers lifted in a dismissive wave. "One does what one can with such raw material."

"So true," she agreed, seemingly oblivious to the fact that Jasper was standing right there. He was literally beside the open door of her carriage, waiting to close it so she could drive off. "You have done all you could for your sister's child. Far more than most, I'm sure. You are to be commended for your efforts."

Redcliffe humbly inclined his head.

Appearing the saint in front of others was one of the devil's greatest charades. Few knew what lay beneath the façade of chiseled aristocratic features, a head full of dark hair barely threaded with silver, a trim physique even for someone approaching his fiftieth year. And, of course, there was his immense wealth.

Men wanted to be him. Women threw themselves at him. And yet, it was never enough.

Redcliffe always wanted more. He especially wanted whatever someone told him he couldn't have. And that made him dangerous.

No one knew that better than Jasper.

"Well, only a barbarian would keep such a delicate bloom out in this weather. So, I shall bid you adieu, Beatrice, and promise to pay a call on you later this week."

"I will hold you to that." She tutted fondly as he bowed over her hand once more.

Then the earl closed the carriage door and touched the faceted handle of his walking stick to the brim of his hat. He waited until the driver set off before starting in on Jasper. His uncle was nothing if not predictable.

Redcliffe regarded the broken umbrella with an imperious sneer. "I see that contraption taxed your intellect."

"It was an accident. My hand slipped."

"'It wath an ac-th-ident,'" Redcliffe mocked in a high-pitched voice, snickering at the lisp that Jasper had developed in childhood after the death of his father. It had been a constant source of derision *and* amusement for Uncle Silas.

Of course, after countless elocution lessons in his youth, Jasper had rid himself of the tendency. It then became a choice to continue the lisp when in society, in addition to speaking in a higher tone. Both were part of a necessary disguise.

If he'd learned anything from his uncle, it was how to expertly conceal one's true self from others. It was the only way to play the game.

There must have been some spark of rebellion in his gaze because his uncle abruptly narrowed his eyes. He took a step toward him, his fist wrapped around the shaft of his walking stick. But Jasper knew Redcliffe would never strike him in public. In truth, he was ever the saintly put-upon uncle when among his peers.

Instead, the earl sniffed, his lip curling with distaste. "Where's my port, buffoon?"

"I'm afraid I dropped it."

As expected, his uncle's temper flared in a slash of dark eyebrows drawn in corrugated furrows above the bridge of an aquiline nose, his hard mouth white-edged with contempt.

"You clumsy ox! You cannot even manage a simple errand," he hissed, ever careful to keep his voice menacingly low so potential passersby would not overhear. "It pains me to know that you are my heir. For the moment, at least. I plan to take a new wife, so be warned. Once I find a bit of baggage capable of breeding a son, you'll be left without a farthing from me. And to give you a taste of that future, you'll have no pittance from me this month." He snapped his fingers to his secretary. "Make note of that."

"Yes, m-my lord," Entwistle said, his hands shaking as he tried to hold the umbrella and pat his coat pockets in search of a writing implement and a scrap of paper.

When Herman Entwistle had begun his post a mere eight years ago, he'd been a robust man in his midthirties, with a head full of brown hair and an eagerness to impress the venerable earl whose fortune and handsomeness had made him a highly revered member of the *ton*.

But now Entwistle was a thin, hunched-shouldered, balding man, who looked about seventy years old.

The earl had broken him, just as he had done to so many others.

But not Jasper. His uncle's harsh criticisms and the horrors of his childhood had done the opposite. It had formed within him a will of iron.

"As for you"—Redcliffe jabbed Jasper's chest with the point of the walking stick—"since you are incapable of performing a menial task, you'll not only use your own coin to replace the bottle but you'll pay a courier to deliver it. Posthaste. I will have my port after dinner this evening or you'll find yourself without any allowance for the entire year. Do you understand? Are my words penetrating that thick simian skull of yours?"

Fighting the compulsion to break that walking stick over his uncle's head and beat his own chest, Jasper inclined his head. "You will have your port, Uncle."

The earl's mouth relaxed into a self-satisfied smirk as his lacquered landau pulled up to the pavement. Then he cast a baleful glance over his shoulder. "Entwistle, have you gone blind? Do you not see the carriage? Well don't just stand there, you sniveling worm, open the door! I have important matters of business to attend."

After that *delightful* encounter, Jasper headed to Maryle-bone, glad for the exercise to dispel some of his rage.

A half an hour later, he arrived at his flat for a change of clothes.

What he found instead was utter mayhem.

As he opened the door, he was greeted by the detritus of a dismembered chair, broken legs and spindles strewn over the floor. That would make the fourth chair this month!

Through the anger buzzing in his ears, he heard urgent voices coming from the drawing room. But no, not *urgent* voices. These were insistent and cajoling. He knew exactly what that meant. And it was the last thing he needed after a morning like this.

Muttering an oath, he marched around the corner to find two men and a boy trying to coax a red-furred, three-legged beast into dropping one of his top boots. *Bloody hell.*

"Garmr, release!" he commanded, his growling voice undisguised.

The massive wolf instantly opened his jaws. Before the boot even hit the floor, a shaggy whip of a tail started wagging as he hopped awkwardly in a quick circle of complete and utter delight, just before leaping in the air.

Jasper barely had the chance to brace himself before his arms were full of a heavy mass of muscle and fur the size of a small horse.

Whining with joy, Garmr licked his face adoringly as if he'd just returned from a yearlong sea voyage instead of an hour's errand.

"It appears as though you were greatly missed, my lord," Allistair Ansonby said, his aging, rawboned face crinkling with a smile. Then the lanky old manservant straightened his livery coat and smoothed back a few wisps of gray hair from his forehead, seemingly oblivious to the fact that he was standing in a room that resembled a battlefield.

As Jasper lowered the dog, he noted that the square-jawed Joe Pitt wasn't meeting his gaze. Instead, his brawny driver began to whistle as he looked up toward the ceiling and surreptitiously tried to slide the condemning evidence behind him with the toe of his boot.

"Garmr was in the stables when I left," Jasper said as he stripped off his useless spectacles and laid them on a scarred console table by the door. "Care to explain how he ended up here?"

Pitt scrubbed a hand over his shaved head, his black brows drawing together in chagrin. "After you left the mews, he started to whimper something awful and he looked so forlorn that I just . . . well, I thought a visit with the boy would lift his spirits."

"Of course you did."

Jasper pinched the bridge of his nose, blocking out the view of a torn cushion, an overturned table, the shredded drapes.

Pitt swept up the boot. "A bit of spit and polish will make it good as new, my lord."

But when he began to scrub the underside of his sleeve over the toe as if the quick motion would miraculously remove tooth marks, it was all Jasper could take.

"That was my last decent pair. Do you have any idea how difficult it is to have boots made for feet my size?"

As if in solidarity, Garmr stood at his side and issued a low *woof* to the others. But when Jasper glared down at the culprit, he lowered his muzzle in contrition.

The boy instantly came to the dog's defense. "'Tweren't Thumper's fault, milord. Just a pup, he is. Don't know any better. So if you've a mind to wallop someone, then wallop me."

Roly wiped his nose with the back of his hand and squared his shoulders. Standing to his full height he barely reached Jasper's elbow. But the erstwhile street urchin never met a fight he wasn't willing to enter. In fact, the reason he'd taken him in was because the fool child had risked his life to save Garmr's.

Jasper drew in a breath and ruffled the lad's carroty curls. "Fear not, Roland the Brave. I don't intend to wallop anyone. Yet. And for the last time, his name is Garmr. I named him after a fierce hellhound. I'm not calling him *Thumper.*"

"But that's how he walks, all wobbly like. And look at how his foot thumps the floor when he gets scratched behind the ears just the way he likes." The last words were practically crooned as the boy proceeded to demonstrate. He never seemed to realize that the wolf was bigger and could likely eat him in two bites if he were so inclined.

Thankfully, Garmr was too grateful, after being saved from a hunter's steel trap and nursed back to health, to ever turn on any of them.

They were an odd lot, to be sure. But they were loyal to each other and had one thing in common—a hatred for the Earl of Redcliffe. And that was all that mattered.

Well, aside from the fact that Jasper was going to need another pair of boots.

"We're still not calling him Thumper," Jasper decreed as he shrugged out of his coat on his way to his bedchamber then tossed it to Ansonby. The butler wrinkled his nose and held the garment at arm's length. "See what you are able to do with that, while I figure out what to sell in order to replace a bottle of port. Pitt, I'm going to need some information about Viscount Abernathy." He stopped and cast a look of warning over his shoulder to Roly and Garmr, who were playing tug-of-war with his boot. "And it's the mews for the two of you."

Chapter Three

𝒯HE PROMISING TINGLE Thea had felt during that rainy morning two days ago had vanished the instant she'd put pen to page. And it hadn't returned since.

Perhaps it never will, the Greek chorus chimed in.

She chose to ignore them.

Besides, she had enough to contend with this evening. This was her first outing of the Season and she had been coerced into attending a party hosted by the snootiest, most abominable woman in all of England—the former Miss Nell Hunnicutt.

Nell had been her neighbor in Addlewick. And, for most of her life, not a day had gone by that she didn't harangue Thea or her sisters, Verity and Honoria. In fact, a legion of toads would sooner fall out of her mouth than a kind word about the Hartley family, or anyone else for that matter.

Then, by happenstance—or witch's spell, Thea suspected—Nell had married the Marquess of Beaucastle and she wanted everyone to grovel at her feet, especially her enemies.

And if the evening's destination wasn't bad enough, the journey there certainly was.

Lady Broadbent's coach had nearly been run into a ditch when a smaller conveyance attempted to overtake them on the narrow lane. Though, to be honest, when their wheel hit a rut and an ominous splintering sound followed, Thea had been more hopeful than alarmed.

Divine intervention, at last!

Unfortunately, Heaven's miracle department was clearly closed for the Season, because the culprit responsible for the accident was also a guest. And the boggle-eyed Baron Chedworth insisted on delivering them to the party, personally. Splendid.

Exclaiming over his great "luck" he grinned as he handed them into his *coupé*. But the small, closed conveyance was designed for two passengers with a driver outside. And between Thea, Lady Broadbent and the four voluminous shoulder puffs of their gowns, they were packed into the tufted bench like sardines in a tin box.

As Chedworth proceeded to wedge himself in beside them, Lady Broadbent suggested on a suffocated breath, "Perhaps you would be more comfortable in the driver's perch, my lord."

"Thank you for your concern, my lady. However, I tolerate snug spaces quite well."

The man was utterly oblivious.

Then he ordered his driver to make haste, giving a hoot of laughter as they tore off with a jolt.

They rode at breakneck speed, sprinting down straightaways, careening around corners. Thea wasn't at all sure they would survive the trip.

By the time they reached the Beaucastle estate, there was one thing she was certain of, however. She knew that the ogling baron couldn't hazard a guess about the color of her eyes or the type of flower she wore in her hair. But she would lay odds that he'd be able to describe every gather, stitch and ruffle along the heart-shaped edge of her pale pink bodice.

"I must say, your misfortune is my great fortune," Chedworth said for the third time that evening . . . to her breasts.

Her breasts offered no reply, but secretly wished they were adorned in porcupine quills that could fire at will.

"Once the gentlemen see such a lovely specimen upon my arm, they will be positively green with envy."

"A bug under glass is a specimen," Thea said sharply. "We are women, my lord."

"You are too right, Miss Hartley. I see my error and shall amend my statement to *two* lovely specimens."

With one hand on the hilt of her cane, Lady Broadbent laid the other on his proffered arm and offered a tight smile that did not reach her glaring eyes. "Your kindness and generosity are as charitable as a single drop of rain in the desert, Chedworth."

"Think nothing of it," he said, the insult soaring over his head. "As your humble servant, I daresay, I am already looking forward to escorting you back to town. My only regret is that I cannot make the journey last longer so that I can enjoy your delightful company for more than half an hour. Rest assured, upon our return, I shall divert you with news of my latest acquisition at Tattersall's. Fine pair of high-steppers. Set me back a pretty penny. Though, I aim to be rather plump in the pocket after this evening's games."

His boasting paused only for a moment as the servants led them inside and took their wraps. But as soon as they mounted the stairs for the ballroom, he began again.

"You must allow me to take you on a tour of the park in my barouche, Miss Hartley."

"I really cannot—"

"I refuse to take no for an answer," he interrupted with smug self-assurance. "While I would never consider the offer as remuneration for my gallant rescue this evening as that would be ungentlemanly, I would however state that your own conveyance will not likely be at your disposal for a number of days. Therefore, I cannot allow you to miss any of the excitement of London."

"I believe you've forgotten that it was your own driver's

negligence that incapacitated the countess's carriage," Thea said tersely. But it was no use.

The pompous arse was already walking away and hailing a newly arrived acquaintance, presumably overwhelmed with the need to talk about his high-steppers.

The instant he was out of earshot, Thea grumbled, "Conceited wretch."

"Insufferable bore," Lady Broadbent said at the same time. They exchanged a wry glance. "Fear not. I will do my utmost to find another party to convey us to my townhouse."

"That will save me the trouble of stealing into the kitchen for a knife to cut off my own ears before we depart."

"Always so morbid, my dear," the countess tutted, yet there was a distinct smile tucked into the corner of her mouth. "Now then, let us make the most of our evening."

"The only way to do that would be to leave, posthaste," Thea muttered as they neared a pair of white-glazed doors, open to reveal the glow of the room beyond.

For that remark, she received a small rap on the wrist from the countess's fan. "You know very well that it would have been bad form for us not to attend, considering we all hail from Addlewick."

"Bad form? Nell stuffed my sister in a closet and left her there." And Verity had always had trouble with confined spaces.

What Nell had done was unforgivable.

"Agreed. However, my grandson settled that matter by returning the favor to the former Miss Hunnicutt before he and Verity eloped to Gretna Green. Besides, it has been three years and a good deal might have changed— *Good gracious!*" Lady Broadbent stopped with a jolt in the doorway.

Thea did the same, her mouth falling slack as she surveyed the ballroom. She barely took note of the butler announcing them.

Gold was . . . *everywhere*. Drapes, mirror frames, the

terrace doors. Golden chandeliers hung from the vaulted ceiling. Wall sconces flickered behind yellowed glass, giving off a jaundice glow to the dozens of guests milling about in evening finery, feathered headdresses seeming to vacillate drunkenly from the blinding overabundance of gilding. Even the potted palms hadn't been spared, their fronds painted and wilting.

"I never thought gold could be grotesque, but this looks as though someone slayed Midas, his aureate blood splattering over the—"

"*Althea*," the countess chided.

Sheepishly, she looked askance to her ever-dignified chaperone. "Too dark?"

"Much too dark. Keep in mind that what is accepted in the more dramatic circles in which you were reared will not likely earn you favor with influential members of society in attendance this evening. And while my good name can open many doors, it is not a battering ram."

In other words, there were many people who still associated the Hartley name with scandal.

"Understood." Thea squinted down at the gilded room as they descended the stairs. "Even so, you must admit that Nell's attempt at letting the *ton* know that she's done well for herself is a bit overstated."

"What matters is that she has made a good match. She now has a husband and a home. If I recall, those were your only requirements before we embarked on this third Season." As the soles of their slippers touched down onto cold white marble tiles, she turned to face her, arching one dove gray brow. "Unless, of course . . . you've changed your mind."

In the hopeful lilt in Lady Broadbent's voice, it was clear that she was asking if Thea had decided to marry for love, as was the tradition of the Hartley family. But falling in love wasn't something she was interested in. At all.

"I have not."

Lady Broadbent issued a nod and drew in a breath as if the task before her was akin to pushing a boulder uphill.

Then her keen gaze skimmed over the gentlemen milling around the ballroom in their black superfine, high shirt points and snowy cravats, and to the others gathered beyond the gilded archway of a card room and puffing on cigars.

Some ingrained part of Thea revolted against the idea of beginning this entire ordeal again.

What she truly wanted was to find her inspiration. To feel it humming inside her like a living breathing fire again. And she would do anything to get it back.

Nevertheless, she also knew that she needed a roof over her head. Unfortunately, bankers weren't doling out houses to poor unmarried, albeit well-bred, women. It just so happened that they required actual money instead of a list of accomplishments, she thought dryly.

Of course, at one time, she'd imagined herself a successful playwright with money of her own . . .

Which brought her back to this Season and her hunt for a husband.

Although, if this quest turned out to be as soul crushing as her artistic aspirations, she would have to consider using her accomplishments to find a post as a governess.

The chorus chimed in with a laugh. *Accomplishments? Like the list of vulgar words and phrases that you learned during your French lessons? The way you paint a landscape and no one can decipher what it is? Or would it be how you made the dancing master give up his profession?*

As if sensing the downward spiral of her mood, Lady Broadbent linked arms with her and steered them toward the open terrace doors. "Before we begin, let us take a breath of fresh air. I know for a fact that Beaucastle employs an excellent gardener. I'm certain that the view will be quite—" She stopped at the balustrade and squinted at the birds waddling around the garden. "Are those . . ."

"Golden geese," Thea concluded, horrified, though not entirely surprised. Ordering a servant to dye-dip live birds seemed like something Nell would do. "Do you think it will wash off?"

"I should hope so. And I believe the birds are of the same opinion, for they are making their way toward the gilded fountain as we speak."

It was just like Nell not to think of anyone or anything other than her own vain desire to appear better than everyone else. To Thea, it seemed unfair that horrible people often received exactly what they wanted.

"Impressive, is it not, Miss Hartley?" a feminine voice purred from just over her shoulder.

"Actually, I was thinking—"

The rest of Thea's opinion stalled on her lips as she turned to find the newly minted marchioness, grinning like a cat who had a mouse beneath her paw. But it wasn't the expression that made her speechless.

While Nell had always bragged about dressing at the height of fashion, the layers upon layers of gold taffeta did nothing for her stick-straight form. In fact, she resembled a chimney brush. To top it off, her yellow hair was twisted into Apollo knots with open braids on either side.

So, a chimney brush with handles, then, Thea thought, holding back an enormous bubble of laughter. She had to press her lips together to keep it from escaping.

"How good it is to see you doing so well, Lady Beaucastle," the countess interjected.

"Lady Broadbent, I am honored that you would accept my humble invitation," Nell said, a simpering grin on her equine countenance. "And Althea, I'm so glad you are here for yet another Season. Your third, is it not?" She tutted as if they were old friends. "But never fear, there are a number of gentlemen in attendance this evening. I would be glad to introduce you. *If* I have the chance."

"That won't be necessary, I'm sure."

Thea would never forgive herself if she met her future husband at Nell's soiree.

"How delightfully naive we are when we are still un-wed. Is that not so, my lady?" she asked on a tittering laugh, looking to the dignified countess in commiseration.

The austere Lady Broadbent gave no reply.

That did not deter Nell one bit. "As a married woman *and* mistress of a great and affluent household, I under-stand what is required to catch a husband. It takes the art of subtlety. Men respond to that, you know." She made a show of adjusting her glove and trilling her fingers so the stacks of bejeweled rings glinted in the sconce light. "Of course, you and your sisters, with your need to be the cen-ter of attention wherever you go, likely wouldn't under-stand. There are so many things I could teach you. And how is your family, by the by? Still performing their little plays on the lawn?"

Thea's amusement fled, but she bared her teeth in some cousin of a smile. "How strange that you should mention a play, for I heard a rumor that you staged a scene of your own to secure Beaucastle. I believe it involved a house party and a turned ankle, did it not? Apparently, you'd taken quite the tumble."

Twin blotches of pink colored Nell's cheeks. Then she laughed again, the sound high and strained as if she were being strangled to death. *If only.*

"I have no idea to what you are referring," she said. "And besides, I'd heard that you were seen following a cer-tain celebrated playwright like a lost puppy . . . until you suddenly scampered back home in the middle of last Sea-son. Hmm. Why was that, I wonder? Oh, but after years of the Hartley name being embroiled in scandal, I'm certain no one gave it a second thought."

Thea felt herself pale, her throat thick.

Nell's gaze turned malevolently bright, her handles twitching as she preened and fluffed her chimney brush bristles.

"I forget, Lady Beaucastle," the countess intoned. "How many Seasons did you have? Six? Or was it seven? Not that it matters, of course." She executed a dismissive wave of her fan. "You found yourself a fine husband. And I can say that with authority because the marquess actually courted me, back when I was a mere debutante. In fact, he and my late husband attended university together . . . with your grandfather."

Nell's condescending expression fell.

With an audible swallow, her gaze flitted over the countess's fine wrinkles and dove gray coiffure. "Isn't that . . . interesting?"

"Yes, quite." Her fan closed with a snap.

"Well, I must be off. After all, a hostess of such a great house has many duties. Including the fact that my cousin will be making her debut this evening. Since I have such an influential position in society, I thought it only right to sponsor her."

"Your cousin is fortunate, indeed. Miss Hartley and I look forward to making her acquaintance. Pray, which debutante is she?"

Somewhat mollified, Nell pulled her lips over her horse teeth into a moue. "Portia will be making a grand entrance just before dinner. Now, if you will excuse me, I have many important guests to greet."

As she flounced away, Lady Broadbent turned to Thea and said, "I do hope you write a grisly demise for her character in your next play."

"A beheading, do you think?"

"Much too quick."

That response brought a grin to her lips and eased some of her tension. "You're positively diabolical, my lady."

"I've never liked that girl. A pity that she's done so well for herself."

"She married a man old enough to be her grandfather. She could not possibly lo—" Thea stopped.

"*Love* him?" Lady Broadbent finished for her. Before Thea could utter a denial, the countess linked their arms and began to take a tour of the room. "Regardless of what Lady Beaucastle may or may not feel for her husband, she delighted in reminding us that this is your *third* Season. I doubt she will be the only one. And without needling a sore point, I'm sure neither you nor I thought we would be in this predicament."

Because both of them had been certain that Sir Kellum Archer would propose, Thea thought glumly, feeling the prick of that needle all the same.

"Granted, considering your artistic sensibilities, I had accepted more invitations from hostesses with similar inclinations. Primarily those with connections to the theatre," the countess continued, her steps punctuated by the tip of her cane on the tiles. "But traveling the same path as before will not yield the desired result. Therefore, I believe it's time we explored new avenues."

Yet, part of her was also wary of taking a path that might ensure that her creative spark remained dim forever.

Thinking about the last year, about all the months she'd spent in Addlewick feeling estranged from her old life and uncertain about the future, Thea liked the idea of something new. She wanted to leave the past far behind her and prove to Kellum that she wasn't the naive country bumpkin he thought she was.

After a moment's hesitation, she asked, "What do you have in mind?"

The countess held up an index finger and her voice lowered conspiratorially. "First, you must tell me this rumor you heard about our peevish hostess."

"There is no rumor."

"Do you mean to say that you invented it? Out of thin air?"

"Well, not entirely. I remembered that, last summer, her mother stopped by to brag about a house party that she and Nell were attending. I also observed that her own dress had been years out of fashion. From which I deduced that having a spoiled daughter was likely taxing on more than just her nerves. A woman as proud as Elaine Hunnicutt wasn't about to be saddled with a spinster beneath her roof who drained the family coffers, exposing them all to ridicule. And since Nell doesn't possess a single feminine wile—hers are more of the feline, claws-out variety—it just made sense that mother and daughter would have conspired to use every trick in the book to snare a husband, even by arranging a compromising position between Nell and Beaucastle."

Lady Broadbent's brows inched higher. "You are alarmingly clever."

"I think I should be offended by your astonishment at my ability to fabricate stories. You have attended many of my plays in Addlewick, after all."

"Nonsense, my dear. I wasn't speaking of your talent as a writer, but of your impressive knack for observation. And I had no idea you possessed the lion's share of the famed Hartley silver tongue." She tsked in admonishment, then pursed her lips thoughtfully. "Tonight I shall think on this development and prepare a plan of action. Something that will take the tarnish off your third Season. Something that will create just enough of a stir to make you the most sought-after debutante in Lon—"

A sudden bang interrupted, the sound reverberating through the ballroom.

Their gazes swerved to the open doors where a butler stood beside a large bronze gong.

"Miss Portia Hunnicutt," the man announced to the guests as he held the gong paddle at his side like a band leader.

Then, the strains of a string quartet began to drift down from the minstrel gallery. Two serving maids entered, standing on either side of the doorway.

"For all the times Nell has spent disparaging my family for their dramatic flair, she is putting on quite the production," Thea said wryly.

"Indeed."

Then a girl appeared. From the spots on her plump cheeks, she could have been no more than fifteen. Twin plaits of bright red hair were twisted into knots on either side of her crown, the ends sticking straight up like rabbit ears. She wore a white gown draped in gold netting with a train that trailed so far behind her that it reached the stairs. And as she smiled, it became abundantly clear that horse teeth ran in the family.

But when the maids on either side reached into their baskets to shower her in flecks of gold, the tableau took a turn for the worse.

For an instant, the glittering spectacle earned admiring *ooh*s from the crowd. At least, until it had the unfortunate result of adhering to Miss Hunnicutt's perspiring skin.

Just as the music stopped, presumably for the debutante to give a soliloquy, someone said, "She looks like a gilded hare."

A few snickers followed, growing into giggles as they washed through the crowd.

Nell rushed up to her cousin, attempting to brush away the gold with her handkerchief.

It didn't work. In fact, it only gave her stripes.

Portia began to shriek at her cousin, stomping her foot. "This was all your idea! You've ruined my debut! Ruined it! I hate you! Just wait till I tell my mother!"

Then she stormed off, shouting at the maids to pick up her train.

Lady Broadbent began to commiserate over the debacle with the Marchioness of Leighton, whose upcoming ball was one of the most coveted invitations among the *ton*. And Thea was about to innocuously insert herself into their conversation when she heard a man's low murmur from just over her shoulder.

"Pity that. The one thing the party needed was a bit more gold," he said dryly.

The comment tugged a grin from her lips and she turned to identify the speaker.

At first, her gaze landed on a somewhat wrinkled ivory cravat, then on a pair of broad, sloped shoulders. She wasn't a petite woman by any means, but it wasn't until she lifted her chin up and up a bit more that she finally alighted on the speaker's face.

The man was Viscount St. James. She couldn't recall ever speaking with him, aside from when they were first introduced two years ago. She wondered why that was.

"My thoughts precisely," she said.

He didn't respond at first. But his lips parted slightly as if he'd become arrested in midthought, his gaze skimming over her face.

Her smile widened. This was not an altogether uncommon occurrence for her, just as it wasn't for her mother and sisters. The Hartley women were all considered beauties in varying degrees, but it was nothing that Thea concerned herself with. After all, she liked to watch people, too, for the purpose of understanding future characters.

So she took note of him, as well.

She didn't recall that he had ash blond hair that grew dark at the roots. Or that he possessed a prominent brow and a square jaw that seemed cut by a military saber to exact precision. And behind a pair of round, wire-rimmed spectacles, his eyes were the color of treacle and moss and—

St. James blinked. So did she.

Then he cleared his throat. "I beg your pardon. I didn't realize that I'd spoken aloud."

His voice was incongruently soft compared with his imposing size and it made her want to lean closer. He also spoke with a slight lisp that drew her attention to the tip of his tongue and the way it flicked against his front teeth.

She felt her cheeks grow warm at the sight of it. The reaction was clearly from embarrassment, in realizing that she—an astute observer—had not noticed this when they'd met before. It definitely seemed like something she should recall.

With a turn of her wrist, she opened her fan. "Ah, but you did speak aloud. And now I know your secret."

"What do you mean?" His brows snapped together, his gaze alert, jaw tense.

Curious about this response, she took her time to answer, all the better to study him. Then her shoulders lifted in an offhand shrug and she leaned conspiratorially closer. "You, sir, have a dry wit."

His breath came out in a puff, his chest falling as if in relief.

"No one would ever believe it."

She waited for him to say more, her gaze darting from his mouth to the eyes that seemed to brim with stories behind the smudged spectacles.

Then the gong rang again.

Thea turned with a start, jolted back to awareness of the soiree she didn't want to attend in the first place. However, as the butler announced that dinner was served, and the man behind her would doubtlessly proffer an arm to escort her, she realized that her mood this evening had improved.

Perhaps a third Season wouldn't be altogether too terrible.

But when she looked back over her shoulder, St. James was gone. Just . . . gone.

Then she caught a glimpse of those broad shoulders moving swiftly through the room, away from her. And after having felt *not even worthy of a footnote* for the past year, this stung.

To make matters worse, Lord Chedworth appeared, proffering *his* arm and already prattling on about his high-steppers.

Was this the best she could hope for in this third Season?

Your tarnish is showing, the chorus chimed in.

Perhaps, Lady Broadbent was right. Thea needed to do something different this year. And if there was anything a Hartley knew how to do, it was to create a stir.

Chapter Four

$\mathcal{2}\mathcal{9}$

$\mathcal{T}$HE MARROW OF a new play began to form during dinner.

Thea felt the first signs as she took her seat at the legion-long mahogany table—adorned with gilded goblets and golden chargers, of course. And as she peered through the branches of a gleaming candelabra, she caught sight of St. James across from her.

He was just removing his spectacles as if to clean them when their gazes met. His eyes widened briefly. Then he lifted a shoulder in something of an apologetic shrug, his dark brows arching sheepishly.

She didn't know enough about St. James to hold a grudge. He might have already promised to escort another woman into the dining room, remembered it suddenly, then left to honor his word.

Whatever the reason, he seemed to be embarrassed. So, she offered a nod of forgiveness.

Then she smiled and watched his face go blank again. Which only made her lips curve all the more, especially when he fumbled his spectacles—one brass earpiece hooked in place, the other slipping cockeyed from his fingers.

She pressed her lips together to subdue a giggle.

When he finally pushed the spectacles up the bridge of his nose and the lenses reflected the flames of the candelabra, that had been the moment when she felt the tightening of her scalp and the telltale tingles of inspiration.

The sensations came as such a relief that she didn't even mind being situated between two of the most pompous gentlemen in all of England, Barons Chedworth and Timsdale.

In fact, it was actually while imagining how lovely it would be to put them in their places that she first imagined the play, the curtains parting to reveal a stage dressed as a shadowy lane in the forest at night. Then, recalling the story Mr. Fife had relayed the other day, she pictured Chedworth and Timsdale at the mercy of a highwayman.

The perfect beginning! She couldn't wait to write it down.

And yet . . . the instant she felt the familiar itch to withdraw the miniature ledger from the pocket of her gown and take the sturdy pencil in hand, the tingles started to fade.

Nooo! A familiar sense of doom and failure pressed in on her, squeezing the air from her lungs, her pulse harried.

If the past year had taught her anything, she knew that giving in to panic only made it worse. Was she really about to give Nell the satisfaction of seeing her in a fit of hysterics over turtle soup?

Perish the thought.

Taking a breath, Thea quickly cast the notion of writing aside. This time, she told herself, she was going to try a different method and let the play form in her mind's eye instead.

At once, the tight rabbiting of her pulse slowed, the constriction around her lungs easing.

Clearly, she would have to sneak up on this reemergence of her old self, or else startle it into hiding.

Thankfully, the remainder of dinner went on without any further attacks. She couldn't say the same for *after* dinner, however.

When the women retired to the opaline and gold—*surprise, surprise*—parlor, the viper Marchioness of Beaucastle was looking to sink her fangs into someone in order to take attention away from the fact that Miss Portia Hunnicutt was still off sulking somewhere.

As usual, Nell's venom sought Hartley blood.

"I just heard the most delicious rumor," she began, looping her way through the arrangement of chairs, the narrow train of her skirts slithering over the rug. "Sir Kellum Archer has returned to London with a new play to entertain—" She stopped short, affecting a gasp. "My apologies, Miss Hartley. This news must be rather troubling for you in particular."

"Not at all."

"My dear, you are among friends, and we are all aware of your . . . history. There's no need to hide your association. Truly, the dismay is written all over your face."

The room fell silent, the hushed whispers in the corner stalling. Even the amiable chat Lady Leighton and Lady Norris were having with the countess stopped midsentence.

The prickling heat of a dozen curious gazes centered on Thea.

She could utter a denial, but that would not guarantee Nell's tail would uncoil from this topic. So, she took a page from the book of Hartley dramatics and used center stage to her advantage.

Rising from the cushion of the settee, she exhaled a bereft breath as she crossed the room toward Lady Broadbent's chair by the hearth. Briefly, she squeezed her chaperone's hand and shook her head. "It is no use, my lady. I must tell them."

"Tell them?" the countess asked warily, then lowered her voice in warning. "There is nothing to tell."

Thea's fingers splayed over her own heart as she looked at the women who were practically salivating to hear the rest. "So brave, even now. Even after that terrible encounter with"—she paused and closed her eyes as if gathering strength to form the words—"the highwayman."

So many gasps abounded through the room that she was surprised when the sudden absence of air didn't extinguish the crackling fire or gutter the sconces.

The playwright inside her smiled.

"If I do wear dismay upon my countenance, then it is because it happened a mere fortnight ago and remains etched in my mind. But I would never think of boring you with the details, not when we have such a . . . golden hostess to entertain us."

"Indeed," Nell muttered, her complexion decidedly green from all the unejaculated venom burning inside her. "Now then, back to more important matters. If you'll direct your attention to the door, you'll see that I have a lovely surprise for all my guests."

As she spoke, a line of maidservants entered the parlor carrying trays of vermillion liquid in small gilded goblets.

"I fashioned this punch myself. It was to be served directly after dinner, of course. Clearly, I'll have to speak with the cook about her tardiness." Nell issued a haughty laugh.

Serving red liqueur in a gold and white room was asking for disaster. But since it would be Nell's disaster . . . Thea plucked a glass from a waiting tray.

Taking a sip, she suppressed a shudder. It tasted cloyingly sweet like over-sugared berries soaked in rum and red wine, with a peculiar aftertaste of rose petals and medicinal tonic.

She set down the glass on a wine table, careful not to spill. This was her favorite gown, after all, and one of only two she'd coerced the modiste to sew pockets into. And these were lined in sumptuous velvet. She already planned to wear it again with an overdress of white eyelet lace.

"You must tell us more, Miss Hartley," Lady Leighton said, swiftly setting her own glass aside. "I will not sleep if I have not heard the whole of it."

After the estimable marchioness spoke, several others chorused, "Yes, tell us."

Thea was about to offer a perfectly executed nod of resignation, then begin her tale.

But Nell stepped in front of her.

Their hostess, who claimed to know everything about the art of subtlety, spread her arms wide and raised her voice as she rattled, "I have another surprise. My cousin will soon demonstrate her singing prowess for us in the ballroom. I have sent a maid to fetch her. So, I believe we should all adjourn to the—"

"*Lady Beaucastle*," the Marchioness of Leighton chided. "Miss Hartley was speaking."

Nell's mouth snapped shut. Then she lowered her arms and inclined her head.

It was not the time to crow, Thea told herself, but even her derogatory chorus was impressed.

"I'm so grateful to each of you for allowing me to unburden the weight that has been pressing upon my soul for so many days," Thea said, humbly. "Though, with the gentlemen surely joining us soon, perhaps it would be best if we adjourned to the ballroom, where I can tell my harrowing tale without interruption."

"Excellent notion, Miss Hartley."

The instant Lady Leighton spoke, Thea heard a strangled squeak of indignation from Nell. It was absolutely wonderful.

⚗

THE ONLY REASON Jasper attended the soiree that evening was because Redcliffe was punishing him for the wine.

Even though Beaucastle was considered his uncle's friend, at least as far as society was concerned, Jasper knew the truth. And the truth was that Redcliffe despised anyone whose wealth was comparable to his own. So he sent the family buffoon in his stead to endure the debut of Miss Portia Hunnicutt.

Nevertheless, the obligation worked out well for Jasper. He wanted to observe Lord Abernathy, study his movements, discover if he was quick to temper or unpredictable. Having this information was a vital component to his next course of action.

The last thing Jasper needed was another complication.

Fortunately, his objective was simple enough. After port and cigars, many gentlemen retired to the gaming tables in the drawing room, where no one took particular notice of him as he milled along the outskirts of the room, a bystander seemingly absorbed in card play.

"A fine piece, Chedworth." Abernathy smirked as he weighed a gold watch in the palm of his hand. "Not as fine as those new grays you lost to me during the last hand, but it'll do nicely. Perhaps I'll give this to my valet."

Baron Chedworth tossed back the last of another whisky and shoved away from the table. Wavering on his feet, he pointed an accusatory finger and slurred, "You, sir, have no honor."

Leaving, he stumbled into a chair and would have fallen flat on his face if someone hadn't steadied him. But seeing that it was Jasper, he jerked away with a sneer. "What are you looking at, you . . . you simpleminded ape?"

Then he staggered off, through the gilded archway.

The trio remaining at the table—the Marquess of Beaucastle, Viscounts Torrington and Abernathy—toasted each other. They were of Redcliffe's ilk, ruthless men who pursued wealth, status and pleasure without conscience.

Abernathy lifted his glass. "To deep pockets, gentlemen."

Jasper gritted his teeth. He couldn't give a fig about Chedworth's circumstance. But he hated that, while Abernathy was reveling in his good fortune, his mother was unable to pay the hatters or wear a decent shawl.

He wanted to charge up to the blackguard, haul him from his chair, hold him upside down and shake him like a piggy pot until all his money fell out.

But he couldn't. At least, not here.

So he took a breath and left the gaming room.

Besides, if he confronted Abernathy in front of all these men, they would merely laugh, each in turn doling out their insults to the ape. The lumbering oaf. The buffoon. Though, after nearly five and twenty years of enduring such barbs, Jasper had long ago accepted society's estimation of him. Even fostered it to suit his own purpose.

Of course, there were a few exceptions—acquaintances who knew him better, or men among the *ton* who didn't care about collective opinions, preferring to decide for themselves.

Beautiful women, on the other hand, usually took one look at him, then did everything possible to appear invisible so he wouldn't talk to them.

Except for Miss Hartley.

Earlier that evening, when she'd first spotted him, he'd been too busy kicking himself for muttering his opinion on the golden debutante to walk away. Then her gaze met his and her lips curved in apparent pleasure at seeing him.

Him?

Initially, he'd thought she mistook him for someone else. Then he'd wondered if she required spectacles to see properly. And finally, he imagined she was drunk.

That really could've been the only explanation.

Therefore, he'd steadied himself, waiting for her inevitable response. Waiting for her confused blink of "You're not who I thought you were," or for her gaze to dart wildly, seeking an escape before she dashed off in the opposite direction.

He wouldn't have blamed her.

But instead, her smile had widened upon recognition. Then his mind went utterly . . . blank.

The sensation was like throwing back the curtains in the morning, the room suffused with so much light that it hurt to look upon.

And yet, even taking the full force of that blinding brilliance, he hadn't been able to look away . . . or to stop blathering.

She'd cast some sort of spell on him.

Alarmed, he'd been relieved when the gong had rung a second time. And the instant her back was turned, he'd disappeared.

As far as he was concerned, the farther he stayed away from Miss Hartley, the better.

Unfortunately, he'd ended up seated across from her at dinner. And there she was again with that unflinching eye contact, peering straight into his soul.

Even so, she'd clearly been cross with him. Not wanting to cause a spectacle that would bring attention to either of them, he'd decided to appear chagrined, hoping to set the matter aside.

It had been a miscalculation on his part.

She'd forgiven him far too easily. And then it happened again—that smile and his subsequent blinding blankness.

By the time he came back to himself, a new course was being served, the old cleared away, and the two matrons on either side of him making no secret about wanting to keep their daughters from *unsavory personages* as they cast not too subtle glances at him. At least they had sense.

It was the reason he hadn't bothered with awkward introductions to debutantes that evening. That alone would save him—or them, as the case may be—from being pressed into dancing. Besides, a display of his clumsiness wasn't necessary if his uncle wasn't present to be embarrassed by it.

Which didn't explain why, as he entered the ballroom, his gaze surveyed the assembly in search of glossy mahogany curls and a pale pink gown with a spray of ruffles around the bodice that looked so delicate they'd likely dissolve with the barest brush of his apish fingers.

He shook his head.

Why in damnation was he thinking about ruffles? More importantly, why was he wondering what they'd do if he touched them? Because he wasn't going to touch them. He wasn't even going to ask her to dance.

Not that she could even accept if she wanted to—which, of course, she wouldn't—because no one was dancing. In fact, he noticed that the majority of the guests were gathering at the far end of the room.

Removing his needless spectacles, he saw the reason.

Miss Hartley.

With a damask rose in her hair, she stood at the center of a pastel bouquet of debutantes, their chaperones in feathered turbans amidst a small grouping of chairs, expressions rapt. Even the gentlemen, who would normally be in want of a partner as the musicians played overhead, were loitering nearby instead, their attention fixed on the dark-haired enchantress.

He couldn't blame them. It was impossible to look away from her in this moment. In the adoring glow of the chandeliers, her animated features were mesmerizing, her graceful arms casting a spell. Whatever she was saying had them all captivated.

But Jasper had his own agenda that night and decided to return to the gaming room.

As he turned on his heel, he caught sight of the new Marchioness of Beaucastle, glaring daggers at the woman holding court. She practically vibrated with animosity. And when her gaze shifted between Miss Hartley and the numerous untended goblets of red punch on a Bombay chest near a gilded potted palm, her intention was clear.

Before he knew his own, he found himself walking in Miss Hartley's direction . . . To do what, precisely? To fall in among her admirers? Ridiculous. To protect her from their hostess? Absurd.

Nevertheless, there he was, still moving along the outskirts of the room. And that was when he heard someone ask, "Is that when you saw the highwayman?"

For a moment Jasper could hear nothing else through the sudden rush of blood in his ears.

Highwayman, the one word guaranteed to snap him out of his miasma.

"Not yet. We chose to ignore the warning from the fortune teller at our last change of horses. After all, a full moon hung in the sky. We thought we could make the next coaching inn without worry . . . until the fog descended on us," Miss Hartley continued, her voice dipping to hushed tones, guaranteeing that her transfixed audience leaned closer to listen. "The uncertain path forced our carriage to a crawl. We could do nothing but stare, unseeing, at the haunting shadows that lurked deep in the forest, the jangle of the rigging echoing eerily like ghostly chains. Lady Broadbent clutched my hand. But neither of us knew true fear until we heard the rapid thunder of hooves and the bloodcurdling howl of a wolf."

"Dear me!" a debutante said, clutching her throat.

Miss Hartley paused, splaying a hand over her bosom as if struggling with the memory of it. "Then our driver called down. He could just make out a stopped carriage up ahead, you see, and he inquired if we should offer assistance. But before the countess could offer a noble reply, we heard the report of a pistol crack through the ether."

The crowd gasped.

"I tell you, the hair at my nape stood on end. And then our driver called down again, speaking the single most terrifying word—*highwayman*."

"No!" a chorus of voices said as Jasper reached the Bombay chest.

"Countess, were you not frightened?" asked the Marchioness of Leighton. "I would have swooned for certain."

Lady Broadbent blinked, her eyes wide as if she were experiencing this tale for the first time. Then, after a subtle nudge from Miss Hartley, she cleared her throat. "Thankfully my driver is quite the fearsome fellow and a crack shot to boot."

"He *shot* the highwayman?" one of the men asked.

"No!" Miss Hartley interjected. "What I mean is, there wasn't time. Because in the very next instant, we saw that dark figure on his mount, man and beast cutting through the fog as if they were comprised of the same unearthly substance. We knew at once that he was—"

Her story ended on a sharp gasp as Jasper tripped and spilled the vermillion punch all over her gown.

Chapter Five

ᴥ

As Thea situated her skirts, grimacing at the red-stained satin pinched between her fingers, she wasn't certain which portion of the evening was the worst.

Was it when her favorite gown was ruined? When Baron Chedworth had abandoned them at Beaucastle's without ensuring they found another way home? Or when the first two circumstances had left Nell beaming with malevolent delight as she bid her fellow Addlewickians farewell?

A plague upon all your houses, Thea thought crossly as Viscount Abernathy's coach drove them away from the cursed party.

"I simply don't know what Chedworth could have been thinking," Lady Broadbent said on an even breath. "Needless to say, Miss Hartley and I are in your debt, Lord Abernathy."

Seated on the bench across from them, the viscount's vulpine face gave way to a half smile that elongated a pointy chin. "Not at all. It isn't often that I have the privilege of escorting two such charming and alluring ladies."

As if this night's abominable feast of catastrophe required a sauce, Abernathy's gaze shifted to Thea, then held for an uncomfortable beat too long.

"You are too kind," the countess interjected sharply. "I'm sure your mother would be proud to know she raised a man who came to our aid without desiring any sort of favor in return."

A pregnant pause followed, her meaning patently clear.

His smile turned sour as he glanced down to brush an invisible speck of lint from his coat sleeve. "Indeed. I had forgotten you shared an acquaintance with my mother."

The creaking of the carriage walls and the whistle of the wind slipping in through the window casings filled the silence that followed.

At his discomfiture, Thea grinned to herself. She was tempted to squeeze Lady Broadbent's hand in gratitude, but the countess was nothing if not proper. Needless displays of affection were frowned upon. Nevertheless, Thea received a nod and a tap on her forearm. For the countess, that was the equivalent of a warm embrace.

Thea shifted deeper onto the bench, a forlorn sigh escaping when her skirts and petticoat stuck to her thighs.

"I'm afraid the red will never come out of the satin," the countess said.

But Thea was lamenting the loss of the velvet pockets most of all. The special lining had been the clever idea from the extraordinary modiste Madame LeBlanc after Thea had told her about having lost a ledger last Season.

That ledger had contained the last of her own work that she'd truly been proud of. But it was gone forever.

"St. James ought to be horsewhipped. Ignorant clod," Abernathy said, leaping onto the change in topic like a flea to a dog's back.

Thea frowned. "It was an accident. Anyone could have tripped and done the same. If that punch hadn't been so unpalatable, then perhaps—"

"You'll find that *accidents* follow that buffoon wherever he goes. He's a menace and a blathering idiot. It's a shame that the Earl of Redcliffe has no better option as heir."

"Just because St. James speaks with a lisp does not make him dim-witted."

Abernathy's eyebrow arched. "Forgive me, I had no notion that he earned such a high place in your esteem."

"He hasn't." When her declaration earned a smug chuckle as if he'd already known the answer, she hastened to add, "But if he were to pay a call and express an interest in courting me, I would give him due consideration, just as I would any true gentleman."

She didn't know why she was rushing to St. James's defense. After all, the red splatters covering her gown gave her good cause to be cross with him. But she hated when proud, pompous men chose to belittle those they deemed beneath them. And she didn't understand the contempt.

It was true that St. James was built on the larger scale, which could account for any clumsiness. Additionally, the clothes he wore made him appear rather unkempt. But if one looked beyond all that, they could see that he had a number of appealing qualities.

She just couldn't remember them at the moment.

It was rather sad to admit—especially under these circumstances when righteous indignation would aid her in putting Abernathy in his place—but, other than brief conversations and St. James's unfortunate stumble in front of her, he hadn't left much of an impression.

As far as potential suitors went, she didn't even know what would impress her. She supposed that, just like with her inspiration, she was searching for an elusive spark.

Best of luck with that, her chorus snickered.

"Ah. Now I understand." Abernathy's thin lips curved in a grin, even though she was fairly certain she hadn't said anything amusing. "You are quite clever, Miss Hartley, and I happily accept your invitation."

"My . . . invitation?"

"To pay a call on you."

Believing she misheard him, she glanced to Lady

Broadbent for clarity only to see perplexity in her creased brow. Then, suddenly, a candle flared to life in Thea's brain.

She'd said she would give any *true gentleman* due consideration. Did he actually mistake her insult to his character as encouragement?

The answer was clear in that smug expression.

Oh, how she looked forward to setting him straight. "Abernathy, I wouldn't—"

Her setdown ended on a gasp as the carriage suddenly lurched, picking up speed. She nearly tumbled forward into the viscount's lap, but braced herself in time.

Lady Broadbent held on, as well. "Good gracious!"

Abernathy scowled and pounded on the roof hatch. "See here! What's the meaning of this?"

In response, several things happened at once. The crack of a gunshot split the air. The piercing howl of a wolf echoed through the trees that lined the forest lane. The driver cursed.

Then the word *highwayman* dropped inside the carriage like a stone.

Chapter Six

✒

$\mathcal{A}$s THE DRIVER sped up, the coach bounced mercilessly until Thea felt like a kernel of popping corn by a fire.

Was it possible to outrace a highwayman?

Even before her inner chorus added their dire prediction, she suspected the odds were rather slim. "Do you have any weapons we might use to protect ourselves, my lord?"

Abernathy ignored her. He seemed far more concerned with stuffing the contents of his pockets into the seams of the bench upholstery than with his guests.

Lady Broadbent clutched her hand, her countenance fraught with worry. "Oh, Miss Hartley, I wish you had not told that tale."

"Surely, you don't imagine that I conjured a highwayman with my story."

An arched brow was her only answer before all the jostling sputtered the lanterns. They were instantly pitched into a darkness tinged with the acrid scent of oil smoke.

This wasn't her fault! Besides, she'd merely taken a few liberties with the tale that Mr. Fife had relayed to her that morning. So, if anyone was to blame . . .

And yet, she rather liked the idea of conjuring a highwayman. There was something altogether intriguing in the notion that words—*her* words—could hold such power. Wasn't that what she'd wanted? To have her words matter enough to be acted out on the London stage?

She couldn't stop herself from remembering how engaged the small crowd surrounding her had been. They had been enthralled by the carriage chase, the mysterious fog, the daring highwayman. They'd liked the danger of it all.

Truth be told, so had she.

It was well-known among her family that she suffered from eternal ennui, without any hope of a cure. But what if this was the cure? What if tales of danger were what she'd been searching for all along?

Perhaps that was the reason her plays had never struck a chord with Kellum.

Not that she wanted to think about him at a time like—

A shot fired. Then the carriage lurched to a stop.

She held her breath, determined to take in every detail of that moment. Even if it was to be her last. Even if she had to use her own blood to write the scene in the dirt on the side of the road . . .

A shiver rolled down her spine, and she realized she'd gone a bit dark again.

Suddenly, the door swung open with a crack. But there was no one there. Just the black of night staring back at them.

Then a figure moved among the forest shadows, large and looming. As it drew closer, a shaft of moonlight broke through a part in the clouds and fell upon a broadbrimmed hat, a tattered black cloak whipping in the wind, and the glint of a pistol in his grasp. And it was aimed directly at Abernathy.

Thea knew that the highwayman's words would seal their fates. And, should she survive this encounter, she suspected that those words would also make the perfect opening line for the play.

She waited, crossing her fingers and silently beseeching the stranger into saying something truly bone chilling.

"Stand and deliver," the highwayman ordered.

Thea bit back a sigh of dismay. That deep, forbidding voice was wasted on such a mundane line. She could have come up with something far more threatening in her sleep.

"I . . . I don't have anything," Abernathy stammered, his arms raised.

A black-gloved thumb cocked the flint lock with an ominous click. "Out with you, maggot, and empty your pockets."

Abernathy did as instructed. Then, after a fruitless search turned up nothing, the highwayman growled.

"See? I t-told you. I have n-nothing."

"And if I search your carriage?"

"No. Please don't." Abernathy went pale as if he feared the highwayman might discover the women tucked away in the shadows.

For just a moment, Thea wondered if he had some redeeming qualities, after all.

Then, raising a trembling hand, Abernathy pointed toward the interior. "The women. They have jewels and reticules filled with baubles and whatnot. Take them. Do whatever you want with them."

Lady Broadbent gasped and strapped a protective arm across her charge.

Thea, on the other hand, was far too incensed to stay hidden in the shadows. "Of all the nerve!"

Her outburst must have shocked the highwayman, for he stood motionless beneath a wedge of silver light bleeding down through the trees as she moved into the open doorway.

But she only spared him a glance. Her target was Abernathy. "You dare to offer us up as collateral in order to conceal all the money you stuffed in the upholstery? Well, this is what I think about despicable men like you!"

As she spoke, her hands began fishing into the nooks and crannies of the opposite bench. Grabbing a fistful of notes, she threw it at him. "There. That's about a hundred pounds,

I'd say. Oh, wait. There's more." Her fingers wrapped around something smooth and solid. "And here's a golden watch— Correction, make that *two* golden watches." She hurled one after the other. "Let's see what's inside this leather coin purse. A ruby signet ring and—"

"Shut up, you worthless wench!" Abernathy lunged, his hands outstretched to strangle her.

Thea was so angry—not just at Abernathy but at Chedworth and Kellum and every man who'd ever disparaged her sex—that she was prepared to fight back.

She had her claws at the ready, but Lady Broadbent grasped her wrist to pull her back to safety. Abernathy grabbed the other an instant before the highwayman knocked him to the ground.

She lost her balance, teetering forward into the night air. And she fell . . .

Directly into the highwayman's arms.

She landed against him on a soundless gasp, her eyes wide.

An instinct for survival attempted to order her to scramble away. A lifelong habit of observation, however, shoved that coward aside and took note of every detail.

As any proper highwayman ought, he masked his identity with a strip of black silk over half of his face. The only thing she could see beneath that broadbrimmed hat was the outline of his mouth and the incipient emergence of a night beard beneath the skin along his chiseled jaw. Below that was a dark neckcloth. And he must have been wearing black shirtsleeves as well because she saw no glimpse of white through the open collar of a caped greatcoat.

He said nothing as he held her against his large body. But she could feel the strong thud of his heart as his breath fanned across her cheek, warm and spicy. His strong hands were positioned beneath her arms in the manner that one would catch a child hurled through the air. And she did, indeed, feel small against him. Fragile, too. He seemed to take additional care to shift his hold to her back as if he feared breaking her.

Dazedly, Thea wondered if she might already be broken. She felt lightheaded and muzzy as if in a dream. Fearing that she might wake up and fall flat on her derriere, she clutched his shoulders for support.

His hands flexed in response, causing a tumult of tingles to cascade over her body, beginning at her scalp and sliding sinuously down her spine.

She drew in a surprised breath, her nostrils filling with some combined scent of pine forest, saddle leather and a spice she couldn't name. Whatever it was, it dipped below her lungs and curled warmly in her midriff. Her stomach felt peculiarly weighted, pressed against his as it was. And she had the insane desire to rest her cheek against his shoulder. Perhaps even bury her nose into the curve of his—

Abernathy suddenly unleashed a cry of attack.

From the corner of her eye, she saw the viscount swing a fallen branch toward the highwayman's head. She barely had time to flinch.

Fast as a whip, the highwayman's arm shot out. Fist closing around the thick branch, he tossed it aside as if it were nothing more than a twig. Then he took Abernathy by the throat and lifted him to his toes.

Yet, even with the villainous viscount thrashing and clawing, the highwayman held her with sureness, keeping her from harm. In the process, his arm had snaked completely around her waist and she was pressed so fully against him that her face ended up an inch away from the crook of his shoulder.

Well, *when in Rome . . .* she thought, and gave in to the impulse.

"Are you"—he turned his head, the stubble along his jaw rasping softly against her cheek, and she went still,

midbreath, like a rabbit caught eating the lettuces—
"unharmed?"

She exhaled in relief, glad he didn't ask if she'd been
sniffing him like fresh linens on the clothesline.

"I believe so," she said, her voice oddly hoarse. "You
should probably put me—"

Abernathy's foot shot out and the highwayman grunted
as it found its target.

"Wolf. Guard," the highwayman commanded.

Then a low bloodcurdling growl came from the shadows.

The hair on Thea's nape lifted and she huddled closer.
There was no way she was going to let him put her down now.

"Call it off. Call it off. Please, I beg you . . ." Abernathy
whimpered, his words choked. But, clearly, he was still breathing. *Pity that.*

As if wholly unbothered by the man dangling from his
other arm and the woman attempting to climb him, the
highwayman took a step toward the open carriage door and
simply deposited her.

She slumped down on the bench, wondering why her
chaperone had stayed so silent. But then she caught the familiar odor of smelling salts wafting in the air.

"Here," Lady Broadbent said, her regal voice quavering
as her trembling hand reached out. "Take our jewelry, but
please leave us unmolested."

The highwayman stiffened. "I do not take from women."

He sounded so affronted that, for some reason, it made
Thea smile. "What do you plan to do with Abernathy? Not
that I care, mind you. I'm merely curious."

"Tie him up and put him in the driver's perch," he said
with an unconcerned shrug. "Do with him what you will."

When the man moved to close the door, she quickly
asked, "Can I offer you a bit of advice?"

The moonlight illuminated the bottom portion of his

face, just enough for her to see the corner of his mouth twitch as he inclined his head.

"'Stand and deliver' is far too cliché. I wrote better dialogue when I was seven. So, if you expect to have a lengthy career as a brigand, perhaps something a bit more ominous next time, hmm?"

He touched the brim of his hat in salute. Then he was gone.

As she leaned back against the squabs, it really did feel like she was waking from a dream. But the best kind of dream, with all the tingles of inspiration dancing through her veins.

This was what she'd been waiting for. And now, she couldn't wait to return to the townhouse and spend the rest of the night writing.

⁓

St. James rode off into the night, cursing himself for being so careless.

Abernathy—that cretin—was supposed to have been alone. Damn it all!

The men he went after were always alone. He ensured it.

When he robbed the men who supported and associated with his uncle, it was as if they were all Redcliffe. They all deserved to know what it felt like to be at someone else's mercy. And besides, he was only doing what he had to do to protect those he cared about, especially his aunt and cousins, who were forever in Redcliffe's sights.

Being a highwayman was a means to an end. On any other night, he could close himself off, just do the job and be done with it.

But then she was there.

The instant he'd seen Miss Hartley, it had been impossible

to remain detached. And remembering the way that Abernathy had been ready to simply dispose of her to save himself made his stomach crawl and rage boil in his veins.

Long ago, Jasper had sworn an oath to his mother that he would never inflict the harm that had been done to him on anyone else. But tonight, he'd been tempted—so bloody tempted—to renounce that promise.

He always left the men he robbed with a threat of death hanging over their heads if they were to speak of the encounter. For the first time, he'd been prepared to follow through.

In the end, that hadn't been necessary. Miss Hartley had proven herself to be braver than he could have imagined. If not for the fact that her brazen display of temper might have put her in more danger, Jasper would admit to being rather impressed.

As for Abernathy, the man had soiled himself so thoroughly that his mortification made murdering him counterproductive. A proud man would sooner die than ever speak of such an encounter.

Besides, the threat of death was merely pragmatic. It kept word from spreading and ensured his continued anonymity. No one could ever discover the truth. If they did, then everyone he was trying to protect would no longer be safe.

For the past two years, there hadn't been a single instance when someone had talked. And yet, considering the story that Miss Hartley relayed at Beaucastle's that evening, it was clear that someone had.

But who?

Jasper didn't know. He only hoped that his elaborate stumble at Beaucastle's would be the most noteworthy thing the guests recalled and the tale would go no further.

Reaching the old tavern with its sloping roof and weathered shingles, he pulled on the reins of his black destrier.

Not many travelers ventured this far from the main road where it cut deep into the forest, which made the place ideally located.

At one time, its seclusion drew the interest of ruffians and thieves. But after making an alliance with one of the men who skirted the line between right and wrong—just as he had to do—this place had become a safe haven.

For the past two years, David and Nan Barrett ran the place. They'd both been former servants of Redcliffe's. Barrett had been a footman and Nan, a serving maid. But during a garden party one day, Redcliffe had cornered Nan in the summerhouse and made improper advances. Hearing word of this, the hotheaded Barrett saw red.

Jasper had just sold his commission and returned to his uncle's house as this tableau had begun. He saw Barrett stride across the lawn in front of a hundred guests, a dueling pistol from the study hanging at his side.

Intervening in his usual fashion, Jasper had pretended to be a clumsy oaf, deftly disarming Barrett before anyone was the wiser, explaining in his ear that Nan was already in safe hands and unharmed. But he knew Redcliffe. His uncle always got what he wanted. And when he did, Barrett would end up at the short end of a hangman's noose.

So, it was clear that they would need new employment, a place far from Redcliffe's reach. That was when Jasper had found this tavern, and the seeds of an idea were first planted—a way to fight back against Redcliffe.

Ever since, the Barretts had been his loyal friends. They were among the trusted few who knew of his midnight escapades and the vital importance of keeping his secret. They knew there were too many lives at stake for anything to go wrong.

Just like it had tonight. And it was his own fault.

Jasper muttered an oath as he dismounted. He was never more in need of pint than he was tonight.

Reaching into the saddlebag, he withdrew a carrot and fed it to his stalwart mount, rubbing the flat of his hand over his black coat. "You did well, Berserker."

As with Garmr, he'd chosen a name from the Norse fables his father had read to him long ago. Berserker was a fitting name for this enormous destrier, whose shaggy fur gave him an almost bearlike appearance. Not to mention a similar appetite, for he gobbled up the carrot and was already snuffling out another that Jasper had hidden up his sleeve.

"There," he said with fond amusement as the horse wasted no time.

Withdrawing a large bone from the bag, he kneeled down to Garmr and scrubbed a hand over his hide in praise. "And you did well, too."

The dog panted in bliss, his leg thumping on the ground as he received a scratch behind the ears.

Behind Jasper, the warped front door cracked against the shingles. As Roly rushed out, a distant feminine voice shouted, "And close the door."

"Aye, Nan," he sighed, doing as he was told before rushing over to fawn all over the dog as if they'd been separated for years instead of hours. "How'd he do? I couldn't sleep a wink for worry. But I heard his howl all the way from the kitchens."

"He played his part well." *Far better than his master*, Jasper thought to himself, wondering about the ramifications that would likely arise after this night's catastrophe. He had a sleepless night ahead of him to formulate potential counterattacks. But for now, he turned his attention to the ever-bedraggled boy. "Worried, hmm? It looks as though all that *worrying* put most of Nan's kitchen on your cheeks and chin."

As the words were spoken, the wolf licked every last smear of food from the giggling boy's face, before lowering to the dirt to gnaw on his bone.

Jasper felt a grin tug at his lips. "He'll need a dish of water. Can you fetch that for him?"

Roly was already bounding across the stable yard to the old stone well. And Jasper gave Garmr and Berserker one last pat before he headed inside.

A welcoming fire crackled in the stone hearth along the far wall. Jasper's footfalls sounded heavier than usual as he crossed the aged hardwood floor, then slumped down onto a sturdy wooden chair, absently tossing his satchel onto a nearby table.

Barrett's stocky frame ambled over to him, a tankard in each hand. His brows inched upward toward a short crop of brown hair. "Long night?"

"You don't know the half of it."

His friend slid one ale across the table then sat down and took a long pull from the other. "Nan's coming with a bowl of stew and loaf of bread. She's already made up a room for you upstairs. Though Pamela will be heartbroken to find out that she wasn't here waiting for you."

"Don't encourage her. The last time I was here she came in to clean the room while I was having a bath. Offered to scrub my back."

"There ain't many men who would have turned her down." That statement earned Barrett a smack on the back of the head from the willowy blonde beauty carrying the tray behind him. "O' course, I wasn't speaking for myself. I knew you were standing there, my love. Just having a go with you."

"Mmm-hmm," his wife murmured, her brown eyes slitted. Nan plunked the earthenware bowl and bread on the table without fanfare, then stabbed the crosshatched loaf, the blade of a carving knife twanging. "Oh, I'm not worried. I know too many ways to slice and cook an animal to be worried," she said sweetly as her husband choked on his ale. Then she patted him on the cheek, offering a taunting grin. "Aww, don't worry, love. Just having a go with you."

As she left them, Barrett leaned forward to wipe the froth from his shirtfront. Even so, he grinned as he watched Nan's hips sway as she sauntered back to the kitchen. "That woman'll be the death of me."

"You wouldn't have it any other way," Jasper said as he tore off a hunk of bread and tucked into his meal. He knew that, as much as the couple enjoyed their verbal sparring, they loved each other.

They actually reminded him of his own parents. At least, what he remembered of them during those brief years of happiness. He'd been about Roly's age when his father died. Then his mother was forced by circumstance to move back into the Redcliffe estate, and they were never happy again.

"Aye," Barrett agreed. "I suppose having such a wife ain't all that bad. And she dotes on that boy, too. Let him eat an entire cake, waiting for you."

Jasper lifted his head, eyebrows raised. "There was cake?"

"Pamela pinched it from the lady she cleans for. Left it here just for you." Barrett hesitated and looked over his shoulder before lowering his voice. "I could still send her a missive. She'd be happy to help you rid yourself of that broody tension."

Jasper returned to his meal. He wasn't interested in Pamela. He'd already said as much and he didn't like to repeat himself. So he took out whatever tension he had on lamb, potato and bread, replaying the events of the night in his mind.

Barrett set down the tankard and jerked a nod toward the satchel. "Why'd it take so long? The prig put up a fight?"

"Not much of one. But the hellion with him sure did."

Barrett cursed. "Some light o' love?"

"No." Jasper shoved the empty bowl away. "A debutante and her chaperone. Apparently, their carriage hit a rut on the way to the party."

"Proper ladies?" He whistled. "Quite the surprise, I'd say."

Both men knew that Jasper was not a man who dealt well with surprises. He liked strategy. He planned things out. Accounted for variables.

But he never counted on her.

Althea Hartley had been nothing more than a distraction all week. Not only had she cost him a bottle of port and his monthly allowance, but the repercussions of her presence in the carriage were yet to be determined. And he hated being unable to calculate an outcome with any degree of certainty.

Abernathy was supposed to have been alone, damn it all!

"You don't know the half of it," Jasper said again and downed the rest of his ale.

He stood and moved to the hearth, bracing his hands against the mantel. Staring into the fire, he briefed Barrett on the main points of the encounter, leaving out the part where she'd fallen from the coach and into his arms. And the fact that she smelled soft like some sort of rare flower with petals so delicate that they'd surely crumple in his gargantuan hands.

But she hadn't crumpled. She hadn't even tried to shove out of his embrace. Every delectable hillock and valley on her lithe body had been molded against him. And when Garmr had growled, the way she'd held on so tightly with her legs wrapping around his hips would fuel his forbidden fantasies for a lifetime.

"But you left her with a warning, right?" Barrett asked, the words more of a statement of common sense than a question.

Jasper didn't like to lie to his friends. He already spent the majority of his life lying to everyone about who he was. So, he looked over at him squarely. "It slipped my mind."

One corner of Barrett's mouth lifted. "Must have been some hellion."

"You have no idea."

Chapter Seven

꩜

$\mathcal{J}$ASPER HAD STAYED awake all night, ruminating over the events.

The strategist in him was certain that neither Lady Broadbent nor her charge would speak of their encounter for fear of jeopardizing Miss Hartley's reputation. Which should have put his mind at ease.

It hadn't.

There was still the mystery of how Miss Hartley had heard her tale about the highwayman. The details that she'd revealed about the thick fog and full moon, however, gave him an approximate timespan, and narrowed it down to one of two different gentlemen.

Yet, no matter what she'd claimed, there had been no other carriages on the road that might have spotted him. Which made him wonder . . . what else did she know?

If that weren't enough to keep his thoughts constantly churning, his conscience was also niggling at him.

Last night, she'd been brave when staring danger in the face. But he knew that, for someone who hadn't dined on daily doses of peril, the aftereffects could leave her shaken. Of course, having her fearful was in his best interest. And yet, he couldn't stomach the thought of being a source of disquiet for her.

He was being a fool, he told himself, as he rapped soundly on Lady Broadbent's townhouse door. He should leave well enough alone.

After all, hadn't he sent his driver, Mr. Pitt, to covertly accompany Abernathy's carriage to ensure that Miss Hartley and her chaperone were delivered home without harm? And hadn't Pitt assured him that neither woman had seemed frail?

But it wasn't enough. Jasper had to see it for himself.

When the door opened, a bejowled butler's eyes widened in either alarm or surprise. But the instant Jasper adjusted his spectacles and lisped his request to have an audience with Miss Hartley, the manservant recovered.

That was another thing his disguise was good for—putting people at ease when face-to-face with a man of his size.

Asked to wait in the foyer, Jasper took note of his pristine surroundings. Everything was dainty lace and delicate porcelain, gleaming white glazed trim and polished wood. There wasn't a dust mote in sight, let alone a tooth-marked chair leg or tattered draperies. Not that he'd expected anything different. It was just disconcerting to see the quantity of fragile bric-a-brac he could destroy with a single misstep.

As the butler escorted him to the breakfast room, Jasper inwardly recited his pretty apology for the punch debacle, along with the few innocuous queries that would answer his questions without raising suspicion.

Then he saw Miss Hartley, and every single thought that had brought him here disappeared. Simply tumbled out of his head like stones over a cliff, one after the other.

She was standing at the buffet in a wedge of morning light, her hair in an artless topknot with rich mahogany tendrils snaking down to rest against the side of her face. Her cheeks held a rosy glow that seemed to make her eyes brighter in their nest of dark, sooty lashes. The word *beautiful* would have to bow down to her because she was something infinitely more. He'd always thought so, even before he'd felt her body pressed against his . . . her surprisingly strong limbs . . . her soft, supple—

"We do not usually have callers at this hour, St. James," Countess Broadbent regally intoned from her chair at the head of an oval rosewood table. "Though, if we did, I'm certain they would not linger in doorways."

Jasper had to blink to remember where he was.

Embarrassed, he cleared his throat and stepped into the room.

"Forgive me, my lady. I clearly owe you more than one apology this morning," he said in the soft-spoken fashion he donned for society. "In fact, that is the reason I am here—to apologize to Miss Hartley for ruining her gown. And to give her these."

Withdrawing the bouquet from behind his back, he took a step forward and thrust them at Althea, as if he'd never given a woman flowers before. Which, come to think of it, he hadn't. His encounters with the fairer sex had been of a less romantic variety.

But when she startled on an *"Oh!"* and her plate dropped onto the buffet with a clatter, he wanted to sink into the floor.

Maintaining his disguise of the lisping lout was more painful than usual, given his audience. Unfortunately, he couldn't afford to do otherwise. Even so, he felt like an utter nodcock, and mostly because not all of his awkwardness was an act.

Carefully, she took the offering. "These are quite . . . interesting."

"They're paper flowers," he said inanely. "My father used to make them for my mother because every flower, except for roses, made her sneeze and I thought you'd already have several rooms filled with hothouse . . ."

With a belated glance around the breakfast room, he noted an array of fancy hothouse bouquets on the buffet. There were others in the center of the table, a few spilling over the mantel. And some were even tucked into the window nook as if she received so many that she had to cram them into every room on any available space. But, of course, she did.

And he had given her paper.

Any other woman would have laughed in his face by now.

He reached out. "I see now that you clearly would have preferred—"

"No," she interrupted, pulling the offering close to her bosom. "I like these very much. Thank you."

His gaze strayed to the way her delicate hands shielded the intricately folded silver paper that he had worked on long into the night, thinking of her.

When her fingertip traced the outer edge of a petal that he'd rubbed smooth with his own, his flesh tingled. It was as though they were touching it together, fingers brushing, tangling. He didn't know why such a mundane thought made his pulse quicken. Or why his hands suddenly ached to splay over her back again, to pull her close. To feel her cling to him in the bright light of morning without any disguises between them.

A jolt of alarm sprinted through him.

What was he thinking? That was the worst idea ever, and not remotely part of his plan. He had a prepared speech, damn it all. *Strategy, man! Strategy!*

"As for last night . . ." he began, collecting himself.

At the same time, she met his gaze and asked, "Are you hungry?"

". . . I hope that you were not too—" He stopped. There she was with that direct eye contact again. No one ever looked at him the way she did. And that blue was so clear and bright it was like looking at a midday summer sky. He blinked. Glanced at her mouth because—bloody hell—she was smiling at him. And he started to feel his mind fuzzing around the edges. "Am I . . . hungry?"

When she giggled, he was gone. Utterly gone.

He didn't know what was wrong with him. Sleep deprivation. That's what it was. It had to be.

"Yes," she said, biting down on her lower lip in a way that sent an unbidden surge of heat through his blood. "Would you like to break your fast with us? That way you can be assured I hold no grudge against you. It was an accident. And anyone who'd sampled that punch would have agreed that it was better used as a fabric dye."

Absently, he hooked a finger in his shirt collar and cleared his throat. "Thank you, but I will tarry on your time no longer. Good day, my lady. Miss Hartley."

⌁

THEA STARED AT St. James's retreating form, her brow knitting in perplexity. "That was rather . . ."

"Charming," the countess said, bemused.

"Curious," she finished. But yes, she thought as she carefully placed her flowers in an empty glass, he'd been charming as well. And sweet. "After all, he'd apologized last evening. Profusely."

"Perhaps your formidable glower as you'd assessed the damage to your skirts had left him unconvinced of his absolution. Or perhaps . . ."

Thea glanced over at Lady Broadbent, sipping her tea, a pair of dove gray eyebrows arched with intrigue. "Or perhaps . . . what?"

The countess set down her cup, a ghost of a smile on her lips. "I believe you have another admirer. It would explain why he was so clumsy in your presence. Your mother had men falling at her feet, as well, and you have the look of her but with your father's pale eyes. The combination is rather striking. Of course, the arrangement of your features leans more toward intensity than welcome, which likely accounts for the fact that we are in this third Season."

"As your ladyship is clearly fond of reminding me," Thea muttered as she picked up her plate again and lifted a cloche.

Her chaperone issued an imperious sniff. "Your parents left you in my charge. I merely aim to direct you. You do wish to find a husband, do you not?"

What Thea wished was to go back to when she felt like herself. To when she felt like she belonged somewhere.

Ever since last Season when she'd returned to her family's home in Addlewick, she'd felt adrift, set apart from all the people and the home that used to provide a sense of comfort and solace.

Everything had changed. There were no more boisterous discussions or sharing of gossip at the breakfast table with her sisters. There had been no more afternoon play rehearsals on the dais in the corner of the drawing room.

Her sisters had both married. They had lives of their own, which was to be expected, she knew. But then her mother and father had changed as well.

Oh, they were still embarrassingly amorous toward each other, always holding hands or giving each other lingering glances across the room. They were still producing and performing plays with the villagers. And Father still recited Shakespeare and jested that Mother was trying to poison him at dinner.

But it wasn't the same.

Perhaps it was because the house had changed, too. There were paintings on the walls that Mother had brought down from the attic. Paintings of a brother and the grandparents that Thea had never known. She'd been born after they'd died. And for almost the entirety of her life, no one had ever spoken of them, as though the pain were too raw.

Now whenever Honoria and her husband, Oscar, popped by for a family dinner, there was always talk of Ernest—Honoria's twin who'd died at the age of four—and of Grandmother and Grandfather.

Of course, Thea understood that the stories and conversations were meant to soothe old wounds, and she was glad for it. Glad for them.

Therefore, it was with immense guilt that, while they had opened a door to healing, she felt like they'd closed a door on her. She'd been cast outside, the stranger that didn't belong to the family who shared a lifetime of memories without her.

The stark reality that the familiar home of her childhood was no longer there had hit her especially hard as she'd been nursing the heart that Kellum had crushed. Not only had she lost the dream of writing a great play for the London stage, but she lost a part of herself that she'd always thought unshakable.

But she didn't want to think about that.

Instead, she lowered the cloche, took her seat at the table and looked squarely at Lady Broadbent. "Yes. I do wish to find a husband."

The countess issued a decisive nod.

"Now then," she said as she spooned marmalade on a triangle of toasted bread. "I do believe that Viscount St. James would make for an interesting prospect. He is nearly five and twenty and, although he has no estate of his own, he is the current heir to an earldom. Unfortunately, his uncle is the Earl of Redcliffe and likely plans to take a third wife."

Over the rim of a teacup, Thea saw the countess's expression sour and assumed it was due to the number of wives. "What happened to the earl's other countesses?"

"A carriage accident took his second wife, along with her traveling companion. As for the first"—she paused to return the unbitten toast to her plate and gestured for a footman to clear it away—"I seem to recall that she'd fallen ill after the loss of her child and was sent to an asylum."

"How dreadful."

"Quite," she said softly, carefully adjusting the gathered cuff of her pale gray morning dress. "Considering Redcliffe's age, the likelihood that he will eventually produce an heir is greater than not. Therefore, perhaps it would behoove us to strike St. James from the list."

Lady Broadbent looked across the table at her as if waiting for an answer.

Until that moment, Thea hadn't been thinking along the lines of marrying St. James. She'd just enjoyed the unexpected pleasure of conversing with him. But now, picturing him as a husband—*her* husband—she felt a sudden jump of nerves and her mouth went dry.

After gulping down the rest of her tea, she nodded. "Consider him stricken."

"A pity, though. St. James reminds me so much of my husband. Pomeroy was also a kind, soft-spoken man, built on the larger scale." She emitted a dreamy sigh and added quietly to herself, "In every sense."

Thea wasn't a fool. She knew that look. With parents who were embarrassingly affectionate, she saw it often enough. And that comment was precisely why she wouldn't consider St. James as a potential husband.

Roxana Hartley had scarred her daughters by performing a play with puppets to explain what a woman was to expect on her wedding night. The characters were Lord Flaccid, Lord Turgid, and Lady Content.

Thea had always had nightmares about Lord Turgid. The puppet was twice the size of Lady Content. He was even bigger than the door of the box stage.

She shuddered at the memory.

Having been reared on plays, she'd seen dozens of battles, actors bathed in silk scarves of blood, and even a cabbage painted to represent a decapitated head rolling across the stage. But nothing had ever frightened her more than Lord Turgid and the way he made Lady Content tremble with fear.

If she had to marry to secure her future, then she would prefer a much smaller man than St. James.

Looking down at the sausage on her plate, she decided she wasn't hungry anymore.

"If you've finished, let us repair to the morning room where our invitations await." Lady Broadbent stood, leaning heavily on her cane. "Come, come, my dear. Don't dawdle and give me your arm. And remove that worry from your countenance. I'm old, not dying."

Thea couldn't help but smile at the terseness, knowing she was all bark and no bite. "You are ageless."

"Stuff and nonsense," she chided as they left the room.

Turning the corner, they entered the cozy little room with hand-painted jonquils on the walls, a fringed violet shawl draped over an upholstered settee, and a fat tufted hassock near a slender writing desk that overlooked the narrow side garden.

"Now then," Lady Broadbent began as she sat in the fiddleback chair behind the desk and uncapped the inkwell. "I believe we shall accept Lady Norris tomorrow, and the Biltons' the day after. We'll attend the musicale the following day, with the Leighton Ball later in the week. You made quite the impression, my dear. Nevertheless"—she paused to look over at Thea who was sitting on the hassock—"I'm sure I don't need to tell you that the unfortunate events of last night should be of a private nature?"

"But it was the tale of the highwayman that earned those invitations."

"Perhaps the make-believe story you invented didn't call your reputation into question but, I can assure you, the truth of our actual encounter surely would. We were quite fortunate to leave with our persons unmolested."

Hearing the censure, Thea protested. "I could hardly stand by and let Abernathy throw us to the wolves. Furthermore, he proved that we were more in danger of him than of the highwayman."

"That may be true. And I'm certain that Abernathy deserved every ounce of humiliation he suffered. However, there would be many who would leap to the wrong conclusion no matter what we claimed. Your reputation would be called into question," she warned, albeit with concern in her gaze.

Thea glanced down at the toes of her slippers peeking out from beneath her ruffled hem. "The thing is . . . I was able to write last night, for the first time since . . . last Season. I haven't told anyone because, frankly, it has been embarrassing, especially when I've written all my life. But worse than that, I'm afraid that if I don't continue to make up stories about the dashing highwayman that I will . . . lose the ability again."

The countess laid down her pen. "I had no idea, my dear. I knew that something between you and Sir Archer had—"

"I don't want to talk about him."

Her chaperone drew in a patient breath. "Very well. But I still have reservations, especially with involving us in the highwayman narrative. After all, there are only so many times I can persuade people to believe that my driver is a crack shot. When we both know that Mr. Dobbins is about as fierce as a titmouse, and his constitution causes him to pass wind whenever he's nervous."

"And he always blames the sound on the horses," Thea added with a small grin, grateful that she wasn't pressed for more details about Kellum. It seemed only fair that she offer a compromise as well. "In regard to your reservations, I will refrain from mentioning our encounter with the highwayman."

"I believe that is the correct—"

"Instead, I will think of something far more clever." She

stood and, before the countess could caution her once more, she bussed a kiss to her cheek and added, "But only if the party is perilously dull and requires a modicum of excitement to keep everyone from perishing. Death by boredom is a grave matter, after all."

Then she swept out of the room and went upstairs to plan her wardrobe. But only after she quickly returned to the breakfast room for her paper flowers.

Her inner Greek chorus hummed with intrigue.

It didn't mean anything, Thea silently told them. This bouquet was just more interesting than her usual gifts, nothing more.

Chapter Eight

ᘓ

THE NORRIS SOIREE was about as thrilling as watching mold grow on a muffin.

"It's called a zoetrope," Lady Norris said, pronouncing each syllable like a governess speaking to an infant. *"Can you say zoetrope?"*

It was a cylindrical bowl with figures painted along the inside, set in various poses between open slats. Then their hostess gave it a spin, grinning as the scene of a horse galloping played before their eyes.

Proud of her accomplishment at setting the bowl into motion, she gave herself a little clap. "Isn't it marvelous?"

Thea sent Lady Broadbent a beseeching look. Clearly, this was the ideal time to begin her tale of the highwayman. But the countess stared back with the stern expression of a general ordering his archers to hold . . . *hollld!*

So, she held.

"Simply marvelous. I've never seen a horse gallop before." When the countess cleared her throat at the slightly sarcastic tone, Thea added, "In quite that fashion."

"Indeed, Miss Hartley. Indeed. It was a gift from my husband. There are some evenings when all we do is gaze into it. Horace is often surprised when the mantel clock chimes and he realizes that we've whiled away an hour or more." She tittered. "I must say it is an entertaining way to pass one's time."

Well, marriage sounds like an absolutely splendid

institution, Thea thought dryly as the hostess and Lady Broadbent walked on to examine another marvel from Horace—a lamp, of all things.

"If the nightly recreation of regarding a revolving bowl won't drive a couple to the altar, then nothing could," a man muttered behind her.

With a laugh on her lips, she turned, surprised to find St. James standing there. Not that he'd startled her, but more that when he spoke under his breath, his voice seemed lower, deeper in a way that his usual softer tone wasn't. Or perhaps, she'd simply imagined it.

"My thoughts precisely," she said.

But he looked just as startled as if he hadn't meant to speak aloud.

Then he said nothing. Behind his spectacles, his gaze dipped to her smile and he swallowed.

Interpreting the silence as nervousness or shyness, and not wishing to scare him off again as she'd done in the breakfast room yesterday, she decided to interject a truth that would put them on equal footing. "Then again, I come from a rather unconventional family where an evening without a well-executed death scene is considered lackluster at best."

His mouth quirked.

Foolishly, she felt as though she'd won a prize of some sort. *Huzzah! I have amused this man, even if reluctantly.* Of course, this achievement wasn't quite up to par with spinning a bowl . . . but she would take it.

"I suppose many would find that rather odd," she continued, eager to encourage conversation with a man who was hardly known for grand speeches. And it was no wonder considering how he was ridiculed. But she hoped he would feel safe with her.

"At Redcliffe Court, I think many a dinner could be improved upon with a dramatic fatality."

"Do you spend much time at your uncle's house?"

He shook his head, the gesture stiff.

She observed that the mention of his uncle was as unpleasant as Kellum was for her. So she quickly changed the topic. "Do you like plays?"

"I do, albeit in the reading of them. Too often, I've found, the performance failed to depict the vibrant world my mind created from the written word of the author," he said.

Even though his words were an observation of what he'd seen on stage, there was a wounded part of Thea that felt the weight of all the failures of which Kellum relished reminding her.

You expect me to hand that rubbish to my actors? The dialogue is wooden. The scene, utterly flat. No audience will be inspired by that drivel.

Oh, don't start pouting. After all, what could you possibly write that has not been written a hundred—nay, a thousand—times before? You haven't even lived. You're still clinging to your mother's apron strings. But, fear not, I am up to the challenge. Now, be a good girl and copy these pages. You might even learn something.

St. James studied her, his mouth pulling into a frown. "I had forgotten that you are a playwright. Forgive me. I hope you know that I meant no insult to—"

"It is the same for me," she interrupted, refusing to let Kellum spoil anything else for her. "After reading a play, I am absolutely certain about the manner it should be performed. Then I see what someone has done to it, or hear an actor miss every cue for comedic timing and I want to groan in frustration. I know I should not say such things, especially when I should be so fortunate as to have the burden of one of my own plays dramatically butchered for a London audience. But I cannot help it." She lifted one shoulder in a negligent shrug. "The curse of being a Hartley, I suppose."

"I admire the ability to create art from thought alone," he

said quietly. "To take from the ether and form a world with your own pen can only have been regarded as a true achievement, whether performed in a London theatre or not."

Her lungs filled like a Montgolfier balloon. In that moment, she felt as though he'd given her back something she'd lost.

"You are most surprising, St. James."

"The fact that I can read?"

At his deadpan reply, she laughed. "No. I highly suspect that you are hiding who you really are from society. Oh, don't look so alarmed. There's nothing for which to be ashamed. It's clear to me that you are a secret romantic. And don't bother to shake your head in denial either. I have proof, after all, in a vase on my bedside table. You'll have to show me how . . . you . . . make . . ."

The sudden intensity in his gaze caused a flood of warmth to rush to her cheeks, and she forgot what she was saying.

There was something about the way his black pupils expanded, spilling over the brown and leaving only a penumbra of mossy green that made her breath catch. Her pulse quickened as if she'd just raced her father's Irish wolfhounds down the towpath at home.

The reaction puzzled her exceedingly.

Seeking relief, she lowered her gaze, letting it drift past the nose that wasn't altogether straight, the generous mouth, square jaw and lopsided cravat. Her perusal skimmed over miles of shoulders and, beneath an ill-fitting black waistcoat, a broad chest that rose and fell as rapidly as her own.

From the corner of her vision, she caught the slight movement of his arm. Then, almost instantly, his hand retracted into a fist and he held it to his side once more.

Had he been about to reach for something but decided against it?

Perhaps he was thirsty. Perhaps that was the reason a

muscle ticked along his jaw. Yet, there was no passing foot-man with a tray of aperitifs, nor was there a convenient table nearby with a waiting glass. So he must have been about to reach for—she swallowed—something else.

It was you, fool, her inner chorus shouted.

Her pulse tried to break through the susceptible skin at her throat. She pressed her gloved fingertips over it, won-dering at this wholly unexpected reaction.

Almost at once, Thea became determined to understand it for the purposes of her writing. She became inordinately curious about those hands and what they might have done if she had not looked. They were so large, broad palmed and long fingered.

It was impossible to imagine that those same hands created such delicate flowers out of colored silver paper.

Thea lifted her gaze and boldly met his, deciding to be direct. "Were you going to take hold of—"

She didn't have the chance to finish.

Without a word, he turned on his heel and walked away, his long legs eating up the drawing room floor in his haste.

He just walked away and left her standing there. Alone.

Well, clearly, she had misunderstood the entirety of their exchange. She'd thought that expanding pupils indi-cated attraction. She'd seen it a number of times in other gentlemen, after all. Then again, pupils also expanded when a room was dark. And since he did wear spectacles, she might have leapt to conclusions, and his poor eyesight might have been the root cause.

Which still didn't explain her own reaction, at all.

Not that it mattered because, at the moment, a wholly new sensation was overtaking her—icy annoyance.

How could St. James have been so engaging one minute then rude in the next? And what had he been reaching for?

Perhaps his arm had lifted to stifle a yawn, the chorus jeered.

Thea grumbled to herself, deciding to write a play where the Greek chorus was brutally murdered.

She was just reaching for a ledger to make note of that— before remembering that this dress didn't have pockets, drat it all—when she was joined by two other gentlemen.

Lord Bromley and Mr. Handscombe were brothers three and two years her senior, respectively. From having met them last Season, she knew they considered themselves art aficionados, so their conversation was usually engaging. And, if their ready smiles were any indication, they appeared to want to be in her company . . . unlike a certain viscount.

Giving them her attention, she did her level best to put any distracting thoughts from her mind.

"I say, Miss Hartley," Lord Bromley said, "we just saved you from quite the harrowing ordeal."

"I'm not certain I know what you mean, Bromley?"

Mr. Handscombe gestured with a jerk of his chin. "St. James appeared to have you trapped in conversation."

"Though I imagine it was rather one-sided. He was likely one incomprehensible utterance away from resorting to his ape self and dragging his knuckles on the floor."

"We heard he nearly crushed you at Beaucastle's fete."

She stiffened, disliking their tones. Just because she was vexed by St. James didn't mean she wanted to hear him disparaged. "He merely tripped over a rug, as anyone might have done."

Even so, she was still lamenting the loss of the gown with the velvet pockets.

"Forgive us, Miss Hartley. We meant nothing by it. Just having a lark." Mr. Handscombe appeared contrite enough for her to offer a short nod and he smiled again. "You have a most forgiving and generous heart, and you've always been kind."

"And fearless as well," Bromley interjected, clapping

his younger brother on the shoulder. "Do not forget, our Miss Hartley faced a highwayman, so the rumor states."

Thea noticed a few sly gazes swivel in her direction, intrigue marking their expressions. But she also saw Lady Broadbent across the room and knew what was at stake.

"You've been misinformed," she said reluctantly, knowing she was missing an opportunity to provide a riveting firsthand account. "It was only through a carriage window that my chaperone and I witnessed the highwayman."

Bromley was undeterred by this fact. "I say you are still fearless. Were an ape to escape the zoological society and stroll through those doors, I doubt even that simian could frighten you."

Even though he winked good-naturedly to his brother, she was irritated by the thinly veiled comparison to the moniker attached to St. James. And besides, he didn't remotely resemble an ape. It was true that he had tremendously broad shoulders and ill-fitting clothes, but his features were every bit striking. Some might even consider them handsome.

Not that St. James would care what she thought, of course.

So, she would put him from her mind. After all, she was on a new path this Season, looking to rekindle her creative spark and to find a husband. As for the latter, she knew she would have to make some allowances.

With that thought in mind, she exhaled her irritation.

"Did I hear my brother mention a highwayman?" a young woman with hair the color of corn silk asked. The newly out Miss Handscombe's dimpled cheeks spread in a grin as she sidled up with her raven-haired friend, Miss Livet. "Oh, my head must be full of feathers. You're the one who saw him, are you not?"

When Thea offered a nod, Miss Livet gasped and leaned closer. "I've heard a few whispers here and there, but not the full story. Could you tell us, do you think? Or is it a great secret?"

The way her brown eyes danced told Thea that she would be the first to spill it if it were a secret. And it didn't bother her. Quite the opposite.

Though, it did make her miss her sisters and the bond they'd once shared—the teasing, the mischief, the laughter, the plays . . .

Thinking of plays, thoughts of Kellum intruded again. Memories spun in her mind like a zoetrope of when she'd met him at the end of that first spring in London, and the sky seemed to open with possibility.

She just never thought the possibility was that everything she knew about herself would disappear.

Kellum hadn't just told her that she'd lacked talent. He'd whittled away at her self-esteem, little by little, shaping her into someone she no longer recognized.

At first, the comments were seemingly insignificant, banal even. One day, he'd frown and ask her what she'd done to her hair. *Slice*. He wouldn't elaborate. He'd simply leave the question between them for her to wonder over as he changed the topic.

There were a few times when they'd been sitting close together, poring over a script, and he'd wrinkled his nose and asked if she'd bathed in cabbage water. *Slice*.

When he'd kissed her, he'd laughed and said that it was obvious she was an ingénue in every way. So she'd tried to be what he wanted, to take his instruction. But he'd complained at every attempt. Her lips were either too firm or too soft. Her mouth was either too broad or too narrow. And she either kissed with no passion or was overzealous. *Slice, slice, slice*.

After a while she'd hated the mere idea of kissing. So she'd stopped altogether. She'd shied away, making excuses that she was afraid her chaperone would discover them, even when Thea had made sure Lady Broadbent never suspected she'd been sneaking away unsupervised at all.

By the time Kellum delivered his final, soul-destroying speech to her, her sense of self had been stripped so bare, so hollowed out, that she'd believed every word. Believed that he had the first and last word on all things regarding Althea Hartley.

Then she'd gone home to find that everything had changed and she no longer belonged anywhere.

But she was here to change that. At least, she hoped.

As her acquaintances awaited her reply, she saw St. James enter the room and cast a dark glower in her direction.

She stiffened, a piece of her old self riling at once.

What did he think, that just because he didn't find her interesting enough to continue a conversation, no one else could?

Well, he was about to learn otherwise. Because if there was one thing she hadn't lost, one precious thing she'd learned from being a Hartley, it was how to captivate an audience.

And there was no time like the present.

◄╼

JASPER SWORE UNDER his breath as he watched those ice blue eyes hurl daggers at him from across the room.

She didn't know it, but he'd had to leave. Standing that close to her and imagining those flowers—*his* flowers—on her bedside table had set off such a flurry of inappropriate thoughts that it took every ounce of restraint not to reach out and touch her.

Ever since the night of Beaucastle's fete, he'd become a stranger to himself, his usual control sorely lacking. He'd even spoken aloud in his actual voice, twice in her presence.

She was making him forget himself.

And when her cheeks had pinkened, her eyes darkening as they skimmed down his body, it made his skin prickle beneath his clothes. His palms and fingertips tingled to the point where the act of not touching her had caused an intense physical ache.

The only thing that stopped him from making a complete and utter fool out of himself was the two young cubs that headed in her direction. He'd felt his hackles rise. A strange, almost primitive compulsion rose inside him that made him want to growl at them, to warn them in no uncertain terms what would happen if they dared approach what was his.

But one last ounce of sanity must have remained in his pia mater, for it reminded him of all that was at stake, of who truly needed his protection, and that Miss Hartley—no matter how tempted he might be—was not his to guard and never would be.

So, he'd walked away. He'd had to.

Perhaps he should have left the party altogether because that same compulsion was still humming through him as he saw the crowd forming around her. She moved gracefully toward the zoetrope, a slew of slathering puppies, debutantes and their chaperones following like acolytes.

"I know you wished to hear about that dreadful night, Miss Livet," she said conspiratorially. "But it pales in comparison to the tale that Lady Broadbent and I overheard at tea."

"Oh, do tell us," one of the ladies chirruped excitedly.

A sense of dread filled Jasper. Surely, she wouldn't. And yet, even before he heard the word *highwayman* whispering through the crowd, he knew she would.

Bloody hell!

"Of course, it would be wrong of me to reveal the identity of this gentleman. For the sake of this tale, however, he shall be named Lord Zed, because he is not deserving of a more elevated letter of the alphabet as this terrible account will soon convey."

Offering up a story with a secret identity was akin to handing a drunkard a bottle of whisky for safekeeping. The mystery of it all would only whet the *ton*'s appetite.

He moved deeper into the room as she began her tale about Lord Zed and his encounter with the highwayman.

"The report of a pistol rent the air." She closed her fan with a snap. "The eerie howl of a wolf echoed off the trees . . ."

Damn it all! He was supposed to be elusive. A shadow. The thief that no one dared speak about out of fear. But because his brain had turned to mush that night, he'd neglected to warn her.

Not that it would have done any good. It was painfully clear that Miss Althea Hartley didn't react to danger in a predictable manner.

Jasper didn't know how he would stop her.

Oh, and she had certainly set the stage for a grand production. With the wave of her open fan, she set the zoetrope spinning, the light of a taper casting shadows all around, inviting her audience to imagine they were on the darkened road as the carriage picked up speed.

It was a clever trick. Too clever.

"Lord Zed thought nothing of the occupants in his carriage, but began to stuff all his valuables in the . . ."

Jasper saw his opportunity as the candle flame grew higher, lengthening in the draft of the fan. The light sparked in his mind and a strategy formed.

"There must be a place deep in the forest where the highwayman waits," she continued, weaving her spell. "He moves like a wraith through the shadows . . ."

Needing to take the focus off her tales of the highwayman and turn it back to his clumsiness, he acted quickly.

First, he stepped behind Miss Hartley. And when she

glanced over her shoulder, he made all appearances of contrition, earning a begrudging nod of forgiveness.

Leaning in to view the spinning bowl, he bumped her fan and caught it on fire. Gasps of alarm followed.

He assisted by grabbing a vase of flowers from the mantel.

Then he expertly tripped over his own feet. And *accidentally* emptied the contents of the vase onto Miss Hartley's gown.

Objective accomplished.

Chapter Nine

꧁꧂

THEA DECIDED THAT she loathed St. James. His mishaps had ruined not one but *two* gowns!

She didn't know if he planned to attend the concert at the music hall tonight. But if he even dared approach her, she might take a pair of scissors to his cravat.

Not that it would make much difference. His cravats were always wrinkled, with the knot slightly askew. Most of the time she'd wanted to fix it for him. Just pull him aside and have a conversation that she actually enjoyed.

But that was before he'd dowsed her with a vase full of putrid flower water.

To think, she'd actually been happy to see him stand by her side while she'd told her tale the other night. At first. Now as she and Lady Broadbent entered the music hall with its tall windows and ornately vaulted ceiling, she was scanning the room with dread.

And yet, it wasn't the abrupt end of her unfinished story of the highwayman and the deluge of smelly water—which had taken three long soaks in the copper bathtub to be rid of—that she'd thought of when a messenger arrived with a new bouquet of paper flowers yesterday morning. It had been their conversation. The way he made her laugh. The tingles that danced over her skin when he looked at her in that intense way of his. And his hands . . .

She swallowed down a groan of frustration. Because

every time she looked at those tiny little petals, she thought of his big hands. And thinking of his hands led her back to the moment he'd reached out before lowering his arm and clenching his fist.

From there, her thoughts gathered momentum as she wondered what might have happened if he hadn't stopped. Wondered if he'd have taken hold of her hand, the warmth of him seeping through her glove. Wondered what it would be like if he'd peeled off her glove, inch by inch, until she felt those hands on her skin.

She shook her head to clear it. This wasn't like her.

Being raised by two overly affectionate parents, their casual touches and saucy looks across the room had embarrassed her. They even kissed in front of their children. It was unheard of in polite society!

At an early age, Thea discovered no other parents did that. Other husbands and wives behaved with decorum. They practically pretended their spouse didn't exist in anything other than name.

When women were breeding, they were hidden away from society. And when they reappeared, they would present their child to visitors like a bauble they'd purchased in a curiosity shop, then send the mewling creature back to the nursery.

Meanwhile, Roxana Hartley performed puppet shows for her daughters to explain that children came into being after Lord Turgid would lie with Lady Content. But only *some* of the time. According to her mother, there were other times when Lady Content and Lord Turgid merely enjoyed each other's companionship.

Until a few years ago, Thea had assumed that Lady Content preferred Lord Turgid because he was tall enough to shield her from the rain. After all, Lady Content was obsessed with the weather, forever talking about becoming wet.

But Thea made the mistake of mentioning this to her mother.

After drying tears of laughter from her eyes, Roxana had explained everything. In detail.

Thorough. Mortifying. Detail.

To make matters worse, her mother threatened her, telling Thea that it was going to be like that for her one day. That she couldn't escape the passion in the Hartley blood.

Was it any wonder that Thea preferred to bury herself in plays? Or why she'd always struggled to understand the full complexity of human behavior with so many opposing viewpoints and confusing examples in her life?

The worst part was that Thea's muse had disappeared again. Just vanished in a poof of smoke. Or rather, in a deluge of rank water.

And just thinking about St. James made her so angry she could— *Argh!*

"Are you quite yourself, my dear?" Lady Broadbent asked in hushed disapproval as they entered the rooms of the music hall. "I merely ask because one does not usually growl in public for one's own amusement."

She had to paste on a smile when a matron near the door glared at her through her quizzing glass.

"As you might have noticed, I'm a bit distracted," she whispered as her chaperone paused to survey the room, seeking the most advantageous seats. "In fact, I feel a sense of ennui returning. Perhaps we should leave and stay in the rest of the evening."

"Stuff and nonsense. You're merely plagued by the thought of encountering St. James this evening."

Thea opened her mouth on a denial, but snapped it closed when the countess slid an imperious glance her way as if daring her to deny it. "Fine. But wouldn't you be wary, too? He's doing his utmost to make a laughingstock of me. I'll never find a suitable husband at this rate."

Or, more importantly, she would never find her muse, who had obviously decided to abandon her in favor of someone more worthy of a footnote.

Her sigh filled the entire room.

Lady Broadbent's fan swatted her lightly on the wrist. "Continue making that infernal sound and I shall send for a physician to examine your lungs. Then I will write to your mother and inform her that her youngest is lovesick."

"I most certainly am not."

"Then stop behaving as though the actions of one man can decide how you proceed from this moment forward."

Though quietly spoken, the reprimand stung. But when Thea glanced up to see compassion and sympathy in her eyes, she wasn't altogether certain if Lady Broadbent was speaking about St. James . . . or about Kellum.

Either way, she offered a nod. It would do her no good to waste time thinking about either of them.

"Now then," the countess continued, "it's perfectly apparent that St. James has done you a service, for we have received an abundance of new invitations."

"Because they all wish to witness the next debacle for themselves," she grumbled. No one was even talking about her tales of the highwayman. It was so unfair.

She would have to be even more creative next time.

"Quite true. Nevertheless, we will use this to our advantage. New avenues, Miss Hartley. I have a very good feeling about these new avenues." Lady Broadbent's lips curved in a pleased grin. Then she pointed to the far side of the room. "Ah, splendid. There is Lady Abernathy, and with three seats open beside her."

As they began walking in that direction, Thea inquired in a whisper, "Are we certain we wish to sit beside a woman who might know about . . . the other night?"

"That is precisely why we should, in order to discover all we can for ourselves," she said, her undaunted trek punctuated by the clip of her cane on the hardwood floor. "When I saw her at the tea shop last week, she was considering removing herself from town, which caused me some worry when I saw the state of her dress and shawl. After making a few inquiries, I learned that she had to let go of several servants because of her son's negligence in ensuring her care."

"That certainly sounds like the man who threw us on the mercy of a—"

"Hush," the countess interrupted before turning to issue a warm smile to the lady in question. "My dear Beatrice, how good it is to see you. You know Miss Hartley, of course. Might we sit beside you? Unless, you're expecting your son, perhaps?"

"Please do," Lady Abernathy said, her face wrinkling like a forgotten apple on the cellar floor. "I was to be joined by Lord Abernathy, but I just received word from his steward that my son has grown tired of town and will reside at his hunting box for a time. Winston mentioned nothing to me himself but that is somewhat commonplace. As we age, our importance to our children ebbs."

Thea exchanged a glance with the countess, wondering if Abernathy would have relayed the events of that night to his mother. Likely not. And she didn't believe it would be prudent to mention that they had shared a carriage.

"How right you are," Lady Broadbent added, tsking in commiseration. "I rarely have word from my own daughter. Of late, Geraldine saves all her attention for her grandchild. Who, as you may recall, is also the nephew of Miss Hartley, here."

"Ah, yes. Miss Hartley, I do hope your family is well."

"They are indeed, thank you, my lady." As rules of social engagement went, Thea knew it was expected of her to add to the conversation. Unfortunately, all she could think about was what an utter sapskull Lord Abernathy was. So she settled for "My, what a lovely shawl you have."

"It is quite handsome, is it not?" the older woman agreed. "It arrived at my door this very day. I believe it was a gift from my son."

Lady Broadbent's brow knitted. "You *believe* it was?"

"I should say that it must have been, for who else?" She leaned closer to the countess to whisper behind her fan. "And directly following this, I received word from my solicitor and my milliner about an accounting error in my favor. Honestly, Olympia, I cannot recall having so much good fortune in one day."

"Can you not? Well, that is quite an interesting coincidence."

Thea could tell by Lady Broadbent's curious expression that they were of like mind and both considering the dubious chance that the despicable Abernathy would be overwhelmed with generosity, if it was not to benefit himself in some way. He certainly didn't seem the type of man to remain anonymous when performing a good deed.

It was possible, she supposed, that she'd misjudged him. Or that, perhaps, his brush with death had altered him for the better.

And yet, she couldn't help but wonder if the gifts were sent by someone who had every reason to remain anonymous . . . like a highwayman, perhaps?

But no. The very notion was ludicrous.

Why would a thief take such risks simply to help an old woman he didn't even know?

Unless, of course, he did know the dowager viscountess . . .

Pondering this errant thought, she revisited the encounter with the highwayman, playing it again in her mind. Come to think of it, he hadn't spoken like a typical brigand. Or at least, how she would imagine a brigand would. There was nothing of high country or low country in his voice. Or even Cockney for that matter. In fact, his tone had an air of authority, his vowels rounded, consonants crisp.

He spoke like a gentleman. Or at least, like a man who had been educated alongside gentlemen. And if that were true, then one could conclude he had an association with members of the *ton*. So it was possible that he was acquainted with Lady Abernathy . . .

Thea was so lost in these fantastical musings, unsure if they were merely a fabrication of her creative mind or a possibility of fact, that she didn't even notice the ushers moving along the outskirts of the room, snuffing out the wall sconces. She paid no attention as the musicians tuned their instruments.

It wasn't until a figure descended into the seat beside hers that she realized the concert had begun . . . and St. James was sitting next to her.

⟶

JASPER DIDN'T KNOW why he'd come.

He'd made his point and taken all the steam out of her tales of the highwayman. All the focus had been on him and his clumsiness. He didn't need to prove anything more. Besides, a musicale wouldn't even provide her the opportunity to engage an audience with her stories.

Yet, for some inexplicable reason, he couldn't stay away.

Knowing that she would be here had set him on edge for hours. He'd paced a groove in the floor between the door and window, deciding whether to stay in town or ride.

Torrington was on his way to his mistress and, according to rumor, prepared to shower her in expensive baubles. Jasper should be saddling his destrier, readying for a night's raid.

Instead, he was here.

He couldn't remember being driven by anything other than his need to ensure that those he cared about were safe and secure and that his uncle—and all the men like him— would pay.

But this? He didn't know how to explain it, even to himself.

It felt like he was drowning, thrashing below the waves, struggling to breach the choppy surface for just one sip of air. Althea Hartley was the air. Hell, she might even be the shore for all he knew.

Whatever this thing was, he didn't like it. But fighting against it was like trying to hold back the tides.

Which brought him here, to the musicale. And sitting so close, he could almost touch her.

His mind sprinted through a quick series of calculations. If he touched her, he could pretend that it was an accident, that his frame was simply too large to be contained in that chair.

A brush of his sleeve to her elbow would hardly be noticed. But what about the knee of his trousers against her skirts?

Bloody hell, he was pathetic!

He let his gaze skim over her arm, to the bare two inches of exposed skin between the cuff of her mutton sleeve and the top of her evening gloves. The pads of his fingers ached to touch her there, drumming an insistent beat to explore the fine gossamer hairs, to follow the slender blue vein running along the inside of her elbow.

If he pressed his lips there, would he feel her blood heat for him? Would she taste of salt or of nectar? Would she gasp and draw away . . . or would she watch him with hooded eyes as he peeled her glove all the way down and traced the lines of her palm with his tongue?

As the music soared through the room, he could feel his pulse race, thicken.

Beside him, she shifted, arranging the fall of her skirt in a way that brought her arm closer to him. Her sleeve brushed his. He drew in a sharp breath, tasting her delicate floral perfume on his tongue. It made his mouth water.

His hands had been fisted over his thighs as if in self-preservation from the moment he sat down. But now a strange sort of madness bade him to open his palm, to slide his hand a fraction closer to that fall of blue silk. Unable to stop there, he arched one finger the slightest degree and brushed a knuckle against the fabric.

He heard her intake of breath. Felt her eyes on him. And when he dared to turn his head to bear the condemnation he deserved, he was nearly undone by the sight of her parted lips and flushed cheeks, her pupils spilling darkly.

But no, it must have been the dim light playing tricks on him. The mere idea that she could be even the smallest degree affected by him was laughable.

Jasper stood abruptly, chair legs scraping on the floor.

Then he dropped a paper flower at her feet and stalked away without looking back.

Chapter Ten

~∽~

$\mathcal{J}$ASPER NEEDED TO leave London before he lost his mind. So, the following morning, he drove out to visit his aunt and cousins.

The two-story cottage stood on a parcel of land situated among grassy hillocks and woodlands just outside of Notting Hill. Though not even half the size of the house they'd had before Uncle Jacob had died, it was clean and had room enough for three women and their cook to live without breathing down each other's necks. He tried to be thankful for that. But it was difficult when he knew the roof over their heads was one of Redcliffe's properties.

Hefting the crate from the boot of his carriage, he ambled toward the kitchen entrance. The whitewashed door flew open before he could call out a greeting.

Standing beneath the lintel was a fiery-haired termagant with her hands perched on her hips. An army of one. A single arching eyebrow rose in her freckled heart-shaped face as she surveyed him from brim to boots. "And just who might you be, stranger?"

"Tempest, let me in."

"And how do you know my name?"

He rolled his eyes at his cousin. "I apologize. I know it has been a few days . . ."

"Ha!"

"More than a week," he amended. "But I've been taking

care of a few matters. Contrary to your belief, I do have a life."

"*Jasper?*" came a soft voice from behind the she-devil. Then a little blonde beauty peered over her shoulder, her face splitting into a grin. "Jasper! Mother, Cousin Jasper's here!"

It was Tempest's turn to roll her green eyes as she stepped aside. "Fine. You may enter. But wipe your bloody boots."

"Tempest, language," came the thready voice of his aunt Clara from the other room.

"Apologies, Mother," she called out, then muttered under her breath, "But Jasper's the one you should blame for teaching me all the words I get scolded for speaking."

He chuckled and stepped sideways through the door. But the instant Tempest glared at him, he stepped back again to wipe his boots on the mat, making a good show of it for her benefit. For a young woman of only one and twenty, she was far too crotchety.

Walking to the center of the snug kitchen, he set the crate down on a scarred table. "Where's your cook?"

Jasper didn't like the fact that he couldn't afford to have them keep more than a cook and a groundskeeper. A maid-of-all-work came twice a week to help, but that was all.

He would much rather keep an army standing by in case Redcliffe should want to look over the property, which he had been known to do on occasion.

"It's her off day," Iris said, standing on tiptoe to peer inside the crate and comb through the straw. At fifteen, she still possessed a girlish roundness in her cheeks and petite frame, and her eyes held a childish innocence that he hoped she would keep for many years to come. "What did you bring this time?"

"Mutton, ham, eggs, cheeses, fruits, nuts, sweetmeats and so forth. There might even be something in there for you."

"For me?" Her pale eyes brightened as if he didn't bring her something special every time. "Where is it?"

Tempest chimed in with a huff. "I suppose you'll have to help me unpack the crate if you want to find out."

"Why are you always so cross?"

"Why are *you* always so lazy?"

"Am not."

In that same moment, Aunt Clara began to cough. "Girls"—*cough*—"try to love each"—*cough*—"other."

His cousins exchanged a worried glance. Then Tempest stepped forward and pressed a kiss to her sister's cheek on her way to pour a glass of water from a waiting ewer before rushing out of the room.

Jasper could hear Tempest's voice soften as she helped her mother through another one of her coughing fits. The physician assured him that it wasn't consumption. Her frailty was a result of a prolonged bout of lung fever shortly after her husband's death six years ago. Back then, there had been times when she'd regained her strength for weeks or months, but those episodes were fewer and farther between. He couldn't remember the last time he'd seen her able to walk more than a few steps at a time without exhaustion claiming her.

Turning his head, he caught Iris's worried expression and tried to reassure her. "I brought more medicine, too, in case the doctor hasn't been by."

"Mr. Lowen won't be stopping by anymore. I heard him telling Tempest that he is needed in Bath and that he was not able to refuse the offer."

Jasper's hands curled into fists. He had no doubt that Redcliffe was behind this. The very same thing had happened to the two previous doctors hired in the parish.

The earl liked to keep people desperate. Desperate people were willing to agree to anything.

Unfortunately, his uncle Jacob had been a desperate

man. He'd made some poor investments that took everything he had.

Then he made the error of striking a bargain with the Earl of Redcliffe.

It had been a generous proposition, of course. With Redcliffe they always were. At first. But Jacob had ended up selling his debt to the devil and the devil had taken everything in return.

In the end, they'd lost their home and were forced to live in one of the properties owned by Redcliffe.

But ever since the death of Uncle Jacob, Jasper had done what he could for his aunt and cousins. He made sure they had enough food and money to pay their servants and rents. Rents that Redcliffe raised more often than not.

Clara, Tempest and Iris were the only family Jasper had left. And they were one of the primary reasons he pretended to be an addlepated oaf, lumbering around town. It was the only way to protect them.

Redcliffe could never know the truth. Whenever he felt threatened, unappreciated or undermined in any way, he could lash out and do the most despicable things. To him, other people were merely objects whose sole purpose was to feed his ego's ever-constant appetite.

"Fear not, Iris," Jasper said. "I'll find a doctor and bring him here."

She offered a tremulous smile, then began unpacking the crate.

He walked into the sparsely furnished yellow parlor and saw his aunt, her chair in a wedge of sunlight streaming in through the window. Tempest sat on the threadbare settee, darning a pair of wool stockings.

Pressing a kiss to his aunt's cheek, he decided to add another log to the fire. "You're looking well, Aunt."

"And you are a terrible liar," she said with a fond smile, her face drawn with violet-tinged hollows beneath her eyes.

Her hair, once a vibrant red like Tempest's, had gone gray from worry. "How are you, my boy? There's something different about you."

As he tended the fire, he lifted his shoulders in a shrug.

For reasons beyond his understanding, a vision of Althea swam to the forefront of his mind. Then again, she was always treading those murky waters in his skull, popping up when he least expected it.

"You've met someone!" his aunt announced, her expression brightening. "That's it, isn't it? My mother had the gift of sight. Did I ever tell you that? Well, now I must know, who is she?"

"There isn't—" He broke off as Tempest looked up expectantly and even Iris swept into the room. He felt the weight of those six eyes as if they were six thousand. And he was glad that the members of the *ton* weren't as perceptive as his own family. After a moment, he expelled a breath. "I might have met a certain Miss Althea Hartley."

As soon as he spoke her name, a jolt of electricity shot down his spine as if he'd been struck by a stray bolt of lightning.

Aunt Clara gasped. "Roxana Hartley's daughter?"

He scrubbed a hand over the back of his neck. "I believe so."

"Ah," she said with a smile, practically singsonging an aria from a single syllable. "Then she must be beautiful. During my first Season, Roxana was the most beautiful woman I'd ever met. Most of the gentlemen in London were half in love with her, your father included. Of course, that all changed the moment he clapped eyes on your mother. After that, no other woman existed. I remember the way John stared at your mother whenever he saw her entering a room or walking down the stairs. Your uncle Jacob used to call him a trout because he'd just stand there, mouth agape for a full minute as if all the words had fallen out of his head."

Well, at least Jasper understood the reason he turned into a driveling sapskull around Althea. It was in his blood.

"Was that the way it was for Father when he met you?" Iris asked, sinking down to her knees beside her mother's chair.

She nodded, her eyes reddening around the edges as she sniffed. "If there's one thing I know for certain, it's that when a Trueblood falls, they fall hard."

Then all eyes turned back to Jasper again.

He held up his hands in surrender. "There has been no falling. There never will be. Miss Hartley is destined for greater things and I have no place in her life."

His aunt frowned. "I don't like hearing you talk like that. She would be lucky to have you. Any woman would be. And if she happens to have a brother . . ."

Tempest scoffed when her mother's gaze shifted to her. "Then that would make him a gentleman, and no gentleman worth his salt would be interested in marrying a penniless spinster who does her own laundry."

Iris made a *pfft* sound. "You? Doing laundry? My pinafore looks like it was washed in rocks and mud when you're done with it. I do a much better job."

"At least I know the difference between a potato and a turnip in the garden."

"Well, I don't like turnips. So I won't pick turnips."

"Girls," Aunt Clara said on a sigh, closing her eyes as she rested her head against the back of the chair. "Go into the kitchen and make a pot of tea."

Tempest bowed her head in regret, setting her needlework aside. Standing, she took her sister by the hand. "Come along, brat. Let's see if there are any biscuits in that crate."

"Nan baked some fresh for you," Jasper said as they disappeared. "There's plum cake, as well."

Seeing his aunt's frailty, and their struggle with this

paltry existence they'd been reduced to living, made Jasper so angry that he didn't know what to do with it. He had been doing everything he could. But his uncle kept a tight rein on his allowance. It was just enough for him to keep up appearances. And Redcliffe demanded that, at the very least, he keep up appearances.

So Jasper had been forced to become creative in making money to help his aunt and cousins.

There was also a part of him that feared Redcliffe's true intentions.

Once, a few years ago, the earl had magnanimously invited Clara, Tempest and Iris to his grand estate for a picnic. A towering maze of boxwood hedgerows twisted and turned in the back garden. The sight had thrilled both Tempest and Iris and they'd been invited to explore it.

Eager, they had ventured in and ended up deciding to take different paths to try their luck, calling out to each other merrily as they went along.

That was when Jasper noticed Redcliffe, watching their progress from one of the balconies of the house, his lips curving into a disturbing smile.

There had been rumors about guests invited to tour the earl's pleasure gardens. If the young woman was pretty, her chaperone might find herself ill from a purgative that had been slipped into her tea. Not too ill to rouse suspicion, just enough to cause embarrassment . . . and to leave their charge unaccompanied and unaware.

Shortly after that particular visit, the earl offered to have Clara and her daughters live beneath his roof. When she refused, he doubled the rent. And that wasn't the last time. He also had enough connections that made it impossible for her to live anywhere else.

But Jasper was determined to do all he could to keep them far from Redcliffe's reach. Even if that meant he would have to continue with his charade as society's clumsy oaf.

Chapter Eleven

❧

THEA AWOKE THE following morning with her head throbbing. She hadn't dozed off until an hour before dawn, and even then her sleep was fitful.

It had been two days and she still couldn't get her encounter with St. James out of her mind. It had been so . . . befuddling. That was the only word for the mixed state of breathless confusion he'd left her in. And all because he'd touched her skirt.

She wondered if there was something wrong with her.

Perhaps having her soul hollowed out last year had left her open to this strange push and pull with St. James, so much so that she couldn't stop thinking about their encounters, long after they'd ended.

It was maddening.

Not only that, but there was this niggling sensation in the center of her brain that seemed to want her attention. It was like her Greek chorus was snapping their fingers in front of her face and telling her, *Wake up! Pay attention. This is important.*

The problem was she couldn't figure out what she was supposed to pay attention to because her thoughts kept returning to the slow graze of his knuckle against blue satin.

Feeling flushed, she shoved the coverlet aside. She *had* to stop thinking about it.

Determined, she clambered out of bed and distracted herself with choosing a dress from her wardrobe.

"Definitely not blue," she muttered.

She even shied away from lavender because it was too close of a cousin to that fretful color. The jonquil was too similar to gold, a color she would forever associate with Beaucastle's soiree and the loss of the velvet pocket gown. She'd been wearing peridot on the evening of the fan debacle, so not green. That left her with burgundy for the day, and her ruffled silver gown for the Leighton Ball that evening.

A short while later, as the maid was plaiting and pinning her hair into a coil, she saw Lady Broadbent in the mirror. She sauntered into the bedchamber with one hand leaning on her cane and the other holding a card.

"We have been summoned to tea, my dear. From Lady Abernathy," she supplied and cast a surreptitious glance to the maid.

Reaching up to sink the last pin, Thea said, "Thank you, Tally. That'll be all for now."

"Yes, miss." The brown-haired maid dipped into a curtsy, then went to the door. But before leaving, she cast a concerned look over her shoulder.

Thea nodded in reassurance.

Tally was like family. She'd been maid to all three of the Hartley sisters. They'd practically grown up together. But being family meant that she also exchanged letters with the servants at Hartley Hall. Which meant that, whatever the countess was about to say, it likely was something that would cause needless worry if reported to those in Addlewick.

In other words, it was about their encounter with the highwayman.

When the door closed, Thea pivoted on the stool and faced the countess. "Do you suspect that Lady Abernathy knows about . . . the other night?"

"Decidedly not or she would have mentioned it. Beatrice

is quite frank," the countess said, her expression thoughtful. "No, I do believe she means to tell more of her mysterious good fortune. Though she could have no idea how eager we are to hear it."

Last evening on the short drive back to the townhouse, they had both admitted immense curiosity over the recent turn of events for the dowager viscountess. A new shawl *and* her accounts paid, directly following her son's encounter with the highwayman, seemed more than mere coincidence.

Which begged the question: Who was responsible?

They were both of the same opinion that Lord Abernathy was incapable of such generosity. Therefore, it must have been the highwayman, for he had not molested either of them and had seemed to have a sense of honor . . . Well, as honorable as a pistol-wielding man who robbed coaches in the dead of night could be.

However, they were not in agreement as to the likely identity of said highwayman.

Lady Broadbent speculated that it was a servant of Lady Abernathy's, someone loyal to his mistress but also tired of not being paid the wages due him.

Thea, on the other hand, thought the highwayman had to have been a relative of Lady Abernathy's. Who other than family would care about her situation?

Additionally, Thea pointed out that it didn't seem as though Abernathy's carriage had been chosen at random. The highwayman had clearly been surprised that she and the countess had been there. And who other than family would have known where Abernathy would have been and likely with his pockets flush?

She was nearly certain she was right. All she needed was an opportunity to slyly question the dowager viscountess.

But what Thea didn't tell Lady Broadbent was the reason

she was determined to discover the identity of this high-wayman.

It was because their encounter had sparked her creativity. She had written long into the night, alive with tingling effervescence as she filled page after page.

But then she'd made the mistake of letting her mind drift to Kellum. Doubt had crept in, sinking its claws into her, and she began to wonder if the play would ever be good enough to make him eat his words. After that, her ability to find the right words was like dropping a wooden pail into an empty well. *Clunk*.

The only sure way to get back what she'd lost was to find the highwayman. He was the key to everything.

Thea knew for certain that he was her muse.

He had to be. There was no other explanation.

"And together, we'll uncover this mystery," she said to her chaperone, hiding her own eagerness.

Eagerness . . . or desperation? the chorus taunted.

She ignored them, her mind set on finding him. Additionally, she hoped the distraction would help her focus her thoughts where they belonged. Which was definitely not thinking about St. James.

⚮

LADY ABERNATHY'S FAVORITE hobby was arranging flowers and then watching them die a slow, shriveling death. At least, that's what Thea thought as she and Lady Broadbent were shown into the somber parlor that afternoon and witnessed bouquets in various states of demise on every table.

The gray room even smelled like a wake. The stale, lingering odor of tallow candle smoke combined with the cloying fragrance of too many flowers in a snug space hung in the air.

Oddly enough, the dowager viscountess shared a resemblance to the arrangement nearest her in the way that their wilted heads appeared hunched over, their leafy shoulders curled forward. But Thea kept this observation to herself.

As the maid carefully laid out the tea on a low table, their hostess impatiently tipped herself to and fro in a fiddleback rocking chair, the top draped with a doily that flapped from the quick syncopated motion.

"Yes, yes. That'll be all, Francine," she huffed with a shooing gesture. As soon as the maid stepped out of the room, she abruptly stopped rocking, poised at the edge of her chair as if ready to pounce. "That girl was born a dawdler. Not an ounce of haste in her. Shall I pour?" she asked, already pouring as if the question were a mere courtesy.

Her gnarled hands shook, her knobby wrists looking ready to snap as she filled three cups without lifting the spout. Tea sloshed over the rim from one to the next, brown liquid pooling in the saucers.

When she finished, she set the pot down with a heavy clatter. "I declare. My cook must fill the bottom with rocks. I'd sack her if she didn't make such a fine scone. Pillowy as clouds. Milk, Olympia?"

"Yes, thank you," Lady Broadbent said and took the proffered cup their hostess rattled over to her.

"Sugar, Miss Hartley?"

"Just milk, if you *ple*—" Thea broke off as their hostess withdrew a heaping spoon from the sugar bowl and plopped it into her cup with a *sploosh*. "Er . . . thank you."

"Let's get down to brass tacks, shall we?" The dowager viscountess issued a sharp clap of her hands. "I should like to know why you were so eager to seek your carriage before the final score had played out at the musicale."

Thea shifted under the weight of the tiny woman's stare. This was not what she imagined they were here to discuss. Now she felt as though the scant few moments next to St. James were painted in scandalous detail on the slats of a zoetrope and Lady Abernathy had her quizzing glass trained on the whirring images.

"I . . . wouldn't say *eager*," she said. "We merely wished to avoid the crush."

"Miss Hartley is always looking out for my best interest, as I'm sure your servants do for you," Lady Broadbent interjected. "In fact, I imagine there's at least one in particular that holds you in great esteem. Perhaps one who might have overheard a passing comment about your desire for a new shawl?"

Oh, the countess was good. A veritable master of redirection.

Their hostess started her metronome rocking again.

"It is a lovely shawl," Thea added, casting her own baited hook into the water. "And such a thoughtful gift to be sent without a card. Then again, this person is likely a member of your own family. My cousin Daphne is the sort of person who would send a letter and forget to sign it. I'm sure you must know someone like that."

Lady Abernathy slid a flinty gaze between the countess and Thea. "Why are the two of you prattling on about my shawl?"

"Prattling? Good gracious, Beatrice. We were merely admiring it." The countess pursed her lips in affront. "Moreover, I should think you would wish to discover the identity of the one who sent it. You might very well have a secret admirer, after all."

Their hostess lifted her knobby fingers in a dismissive wave. "Trivial matter. What I must know is why Miss Hartley is encouraging the attentions of a man like St. James."

Regrettably, Thea had decided to take a sip of her tea in that same instant. She nearly choked. The brew was like drinking syrup. Knowing that it was the worst possible moment to give in to a fit of coughing for it would only make her look guilty, she did her best to suppress the urge.

"I—I don't know what you mean," she croaked, her throat constricting.

The countess tutted. "Miss Hartley is hardly at fault if a gentleman sits beside her at a musicale. She is quite lovely, after all. It would be like asking the bees to stay far afield of the prettiest flowers."

"True. True," their hostess said dismissively. "Though, if she is seen in the company of a man who brings ridicule upon himself, it will make her ridiculous by association and diminish any offers she might receive."

"If the gentlemen vying for Miss Hartley's hand are unable to see her worth simply because of the suitors she attracts, then they are not worthy of her."

"But she will not be the only one who suffers. Society's low opinion would also reflect poorly on her parents for allowing such an unfit man to court their daughter. Which would, in turn, shine a skeptical—if not wholly unfavorable—light on her sisters and their unions."

The countess stiffened. "You forget that one of those unions happens to be with my grandson."

"I assure you, no one has forgotten that the venerable Duke of Longhurst dashed off to Gretna Green to marry. Over an anvil," she stressed.

Lady Broadbent's eyes flashed and Thea wondered if she would soon see smoke coming out of her ears. She was fiercely protective of her family. "Magnus married for love. While you may think that a trivial matter, I do not."

"Now, now, Olympia. I did not intend to ruffle your feathers. We have been friends these many years, and it is with that very friendship that I offer a word of warning that Miss Hartley's third Season should be considered with the gravity it deserves. Tongues are already wagging." Her finger pointed toward the window as if all of society were just outside and trying to peer into her parlor. "Such rumors could spread like the plague, sending our poor Miss Hartley to the shelf instead of the altar."

Lady Broadbent expelled a slow breath, darting a glance to her charge.

"I made a handsome match for my daughter," she said. "While Geraldine's marriage with a duke won society's approval, it left her hardened in the end. She lived many unhappy years with a feckless husband. And there were countless times I wished that I could have spared her such a fate. Therefore, as my friend, I'm sure you'll understand when I tell you that I'll support whatever decision Miss Hartley makes."

Thea felt a wealth of fondness and the prickle of incipient tears at the corners of her eyes. The countess was all decorum and propriety. But when it came to matters of the heart, she was soft as syllabub.

She was tempted to launch herself across the table and hug the dour curmudgeon.

As if sensing this desire, the countess arched an imperious brow that shut down any of that nonsense. Thea grinned and sniffed.

"Very well," the dowager viscountess said offhandedly as if the matter were suddenly of little consequence. Leaning forward, she put a scone on a plate, added a spoonful of red currant jam and a dollop of clotted cream, then offered it. "Olympia, you must try my cook's scones."

"Thank you, I—"

Suddenly, the plate toppled from her fingers and landed face down onto Lady Broadbent's lap.

"Oh, how clumsy of me! I do apologize. I would ring for my girl but she would take an age." Vaulting up from her chair with surprising speed, Lady Abernathy ushered her friend to the door. "If you would but go to the kitchen, I'm certain my cook will see that your skirts are put back to rights. Fear not, I'll keep Miss Hartley entertained until you return."

As the countess left the room, Thea went to the other side of the table and tidied up. Coming from a family of actors, she wasn't at all convinced that the spilled plate was an accident. And when her hostess returned to her rocker and clapped her hands once and chafed them in greedy anticipation, she was sure of it.

Thea set the dish off to the side. "I presume you wished to speak with me alone?"

"You are indeed a bright gel," Lady Abernathy said with a creased grin as she began to rock. "I shall speak my piece then say no more. My advice to you is to stop this nonsense with St. James. He is not a candidate for marriage. There's nothing left of his father's estate other than a worthless title and a handful of acres of fallow land."

"Be that as it may, and even though it is of no concern of mine, I have heard that St. James stands to inherit an earldom."

"That will never happen," her hostess added with authority. "Though, thankfully for St. James, his uncle has been magnanimous enough to look out for him. Paid for his education. And when he failed, time and again, it was the Earl of Redcliffe who purchased a commission for him. I daresay there has been no one who could find fault with the earl. And Redcliffe is still young and handsome enough to take a third bride that could yield a legitimate issue.

"Besides," she continued, "Redcliffe will never approve of a match for his nephew. He was appointed guardian over his nephew's estate years ago. And it is Redcliffe who will make any and all decisions for him, because—as nearly everyone knows—St. James lacks intellect."

Thea let out a huff. "I don't understand why people keep saying that. St. James is as intelligent as any man in our circle."

Lady Abernathy cackled like a Shakespearean witch over a bubbling cauldron. "Then you haven't seen much of the right society. Though I trust that you will now that your fascination with the playwright has ended?"

She didn't answer. All at once her throat felt too thick. *Her* fascination was truly all it ever had been, and it seemed that everyone knew it.

"I'm sure you know that Olympia has a great fondness for you," her hostess said, not unkindly. "It is because of that, as well as my fondness for her, that I wanted to make it clear that you will not be the only one who suffers ridicule."

Thea swallowed. She thought about all the support the countess had given her. All the times she'd procured invitations to assemblies that Kellum would attend. All the times that she'd been patient when her charge became distracted by plays.

Was it really asking so much for Thea to try her best to make a good impression this Season?

Staying away from St. James seemed the least she could do. After all, hadn't she wasted enough time on men who left her feeling uncertain?

"I understand, and I would never wish to bring disfavor on Lady Broadbent. Therefore, I'll keep my distance from St. James," she said, wondering why her lungs felt so heavy all of a sudden. He meant nothing to her.

And besides, she was more interested in discovering the identity of her muse.

"Splendid." Her hostess gave her an appraising glance. "Have you been introduced to Redcliffe?"

"I have not."

"Hmm . . . He is a man of considerable consequence. The connection would do well for you, I should think. Perhaps I'll introduce you."

"Introduce Miss Hartley to whom?" Lady Broadbent

asked as she sauntered back into the room, her stony countenance revealing her displeasure at the dark stain that lingered upon her lavender skirts.

The dowager viscountess stopped rocking and held up a gnarled finger. "I just thought of something. Or someone, rather. A certain Captain Summerhayes. He is the brother of my son's late wife and recently retired from the navy. He was always quite the rascal, if you ask me," she said with a broad smile. "I wonder if he is the one who sent me this shawl."

"Captain Summerhayes, did you say?" the countess asked as she regally lowered onto her cushion. "I don't recall meeting him. Do you, Miss Hartley?"

The change of topic was just the distraction Thea needed. Because, for a moment, she caught herself thinking about St. James a good deal more than her highwayman.

Chapter Twelve

❧

THE INSTANT JASPER stepped through the doors of the Leightons' ballroom, his gaze found Miss Hartley. She was a vision in a gown the color of silver moonlight, curls of glossy mahogany hair cascading down from an artful twist.

It almost hurt to look at her.

It was worse to crave her smile. But he'd made sure she wouldn't smile at him again.

This searching for her in a crowded room had to stop. It was turning into a bad habit. Then again, with a habit a man could control his actions. This felt more . . . reflexive, like breathing in and out.

Disliking that observation, his hands clenched into fists.

A matron and her charge standing nearby squeaked in startlement at the sound of his knuckles popping. Then they looked up and recognized him. Eyes wide, they scurried down the stairs.

When his gaze immediately swiveled back to Miss Hartley, he saw her being introduced to a tall, black-haired man with a military bearing.

Because it served his purpose to have a basic knowledge of all guests at a party he attended, he knew that a certain Captain Summerhayes had joined the ranks of the gentlemen in want of a wife. Since there were no dark deeds or scandals associated with the recently retired naval hero, Jasper didn't consider him a man who might fall into step with the likes of Redcliffe. So he had no qualms against him.

And yet, as he watched Summerhayes earn a smile from Miss Hartley, he wondered if he should keep an eye on the man, just in case.

Feeling the beginning rumble of a growl in his throat, he subdued it. He needed to focus. There was a reason he was here, and it wasn't because of her.

He'd been summoned.

It wasn't often that the Earl of Redcliffe ordered his idiot nephew to appear at a society event where he would also be in attendance. He usually preferred to ignore the familial connection altogether. Unless he could use it to his advantage.

It didn't take long for Jasper to discern what that was.

His uncle was seeking a young bride, preferably one from a large family of males to better his chances for producing an heir. If she should happen to possess a sizeable dowry then all the better. For this Season, Miss Handscombe was the woman to woo.

Unfortunately for Redcliffe there were a half dozen younger men who were currently pursuing her.

But Redcliffe was nothing if not a master at understanding how to worm his way into someone's good graces. He'd been manipulating society into believing what he wanted them to for decades. Most never knew how ruthless and wicked he truly was.

Jasper did. And he knew precisely why his uncle had summoned him this evening.

Redcliffe wanted to play the woebegotten earl, who'd been saddled with a numbskull heir. It was a familiar tactic he used to earn a woman's sympathy, forging a path toward courtship.

Regrettably, there was no way for Jasper to stop these first paving stones from being laid without revealing his true self. And he couldn't afford to do that.

Besides, warning Miss Handscombe directly would

never work. No one had ever believed him about Redcliffe, not when it mattered most.

Therefore, after this night was over, Jasper would do his utmost to play matchmaker for Miss Handscombe and find her a suitable candidate. Literally anyone else would do. And the sooner, the better.

Over the years, he'd shielded over a dozen different debutantes from Redcliffe's intentions. And he would continue to do so for the rest of that blackguard's life.

He only wished he'd been able to save all his uncle's victims.

With dark memories dogging his heels, he made his way along the outskirts of the room and toward the open terrace doors where his uncle was holding court. When their gazes met, the constant hatred and revulsion that was always between them flashed for an instant before it was blinked away.

Redcliffe made a show of lifting his watch fob to check the time, then leveled Jasper with a glare as he snapped it closed. "I see you decided to join us."

Jasper inclined his head and mentioned nothing of the missive threatening the withdrawal of next month's allowance should he not make an appearance.

"And this, Miss Handscombe, is my"—Redcliffe paused to take a long-suffering breath—"nephew, Viscount St. James."

"A pleasure, my lord," she said with a curtsy.

Jasper bowed and lisped, "Miss Handscombe."

Her eyes widened for an instant before softening with pity as one looked upon a wounded animal. It was one of the typical responses, especially from beautiful women. There were some who'd recoiled in horror either at his size or the fact that they were worried the lisp was a contagion and would make idiots of anyone within earshot. Some had even laughed in his face.

Of course, there had been two or three exceptions, most notably Miss Althea Hartley.

At the mere thought of her, his gaze surreptitiously sought her again. She was dancing the quadrille with Summerhayes.

Jasper took an immediate dislike to the swarthy naval hero. The man lingered far too long at Miss Hartley's and her chaperone's sides. Hell, he'd barely stepped away since they'd been introduced. And considering it was only their first introduction, he certainly didn't deserve so many of Miss Hartley's smiles. Three, by last count.

But Jasper forced himself to return his attention to his uncle.

Redcliffe was in the middle of explaining how magnanimous he was. ". . . Of course, given that he's my late sister's only child, I've done whatever I could for him. It was what she would have wanted."

"Your commitment to family is admirable, my lord," Miss Handscombe said.

Commitment was a more apt word than she knew. If it wasn't for Redcliffe having Jasper's mother committed to an asylum after a supposed fall down the stairs, she might still be alive. But that was what happened to those who opposed his uncle—they were made to disappear as if through no fault of his own.

"You may run off to the refreshment table, nephew," Redcliffe said now that his usefulness was over. "Just do your best not to spill it this time, hmm?"

Without waiting for a response, his uncle led his latest quarry away, bending his head to murmur, "The poor boy never gained an ounce of coordination, no matter how many dancing masters I hired for him. I, on the other hand, would be honored to demonstrate that some men can be graceful at any age. During the dinner waltz, perhaps?"

"I'd be delighted, my lord."

Jasper walked away, thinking about Miss Handscombe and how to keep her from becoming his uncle's next target.

As the music ended, his attention swerved to the dance floor as Summerhayes escorted Miss Hartley back to Lady Broadbent. He said something that earned a nod and Althea presented a tile at her wrist for him to sign.

So it would be two dances with the naval captain, would it? And considering her next partner was there to escort her to the floor, Jasper would hazard a guess that she had just given Summerhayes her waltz.

The growl he'd been holding back rumbled in his throat, startling a pair of wallflowers with a squeak as they scampered on by, glancing over their shoulders as they whispered.

"If I had to dance with St. James, I don't know what I'd do. Faint, likely."

"Well, if he ever asked me to dance, I'd find another partner even if I had to drag them to the floor myself."

Behind his spectacles, Jasper's gaze swiveled from Miss Hartley to Miss Handscombe to Captain Summerhayes as an idea began to form.

THEA SPENT THE evening avoiding St. James, while trying to appear as though she wasn't avoiding him.

She'd fielded more than one teasing comment about his presence at the ball and speculations regarding what he might spill on her next. And she was tired of the snickering.

She needed attention, of course. An invisible woman could not find a husband, after all. But she hated this kind of attention. Hated being an object of ridicule. It reminded her too much of her time with Kellum.

Yet, even more than that, she hated what those episodes had cost St. James. They'd further cemented the *ton*'s low opinion of him. Knowing they were wrong, but being able to do nothing to alter their judgment, only left her conflicted and, frankly, irritated.

Of late, she was always irritated. And even *that* irritated her.

Gone were the days of eternal ennui, and vexation swept in like a thunder cloud.

To make matters worse, she missed talking to St. James. Which made her a complete dunderhead because he obviously hadn't enjoyed talking to her. He'd proved it by walking away every time they were in the middle of a conversation.

Enough, she thought. She would think no more of him.

Saints be praised, the chorus jeered.

Wanting a break between sets, she'd left the tarantella open and stood with Lady Broadbent between the pilasters and potted topiaries in urns that lined the room.

"Who was that gentleman I saw you with when I was dancing the quadrille?" Thea asked.

"I assure you, I was with no gentleman."

The harshness in her chaperone's tone piqued her interest. Especially because, from her vantage point, it almost looked as though the countess had given him the cut direct. But clearly she didn't want to discuss the matter.

The countess opened her fan and turned her head to whisper. "I must say, if Captain Summerhayes is our highwayman, as we suspect, he is rather charming."

Accepting the change of topic without argument, Thea's gaze skimmed the crush.

She found the captain on the far side of the ballroom, standing in the midst of a handful of younger gentlemen who looked at the naval hero with godlike adoration. "A man renowned for heroism would also explain why he'd targeted that dreadful Lord Abernathy."

"Quite. In a sense, one could almost overlook that entire episode as something just shy of chivalrous. While I may have experienced a bit of dismay, he didn't harm either of us. And whatever the viscount received was well deserved, if you ask me."

"It seems that this hindsight philosophy of yours is working in Captain Summerhayes's favor."

The countess slanted her a look. "That's too much cheek, Miss Hartley. Even for you."

Thea grinned impishly. "Well, he has already asked to call on me tomorrow."

"Pray tell, what did you say in response?"

"That I would see how well he waltzed first."

Lady Broadbent smiled and closed her fan to tap it against Thea's shoulder. "Clever girl."

Summerhayes was a devilishly attractive man, tall and broad-shouldered with a wealth of dark hair. He had a deep voice, too, as if seasoned by years of salty air. Not only that, but he'd lived an exciting life and had a way of sharing those stories that kept her enthralled.

There was only one problem . . . she didn't feel any tingles.

That feeling of being suffused with so much static electricity that she was certain that lightning would explode from her body if she didn't write something down immediately was absent. If he was her highwayman, wouldn't she feel something extraordinary?

Then again, perhaps she'd built up her expectations to the point where anything less than lightning was a disappointment.

It was too soon to tell for certain. After all, their bodies hadn't been as close as they were that one night. Surely the waltz would settle the matter for good.

As the tarantella was drawing to a close, Thea's gaze crossed the room again just as a footman approached the captain and presented a missive. With a flick of his thumb,

Summerhayes read the contents. Then with a glance toward the terrace doors, he set off for them.

She absently wondered where he was going since the dinner waltz would be next. Turning her head to voice this thought, she saw Lady Broadbent's eyes go round as she laid a hand against her side.

"Whatever's the matter? Are you unwell?" she asked in a hushed voice so as not to draw attention.

The countess stifled a gasp. "I'm quite hale. My corset, however, has likely met an early demise. It seems that the ghost of a whale is having its revenge upon me."

"Don't tell me you're still wearing that old thing," Thea chided as they walked discreetly toward the stairs that led to the ladies' retiring room. "Madame LeBlanc told you this would happen."

"Well, I wasn't about to wear those confounded metal contraptions that creak and groan every time a woman moves as if she were an old door in need of oil on its hinges. Absolute abominations."

Thea suppressed a laugh. "Lean on me then, and I'll escort you up the stairs."

"I'm not an invalid, Miss Hartley. I shall find a maid-servant to assist me and return in a trice. Off with you now." She made a shooing motion. "They are cueing up the waltz as we speak and I'll not allow you to miss your dance with our heroic captain."

"If you're certain."

An imperious brow arched in answer. One did not ask Countess Broadbent to repeat herself.

"I'll find you before dinner," Thea said. "Until then, be sure to light a candle in the retiring room."

"Whyever would I do that?"

"So that your whale finds its way to the afterlife," Thea teased and sauntered off before her chaperone could affectionately scold her for having too much cheek.

She was still smiling when she rounded the corner to the ballroom . . . until she saw Captain Summerhayes take the floor with Miss Handscombe.

Thea had only been away for a minute. Surely he wouldn't have given her up for lost and sought another partner so quickly. He hadn't seemed like that kind of man.

Then again, she'd never expected half the things Kellum had said and done.

The unkind reminder sent a cold shiver over her like a shroud. Her own ghost of insecurity whispered, *No one will remember you. You're not even worthy of a footnote . . .*

A shadow fell over her then.

Distracted, she looked up, surprised to see St. James standing in front of her.

"I'm here on behalf of the captain," he said, proffering his hand.

She felt her brow knit. "Summerhayes asked you to dance with me?"

"I'll clarify the moment we are on the floor." St. James looked askance at those standing on either side, some looking on with horror, some with malevolent humor. Others were already whispering behind cupped hands.

The situation would only become worse if she accepted.

Fortunately, as a Hartley, Thea had a plethora of stage-ready performances in her repertoire. Drawing in a breath, she winced slightly, shifting tenderly onto one foot. "My apologies. But I believe I turned my ankle during the last—"

St. James cut off her excuse by stealing a hand around her waist and pulling her forward on a gasp. Her gaze flew up to his an instant before he swept her into a turn, joining the others on the dance floor.

Reflexively, her free hand gripped her skirts, lifting them out of the way even as her heart raced in panic. "I didn't agree to this."

"You left me no other option," he said, matter-of-factly, taking another turn.

Everything was a blur, her thoughts scattering into the ether. She tried to clear her head and find a fixed point. But what she saw when she glanced at the couple just beyond St. James's shoulder was the frown that Summerhayes cast toward her.

No, not at her, but at her partner.

She looked up to the eyes behind the crooked spectacles. "Summerhayes didn't ask you to dance with me, did he?"

"I approached the captain with a conundrum. Miss Handscombe had given the dance to my uncle, who had become unavoidably detained," St. James said. "I would have offered in his stead, but the debutante in question would likely have fainted."

"Did Summerhayes not explain that he was already engaged for the dinner waltz?"

"He did."

Her eyes narrowed. "And what was your reply to that fact?"

"Merely that you had asked me to relay your regrets that you'd turned your ankle during the previous set."

"Why you underhanded, scheming—"

She broke off as all those scattered thoughts started coming back to her like stars falling to the earth in a blaze of fire.

And in a conflagration of tingles.

Thea's breath caught as she studied the chiseled edge of his jawline, the dark stubble visible beneath the surface of his skin and the impossibly broad shoulders. Her nostrils flared on the familiar woodsy scent of evergreen and the earthy notes of saddle leather. And with every turn, she felt the sure press of the large hand that spanned her waist.

No. It couldn't be.

And yet, it all started to make sense . . . the fact that he came to call on her the day after the robbery, the way he continuously interrupted her stories, the reason that he pretended—and she had no doubt it was all a contrived pretense—to play a clumsy fool in front of the *ton*.

Because Jasper Trueblood, Viscount St. James, was the highwayman.

Her highwayman!

She couldn't believe that he'd been under her nose this entire time. And more than that, she couldn't believe that he'd ruined two of her gowns all to keep his secret. Drat him!

"You are a surprisingly graceful dancer, St. James."

He stiffened almost imperceptibly just before he stumbled out of rhythm. Then, as if carried by momentum, he spun them in a haphazard arc. They narrowly missed colliding with the couple in front of them.

In that moment, she might have questioned her certainty of his identity, if not for the fact that he righted their course at the very last second, tucking her body against his in a brief but startling collision.

She gasped. Beneath that ill-fitting suit of clothes, his body was a solid wall of muscle. And being pressed against a form like his wasn't something a woman could ever forget.

"My apologies," St. James said with an exaggerated lisp, appearing every bit embarrassed.

And yet it was all pretense. Only now did she notice how controlled his movements were. How every misstep never caused harm. He didn't tread on her toes or even her hem.

Clumsy catastrophe had never been so elegant.

She could have kicked herself for not seeing it before. After all, she'd spent her entire life around actors. And that was all this was—a performance.

But for what purpose?

She didn't know enough about St. James to answer the question. At least, not yet.

Now that she had found her muse, however, she was

going to do whatever she could to unearth every one of St. James's secrets.

When the waltz ended, he began to escort her to a mortified Lady Broadbent waiting on the outskirts of the ballroom.

Thea glanced up at him, her brow arched with cunning. "You never should have danced with me, my lord. A woman can glean quite a bit about a man when he holds her close."

Behind the spectacles, his gaze sharpened on hers. And even though he admitted nothing, she saw that her accusation hit the mark.

She felt a triumphant smirk tug at her lips . . . until he stepped on her ruffled hem and ruined another gown.

Chapter Thirteen

❧

*T*HE HISS OF rending silk had drawn every eye around them and a few startled gasps.

Thea had looked down to find that St. James hadn't just torn her hem. The stitching at her waist sagged on one side, as well, leaving a hole that revealed her petticoat beneath.

A torn hem might have been easily repaired in a retiring room. But exposing one's undergarments guaranteed that she would have to leave the ball *and* leave her conversation with St. James unfinished.

She was absolutely incensed!

With two wardrobe mishaps between them, not to mention all the tongues wagging, both Thea and Lady Broadbent returned to the townhouse.

On the short drive, she explained to the countess how the events led to her waltz with St. James, about Miss Handscombe's partner changing from Redcliffe to Summerhayes, and that anyone nearby would have noted that she had been quite unprepared to take the floor with St. James.

She did not, however, reveal her startling discovery.

Without knowing the reason behind his subterfuge, she felt it would be best to keep the true identity of the highwayman to herself.

Still, she was being much kinder to St. James than he'd been to her. Three gowns ruined! Three! She was going to start carrying a pair of scissors with her so that she could even the score.

Although, it went without saying that she wouldn't be able to see him in public again. His escapades had made sure of that. Any woman who welcomed the attentions of that man would become a pariah.

So her encounters with him would have to be kept in secret. Since he'd already proven just how skilled he was at hiding the truth beneath the *ton*'s nose, she wasn't worried. But she was determined.

Now that she'd found her muse, she wasn't about to let him go.

It was half past midnight and she'd already written ten pages of a new play, drawing her inspiration from true events. And it was good, too.

As the tip of her pen scratched over the page, it was as if the curtains of the stage had been wrenched apart and she could see every scene and character, feel every line as it coursed through her blood. A sense of unshakable knowing filled her, banishing the crippling doubt that had plagued her for a year.

This would be her best work yet.

Her stomach chose at that moment to issue a mournful growl, reminding her that she hadn't eaten since breaking her fast that morning.

When they had returned early from the ball, the housekeeper offered to prepare a meal of cold meats, cheese and fruit for them. But Lady Broadbent had been too agitated and chose to have a glass of claret sent to her rooms before she retired for the evening. Thea, in a display of solidarity coupled with a smidgen of guilt, decided against it as well and went up to her own bedchamber to prepare for bed.

But now there was no quieting the beast.

Deciding to slip downstairs to raid the larder and, perhaps, write a few more pages afterward, she stood up from the slender writing desk by the window and stretched. When she reached for the lamp, she grinned at the ink staining her fingers. It had been so long since she'd written with such abandon that she felt rather proud of the mark of her labors.

Just before she moved away from the desk, she heard a faint tap and clatter against the glass.

It sounded like hail. Absently, she wondered if a storm was brewing. If so, she should close her window.

Setting down the lamp, she parted the sheer curtain and positioned her fingertips on the sill. That was when she saw movement in the back garden, a shadow passing along the hedgerow toward the gate. Her pulse quickened.

Cupping her hands around her eyes, she pressed her forehead against the glass and peered closer. But there was no one there. And yet . . .

As her gaze skimmed the small garden once more, she caught sight of something fluttering amidst the hedges. There was just enough light to see the cluster of colors.

She smiled. Oh, St. James and his paper flowers. She could almost forgive him for ruining another dress. Almost. But she wasn't that forgiving.

Slipping into her dressing gown, she tied the sash at her waist in a hasty knot, picked up the chamberstick and went downstairs to collect her bouquet.

Thea never saw the man move out of the shadows until it was too late.

"DON'T EVEN THINK about biting me," Jasper warned, low in her ear when her lips parted beneath his hand.

At the commanding growl of his voice—his true voice—her struggles instantly ceased. But she huffed and muttered an indecipherable string of words that sounded suspiciously like a scolding.

Once they were inside his carriage and it was clipping along the street, he asked, "If I remove my hand, are you going to scream?"

She shook her head tersely.

The instant he did, her rant began.

"I wasn't going to bite you. I was warning you that if you've ruined my dressing gown, I am going to take a pair of scissors and slice your coat to ribbons."

When she bent forward to examine the state of her garments, he regretted holding her on his lap with an arm braced over her middle. He'd only wanted to keep her from injuring herself in case she tried to flee.

But now he was all too aware of the warm, softly scented, curvaceous woman in her nightclothes—and little else—on his lap.

He swallowed. Then quickly deposited her down onto the bench beside him. Even then she was still too close. He wished he owned a larger carriage with enough room for two benches.

"Why did you venture into the garden dressed like that? Where is your pelisse?"

"Well, I was hardly expecting to be kidnapped."

When she crossed her arms beneath her unbound breasts, he jerked out of his caped greatcoat as if she were on fire and draped it over her to smother the flames.

"Thank you, I suppose. I was rather cold," she said, offering information he'd discerned for himself. "You are surprisingly considerate for one who is carting me off in the dead of night."

Trying to replace the vision that burned hotly through his eyes, he slid a finger beneath the leather window shade and peered out at the lamplit street. "For town it is hardly that late. The festivities are still transpiring at the Leighton Ball. Many revelers at other parties won't return to their houses until it is near dawn, which is when I intend to return you . . . *if* you cooperate."

"And what is that supposed to mean?"

"I'm taking preemptive measures against blackmail. In short, if anyone were to discover that you spent time alone with me"—*in your nightdress*, he thought and blew out a breath—"then your reputation, as well as that of your chaperone, would be ruined."

He anticipated one of two reactions. Either she would be in hysterics and begin pleading and negotiating in tearful sobs, or she'd lose her temper as she had done in Abernathy's carriage and would begin to rant, cursing his very existence. Given her frank nature, he expected the latter more than the former.

Yet, as he waited a breath—*two, three*—and heard neither, he let the shade fall then turned to face her.

Without the ambient light reflecting off her white garments, the interior of the carriage was too dim for him to read her expression. Even so, he could feel her gaze on him.

"Are you always this calculating?" she asked.

He detected nothing other than curiosity in her tone, which had the unfortunate result of making him more curious about her. But it also made him aware that he'd miscalculated her reaction. Again.

"Always," he said.

"It must be exhausting."

He tensed, knowing precisely where this was going. "We are not discussing the reasons behind my charade. Do not think you can manipulate me or worm your way out of the situation with a show of sympathy."

"Very well." She heaved out a sigh. "Are we just going to drive around London all night? Because I'm rather hungry, and my sisters have informed me countless times that my demeanor is not entirely pleasant when I'm hungry."

Against all reason, Jasper felt a corner of his mouth twitch. "No, we have a destination. My driver is taking us to an establishment with a lodging where we will sleep."

At this, she sat straighter, his coat slipping down to her lap. "*Sleep?* You said I would be returned before dawn."

"It would hardly be blackmail if I were the only witness. Then it would be your word against mine, and it couldn't have escaped your notice that my word carries little weight. But you need not fear about your virtue. At least, in *fact*. It is only the illusion of your virtue that I hold in the palm of my hands."

"And if someone I know should see us in this *establishment*, are you prepared to marry me?" she asked, her voice rising.

At last, he thought. It was starting to settle in.

Preferring predictable behavior, he eased back into the corner. "My uncle will never permit me to marry, no matter the reason. He has decreed as much. So the answer is no. If you are seen by anyone other than my trusted allies, then the black mark would be yours to bear alone."

She was quiet for a moment, but her whirring thoughts filled the snug silence.

He was almost tempted to ask her what she was thinking or planning, and he was never interested in the inner workings of other people. They were too easy to decipher on his own. But she had always shown herself to be clever. This trait had tempted him into lingering in conversation with her against his better judgment, and more than once.

It was a pity it had to be this way.

"It is a double-edged sword," she said quietly, pulling her shade aside to peer out. "I could not marry you regardless, without bringing shame on my family. You've made sure of that, your uncle's decree notwithstanding."

Oh, but his uncle was the rotten core at the center of everything. But she would never know that. This burden was his to bear alone.

"The truly shameful part of all this"—she let the shade fall—"is that I actually liked you, even after you ruined my favorite dress. When you had come to call with those paper flowers in hand, I thought you were bashful and charming." She issued a huff of disdain. "I thought you were going to ask permission to court me."

He stared at her, incredulous. "Would you have wanted *me* to court you?"

Women did not say things like this to him, especially not beautiful women. And classifying Althea Hartley as merely beautiful was understating her entire existence. She was something otherworldly. Men like him didn't even belong in her realm.

"Well, not now," she clarified testily and jerked his coat up to her neck.

Not now. Jasper sensed that those words would haunt him for the rest of his life.

Chapter Fourteen

𝔍T TOOK LITTLE more than a half an hour to arrive at
Barrett's tavern. The windows were dark, informing him
that David and Nan were already abed. But he didn't need
them to be awake in order to serve as witnesses to ce-
ment this blackmail. He'd tell all come morning, after he
returned Miss Hartley.

Then Nan would likely give him an earful. And he'd
simply tell her that he had no choice.

He was doing this for all their sakes, not just his own.

Jasper left Mr. Pitt to see to the horses and carriage as
he escorted Miss Hartley in through the kitchen door at
the back.

Lying in front of the hearth, Garmr lifted his head, his
tail swishing across the stone floor at the sight of him. Then
he sniffed the air and leapt up, his body poised to guard and
protect his master from the new smell.

"Good, Garmr," he said and brought Miss Hartley out
from behind him. "Now, guard."

The wolf growled and stood at attention. Jasper gave
a cursory glance to his prisoner to ensure she wasn't too
frightened, only to see her roll her eyes at him.

"Is this truly necessary?"

"You said you were hungry, but I'm not about to turn my
back on you to find something for you to eat. Garmr will
keep you in line."

Standing there in his greatcoat, she set her hands on her hips. "Oh, he will, will he?"

He ignored the challenging arch of her brow and the smirk on her lips as he stepped into the larder to grab a loaf of bread.

Coming back into the kitchen a minute later, he stopped midstride. His vicious guardian was on his back, exposing his belly as she kneeled on the floor to give him a thorough scratch.

"Who's a big handsome boy?" she crooned. "You are. Oooh, such a cuddly ferocious beast, too. Yes, you are. Don't let anyone tell you differently."

Garmr's tongue lolled off to the side as he panted in pure bliss.

Jasper expelled a heavy breath and walked to the trestle table. "I see you are able to tame both man and beast."

"Not *all* men."

He scoffed, then went back into the larder. His prisoner might want more than just a ration of bread.

But as he stood contemplating the baskets of vegetables, jars of compotes and various meats, he heard noises from the kitchen. So, he tucked a wedge of cheese beneath one arm, a pot of jam under the other, grabbed a platter of ham, then returned.

Once again, he stopped, his feet rooted to the floor as he took in the sight before him.

He'd stepped away for two minutes. *Two!* Only to find Roly in his nightshirt, giggling at the way Garmr put his paw in Miss Hartley's hand when she said, "Shake."

"A right solid gentleman, he is, shaking our hands."

She agreed with a nod. "He is quite the intelligent fellow. Aren't you, boy?"

In response, Garmr licked her cheek.

Roly giggled again, his grin reaching all the way to his ears. "He likes you. Thumper's never like this with outsiders."

"Thumper?"

"See the way he thumps his leg when you scratch him behind the ears, just like—"

"His name is Garmr." Jasper set down the carving board of ham with a whack on the table. "And shouldn't you be in bed?"

The boy stood, his hair sticking up on one side as he cast a ravenous glance over the food. "Heard someone rustling about. Thought I'd make sure 'tweren't bandits and such."

He was about to order the boy back to bed until Miss Hartley stood beside Roly and laid a hand on his shoulder.

"That was very brave of you," she said. "I think that deserves a glass of milk before you go back to bed. Don't you, St. James?"

"*Man, beast* and *boy*," he muttered under his breath. Swiping up an earthenware cup, he slapped a few glugs of milk into it, then held it out. "There you are, Roland the Brave. Now off to bed, hmm?"

The boy gulped down the milk so fast that he belched, and grinned proudly at the sound he made. Wiping off the lingering line of milk along his upper lip, he turned back to her. "Will you still be here when I wake up?"

"I don't believe so. But it has been a pleasure to make your acquaintance, Master Roland." She extended her hand and they shook.

"And you, Miss Hartley."

Her brow furrowed in perplexity. "How did you know my name?"

The boy was halfway through the door when he tossed over his shoulder, "You're the only girl he ever talks about."

Her eyebrows inched slyly toward her hairline as she fixed her attention on Jasper.

Ignoring the uncomfortable warmth creeping along his neck, he busied himself with preparing her a plate. "There's water in the pitcher by the basin if you feel like washing up. I imagine you're covered in dog fur."

"Thank you, I will. Though, your coat took the brunt of the fur. I'm afraid it will need to be brushed," she said as she slipped out of it and lifted it onto a hook.

But on her way to the sink, she passed in front of the fire, the light revealing the shadowy outline of her body.

It was only a glimpse, taking no longer than two graceful passing steps, but the vision of her high, pert breasts, soft belly and amply rounded bottom made his tongue grow thick. And not only his tongue.

He shut his eyes.

"Best take care, St. James. I don't particularly want any of your finger with my ham."

His eyes flew open to see her walking toward him, drying her hands on a square of flannel, her lips curving in a grin.

"Perhaps you don't deserve any ham for the way you've undermined my authority."

"Such a curmudgeon," she chided, dipping her finger into the jam pot and sucking it off the tip. "Mmm . . . this is delicious. Have you ever noticed that when you're ravenous everything tastes extraordinarily good?"

Jasper knew she was speaking. He recognized the sounds by the way the consonants and vowels connected to form words. The only problem was, he forgot what words were.

Most of the blood in his brain had descended *en masse* to southern climes. And the small amount that remained in his skull was busy conjuring a vision of painting her entire body with jam then slowly licking it off. Very, very slowly.

"Mmm . . . this cheese is heavenly. St. James? Are you making paper flowers in your mind? Is that what happens when you look at me and your eyes go dark?"

He blinked. Glancing down, he realized that he still had

the knife poised above the ham. Clearing his throat, he made the first cut.

Tired, that's all he was. Just tired.

"Have you always had a way with animals?" he asked, diverting the topic.

"Usually," she said, dipping a sliver of cheese into the jam pot. "Or rather, until I try to bring them into the drawing room. The pigs still don't trust me. Neither do the ducks for that matter. And don't ask about the chickens. But the Queen's council are far more understanding when I need to dress them in neckcloths to stand in for footmen in a play."

"The Queen's council?"

"Barrister and Serjeant at Arms. My father's Irish wolf-hounds," she said, absently nibbling on her cheese. "But don't think it escaped my notice that you haven't answered any of my questions."

He didn't pretend to misunderstand which questions. "No, I wasn't making paper flowers in my mind, of all things. I was thinking about"—he took a breath, briefly deliberated, and decided to be honest, *mostly*—"jam."

"Then you must be ravenous, too."

She had no idea. And never would, he reminded himself.

"Here. Eat," he said handing her a plate. "I would prefer to catch some sleep before I return you."

He had a sense that this night was going to take a good deal out of him.

The thought was confirmed as he watched her stack the cheese and ham on the jam-slathered bread and fold it in half before lifting it to her mouth.

She frowned. "You've cut the bread too thick. I can't fit it all."

He ordered his mind not to take another salacious sojourn.

"Come, come, give it here." He waved his fingers in an impatient gesture. When she did, he proceeded to cut it into fourths, essentially creating finger sandwiches. "There."

She beamed at him as if he'd just invented food. "Brilliant."

Then she proceeded to eat one—*one!*—before pushing the plate away with a grunt as if she'd eaten an entire hog. "That was positively scrumptious."

"That's it?"

"Couldn't eat another bite."

"You claimed you were ravenous and that's all you're eating?"

She stared at him as if he was the one not making sense. "Yes. I *was* ravenous, and now I'm sleepy. Don't look at me that way. You're the one who chose to kidnap me."

Jasper opened his mouth to reply, then decided against it. This had already been an immensely long night and he hadn't even shown her to their room yet.

⚜

THEA DIDN'T KNOW why St. James was so cross. *She* was the one here under duress. Well . . . mostly.

Truth be told, as he led her through the dark tavern and up a narrow set of stairs, she was more curious than anything. This was the biggest adventure she'd ever had.

Just imagine, being kidnapped by a highwayman! What a play that would make! And she was determined to absorb every detail.

He opened a door at the end of the hall and waited for her to precede him. Absently, she noticed that he hadn't touched her since he'd handed her down from his carriage. In fact, he'd hardly even looked at her for more than a minute, his expression hard as etched stone.

Was he really so angry with her for having figured out his ruse? If he took a moment to learn anything about her character, he would know that she could keep a secret. Even one as juicy as this.

She stopped in the center of the snug lodging room. It was sparsely furnished with a spindled washstand in the corner, a sturdy wooden chair and side table by the stone hearth, a low chest of drawers by the door, and a small bed pushed against the far wall. But it was also clean and tidy.

With the addition of the faded frilled curtains, patchwork coverlet and the glow of a warm crackling fire, it might have felt cozy . . . if it wasn't her prison cell.

Though, reluctantly she had to admit that St. James made quite the dashing gaoler, garbed all in black from neckcloth to top boots. Unlike his gentleman's attire, these clothes seemed tailor fit.

Which begged the question: Where did a highwayman find a tailor?

She was about to ask but, as he crossed the room to stoke the embers and stack a few logs in the grate, she couldn't help but notice that his snug breeches molded to his form so well that she could see the bunch and shift of his thighs and taut buttocks. Her mouth went dry. And when he moved to stack a few logs onto the grate, his shirt stretched over his back, revealing the delineation of broad muscles tapering down to his waist. A peculiar warmth curled in her belly.

Thea swallowed and surveyed the room for a glass of water. Her gaze went from St. James, to the table and chair, to the bed.

Hmm . . . there seemed to be something missing. And it wasn't the water.

As he stood, her attention drifted back to the bed. "Where do you plan to sleep?"

"In that bed."

Her brow furrowed as she slid a glance to him. "And where will I sleep?"

"With me, of course." His matter-of-fact delivery did nothing to quell the sudden jump of her pulse as he casually untied his cravat. "I can hardly trust you alone. But fear not, there will be no improper advances. You will be beneath the coverlet. I will be on top of it with a bolster pillow wedged between us. I presume that would be preferable to being tied to that chair?"

"*Tied to the*—" Her mouth snapped shut as she stared at the length of black silk he absently tossed onto the table. If she needed further proof that he found her conversation utterly boring and saw her as little more than a nuisance, she certainly had it. "How magnanimous of you."

Though, as she looked from the chair to the narrow bed, then to his large form, she wondered how they would even fit themselves, let alone a bolster.

Thea was no longer concerned about impropriety. And, strangely enough, she trusted him.

She had no idea why. Their acquaintance had been of a much shorter duration than hers with Kellum. Then again, she would never have trusted Kellum in this situation. He may have called her a child on a number of occasions, but it was only after he'd attempted to instruct her on the ways of the world.

But she didn't want to think about that.

"You look troubled. Because of me," St. James concluded, raking a hand through his hair. "Because I'm being an arse."

"I won't disagree."

He scratched the side of his neck. "Contrary to the impression I've made, I don't wish to cause you any disquiet. So I'll . . . sleep in front of the door. I just wanted to make sure that you weren't going to run off and injure yourself, or charm the horses into harnessing themselves to the carriage and driving you all the way back. You're not going to try to climb out the window, are you?"

Thea shook her head. As she looked at him, she no longer saw the blackmailing kidnapper. He was, once again, the bashful man who'd come into the parlor and handed her a bouquet that he'd labored over with his own hands.

Something warm seemed to glow from the empty husk of her heart.

"I don't mind sharing," she said before she lost her nerve. "Besides, you'll get no sleep on the floor."

"But you were frowning just now, and your eyes were"—he made an offhand gesture—"distant."

She wasn't about to mention Kellum. So she tapped a finger to her temple. "Just making paper flowers."

"Mmm," he grumbled in disbelief. Then jerked his chin toward the bed. "Go on with you, then."

Only in that moment did a flush creep to her cheeks. She'd been in her nightclothes in front of this man for an hour and yet she hadn't been truly embarrassed until the moment she folded back the coverlet.

Staring down at the worn but clean linens, her knees wobbled. She was climbing into bed with a man. It didn't matter that he was going to lie atop the coverlet. She was getting into bed. With. A. Man.

As she slipped inside and scooted over toward the wall, all she could think about was the trembling Lady Content. And when St. James leaned over to pull the bedclothes up to her chin, tucking her in tightly, she kept her gaze on anything other than him.

Then he lay down, the bed ropes creaking beneath his weight. Gravity immediately took hold, rolling her toward him. He shoved the bolster between them, pinioning her in place until she was snug as a sausage.

Linking his hands behind his head, he blew out a breath. "The sooner we sleep, the faster the night will pass. Then you'll be rid of me for good."

Rid of him. For good . . .

She frowned at the thought. Doubtless, it would be for the best. He certainly wanted it. After he'd ruined three of her gowns, and just admitted that he thought of her as nothing more than a bother, she should want the same. And yet . . .

Her experience with Kellum had not only hollowed her out, but left her with a lingering sense of fear about asserting herself and acknowledging her own desires. And the only way to conquer that fear and sense of unworthiness seemed to be asking for what she wanted.

Because what she wanted—what she needed—was to write. And, no matter how inconvenient it was for either of them, St. James was the key.

Her head crunched into the straw-filled pillow as she situated herself on her back as well. "What if . . . I don't want to be rid of you?"

"We already discussed that."

"And by your clipped tone, I gather that you abhor repeating yourself," she muttered and he grunted in affirmation. "But, for the sake of argument, what if we did meet on occasion . . . perhaps in secret?"

"That wouldn't be wise. Now go to sleep."

She turned her head and watched his profile in the firelight as he stared at the ceiling. "What if there is a reason that I need to see you?"

"You have scores of men at your beck and call. I'm sure any number of them would be willing to jump through fiery hoops at your whim."

"Well, they won't do," she said, her irritation mounting at his flippant reply and the smirk at the corner of his mouth. "In fact, there is something only you are able to do for me."

As her words sank in, the smirk faded and his throat worked on a swallow. "And what might that be?"

That was an excellent question. How did one engage with one's muse? What method of contact inspired the most pages? Would it always need to be a waltz? Should he kidnap her at least once a week? *Hmm* . . .

"The answer is unclear at the moment," she said. "Perhaps it would be better if I explained that for the last year, I hadn't been able to write. All the words just . . . vanished when I tried to put them on the page. It felt like there was nothing inside me any longer."

"What happened a year ago?" He rolled his head to look at her.

It was her turn to stare at the ceiling. "Someone I admired might have mentioned that I was too countrified, unworldly"—*not worthy of a footnote*—"and that I lacked the talent, skills and just about everything required to become the playwright I've always wanted to be."

He raised up on one elbow. Peering down at her, his heavy brows drew together in an intimidating scowl. "Who said these things to you?"

"It doesn't matter. Besides, I'd asked for his advice."

"Of course it matters. If this blackguard used his influence to attack and undermine, not only you but your dreams, then he is the vilest of villains. Tell me, who is this despicable cretin?"

She shook her head, adamant. "I'm not sharing that part of the story. You have your reasons for pretending you're someone else, and I have my reason for not being able to write."

"I can hazard a guess," he grumbled under his breath as he flopped down onto his back once more.

"The point I'm making," she said, "is that the night I fell out of Abernathy's carriage and you caught me, I wrote again."

"If you are asking me to play the highwayman for you in order to conjure inspiration, then the answer is—"

"No. I'm not," she interrupted. Overhead, the shadows from the firelight danced and weaved, much like the apprehension over what she was about to admit seemed to sway back and forth with her need to take the risk, even though she knew very well that he could laugh at her.

She took a deep breath. "It happened again when we danced. I wrote ten pages this evening before all this"—she flitted her ink-stained fingers—"transpired."

"I'm not certain I understand. What exactly happened?"

"Well, I believe that I have . . . found my muse."

He paused and she could hear the scrunch of his pillow as he turned his head. "Surely you're not suggesting that *I* am your muse?"

Feeling even more vulnerable and exposed than when she'd slipped beneath the coverlet, she pressed her lips together. "Mmm-hmm."

"Because you were able to write? That could have happened for a number of reasons."

"No. I know for a fact that it's you. Because of the tingles."

"The tingles," he parroted.

"Ever since I was little and knew I had something worth writing, I'd feel a rush of tingles tightening my scalp. They'd gone absent this past year. But when I'm with you—*only* when I'm with you—I feel them again, stronger than ever," she confessed, barely able to breathe because she was afraid of hearing him laugh at her.

Would he think she was gauche, like Kellum had? An ignorant country girl who knew nothing about life?

A minute passed in silence. Then another. And when St. James didn't respond, she felt the shameful prickle of tears behind her eyes.

She swallowed and surreptitiously knuckled a droplet away from the corner of her eye.

Then she felt the bed shift. She turned her head and suddenly he was there, looking at her, their faces only a breath apart.

"I'm going to regret asking this, but . . . what are the tingles like?" His voice was different, deeper and scratchy as if the words were dragged over rocks.

Thea was suddenly aware of the heat rolling off his body in waves. Her body seemed caught up in the current, rippling low in her belly as her breasts swelled beneath the tight casing of the bedclothes.

She licked her lips, tasting the spice of his exhale on her tongue. "They cascade down my spine and over my skin. They make my fingertips itch with the need to—"

Their noses touched. Bumped really. She wasn't even certain which one of them had moved. But they both went still, their breaths caught in the sliver of space between them.

In that moment, she noticed that his pupils eclipsed his irises and wondered again if she was only imagining that he might be attracted to her.

He searched her gaze. "Then what happens?"

"Then it feels like the whole world just"—her breath hitched when he reached up and his fingertips dragged softly against her cheek, tucking an errant tendril behind her ear—"opens up, and I feel . . ."

His nose slid along hers and he closed his eyes as if the sensation needed to be savored. But still there was something tentative in the way he touched her, the barest tremor in his hand as if he was struggling with some internal debate.

"What do you feel?" he prodded, his voice rougher now, hoarse.

"Alive." Her lips brushed his as she spoke. "Every part of me feels a—"

St. James didn't let her finish.

Sliding a strong hand to her nape, he captured her mouth with his.

Chapter Fifteen

〜

$\mathcal{T}$HEA FORGOT THAT she wasn't particularly fond of kissing.

As St. James moved his mouth over hers, she forgot about a lot of things, like how to breathe. How to think.

Her entire existence centered on the place where their lips met, the warm press, the slow slide, the tingling friction. It all seemed vital somehow. This was what lips were meant to do. Always.

She couldn't remember feeling this way before. Then again, her last experience had left a bad taste in her mouth.

With Kellum, she was always lacking in some way. He was subtle with his insults, however, pretending to be endeared by all her faults.

You're so pretty when you laugh, even if it makes you sound like an empty-headed ninny . . . The other men are obviously entranced by your every smile, though likely because the display of your molars reminds them of buying a horse at Tattersall's.

But when they'd shared a few stolen moments, he didn't bother with subtlety.

Your mouth is too small, too hard. Your lips are too wide, too soft. You're about as enthralling as kissing a head of cabbage. The least you could do is let me touch you . . .

Even though she never wanted to think of those moments again, the unending list of her deficiencies flashed through her mind the instant St. James drew back.

She braced herself for his disappointed frown. For him to tell her what was wrong with her.

"Your lips are so . . ."

In the fraction of a second that he paused to let out a shaky breath, she tensed.

". . . soft. And you taste so"—he swallowed—"sweet. So bloody sweet."

Then he took her mouth again, swallowing down her gasp on a growl of hunger.

Their lips bumped, slid off-center, caught, nibbled, tasted. It was both frenzied and soothing, raw and strangely eloquent as if they were telling each other things that had no words. In her opinion, there had never been a more perfect imperfect kiss.

Perhaps the reason she'd never enjoyed it before was because she'd had the wrong partner. But this felt right in so many ways that it should have terrified her. After all, one did not recover from the horror of her mother's puppet show with a single kiss.

And yet, she couldn't stop wanting more, more tingles, more kisses, more . . . everything.

"*Just* . . ." He brushed his lips over hers, the heat of his breath stealing into her mouth. "*Just one more. That's all I'll take.*"

The way he spoke with his tone so low and earnest, it was as though he were talking to himself and not to her. And something inside her gave way in that instant, another barrier toppling as she stopped thinking about her deficiencies and simply surrendered to the moment.

She wanted to touch him, to hold him. Fingers skimming over his flushed cheek, they threaded into the thick layers of his hair, his scalp warm beneath her touch. She thrilled at his grunt of pleasure and the possessive way his grip tightened around her waist, hand splaying into the small of her back as he tugged her closer.

The kiss transformed into something no longer tentative but seeking . . . wanting . . . needing. His tongue tested the seam of her lips, feeding her the taste of salt and him as he nudged inside. He was all heat and texture, the invasion sending a pulse of heat between her thighs.

Tentatively, she slid her flesh against his, tongues twining. A rough sound vibrated in his throat as a needy mewl purred in her own and his body moved on top of hers, his leg pressing between—

The kiss ended abruptly.

St. James rolled onto his back, breathing hard, his chest rising and falling like a bellows. Then he cursed.

"Have I done something wrong?" Her heart was racing so fast that she feared it would sprint right through the cage of her ribs. She swallowed. "Because I could try to—"

"You've done nothing wrong." He lifted the hands that had been touching her mere seconds ago and laced them behind his head. "Go to sleep, Miss Hartley."

Sleep? With her lips plump and aching from their kiss and her surrounding flesh tender from the rasp of his emerging night beard? Not that she minded. In fact, she was willing to suffer through it all over again. For hours.

She studied his hard profile in the flicker of firelight, the furrowed intensity as he stared up at the ceiling, and she wondered why she could never seem to understand people as well as Shakespeare had done. He had written eloquently about loss, betrayal, jealousy, hatred, anger, love, and passion . . .

But Thea couldn't even understand why St. James, who had seemed to enjoy kissing her, didn't want to any longer.

Perhaps Kellum had been right. Kissing her was like kissing a head of cabbage.

She shivered, feeling alone and hopelessly untethered.

A pent-up exhale left him as he turned his head. "Don't look at me like that."

"I don't know what you mean." She sniffed. "I'm not looking at you in any particular way."

"Aye, you are. Like I've burned your entire village to the ground, kicked your dog and now I'm just going to drive away and leave you to live in a potato sack beneath the bridge."

That was peculiarly accurate in sentiment. "Well, can you blame me? Potato sacks aren't exactly ideal living quarters, and it's terribly chilly beneath bridges."

"Are you trying to tell me that you're cold?"

That wasn't the truth, but she pressed her lips together and nodded all the same.

He expelled another weighty breath. "Come here, then."

Lowering the arm closest to her, he settled her against the crook of his shoulder. When she reached down to pull the barrier free, he stopped her with a sharp command.

"The bolster stays."

With her mind suffering from the plague of uncertainty and her body from the abrupt ebb of passion that seemed to have been nearing some sort of tidal swell, it took a moment to get comfortable. She still had questions. But she wasn't sure she wanted the answers.

So when she finally stopped fidgeting, she was surprised by how heavy her eyes felt and how quickly her heart matched the steady cadence of the one residing beneath the palm of her hand.

After that, she didn't remember anything aside from hearing his long, slow exhale. And she was sure she was already asleep when St. James pressed a kiss to the top of her head and whispered, "Sweet dreams . . . Althea."

⚜

IN THE FAINT glow of embers, Jasper stretched and drew in a deep breath, savoring the sweet fragrance that lingered on his clothes. Those stolen moments were—

He didn't allow himself to finish that thought because he was fairly certain the word *mistake* hadn't been about to cross his mind.

But that's exactly what it was. A mistake.

With that thought in mind, he turned his head to wake Miss Hartley . . . and found the space beside him empty.

He jolted up with a start. Launching to his feet, his boots landed with a bone-jarring thud against the hardwood floor.

"Fool," he muttered as he stormed across the room.

How did she get past him? He always awoke at the slightest sound, *if* he slept at all. Yet, for some incredulous reason, he chose last night to fall into a deep and trancelike sleep?

Before he ran out the door, he looked through the window.

It was still dark outside. That was . . . good? No, damn it all, that wasn't good.

How long ago did she leave? Long enough to venture outside? What if she'd gone off alone? What if she was lost or hurt?

It would be his fault.

The thought screamed through his head as he ran down the short corridor, checking the two other rooms. Seeing that they were empty, he bolted down the stairs.

The taproom was still dark. Throwing open the front door, he searched the violet of fading night and the shadows of the forest. Dawn would begin soon. He held his breath and listened for the sound of a footfall, the snap of a twig, but all he heard was the low hoot of an owl.

But no, that wasn't exactly true. He also heard the low rumble of voices.

Turning around, he rushed through the tavern, past the stairs, down the narrow hall. Seeing a wedge of light bleeding through the gap beneath the kitchen door, he ran toward it, forgetting his size as he barreled through the archway.

Then he juddered to a full stop. Not just because he'd knocked his skull on the lintel, but because there she was.

Draped in his greatcoat, she sat on a stool, holding the toasting fork to the fire, while chatting amiably with Nan and David as Roly tried to get Garmr to shake his hand.

Then Althea Hartley smiled at him, her cheeks tinged with a rosy glow. "Good morning, St. James. Sleep well?"

If it wasn't for the splitting pain at his hairline or Garmr bounding over to him like a lunatic, yipping and leaping around in his lopsided way as if this was the best day in existence, Jasper would have thought he was still abed, dreaming.

Women like her weren't supposed to smile at the likes of him. Or sit in his greatcoat with the cuffs rolled up and look perfectly at home in a slope-roofed tavern with cracks in the soot-stained plaster. They were supposed to sit in fancy parlors and ring the bell for tea.

They certainly didn't kiss the man that kidnapped them or sleep curled up alongside him.

If it wasn't for the fact that every inhale brought him to the stunning awareness that his clothes were covered in her delicate scent, he never would have believed it happened at all.

Even so, it didn't mean anything, or change anything. He'd only brought her here out of necessity. As soon as he took her back, they would never have a need to see each other again. In fact, he would ensure they didn't.

Lowering his hand from the small welt rising, he absently scrubbed a hand over the dog's fur and dragged his gaze away from her mouth.

"Aye, St. James. *Did* you sleep well?" Barrett asked, lifting an earthenware mug to his lips to hide his smirk.

Kneading bread dough beside him, Nan paused to flick flour at her husband. "Behave."

"*Whot?* It was just a question."

"And sometimes an arse is just an arse," she scolded, then turned to Jasper. Her eyes narrowed a fraction and he knew he was about to get an earful. But instead, she said, "You'd best be on your way before first light. There's bound to be servants up and about soon enough. Mr. Pitt is bringing the carriage around."

Not willing to question his luck at avoiding a railing, he nodded.

Then he dared another glance at Althea, hoping she wasn't going to smile again. There was only so much a man could take. "If you've finished toasting your bread, we can leave."

"Oh, this isn't for me. I've already eaten mine. This is for you." And she smiled, damn it all. "Would you like me to spread some jam on it?"

"No." Not wanting her to come any closer, he reached out and snatched the bread from the toasting fork. It nearly burned his fingers. When he hopped it from one hand to the other, he caught Nan's curious expression. Before she asked a question or Barrett spewed whatever thought was making him grin, Jasper shooed his toast toward the door. "Best be off, Miss Hartley."

Roly blocked his path, looking up at him with beseeching brown doe eyes. "Can I go, too? And Thumper?"

He thought about Althea's tales and her mention of a howling wolf and decided against it.

"*Garmr*," he stressed, "needs to stay here for a day or two. How about you stay with him and teach him another trick?"

He passed a glance to Barrett and his wife over his shoulder.

Nan nodded, smiling fondly at the boy. "You know we always like having him here. And your beast is welcome, too." Then her expression hardened and she held up a finger. "As long as he doesn't bring another mangled animal to my doorstep."

"Aww, come on, wife. That was just a gift," Barrett chuckled at her squeamish shudder. "He was protecting your chickens from that fox."

Jasper scrubbed a hand over Roly's head. "Be good until I return." Then he pointed a warning finger at Garmr. "You, too."

"Farewell, Mr. and Mrs. Barrett. It was indeed a pleasure to make your acquaintance." She offered a wave, then bent down to whisper something to Roly.

He stood up straight as a tin soldier and nodded. "You can count on me."

"There's a good lad," she said and pressed a kiss to his cheek. Then she turned and whispered something to Garmr and received a *woof* in response before she kissed the top of his head.

Jasper felt a frown tighten his mouth as they walked outside. When he handed her into the carriage, he told himself that he wasn't jealous of those kisses she seemed to give out so freely. That would have been ridiculous.

He made sure his tone was merely conversational when he asked, "What did you say to the boy?"

"I asked him to look after Garmr for you because sometimes the men who carry the most weight on their shoulders often forget to ask for assistance from others, and that I could tell straightaway that he was reliable and steadfast."

"And what did you say to the dog?"

"The same thing—to look after the boy and keep him out of trouble."

An unexpected grin tugged at his mouth. And since it was dark inside the carriage as it trundled down the forest lane, he gave in to it.

When he heard her yawn, he moved without thinking, wrapping an arm around her to settle her against his side. But it was only for her comfort. It had nothing to do with him.

She accepted this position without a word of protest, the

weight of her head finding the perfect nook between his chest and shoulder to rest against, the warmth of her body coaxing him into relaxation as the scent of her hair filled his nostrils.

"Does this mean you don't abhor touching me, after all?" she asked sleepily.

"Wherever did you get that idea?"

"The kiss," she said, her voice quiet and almost fragile. "It ended rather abruptly. I know I'm not very good at it."

He stared into the darkness with incredulity, then a slow simmering anger as her statement sank in. "Whoever told you such a blatant falsehood should be flogged. The reason I stopped is because you are an innocent."

"So, you ended the kiss because of my inexperience?"

When he heard the hurt in her tone, he knew he'd said the wrong thing. But telling her the truth made him feel like he was approaching a bear trap and was about to lose a foot. Nothing good could come of it.

And yet, even in this darkness, he sensed her light dimming.

"I had to stop before I lost the ability to do so. You do something to me that makes it bloody hard to think. I made a vow, years ago, not to bring dishonor to any woman and I would never forgive myself if I . . . made it impossible for you to return to your life. Intact." He blew out a long breath as if he'd just run all the way to London and back. It was suddenly quite warm in the carriage. "There. Have I made myself clear?"

In response, she pressed her cheek harder against his chest. "Your heart is thundering exceedingly. I can hear it all the way through the cage of your ribs. Was saying all that so dreadful?"

"Hurling oneself off a cliff might have been less painful," he said dryly. "But you haven't answered my question."

She curled closer to him, drawing her knees up, her feet

tucked beneath her on the bench. "You have made yourself exceptionally clear."

He wasn't sure but, for an instant, he thought he felt her press a kiss to his rib cage. Though, it was clearly his imagination.

"Is Roly yours?"

"My what?" he asked, his thoughts elsewhere. But then he caught up with them all at once. "No. Roly is an orphan, a street urchin. Last year, Garmr lost his head over a French poodle and dashed off into traffic to woo her. He found himself at the mercy of a coachman's whip. Roland the Brave, as I call him, came to his defense, shielding the beast with his own body. In turn, I gave the lad a place to live and food in his belly."

"Ah. Then you don't live in the tavern?"

"I have a furnished flat of rooms in Marylebone. At least until the landlord finds out that whenever I leave Garmr alone he eats one of the chairs."

She laughed softly. "Where did you find such a massive dog?"

"He was just a pup, though still fairly large. I heard him baying one day and found that he'd stumbled into a huntsman's trap. I opened the jaws, wrapped him up, took him to a farrier that I know." He shrugged. "And there you have it."

She was quiet for so long that he thought she'd drifted to sleep, but then she yawned. "I think I know how to keep him from eating your chairs."

"If such a miracle exists, I have no doubt you hold it in the palm of your hand."

"I suspect that you're teasing me, but I'm too tired to care," she said, curling closer to him and carelessly resting her hand on his thigh. It made his muscles jump. *All* of them. "Big dogs require an occupation. They want to know that they're helping their pack. If he was still in the wild, the alpha wouldn't allow him to eat unless he'd helped supply the meal."

To keep his thoughts centered on the conversation, he took her hand in his. "So, you're saying he wants to earn his food?"

Her head moved in a nod of agreement. "When he accompanies the highwayman-who-shall-not-be-named, I imagine he receives some sort of reward for a job well done. He simply needs a task to perform when he's in town. Something that he believes is important to you."

"Mmm . . ." he murmured thoughtfully, his thumb passing aimlessly over the delicate bones of her fingers.

He had to remind himself that this wasn't normal. They barely knew each other. Had only spoken a handful of times. Yet, even if they'd been in each other's confidence for years, this degree of comfort and ease was not something he'd experienced before.

He knew he shouldn't even indulge in this small show of affection. It was only tempting fate.

"You were the one who held the umbrella for me, that day when I came out of Fife's," she said.

"Did I?" he asked as if he didn't know what she was talking about.

"You'd forgotten to disguise your voice."

When he'd seen her that day, he wasn't thinking about protecting himself. He'd only been thinking about her and that haunted look in her eyes. "Why do you suspect I was the one, then?"

"Tingles," she said, matter-of-fact. "I wonder if they've appeared all the other times and I simply didn't pay attention. I still remember the day we were introduced, when my parasol flew out of my hands and you rescued it just before it toppled into the river." She shook her head on a quiet laugh. "Honestly, I should have seen through your disguise then."

Damn. He frowned. Had he always revealed too much around her?

If he did, it was her fault. There was just something about her that made his strategies fall into the background and she became the center of his focus. That was dangerous. And he was sure it would only become worse if they were to spend any more time together in public. Because after spending just a few clandestine hours with her, he already wanted more.

He released her hand and shifted to peer through the slit in the shade. "We'll be at the townhouse shortly."

"So soon? It hardly seemed to take long at all."

"Aye," he said, wishing he didn't feel the same, like they were running out of time.

This night had not turned out the way he'd imagined. He'd expected ranting and arguing, some hysterics.

Instead, he'd found that she was just as extraordinary as she'd seemed. More so. And after all he'd done, she'd still trusted him with something that had hurt her and made her feel vulnerable. It made him want to shield and protect her. To slay dragons for her.

But how could he do that and keep his distance? He didn't have an answer.

"My mum used to say, 'Don't ever let anyone make you doubt yourself, for they cannot fathom all the greatness that resides inside of you. Trust in yourself, and in doing so you will find that greatness,'" he said and heard her breath hitch.

"Thank you," she said softly.

They were silent for a while. Both lost to their own thoughts.

Then she sat forward. "I suppose I should remove your greatcoat."

Without a word, he helped her. Sliding his hands to her shoulders, he lifted the weight of the garment so she could slip her arms from the sleeves. Then the white of her nightdress seemed to fill the interior of the carriage with moonlight, and he could see her chafe her hands over her arms.

She blew out a shaky breath. "It's cold in here. The next time you kidnap a woman, be sure to have a foot warmer."

He acted without forethought or strategy and pulled her onto his lap. Every warning in his head faded into the background as he drew her against him. He felt her turn. Then her hands cupped his face and she drew him down to press her lips to his forehead.

"You should be more careful before dashing into rooms," she whispered against his skin.

"I was hoping you didn't notice," he grumbled, embarrassed, not to mention unbearably aroused as she continued her soft kisses over his brow, down his cheeks.

"Does it still hurt?"

When he shook his head, their mouths found each other, instantly sparking, seeking, searching. She stripped bare all of his defenses.

He never should have kissed her the first time, let alone now. But there was only so much a man could resist. Besides, in a moment, it wouldn't matter. They would go their separate ways once this carriage stopped.

"I can never have you," he said against the corner of her mouth, more to himself than to her. His hands splayed over her back, pulling her flush against the frantic beating of his heart. And he regretted every moment he'd spent with her.

"I know," she said on an exhale. "We're facing insurmountable obstacles, helplessly drawn to each other like star-crossed lovers."

He shook his head, sensing the direction of her thoughts. "Althea, I won't allow myself to fall in love with you. This isn't a work of fiction."

"Then why does it feel like all we need to do is write the perfect ending?"

She pressed her lips to his one last time, then slipped out of the carriage.

He hadn't even realized they'd arrived. All he could do was watch her dash through the garden gate, the thick morning fog swirling in curlicues behind her until she reached the way to the terrace door. She could even make fog beautiful.

Jasper sank back against the squabs on a self-disparaging groan. He was not some besotted fool. Life had taught him that insurmountable obstacles were just that—*insurmountable!* Only a romantic would find anything remotely promising in their situation.

He couldn't afford to be that delusional. There was far too much at stake.

Chapter Sixteen

❧

"Good gracious! You're not even dressed. Up! Up! You have a caller," Lady Broadbent said, her cane tapping on the floor as she entered the bedchamber.

Confused by the commotion, Thea lifted her head from her desk on a groan. Her eyelids weighed twenty stone. Each.

She opened her mouth to speak, but her tongue felt like a lump of cotton wool. "What time is it?"

"After ten, slugabed. Don't tell me that is where you slept." Tutting, the countess peeled a sheet of paper from her cheek. "Oh dear, you look as though you've been tattooed like those tribesmen that your brother encountered on his travels. I'll ring for some lemon. Your maid would have come but I've been informed that both Tally and Beth have come down with colds. So we'll have to make do."

"That's awful," she said through a yawn and received an arched eyebrow as the countess tied back the curtains.

"Indeed. The physician has been here and gone. He assured me that it is nothing a bit of rest and hot broth won't cure. You see, *some* of us have already accomplished a great deal this morning." That last remark was tossed over her shoulder as she ambled to the wardrobe. "Come, come, my dear. Don't dawdle."

Thea did her best to stand up from the chair, but every

bone in her body seemed to be fused in a slumped-over position. It felt as though she were wading through reeds, her progress slow and crackling. And the farther she moved away from her desk, the more she felt as though she were leaving her night with St. James behind.

But wait, she thought, her pulse leaping in hopeful speculation. "You said I have a caller?"

"And one who is pacing in the morning room as we speak. I implored him to break his fast, but he said he couldn't eat until he'd spoken with you. Which, I must admit, reveals a strong, upstanding character."

Thea's pulse hammered excitedly at the thought that St. James was unable to stay away. She swiftly started to unplait her hair, her fingers tangling in her haste. "He does have a fine character, does he not?"

"Even so, I am still quite vexed," the countess continued as she withdrew a Pomona green day dress with scalloped lace along the sleeves and bodice. "He never should have left you at the mercy of St. James."

Thea stopped, understanding dawning in her sluggish brain. "Captain Summerhayes. He is my caller."

"Yes, of course. Though I am ready to rail at him for taking Miss Handscombe to the floor."

"I'm sure it was simply a misunderstanding," she said, trying to stifle her disappointment.

"That may be true, but it is not he who bears the weight of the scandal." Lady Broadbent expelled a breath and shook her head. "A dozen missives have arrived already, sending regrets that our invitations were made in error. We must repair the damage that has been done. Though, at the moment, I know not how."

Feeling guilty for having enjoyed most of her evening, Thea took the countess's hand and offered an affectionate squeeze. "Together, we shall think of something."

It took the better part of an hour before Thea was presentable. A faint blue scrawl lingered on her left cheek, but she did her best to angle her face so that he would not see it.

As she'd taken the lemon water to her face, she'd had to bite down a hysterical laugh the instant she'd deciphered the *namyawhgih* emblazoned on her skin.

After last night, it somehow seemed apt that the mark she bore read *highwayman* in reverse.

The instant she and the countess stepped into the parlor, the captain turned from his thoughtful pose by the window and strode directly to her.

"Allow me to beg your forgiveness, Miss Hartley," he said, bowing his dark head, his handsome features stricken in self-contempt. "Had I known that you had not turned your ankle as I'd been informed, I would never have agreed to the favor asked of me. The plot only became apparent as the very one who'd presented himself as a champion for Miss Handscombe was actually deceiving me in order to dance with you."

"What's all this?" Lady Broadbent asked. "Are you saying that St. James had you dance with Miss Handscombe?"

"Aye, my lady. His uncle, Lord Redcliffe, had the honor of the dinner waltz with Miss Handscombe. St. James informed me that his uncle had taken ill quite suddenly, but feared that if he offered to step in, then Miss Handscombe would feel doubly slighted," he said. "Then, he informed me that Miss Hartley had turned her ankle during the previous dance. Since I didn't see her when I first returned from the terrace, where he and I had been in conference, I believed him. For that, I owe you my humblest apology, Miss Hartley. I should've sought you out."

She offered a nod of acceptance. At the time, she had

been hurt. And yet, without the dance with St. James, she never would have experienced the most thrilling night of her life.

A wave of guilt flooded her cheeks as she realized that while the captain had been fretting over this, she had been kissing St. James. "I accept your apology and hold no ill will toward you. It is clear that you were misinformed."

"Though you are most generous, I cannot accept your forgiveness. You suffered grievously and I am, at least in part, to blame."

A bubble of laughter escaped her. "Then we have just played a very poor game of badminton with the apology dead on the floor between us."

His mouth quirked as he inclined his head. "Perhaps there is a way for me to earn your forgiveness, or to believe as though I have done. If you would permit me, I should like to take you for a drive through the park some afternoon when the weather is fine."

She thought again of St. James. How would he take the sight of her out with another man? Being courted by another man?

It was foolish to wonder such things. He made it clear that he wouldn't pursue her and that they couldn't be seen together. She knew this as well, even if every drop of blood in her body longed to sprint through her veins as it only did with him.

"I would be honored, Captain Summerhayes," she said with a resolute smile.

Then he bent as if to pick up something from the floor and held out his open palm. "I will leave you in charge of our badminton until then, Miss Hartley."

After she pantomimed pinching the invisible offering by the feathers, he grinned, a spray of attractive creases beside his eyes.

"My lady," he said, bowing to the countess, then took his leave.

Lady Broadbent waited for the sound of the front door closing, then she waggled her fan at Thea. "To have such an important man—not to mention a devilishly handsome one—take such consideration clearly means that you have another admirer. Well done, my dear."

"I did nothing to earn his regard, and the brief conversation we had at the ball contained little importance." She shrugged.

"Clearly, it was enough for him. And that witticism with the badminton was quite clever. He certainly seemed taken by you." Lady Broadbent's lips pursed, a *however* hovering in the air like the odor of cigars in the dining room after a dinner party. "However, this one will not linger long as a bachelor, I should think, especially if the matrons of the *ton* have their way. There are many young women who would leap at the chance to secure such a man. Though not many of those would be in their third Season."

Thea understood perfectly. If she had any interest in the captain, she should make him aware of her regard at once to secure him.

"I have it," Lady Broadbent declared with a rap of her fan against the arm of the chair. Then she waved her hand in an impatient gesture toward the escritoire on the far side of the room. "Take down a missive, my dear. I know precisely how to extricate us from the grip of scandal."

Lowering the hinged table, Thea withdrew a sheet of paper and uncapped the ink. "To whom should I address it?"

"To Madame LeBlanc. We shall request an audience with her at once. After all, who better than the premier modiste to turn the tides in our favor by discreetly supplying the correct view of events at the Leighton Ball."

Thea didn't like the sound of this. "And what exactly is the correct view?"

"Why, that you have bewitched St. James, through no fault of your own, of course. And his villainous actions left the honorable Captain Summerhayes with no choice other than to escort Miss Handscombe to the floor."

"But you heard the captain. St. James knew that Miss Handscombe wouldn't wish to dance with him, so he merely offered her a replacement. Then, so that I wouldn't feel slighted, he danced with me."

"Pish tosh. No one will believe him capable of orchestrating such a farce. And one could hardly accuse him of being noble after all that he's done to ruin your gowns."

Lady Broadbent wasn't saying anything that hadn't been said before. But she didn't know St. James the way Thea did. Though, to be honest, she didn't know much about him either. Certainly not enough. But what she did know was good and clever and sweet. And he was capable of a great many things.

Like kissing, she thought as another flush of heat crept to her cheeks.

But even before the kissing, she had seen more inside him. Surely the countess had to see something more as well. "That day when he came to call, you said he was charming."

"Did I?"

As a pair of dove gray eyebrows inched higher, Thea felt her lungs fill with hope. Perhaps the countess would understand and even invite him to dinner one evening. Once they were better acquainted, she was certain that—

"I cannot imagine what I'd been thinking," Lady Broadbent said dismissively.

Thea remembered reading about one of the first flights of the Montgolfier balloon. It had soared up over the trees in a magnificent display. But as it descended in a nearby village, the people were so frightened that they came at it with pitchforks and spades until that wonderful thing was nothing more than a sad, defeated lump on the ground.

In that moment, she knew exactly how the balloon had felt.

"Trust me," the countess continued, "this way is much better. Mark my words, in two days' time, you will be the most sought-after debutante this Season. No one will even recall that it's your third."

⟜

THAT AFTERNOON, THEY managed to secure an appointment with Madame LeBlanc. Thea had no idea how much Lady Broadbent had paid for the privilege, but the cost had to have been dear.

"I fear you have been far too generous, my lady," she said over a lump of guilt the size of a toad in her throat. "Three Seasons, my ennui, that entire ordeal last year, and now this."

As they left the shop, Lady Broadbent squeezed her hand. "None of that, my dear. I would do it all again in a trice if it meant finding you a proper husband."

If Thea hadn't told that story about the highwayman, then none of this would have happened. None of it.

She never would have had a gown ruined, let alone three. She would have smiled politely at parties. Would have been introduced to a few potential prospects, with at least one who wanted to court her. And by the end of the Season she might have been betrothed to a proper gentleman.

But if none of it ever happened, then she never would have talked to St. James. He never would have carried her away in the middle of the night. She never would have found her spark. And the rest of her life would have continued on as a sea of empty pages in a world without ink.

Thinking about all of it only made her feel selfish. She wasn't even certain she was worth all this trouble.

As soon as the thought registered, a wave of nausea

rolled through her. Kellum would have said something like that. Not her. Before she met him, she never would have believed that she wasn't worth living a life that made her happy.

She needed to stop thinking that way and shove any trace of him out of her head.

Determined to do just that, she lifted her head high and saw Miss Handscombe and Miss Livet coming toward them on the pavement. With a ready smile, she offered a wave.

Miss Handscombe did the same until her mother quickly intercepted the gesture. Lady Bromley shook her head so adamantly it looked as though she had an actual bee in her bonnet, then the trio swiftly altered course, disappearing into the nearest shop.

As the sharp ping of a bell faded and the door closed, Thea felt that toad in her throat plummet to the pit of her stomach.

"Never mind all that," the countess said with a pat. "By tomorrow everything will be different. Just wait and see."

She'd said the same thing last year as they'd left London with Thea in tears. And everything had been decidedly different, but not in a good way.

"Now, we'll simply have ourselves a lovely cup of tea and a few biscuits and then—" She stopped and a smile bloomed on her face. "And here is a friend that I'm certain will brighten your day."

Thea didn't even realize that she'd been staring down at the pavement until she looked up and saw the approach of Anna Snow, her porcelain skin adorned with a cheerful smile, black ringlets bouncing under a blue bonnet as she quickened her step to greet them.

Miss Snow was a dear friend of Verity's, Thea's eldest sister. And, in a way, had become something of a sister to all of them. In fact, she was partly the reason that the true swindler behind the scandal that had blackened the Hartley name had been caught and brought to justice.

However, ten years ago, it was a different story.

Thea had been just thirteen when it happened. She remembered her father's excitement about an investment opportunity that would provide handsomely for their family. Unfortunately, his famed silver tongue also lured many members of the *ton* into sinking their fortunes into the endeavor. Before anyone was aware that they were all being swindled.

When the truth was revealed, most of society blamed Conchobar Hartley, ignoring the fact that he'd lost a fortune as well.

Seven years passed and the Hartley family kept to themselves in their small hamlet. Until, one day, Verity told a lie that brought the Duke of Longhurst—*Lady Broadbent's grandson*—to their door.

The very same duke who'd been on the precipice of marrying Miss Anna Snow.

It was almost comical to think that one little lie could change so many lives for the better. And yet, Thea didn't believe that the tale the countess had just spun for Madame LeBlanc would have quite the same result.

After all, there were still many in society who likened the Hartley name with scandal, and she would do well to remember that.

"Why, Lady Broadbent and Miss Hartley, as I live and breathe. It has been far too long since we've seen each other," Anna said, reaching out to squeeze both of their hands. "Thea, I believe it was at the christening of your sister's son. Come to think of it, I just had a letter from Verity the other day. How is the rest of your family?"

In the presence of Anna's effervescence, Thea's smile was genuine as the tightness in her lungs receded on a relieved breath. "They are all well. And it is exceedingly good to see you, Miss Snow."

"Hearing 'Miss Snow' only reminds me of the Season I

spent as the common-born heiress who once darkened the *ton*'s door. It is *Anna* to you," she corrected affectionately. "After all, I think of you, Honoria and Verity as near to sisters as anyone could be. Therefore, we are practically family."

"Well said, Miss Sn—" Lady Broadbent hesitated with a wince as if delivering an improper address pained her. "Anna."

Thea and Anna exchanged a playful look. Even during the short time that Magnus had been courting Anna—*before* he'd met and fallen head over heels for Verity—Lady Broadbent had never called her by her given name.

"And how is your father?" the countess continued. "Well, I hope."

"Indeed, he is. However, he would be happier if the world had more buttons in it, and he was the one to make them," she said wryly of the man once known by all of England as the Button King before he lost his fortune. But Phineas Snow wasn't the type to give up, even if he had to start over. "In fact, I was just running an errand for his business partner, Mr. Dashing, when I saw the pair of you."

"And we are ever so glad you did. As for us, we were about to have tea. It would be lovely if you were to join us."

"That is," Thea added ominously, "*if* you dare to be seen with two pariahs."

One of the things that she liked about Anna was that she didn't possess an ounce of artifice in her character. She was wholly genuine, and so was her look of understanding.

"I have seen the papers and I can tell you that I am heartily sorry for this nonsense you are being forced to endure. However, as one who has lived through a scandal or two, I can tell you that they live a half life. Like fireflies in a jar, they will soon lose their power to glow." Then Anna linked her arms through Lady Broadbent's and Thea's.

"Besides, I've always thought that three pariahs make a far better number for tea. Don't you?"

⁓

BEFORE THE END of the following day, dozens of new invitations arrived, as well as missives claiming to have sent earlier regrets in error. The scandal sheets laid all the blame at St. James's feet, while Miss Hartley was dubbed the *enchantress*.

Lady Broadbent's plan was a smashing success.

Thea expected to feel a wave of relief. But all she felt was guilt.

She wanted to send Jasper a letter in order to . . . To what? Warn him? Explain that casting him as the villain hadn't been her idea?

In the end, she knew that anything she might have said to her chaperone would only have worsened the situation for both of them, risking her reputation and exposing him. And she wouldn't do that to him.

Of course, all of this would be so much easier if she knew his reason for becoming a highwayman and his ongoing disguise for the *ton*. After being deceived by Kellum's character, it was difficult for her to trust, not only others but her own judgment.

Was she wrong to feel this peculiarly potent connection to Jasper? Or should she simply accept what he'd told her— that they could be nothing to each other?

Ugh! She hated the sense of hopelessness that came from all this uncertainty.

After the discussion she'd had at tea with Anna, she wished she could be more like her.

When Mr. Snow's business had gone down in flames, she'd offered up her considerable dowry to rebuild it, but only if her father allowed her to manage the factory.

Even though she was six and twenty, she was unconcerned with finding a husband. Her dream was to become a businesswoman in her own right, and she was doggedly pursuing that dream, no matter the cost.

"We have two for Thursday next," Lady Broadbent said from a tufted chair by the hearth in the parlor.

"Oh?" Thea answered distractedly as she sat at the desk by the window and attempted to fold pieces of silver paper into a bachelor's button. So far it looked more like a miniature elephant.

"To narrow it down to one, we need to decide which . . . Oh." The countess stopped and her expression shuttered closed. "Never mind, my dear. I spoke in error. The second option is simply . . . well . . . unsuitable."

Thea's interest was sparked at once. To her mind, anyone hosting a soiree deemed *unsuitable* would likely have invited St. James as well.

She set the elephant flower aside. "What is the second option?"

"The Buxton Ball."

"Oh," she said, the weighted syllable practically pachydermic.

Lord Buxton and Lady Buxton were patrons of the arts. Because of their affinity for the theatre, they had once been friends of Thea's parents. However, when the scandal blackened her family name ten years ago, they chose not to be their champions. After her father had been exonerated, they'd extended an olive branch and were more than pleased to add Thea's name to their invitation list.

That was how she had met Kellum.

The Buxtons often invited him to their home, and had even taken holidays with him. And considering the fact that they were well aware of Kellum's attentions to Thea last Season—*and* the abrupt end of his attentions—their primary interest was likely in the drama created in having the two of them encounter each other.

"Fear not, my dear. I shall send our regrets."

"No. I think we should attend," Thea said, surprising herself. "It would only make tongues wag if we didn't, with the *ton* whispering and speculating that I am still"—she swallowed—"heartbroken. But I would rather not give Sir Archer the satisfaction of believing he has any effect on me whatsoever."

Not only that, but she didn't want St. James to hear those rumors either. Because even though he said they could be nothing to each other, she wanted to give him every reason to reconsider.

Lady Broadbent's lips curved, her eyes softly creased at the corners. "I am in full agreement. Let us make him rue the day he ever let *the enchantress* slip through his fingers."

Later that night, and feeling a rise of her own dogged determination, Thea decided to send a missive to St. James.

> *Please come to the Buxton Ball.*
> > > *Yours,*
> > > *A*

Chapter Seventeen

༄

*T*HEA SPENT THE entire week waiting for Jasper's response. And for an entire week she received nothing.

Clearly, he didn't harbor a doubt over his decision to avoid her.

The twinge of hurt she initially felt transformed multiple times. At first, when she believed he was cross with her for the rumor they'd spoon-fed to the *ton*, she began to eat everything in sight—much like a caterpillar—until her corset left her unable to breathe.

Then when she was convinced he hated her, she'd burrowed indoors during the gloomy wet days that followed, grousing at anyone who dared look at her the wrong way.

But when seven sparkless days and nights had passed without a word from him, she emerged from her self-imposed chrysalis, unfurling wings of glorious vexation. How dare he ignore her!

So she decided to make him regret his choice. It was time to prove herself the *ton*'s enchantress.

Garbed in Madame LeBlanc's latest creation—an ethereal moonlight satin gown *with* velvet-lined pockets—she squared her shoulders and approached the doors to the Buxton ballroom.

This was it, she thought on a breath.

She had prepared herself for this night, assured that her anger would be the perfect armor against seeing Kellum. His opinions had no hold over her. And from the gasps she received when guests saw her with her shoulders bare and her coiffure accented by silver and glittering gems, she knew that not even he could find fault in her appearance.

"Miss Hartley, as I live and breathe," Lord Buxton said when she reached him. His voice had a booming quality as if the camel satin waistcoat, stretched taut over his rotund belly, was the skin of an enormous drum. Taking hold of her fingertips, he leaned forward and offered a wink. "Dare I say, you look *enchanting* this evening?"

"You are too kind, my lord."

She expertly concealed any lingering disquiet with a ready smile. Beside her, Lady Broadbent issued an almost laugh to Lady Buxton, likely encountering a similar greeting.

"My wife and I were only too delighted to learn that you've returned for another Season. Back to have another go at it, hmm? I'm sure you'll find there are an ample number of gentlemen who'll . . ."

As her host rattled on with a sweeping gesture toward the crush below, she caught sight of Kellum at the bottom of the stairs.

The instant their eyes clashed, a clutch of icy dread gripped her heart. A sudden barrage of inadequacies flooded her and her smile froze, feeling brittle around the edges.

"I say, Buxton," came a familiar voice behind her. "You're holding up the line."

Thea spun on her heel to see her brother standing there. "Truman!"

His returning grin stopped at the thin scar he refused to talk about, but there was warm affection in his gaze. "Hullo, imp."

He looked ever so dashing dressed in black superfine with a high snowy cravat, his skin still retaining a lingering tan from his years as a merchant sailor. And there was no taming the barley and gold feathering of his hair that had earned him the moniker of Hawk.

Buxton gripped Truman's hand, shaking it like a pump handle. "Hartley! You have just made my soiree a tour de force. Why, no one has seen much of you in society for nigh on—"

"Tell you what," Truman interrupted, clapping their host on the shoulder, "let's meet up at Stirling's one night and we'll have a chat over cards and whisky. But now, I have two beautiful women to escort down the stairs."

"Of course, of course," Buxton said, his jowls quivering with the thrill of having his party being the *pièce de résistance* in tomorrow's scandal sheets.

As Truman turned away, there was a certain stiffness in his posture that made it clear he wasn't altogether comfortable with being out in society. At least, not any longer.

Before the scandal, he'd been a man-about-town, attending parties and stirring up mischief as any gentleman of two and twenty would. He was apprenticing to become an architect and had even been set to marry. But, like a house of cards, his betrothal and dreams of the future he'd envisioned toppled beneath the weight of the scandal.

Thea loved him all the more, knowing that he'd come out, willing to endure dredging up those memories, just for her.

"You never attend these gatherings. I have to wonder what Lady Broadbent said in the missive she must have sent you to persuade you here."

"Whatever could you mean?" He blinked, feigning ignorance. "I've been planning to attend Buxton's ball for weeks now."

Her smile twisted wryly at the lie and she rolled her eyes as she threaded her arm through his. "Well, no matter the reason, I am glad you're here."

"As am I," Lady Broadbent chimed in, taking his other

arm as they descended the stairs. "There are sure to be a number of young ladies who'll catch your eye."

He squinted, tilting his head. "I beg your pardon, my lady, but I could not hear you. I'm a trifle deaf in both ears."

For that, he received a swat with the fingers she had curled over his arm, but there was a grin tucked into the corner of her mouth. "Cheeky, scamp."

Nevertheless, Lady Broadbent took every opportunity to ensure that he was introduced to any debutante who happened to be standing near, whenever Thea was stopped by a gentleman to add a dance to her card.

When her card was as full as she wanted a short while later, the countess retired to the upper gallery to watch the dancers from a comfortable chair or as she preferred, "a worthy vantage point."

To appease the lady, Truman accepted her cajoling and agreed to dance the first set with Thea. When it ended, he embraced the Hartley acting prowess in his blood and affected a limp.

"You are abominable," Thea whispered with a laugh as he pretended to lean on her arm. "All this to avoid dancing with a woman who may strike your fancy?"

"It's not the women I mind, it's their matchmaking mamas. They're wily creatures. First you agree to a dance, then to a tour of the park on Sunday and, before you know it, you're attending picnics and buying flowers and . . ." He shook his head. "I've no stomach for that."

"Surely you don't intend to remain a bachelor. You are Father's heir, after all."

She often wondered if his heart had been irrevocably broken when his fiancée had married another, following the scandal. More than anything, she wanted to believe that hearts could be mended.

He slid her a look. "So, your third Season, hmm? Surely you don't intend to become a spinster."

"Point taken," she grumbled. "Even so, you are nearly ten years my senior. Why is the insulting title of spinster only applied to women who are unwed?"

He shrugged in that "I don't make the rules" sort of way, but there was a smug tilt to his lips as they paused near the terrace doors.

A cool breeze filtered in, stealing across the skin of her nape. She felt as though she were being watched and quickly surveyed the room to see if Kellum was nearby. He wasn't.

Sir Archer was standing through the doorway of an adjacent room, gesticulating as he told a story. The women around him were clearly enraptured by his handsome features, the resonant sound of his voice and the graceful movement of his hands. Then he must have made a quip because he laughed in that superior way of his.

The sound of it had always grated on her nerves. It was part scoff, part chuckle. A *scuckle*.

As his *scuckle*, *scuckle*, *scuckle* drifted into the ballroom, she wondered how she'd ever been able to bear that annoying sound. He was just so pompous. Why hadn't she seen that from the beginning?

Irritated with herself, she lifted her gaze to the gallery to find Lady Broadbent shaking her head at Truman, who made a poor show of clutching his side and wincing.

"She is leaning heavily on her cane," her brother said as they stepped outside and walked toward the stone balustrade. "I imagine this will be the last Season she will be able to chaperone."

Thea blew out a slow breath, the chill in the air turning it to vapor in the fan of light spilling from the ballroom. "I know. She has been more than generous. I could never thank her enough, and all she asks in return is . . ."

"For you to be swept off your feet and fall happily into the shackles of wedded bliss?"

"Precisely," she said dryly.

"Well, you are either here to find a husband or"—he widened his eyes in mock horror—"to escape a life with our parents."

At the moment, she didn't particularly like either option. "Did you hear how they scandalized Reverend Tobias when they thought they could cavort like the fairies in *A Midsummer Night's Dream* after they'd sent all the servants on a picnic for the afternoon?"

He nodded gravely. "Ben Lawson wrote to me about it. According to him, it wasn't the nudity that bothered Tobias, it was finding them in the middle of some rather acrobatic"—he stopped and cleared his throat as if he'd just remembered his audience—"activities."

"I'm not a child. I've known for most of my life that our parents are abnormally passionate," Thea said with a long-suffering sigh.

And yet, now she had a much better understanding.

The mere thought of St. James sent a rush of heat to the surface of her skin, and she was glad to be standing in the cool night air.

Although, she wished he was here. Her gaze had skimmed the crowd at least a hundred times, but he wasn't in attendance. At least, not yet. She still had hope that he would decide that he couldn't stay away from her like he'd vowed he would.

"You think *you've* been embarrassed?" her brother asked, drawing her back to their conversation. "Imagine being their firstborn. I had no one to shield my eyes."

"Imagine being their last born and hearing Mother giggling as Father promises to reenact their scandalous courtship once their children are no longer at home."

In their defense, they didn't know that Thea had been passing by the parlor on the way to the library for a book late one night when she'd overheard their conversation.

She couldn't blame them for being eager to be rid of

her, she supposed. She'd been rattling around the house and dragging the corpse of her soul behind her for nearly a year. Who would wish to subject themselves to that?

"A scandalous courtship? Are you suggesting that I wasn't born three months prematurely?" Truman gasped.

"Yes, well, you might say it encouraged me to return to London for another Season."

"Whether you wanted to or not, hmm?" He turned his head back toward the ballroom, his look dark and foreboding.

She followed his gaze to find Kellum standing with one elbow resting on the spiral newel-post at the base of the ballroom stairs, holding court for a passel of adoring sycophants. His annoying *scuckle* bounded through the crush like a pig on the loose.

"I noticed you kept two dances available on your card. You weren't hoping for . . ."

"No," she said at once. Then repeated herself for good measure. "No. I'm not a dimwit."

There was a hardness lingering in the gaze that studied hers, an unspoken promise of retribution if she should but ask. But he must have been satisfied with her answer, because he offered a short nod.

"And yet, you're still the sister who brought chickens into the drawing room," he said, the light catching the silver skin of that scarred brow as it arched in teasing.

She felt her lips twitch despite herself. "I'll never live that down, will I?"

"Never." He grinned and proffered his arm. "Care to return to the horde? I'm sure your next partner is ready to impress you with superior form and grace."

His inflection was the exact imitation of their old dancing master, whom they'd dubbed Mr. Bumbleton because he was forever warning them against the *bumbling offenses* of slouching and stumbling.

Thea was laughing as they turned, just when Captain

Summerhayes appeared. She hadn't realized he would be among the guests this evening.

The instant he saw her brother, he stopped at the threshold, his expression one of surprise. "*Hawk?*"

Truman blinked. "Summerhayes. I heard you were in town."

"I imagine you did. As I recall, very little escapes your notice." His momentary surprise faded as he extended his hand. "It's good to see you under better circumstances."

Thea pretended not to notice the way her brother discreetly shook his head or the way his arm tensed beneath her hand. Dutifully, she tamped down her curiosity. For the moment. There was a story there that she very much wanted to hear. But this was clearly not the time.

"I have recently become acquainted with your sister," he continued. "And if it is acceptable to you, I should like to request a dance. That is"—he turned to her—"if Miss Hartley is amenable."

It was clear in her brother's curious expression that he was wondering if Summerhayes was the reason she'd kept those dances empty on her card.

She knew it had been foolish to hold out hope that St. James would have been in attendance. That he might have asked her. She couldn't have accepted, regardless. And yet, she had still hoped.

But not any longer.

"I would be delighted, Captain," she said with practiced alacrity worthy of the stage.

He glanced down at her card and smiled. "Shall we attempt the dinner waltz again?"

Ignoring the pang in the center of her chest, she nodded.

AFTER THE DINNER waltz, she'd ended up offering Summerhayes the last dance she'd left open, as well. But when it came time to take her to the floor, she asked if he wouldn't mind taking some air instead. Her heart simply wasn't into dancing.

They ventured out onto the terrace with Truman's nod of approval as he lingered inside and spoke with an old friend.

Earlier, her brother had remarked that Summerhayes was a good man, but a serious one. "He's looking for marriage," he'd said. "Not simply wanting to pass the time on the arm of a pretty girl."

In other words, she should be serious as well about her choice.

And yet, the last time she had thought she'd been serious, she had chosen wrong. How could she trust herself again?

As if conjured by her thoughts, Kellum appeared on the terrace. And framed in the glow of the ballroom, he looked all too smug.

Beside him was Lord Buxton, puffing on a cigar. They were deep in conversation and didn't seem to notice her. But she had little faith that Buxton would allow her to escape this evening without having his drama.

Believing she could steal inside before they saw her, she turned to her escort.

Summerhayes had his face tilted toward the night sky with the quiet reverence of a man who'd used the stars to guide him home a time or two.

"Do you miss it?" she asked, curious despite her need to slink away unnoticed.

"When the nights are clear like this one, aye." He breathed in deeply, then looked down at her. "But my feet are firmly planted on English soil, where I hope to build a home."

"If you are building a house, you should consider my brother as your architect," she said quickly, purposely misunderstanding his meaning.

The flesh around his eyes creased attractively when he grinned. "I believe you know that isn't what I meant. But I understand you. These things take careful consideration, after all. Though, I will assuredly think of your brother for the design of my country home."

She was grateful that he wasn't pressuring her. He was kind, considerate and patient, not to mention handsome and intelligent. He was precisely the type of man she'd hoped to find after last Season.

So then why couldn't she stop thinking about St. James?

Before the chorus could chime in with their opinion, she decided to embrace her eldest sister's more sensible nature. Looking up at him—and trying not to compare his height and coloring to St. James—she said, "I suppose this is when I ask where you intend to live."

He grinned again in approval. "I actually have several properties. One, most notably in Lincolnshire where, I believe, your parents live." At her nod, he continued. "But I've yet to make a firm decision."

He was good enough to turn his gaze toward the gardens instead of handing her the weight of an expected response. And he continued conversationally, remarking on the merits of each parcel.

She listened with a distracted ear when she thought she heard her name mentioned between the pair of gentlemen at the far end.

Her shoulders tensed. She'd been spotted. But surely Buxton and Kellum wouldn't have the audacity to approach her when she was with Captain Summerhayes.

Oh, who was she fooling? Of course they would. Where one loved drama, the other loved being the center of attention.

She stole a wary glance down to the men just as Kellum's gaze met hers.

The instant she saw him move in her direction, she felt the clutch of panic root her to the terrace stones. She wanted to turn away. But it was as if those roots were slowly dragging her down, encircling her ankles, vining upward to curl around her throat . . .

"Miss Hartley, what a delight to see you again," Kellum said, sweeping up her unoffered hand and pressing his lips to it before she could pull away.

When she did, she shored up her spine. She wouldn't reveal that just the sound of his voice could make her feel smaller. As if she were slowly sinking into the earth, disappearing without a trace, without even a footnote.

"Sir Archer," she said.

Years of performances on the family stages had taught her how to hold her features unmovable. Therefore, Captain Summerhayes wouldn't detect her disquiet, and Lord Buxton wouldn't have his entertainment. But more importantly, Kellum couldn't feed off her reaction as he'd always done, practically crowing in triumph whenever he'd reduced her to tears.

As if her lack of reaction posed a delightful challenge, Kellum's eyes brightened. "It has been nigh on a year since we've last been in such close confines, has it not? Then again, I'm sure you could tell me the exact day. You likely wrote it down in one of those little ledgers you like to keep."

"I'm sure I cannot recall." She swallowed. "Have you met Captain Summerhayes?"

Without missing a beat, Kellum turned with a genial smile that won over nearly everyone he met. "Captain Summerhayes, a pleasure. We haven't been introduced, but I've heard many good things about you and I was looking forward to making your acquaintance."

As Summerhayes shook his hand, Thea was struck by how easy it was for Kellum to appear the amiable man-about-town. Manipulation was mother's milk to him.

The evening they'd met flashed through her mind. How impressed he'd been that she knew so much about the structure of a play. His woebegotten tale of his secretary running off and leaving him in a bind, and Thea's innocent offer to assist him.

Admittedly, she'd been dazzled by him. That was the reason she hadn't seen it. How nothing she did was ever good enough. She would stay up all through the night making copies of his plays because he said he didn't trust anyone else. Then he would look the pages over and find displeasure in her penmanship, her margins, a stray drop of ink . . .

From there, after he affectionately said she made a worthless secretary, he invited her to watch one of his plays from his own box. Then he'd begun to court her. He'd showered her with comfits, popped by for surprise visits, overwhelmed her with his attention . . . and apologized for being so jealous after he'd lost his temper, time and again.

Looking back, she didn't know how she hadn't seen it while it was happening.

"Lost in your own little world again, Miss Hartley?" Kellum smirked when she blinked and chafed her hands over her arms. "You had the faraway look of reminiscence on your face."

Thea shook her head. For him to say such a thing was unspeakably rude to Captain Summerhayes.

"No, indeed. I simply did not want to interrupt your conversation." She remembered how much he despised being interrupted. "However, if you are through, then the captain and I'll leave you and Lord Buxton to your cigars."

When she put her hand on her escort's arm, Kellum stepped forward.

"Actually, if Summerhayes doesn't mind, I should like to have a private word with *yooo*—"

A surprised squawk came out of him as he stumbled. Then, the estimable Sir Kellum Archer fell to his hands and knees at her feet.

He howled with incredulity, cursing out accusations of someone having the nerve to trip him. But it wasn't until he glanced back that they all noticed the ropes of ivy wrapped around his ankle.

Thea was no expert in horticulture. However, she was fairly certain ivy didn't grow that quickly. Which meant that something, or *someone*, made certain that Kellum would fall.

It seemed impossible. The terrace was six feet from the garden below. It would have taken a very tall man to reach up, to loop the ivy around an ankle without anyone noticing.

There was only one man who could have done it. One man who blended in with the shadows. One giant of a man that no one would ever suspect of being that clever.

Her breath caught at the possibility, her heart thumping like a rabbit beneath her breast.

She spun around to search the shadows. And just then, she heard a rustling sound on the stones at her feet. And there, perched on the very edge of the terrace, lay a small paper rose.

As Summerhayes and Buxton assisted Kellum, she bent down and just managed to slip her arm through the balustrade when her hand was clasped by someone below. Someone in the shadows. It was just a brief touch and over before she could even form a gasp. But she knew precisely who it was as warm tingles raced up her arm.

St. James.

Standing, she tucked the flower into her bodice and smiled toward the darkness.

He couldn't stay away, she thought. And that changed everything.

Chapter Eighteen

༄

JASPER PASSED A rider on the way to his aunt's cottage. Looking over from the seat of the old dray, he recognized the man at once and tipped his hat. The dark-haired rider did the same as they went on their own way.

But he wondered why Willie Raintree was this far west. There was nothing for miles except pastureland and a handful of houses, owned by Redcliffe. And the possibility that Raintree would ever ally himself with Redcliffe was highly improbable.

Raintree harbored an intense loathing toward the aristocracy. He was the eldest son of Baron Fauconberg, but because he was born on the wrong side of the blanket, he would never inherit. The unfairness of it left him embittered and fueled a thirst for rebellion and revenge.

He was considered an outlaw with a band of ne'er-do-wells who followed him. And he was also an opportunist.

So when Jasper approached him with an arrangement that would keep hooligans and thugs from Barrett's tavern in return for a cut from the highwayman's ill-gotten gains, Raintree readily agreed.

But even though they had formed something of an alliance, Raintree had no business being on this particular country lane.

A dark suspicion niggled at the back of Jasper's mind as he drove the horse cart around to the back of the cottage. Spotting Tempest and Iris in the garden, he waved a hand in greeting before hefting up the crate. Then he went inside to his aunt.

That was when he saw the bunch of posies on the kitchen table.

"Good morning, Mrs. Bidwell," he said to the cook as he set down the crate of various meats, cheeses and whatnots. "Is my aunt in her sitting room?"

Turning away from the sink, she smiled at him and tucked a hank of grizzled hair back beneath a frilled mob-cap. "She is, my lord. I was just bringing her a tea tray to take the chill off."

"I'll do that, if you don't mind."

"You're too good to us. Why, I still have a bit of ham left from your last visit. I'll make a nice hearty bean stew with what's left." As he took up the tray, she began unpacking the crate, then gasped. "Oh! Those jelly comfits I like so well. My lord, you shouldn't have."

"I've no idea how those found their way into the crate," he said. Then, just before he turned to fit his shoulders through the doorway, he added, "Happy birthday, Mrs. Bidwell."

There was a grin tucked into the corner of his mouth as she prattled on and on about what he should or shouldn't have done. In his opinion, it was the least he could do for all her years of service and her work consisting of far more than cooking.

He found his aunt in a chair by a window that over-looked the garden. She was looking paler and frailer than she had the week before. When she saw him, she hastily lowered a handkerchief to her lap, but her eyes were still glistening with tears.

Alarmed, he set down the tray and went to her, kneeling to take her hand. "What is it? Are you unwell? Shall I send for a doctor?"

She patted his hand in reassurance. "I am as well as to

be expected with these lungs of mine. Besides, there is no doctor, remember?"

Redcliffe, he thought, biting down a curse. But the fury must have shown in his eyes because she shook her head.

"Anger solves nothing, as you well know, and neither will allowing him to corrupt the goodness in you. He has already taken so much. Don't let him take that, too."

"For your sake alone," he agreed with a nod, swallowing down the burning rage where it would join the mountain of embers already inside him. Yet, he feared that, at some point, there would be no possible way to hold back the inferno that begged for release.

Redcliffe needed to pay. But that was a thought for another time.

As for today, he had other matters to deal with, like who might be paying a call on his cousins.

He pressed a kiss to his aunt's hand, her fingers chilled beneath his lips. "You're cold. I'll add another log to the fire."

Rising, he went to the hearth and noticed the wood box was nearly empty. He made a mental note to chop more before he left.

"I happened to pass a certain Mr. Raintree on the way here," he said casually as he stacked the logs on the grate. "He hasn't been stopping by, has he?"

His aunt was silent as she looked down at her lap, twisting the handkerchief around a finger.

"Aunt Clara?"

She expelled a breath. "Tempest asked me not to tell you. She said you wouldn't understand. And he has behaved most honorably toward her."

"*Honorably?*"

"I wouldn't say it if it wasn't true. I've witnessed it for myself." She straightened in her chair, her dander up. "My daughter is one and twenty and she's never been in society. Has never been courted by a young man who fancied her.

She lost her father before her life could begin and, ever since, she has been here playing nursemaid to me, mother to Iris, and maid of all work. I just wanted her to have something. Someone."

He was about to point out that Raintree was a criminal, practiced in the art of showing his good side to get what he wanted. But when he saw tears well up in his aunt's eyes, he didn't have the heart to reprimand her. She was doing what she thought was best for her family.

And he, when he saw Raintree again, would do what he had to do.

"Oh, Jasper," she cried, patting the consoling hand he laid on her shoulder. "They deserve so much better, but here I sit as they labor in the garden to put food on the table. All I've been able to teach them are lessons in decorum, needlework and my abominable French. On good days, I've taught them dancing and painting. However, those days are fewer and farther between."

Kneeling down again, he dried her eyes, wishing that he could do more. Wishing that his hands weren't tied with so many different knots.

Years ago, at the end of school, he'd saved a little money and tried to invest in the railroad, certain that it was going to change the world. It would certainly have changed his.

But then Redcliffe arrived in the broker's office, explained that it was all a mistake. When the broker tried to tell him that every man was entitled to invest money, and even that Jasper's proposal had merit, Redcliffe had laughed.

"My idiot nephew is a clever mimic. Whatever utterance he offered to convince you that he has a brain, I can assure you that it was merely a facsimile of a conversation he'd heard elsewhere. And more to the point, I am guardian of his trust. Any and all financial dealings must go through me."

Shortly thereafter, the broker had lost his position at the

exchange, then his home when no one would hire him, not even as a clerk in a haberdashery.

The guardianship was supposed to have ended when Jasper turned one and twenty. However, because of Redcliffe's financial ties to certain members of the court, his guardianship—on grounds of Jasper's mental incompetence—would remain until the next hearing when Jasper turned five and twenty.

That was three weeks away. And even though Jasper had never pretended to be dimwitted, Redcliffe's constant declarations to that fact had been what most of society bothered to believe.

"You are doing the best you are able. None of this is your fault," he said, adjusting the shawl around her shoulders. "I will think of something. In the meantime, is there not one of your society friends you can write to and propose a visit, even for a short while?"

She began to shake her head, but hesitated. "There is that busybody Lady Deardorff, who pops by once a month with her pair of ankle-biting dogs. But I was afraid she was trying to play matchmaker for that sniveling son of hers."

"Tempest would likely eat that lordling alive," he quipped, trying to ease her worries. But his aunt's expression remained fraught and for good reason.

"Normally, I would never consider allowing a man of no consequence like Mr. Raintree to court my daughter, but Redcliffe has closed all other doors, waiting like a rat in the dark."

"I will get you out of here and away from Redcliffe's reach."

"But who will keep you out of his?" She shook her head. "I hate to think of all that he's done to keep you from having your rightful place. My husband never would have agreed to him overseeing the St. James property if he'd known how despicable Redcliffe truly was."

Jasper shook his head. "It wasn't Uncle Jacob's fault. Redcliffe has always been good at hiding who he really is. That is the one thing I learned from him. But I will get the land back, somehow."

"And whatever happens to me"—she clutched his hand, searching his gaze—"you'll take care of my girls?"

"I promise."

She sank back into the curve of the chair and closed her eyes. "No more of that now. Tell me about your Miss Hartley."

"She's not my—"

"Is she beautiful?" she interrupted with a squeeze of her hand.

Letting out a breath, he sat down beside her, his gaze turning toward the fire crackling in the hearth. He supposed it wouldn't hurt to indulge his aunt just this once.

"Aye," he said. "Like a fey creature that isn't part of this world."

"Pale hair or dark?"

He pictured her as she'd been last night on the terrace, dressed in a gown of moonlight with stars glinting in her hair. "A glossy mane as rich and dark as mahogany."

"Blue eyes or brown?"

"A blue that glitters like jewels caught in a ray of sunlight—" Hearing himself, he stopped, the heat of the fire stinging his cheeks.

The curve of a soft smile brushed Aunt Clara's lips when she looked at him. "Thank you. For a moment, I could see her. See the way she looks through your eyes. The way she sees you like no one else has done before."

"There's nothing between us," he said, attempting a lighthearted laugh.

"I fear you'll have to make a choice," she persisted, her gaze searching his as she lifted a hand to his cheek. "Hold fast to her, my darling boy. We aren't granted too many chances in this life to find love."

"I think the soothsayer in you is peering through rose-colored glass," he said as he drew her hand down. "But here, on the physical plane, there is a wood box that needs to be filled."

And he had a matter to discuss with Tempest.

He stood, pressed a kiss to his aunt's cheek and went to the door. But before he could leave, she left him with a notion that would likely plague him until the end of his days.

"If Miss Hartley is anything like her mother," she said, "then I know she will hold on to you just as fiercely, and no one—not even Redcliffe—could separate you."

A chill slithered down his spine.

Jasper hadn't seen his uncle since the Leighton Ball when he'd become unexpectedly ill and was unable to partner Miss Handscombe. But Redcliffe's pursuit of a new heiress to wed would not end. Therefore, as always, Jasper kept watch over his activities with the assistance of a few loyal servants who knew the kind of monster the earl actually was.

If there was one thing he was grateful for, it was the fact that Althea wasn't an heiress. Because, if she were, there was likely nothing Redcliffe wouldn't do to have her. Thankfully, Countess Broadbent had prevented an introduction by delivering a subtle cut direct, but a cut nonetheless.

⚜

WHEN THEA OPENED her eyes that morning, the first thing she saw was a sliver of sunlight brushing the tip of the paper rose on her bedside table. She wasn't sure if she wanted to smile or sigh.

Before the ball had ended, she'd wanted to ask Truman what he knew about St. James. Since her brother had an annoying affinity for seeing through people and knowing all their secrets, she imagined he could tell her a good deal about Jasper.

But before she had the chance to pose the question, he began doling out the foreboding wisdom of an elder brother.

Apparently, Summerhayes had asked for permission to court her. When Truman informed her of that, she'd confessed to her uncertainty regarding the captain.

"I simply don't feel a spark."

"Gently bred women are left with few options," Truman had said, raising a hand in defense. "And before you rail at me for being able to pursue my own dreams as an architect, I will state that I know it is unfair. Nevertheless, you'll have to decide. Do you want to live with our parents? Or do you want to make a life of your own with someone you can respect? Someone you could like and, perhaps, could grow to love in time?"

In that moment, she'd felt as if stones were being placed on top of her chest, one after the other.

Her first option was to live in the house she'd grown up in, but her parents would be disappointed. Her second was to continue on with the rest of this Season, but at great cost and physical toll to Lady Broadbent. And third, to marry and have a home, but not with the man she wanted.

On top of all this was the ever-present reminder that her dreams didn't factor into any of her choices. Not to mention, the heap of secrets she was keeping.

Thinking about it this morning, she felt crushed beneath the unbearable weight of it all.

Finding it hard to breathe, Thea threw off the coverlet and sat with her legs dangling over the side as she dragged in a gulp of air, her hands gripping the edge of the mattress. What was she going to do? What was she going to tell Captain Summerhayes when he came to call? What if she never wrote again?

Her anxious gaze fell on the paper flower once more. It

made her think of cool night air, of longing and of impossible things that turned out not to be so impossible after all.

Gradually, her breathing slowed. She realized that she needed to step away from this. All this obsessive thinking wasn't getting her anywhere. So, she decided to focus on someone else.

Crossing the room, she splashed cold water on her face, then dressed for the day. Since her maid was still in the grips of a cold, she went upstairs to sit with her.

<hr>

"THE COOK MADE this tea with elderflowers and says it will do the trick," Thea said as she set a tray over the maid's lap.

With a scraggily plait of brown hair over her shoulder, Tally blinked with puffy eyes, her face pale and her nose red as she sniffed into a balled-up handkerchief. "Forgive me, miss. I hate to be such a bother."

"You're no bother at all. All that matters is that you are yourself again," Thea said, feeling those words to her very soul as she fluffed her pillows. "In the meantime, what can I do for you? Take down a letter? Read one of those gothic romances you are so fond of? Or . . . I could dash off to Gunter's for the parmesan ice you like, hmm?"

"You are ever so kind, miss. With my nose all stuffed, I cannot taste a single thing and Gunter's would be lost on me. And I've already written my letter."

"Then I shall post it for you." Seeing Tally's eyes dart to the table where there was a folded missive, she crossed the room.

"Oh, no, miss. That won't be—"

Before her maid could stop her, Thea picked up the letter and distractedly skimmed the address. Her brows arched with intrigue. "Mr. Lawson?"

Tally's cheeks flooded with color that had nothing to do with fever.

Ben Lawson lived in the dower house near Hartley Hall. He was neither servant nor tenant, but looked after the place and kept it in good standing. His background was a mystery, but Father frequently welcomed men who'd run into a bit of bad luck to live there until they were on their feet again. And Ben Lawson had been there so long that he was like a member of the family.

Tally looked down to the handkerchief in her hand. "He wrote to me, stating that he knew of my cold from your letter to Lord and Lady Hartley and sent his best wishes for my swift return to health."

"Did he, indeed?" Thea asked, grinning from ear to ear. "So . . . you and Mr. Lawson, hmm?"

Tally swallowed and shyly glanced up. "Nothing untoward has happened. He is a good man and he would never . . ."

"Oh, but you want him to, don't you?" she teased.

Her color deepened. "I am six and twenty and he is rather handsome . . . I mean . . . He is good and kind and . . ."

"Fear not, Tally. I will be happy to post your scandalous correspondence with a bachelor."

Her gaze flew up to Thea's. "I hope you know that, if he had a sister, I would write to her instead. I'm not . . ." She swallowed again. "Well, I'm rather shy . . . around men."

"You are a beautiful woman, Tally, who is also good and kind. It isn't any wonder why Mr. Lawson would be drawn to you."

"Oh, miss, you're going to make me cry." Even as she spoke, her red-rimmed eyes began to shimmer. And when Thea withdrew her own handkerchief from her sleeve and gave it to her, she tentatively took it and said, "But I haven't made any plans with him. For the future, I mean. Your family has been most kind to me, and I am ever loyal to each of you."

It took Thea a moment to understand what she was trying to say. Then it struck her. Her maid wasn't making any plans of her own because she was waiting for Thea to marry.

"Do you want to hear something I just realized, Miss Evans?" she asked as she brushed back a hank of hair from Tally's warm forehead. "There are times when a woman must do whatever she has to do in order to make her own heart happy."

As she left the attic and walked downstairs with the letter, she thought about her own epiphany as well as what Tally said regarding Mr. Lawson's sister. That was what a woman did in order to get to know a man better—she spoke to a member of his family.

By the time Thea reached the foyer, she had tingles. And suddenly she knew how she was going to learn more about St. James. And, perhaps, worm her way into his heart.

Yet, as far as she knew, his only family was the Earl of Redcliffe.

Well then, it seemed that she would need an introduction. And who better to do the honors than Lady Abernathy?

Chapter Nineteen

✑

"Poor Olympia," Lady Abernathy said that afternoon. "I do hope she feels better soon."

"I believe it's just a cold, my lady. She intends to rest in her rooms for the day."

"Splendid. There's nothing better than a good, lengthy lie-about. Besides, she doesn't always have a sense for these things."

"These . . . things?"

The dowager viscountess offered a dismissive wave, a pleased grin wrinkling her cheeks. "As soon as I received your card, I sent a runner. You see, I happen to know of a gentleman who very much wishes to make your acquaintance. Thus far, his attempts seem to have been thwarted." The rapping of the doorknocker pulled her excited gaze to the archway. "Oh, I believe he is here."

Thea was still wondering about what Lady Broadbent *didn't have a sense for* when a tall, distinguished gentleman briefly paused in the doorway, his gaze assessing as he crossed the threshold.

He had a wealth of dark hair, liberally threaded with silver. His features were finely sculpted with high cheekbones and darkly arched eyebrows. He was lean and fit, and carried himself with an air of confidence that doubtless made him appealing to women of any age.

Lady Abernathy was no exception. When he bowed in

greeting, she began to titter breathlessly. "Redcliffe, how good of you to pay a call on an old woman."

"You are still in the bloom of youth, Beatrice," he said with a practiced air.

Then he turned his full attention to Thea. She noticed that his brown eyes flashed in the way that men's sometimes did when they looked at her, as if they were seeing a fresh apple tart in a baker's window. But in an instant that look shuttered closed and he was all politeness, bowing over her hand as their hostess introduced them.

"I understand why my nephew has made such a cake of himself, Miss Hartley." He laid a hand over his heart. "It falls to me to make amends for his behavior. Rest assured, I will replace every gown that he has ruined."

"Thank you, my lord, but that isn't necessary. It was only an accident and I harbor no ill will toward your nephew. At all."

He smiled. "Your compassion does you credit. It isn't often that one finds such beauty both inside and out." He paused long enough for her to acknowledge an obligation to thank him for the compliment, which she did with a nod before he continued. "And I concede that the topic of replacing garments is rather bold, especially for the first of what I hope will be many encounters. So I will say this—if you ever have need of my services, consider me your humble servant."

"Thank you, my lord," she said again, an uncomfortable feeling settling in her stomach.

She remembered the way Kellum's nature demanded constant appreciation. He could rip apart everything about her—her writing, her laugh, her smile, the apparently annoying inflection in her voice, even accuse her of purposely dressing in clothes that made her look dowdy—and go on one of these endless tirades until she felt like a kicked puppy.

Afterward, he'd issue a mollifying smile and confess that she made him act that way because he wanted her so much. It was her fault. *She* made him insane.

Then, he'd offer a consolation, like "I enjoyed the first line of your character's soliloquy. It shows promise."

By that point, she would be so grateful to hear something nice that tears would clog her throat. Then he would wait, expectantly. And she knew that if she missed her cue to say *thank you*, his tirade would start all over again.

In a way, she had been relieved with the end of their courtship.

"Shall I ring for tea, Redcliffe?" their hostess asked.

"One hates to waste such a lovely day," he said. "Perhaps we might have our tea after a quick jaunt through the park?"

Lady Abernathy looked to her. "I'm sure Olympia can do without you for an afternoon."

At the seemingly orchestrated convenience of this entire meeting, that sense of unease niggled at the back of Thea's mind. But it was nothing, surely.

After all, hadn't she come here for the explicit purpose of learning more about St. James and helping him? There didn't seem to be any harm in spending an afternoon in the company of his uncle.

❦

JASPER ROLLED UP his shirtsleeves and stood a thick section of a branch on an old tree stump. Out of the corner of his eye, he saw Tempest cross from the kitchen garden and head toward the stone potting shed that stood behind him.

"I passed Willie Raintree on the lane this morning," Jasper said without preamble as he swung the axe down and split the waiting wood with a satisfying crack. "Is there something you wish to tell me?"

His fiery-haired cousin stopped, the tines of the spading fork in her grip stabbing into the earth as she raised her brows. "Only to ask why it's any concern of yours."

"He's no gentleman, Tempest. Men like him aren't after marriage and respectability."

"Then what are they after, cousin?" She batted her lashes coyly, her green eyes already flashing with temper.

Standing another thick section of branch on the stump, he drew in a breath and started again. It would do no good if they were both irritated from the outset.

"What I'm trying to say is that men like him have used flattery to get what they want since the dawn of time. I simply don't want you to fall for pretty words and shallow promises, only to find yourself in a situation where you expect him to behave like a gentleman."

"And I suppose you always act like a gentleman, hmm?"

At her flippant tone, he narrowed his eyes, his grip tightening on the handle of the axe. "Has Raintree tried to kiss you?"

"I would have slapped him if he didn't. I am one and twenty, after all. And, contrary to your apparent belief, this cottage hasn't become an abbey and while this dress may be years out of fashion, it isn't a nun's habit."

"I'll kill him," he growled and swung the axe down. *Crack.*

"Oh? And I suppose you've never kissed a gentleman's daughter? Miss Hartley, for example?"

Lifting one of the halves to the stump, he took care in arranging it, his face warm from his exertions. "We're not discussing my behavior or Miss Hartley. We are discussing you and your association with that ruffian. It needs to end."

"And I disagree," she said, hiking her stubborn chin. "He and I are the same, after all. We both have aristocratic blood, but neither of us have ties to society. And if we married, then—"

"No. Absolutely not," he fired back. "It is my duty to protect you and I'm telling you that Raintree is not an honorable man."

"*Protect* me? Or keep me from living any sort of life at all?"

The axe swung again. *Crack.* "You know the answer isn't that simple."

"Do I? Or are you being just like Redcliffe and trying to keep everyone under your thumb?" Seething, she stormed toward the shed, oblivious to the blow she'd just struck. Then she stopped, whirling to face him. "Sometimes, I think that you and Mother use him as an excuse to make certain that nothing ever changes."

Feeling the sharp slice of her words, he took a moment before responding. It was true that he'd sheltered his cousins as much as possible in an effort to maintain their innocence. But he never imagined his warning would be called into question.

Taking a breath, he turned and held her angry gaze. "As you said, you are one and twenty. I realize how difficult it must be to live apart from society. For now, I can see no other way to—"

He didn't finish. The sound of a rider approaching, hard and fast, had both of them turning to look down the winding lane.

Unexpected company had a way of sending a shiver of foreboding down his spine.

Axe on his shoulder, he walked toward the drive. Shielding his eyes from the sun, he saw Barrett pulling hard on the reins of his horse. That shiver of foreboding abruptly settled in his gut like a rock.

Swinging his leg over, Barrett dismounted in haste, a cloud of dust beneath his boots when he hit the ground and strode directly to Jasper. "A missive came from the man you hired to watch Redcliffe's house. He arrived some time ago with a debutante and her chaperone."

"Bloody hell," Jasper muttered and handed the axe to Tempest. "We'll finish this discussion later, hmm?"

All the fury drained from her face and she swallowed. "You'll be careful?"

He nodded and walked away with Barrett, hating that he was such a far distance from Redcliffe's estate. He needed to leave immediately to have even a remote chance of saving the debutante from ruination. "And Pitt?"

"He's just behind me with your carriage," Barrett said as the jangle of rigging reached them. Then he gripped Jasper's arm, his expression unreadable. "Then a letter arrived from the man you have watching Miss Hartley."

Jasper stopped cold. His heart stopped, too. And in that moment he knew . . . he just knew . . .

"Miss Hartley is the debutante with Redcliffe."

Chapter Twenty

❧

𝒯HE MOMENT THEA saw the immense stone mansion on the grounds of—what Redcliffe liked to call—his pleasure gardens, she wondered why Jasper had become a highwayman if his uncle was this wealthy.

All this time, she'd thought he'd been forced by circumstance to play the fool for the *ton* in order to conceal his nocturnal raids against despicable men. Especially since she'd learned that St. James had an aunt and cousins on his father's side who depended upon him. Therefore, wouldn't Redcliffe understand those responsibilities and make allowances?

It was all a great puzzle.

"Can you imagine, Miss Hartley," Lady Abernathy said, her eyes wide and bright with wonder as they approached the house, "the woman who might become mistress to such an awe-inspiring demesne?"

Thea gaped at the ostentation of peacocks sashaying over a grassy knoll. "Nay, my lady. For this is almost too grand, even for one's imagination."

Not even Nell Hunnicutt could compete with this sort of wealth.

"I shall take that as a compliment, Miss Hartley," Redcliffe chuckled. "One day, I hope to have an heir worthy of inheriting all that I have amassed."

Thea would have thought the statement a rather abrupt change of topic. Although, since she'd been wondering for nearly an hour how to insert St. James into the conversation, she didn't look a gift horse in the mouth.

"Your nephew would inherit. Would he not?"

Redcliffe visibly stiffened, his jaw tight as if she'd insulted him.

"Regrettably, you are correct. The Fates have been unkind to me," he said without a trace of irony as his gaze traveled over his expansive grounds, including stables that were practically larger than the entire village of Addlewick. "To take not one, but two wives, then leave me without issue. Then my beloved sister was also taken, saddling me with a simpleton to raise."

"He isn't a simpleton," she interrupted. However, knowing she couldn't reveal too much or else it could expose him, she softened her tone. "I've spoken with St. James on a few occasions and he has proven himself to be as intelligent as any man."

Far above any man, she wanted to say. But to *know one's audience* was something her father had always taught her. She probably should have remembered that before she'd interrupted.

"I did hire the best tutors for my nephew," Redcliffe offered magnanimously, as if any accomplishment of St. James's were his own doing. "I sent him to school. And when he was dismissed from one, I sent him to another. I have done all that I could for my sister's child. More than most. I also tried to make a man out of him and purchased a commission, but all for naught." He shrugged. "Even his father's younger brother saw that the boy was unfit to manage what was left of the estate and entrusted it to me. I, and I alone, look after his tenants and his land because he is utterly incapable of doing so."

She didn't understand how any of that could be true. "Surely, he should be in charge of his own estate. He has reached his majority."

"And when he did, the courts ruled him mentally incompetent, Miss Hartley." His resolute tone brooked no further argument.

Thea felt her brow knit. She knew Jasper. He wasn't a man who would lie to her about who he really was. He wasn't like Kellum who'd wear one face for the public while in private he . . .

Her thoughts stalled. Wasn't that precisely what Jasper was doing, showing the *ton* one face and her the other?

The truth of the matter was, Jasper hadn't trusted her enough to tell her his reasons for what he did. In that sense, she didn't know him. Not really. And hadn't she already traveled that road before?

How much more of herself was she willing to risk losing?

The carriage stopped at the mouth of a yawning doorway, flanked by three liveried footmen on either side, all standing at attention.

Before climbing out, Redcliffe turned to her, a frown bracketing his mouth. "You seem to take a great interest in my nephew."

"She merely has a soft and forgiving heart, my lord," Lady Abernathy interjected. "Surely those are accomplishments as much as beauty and grace."

"They are indeed," he conceded, then extended his palm to hand Thea down. "A man could ask for no more in a wife."

Distracted by her thoughts, she placed her hand in his before he'd finished that sentence. Too late, she saw the hungry gleam in his eyes. It churned uneasily in her stomach.

The sensation only intensified when, upon crossing the threshold to the vaulted marble foyer, the housekeeper made it known that tea was waiting on the terrace. Clearly, this entire supposedly impromptu outing had been arranged.

So why the conspiracy? The secrecy? If he wanted to

change the agreement from a tour of Hyde Park to his own pleasure gardens, why not simply invite them?

Honestly, she was exhausted by lies.

Furthermore, as someone who'd been reared on plays her entire life, she usually found that it was the villain who consorted and conspired. And she wondered if she was the oblivious character being led into a trap.

"*Suspicion always haunts the guilty mind*," the chorus quoted.

Uneasy, she lingered at the railing and gazed out at a maze with a serpentine path between the hedgerows on the far side of the back garden. Seeing it from above, she thought that the pattern was simple. Even she could navigate it to the domed Grecian folly in the center.

"It's deceptively simple," Redcliffe said as if reading her mind as he sidled up to her, his hand resting so close to hers on the railing that she could feel the heat of it through her glove.

Retreating a half step, she pursed her lips and studied the maze once more. "It is hardly a challenge. All one must do is memorize the turns from up here."

His arm extended in a sweeping gesture. "You are welcome to try. I will remain with Lady Abernathy. Then, if you have not returned in, say, half an hour, I will come to your rescue."

"Gallantly said, Redcliffe," Lady Abernathy offered from the ease of an upholstered chair, her knobby fingers pinched around the handle of a teacup. And when Thea looked at her for permission, she jerked her chin in a nod. "Off with you, Miss Hartley. Redcliffe and I have much to discuss."

As she curtsied and took her leave, she silently hoped that they weren't fools enough to think they had anything to discuss regarding her.

Striding away, she couldn't wait to distance herself from the pair. Lady Abernathy seemed to forget that her opinion had no bearing on Thea's future. And as far as she was concerned, she'd rather lose herself in the maze until nightfall than spend one more minute in the company of Redcliffe.

As she walked toward the pebbled path between the tall boxwood spires, she felt a taut, gnawing sensation on the nape of her neck as if she were being watched.

She shrugged it off and continued her trek, keeping track of every turn she'd memorized.

It wouldn't take long before she reached the middle. Then, with any luck, Lady Abernathy would be ready to depart. The sooner this entire outing ended, the better.

"What a waste of an afternoon," she muttered to herself after a few minutes. "I learned nothing of what I intended, and am only left to feel more hopeless than—"

She stopped, surrounded by three boxwood walls. A dead end. Drat!

Redcliffe was likely looking down and chuckling to himself.

She cast a surreptitious glance over her shoulder. "Was that left, right, right? Or right, left, left?"

Unfortunately in retracing her steps, she soon discovered that there was an identical dead end in another part of the maze.

Unless . . . of course, she'd circled back to the first one.

She sighed. Lady Broadbent was right. She truly did have the directionality of dandelion fluff. Even so, at least a downy seed would have the ability to fly over the top of these hedges.

Perhaps, she should start again. Unfortunately, finding the two spires wasn't as simple as it seemed. And when she looked down, she definitely saw footprints in the gravel that looked suspiciously similar to her own.

The sun must have been caught behind a cloud because she shivered for no apparent reason.

Then she heard a footfall on the gravel.

"Oh, Miss Hartley?" Redcliffe called. "I've come to rescue you."

She swallowed and for some reason, she didn't want to respond.

After a minute, he chuckled. "I do enjoy a game of cat and mouse."

Her throat tightened, the pulse beating in a harried rhythm beneath her skin. She had played blindman's bluff with officers at a garden party. Hide-and-seek in Addlewick with Percival, Peter and Carlton Culpepper. But never before had she felt the utter certainty that what she was playing was definitely not a game.

All at once, Thea didn't want to be in the maze. And most assuredly, she didn't want Redcliffe to find her.

Her steps quickened on the path.

"Ah, there you are," he said, his voice an indeterminate distance away. And then his steps were faster, too.

She hated this cornered feeling. There were debutantes who'd shared stories about the men who took liberties. Men who'd held them too tightly. And men who'd done much worse.

But this was the Earl of Redcliffe. Surely, she needn't worry about impropriety with Lady Abernathy watching on. Then again, the dowager viscountess might simply turn her head, believing herself to be a matchmaker.

Biting down on her panic, Thea dashed around the curve of a long, winding path and stopped short at another wall in front of her.

"I believe you've reached the serpent's tail. That's what I like to call this path," he said, the crunch of his steps slowing.

They slowed, she realized, because there was no exit for her from this vantage. If she ran back the way she came, she'd only meet up with him sooner.

Her gaze darted around at all the possibilities . . . just before she heard the crackle of branches behind her and a hand clamped over her mouth.

Chapter Twenty-One

꙰

*T*HEA SCRATCHED AND clawed at the hand covering her mouth, thrashing to be free of the brawny arm around her waist.

But her assailant was immovable, unfazed by her attempts. He simply picked her up and stole through some unseen part in the hedgerow, disappearing into the shadows.

Icy dread filled her, her pulse rushing in her ears.

Still, she kicked and pounded her fists on every part she could reach. And when that did nothing, she drew in a breath through her nostrils and began to scream, hoping that the sound would carry beyond the muzzle of his palm.

"Shhh . . ." a voice whispered in her ear. "Althea, it's Jasper. I won't hurt you."

Even before he spoke the last sentence, relief flooded her, easing the constriction around her lungs.

She wanted to turn in his embrace and wrap herself around him. But he altered his grip, tucking her under one arm like a valise. Then he began to move too swiftly for her to do more than hold on for dear life.

She squinted against the rapid shifting of light to shadow, light to shadow, as they slipped out of the maze and into a break of pine trees that bordered the property. Even then, St. James did not slow.

He picked up the pace, his hard breaths punctuated by every footfall as he raced toward a destination that was concealed in the darkness below the evergreen canopy.

Then suddenly, they were inside a carriage, the horses spurring into motion before the door was even closed.

Jasper's arms were still around her, but this time he was pulling her onto his lap, his hand cradling the back of her head. The gust of his ragged breath drifted across the shell of her ear. "You're safe. I found you in time. You're safe. You're safe. I'll never let him near you again."

The words tunneled through her, quieting the last traces of panic. A thousand questions whirled around her mind but the only thing that mattered—truly mattered—was that she hadn't been wrong about him.

Her heart told her the truth all along. She was safe with Jasper. She could trust him.

Burying her face in his neck, she breathed in his scent the way people do over the vapor that rises from a copper pot of steamed pudding or mulled wine on a cold day. If he was pudding, she would devour him. If he was wine, she would get drunk off him. He was sustenance to her. Necessary in a way that she'd never known.

She wrapped her arms around him. "Don't ever let me go."

"I cannot. I've tried, but I—" Jasper shook his head and their lips brushed.

He didn't finish speaking. A raw sound of desperation left him as he claimed her mouth.

The kiss was hard and hungry. Nothing else would do.

Slanting her mouth beneath his, she opened for him, welcoming the invasion of his tongue. He tasted of spice and need and when he growled deep in his throat, she wanted to taste that, too.

His grip tightened, pulling her flush and flattening her breasts against the harried pounding of his heart. The heat of his long-fingered hands along her back was soothing yet urgent. She sensed that he needed the contact as much as she did. So she shifted on his lap, lifting her skirts out of the way to straddle him. Then her hands were in his hair, the locks thick and damp with perspiration as the kiss ignited a coiling heat inside her.

Thea didn't understand this strange new need burning inside her, consuming her. All she could think of when his tongue withdrew was *more*, and she followed his retreat, stealing inside his mouth, tasting his heat and spice and feeling a bit drunk.

She'd been shy with Kellum's advances, ever aware of the line of propriety and impropriety. But with Jasper . . . only with Jasper, she wondered why the line ever existed. It seemed unfair to keep two people apart when this felt so vital. It was like asking someone to breathe for only half the day. *No, you cannot have more air. You've reached your allotment and now you must suffocate.*

But Jasper was air. He was food. Water. Shelter. Everything she needed.

"Hold me tighter," she whispered against his lips, unable to move closer because her knees were pressed against the back of the bench.

He slid to the edge, tucking her hips down onto his. The new position pulled a needy whimper from her throat, a growl from his. At the sound, heat pooled low and liquid in her body and she hitched reflexively against him.

A shared shudder went through them. His breath caught, his hips arching, pressing her against a thick shape, hard and hot.

A vague notion of what that part of him was began to filter into her thoughts, a memory of the sock puppet play about Lord Turgid and Lady Content. And an unexpected giggle burst from her lips.

"The puppets . . . never warned me . . . about this," she said between kisses, squirming to find the perfect spot to alleviate the thrumming ache between her thighs.

When she found it, she pressed down again, the pleasure so excruciating, she had to close her eyes. Her neck arched on a foreign mewling sound as his mouth coasted down her throat, licking the salt from her skin, sampling the flutter of her pulse.

He nuzzled a spot just behind her ear sending a torrent of delicious quivers to her midriff. His teeth raked gently against the shell of her ear, drawing a gasp from her. But when his tongue drew the tender lobe into his mouth and he suckled gently, she was fairly certain she purred.

"You taste so good. I want my mouth on every single inch of you," he rasped, his hands roaming down her back, to her hips, gripping, then gliding up her sides, his thumbs pausing just beneath the swell of her breasts. Then his lips parted, a gust of warm breath stealing into her mouth as a furrow formed between his brows. "Did you say . . . *puppets*?"

She nodded, trailing kisses across the high crests of his cheekbones, the bridge of his nose . . . "My mother performed a puppet theatre to inform her daughters about relations between men and women. The shy, drooping Lord Flaccid would turn into the monstrous Lord Turgid who was never satisfied until he had Lady Content quivering. I had nightmares for months. I was certain he was torturing Lady Content. But I think I might understand a bit better."

She pressed down onto him and watched his eyes glaze over, his pupils full-blown, black and hungry.

Lord Turgid was definitely something she never imagined would spark her curiosity. She'd thought he was the villain of the play. And yet, now that she was so close to *his* Lord Turgid, she wanted to know more—the temperature, the texture, the precise dimensions.

A new kind of tingle cascaded down her spine, gathering low and tightening. And she wondered what would happen if she could just . . . press . . . a little . . . closer . . .

Jasper's breath stuttered to a halt. His hands descended to her hips to hold her still.

That didn't stop the steady rocking of the carriage beneath them that kept their bodies undulating, thrumming. She licked her lips, a plea for more of this—whatever this was—on the tip of her tongue.

But then he suddenly set her apart from him. Depositing her unceremoniously on the bench beside him.

⁂

JASPER LOWERED HIS face into his hands, his breathing erratic, his heart hammering, his cock—

No. Better not think about his cock. Not when she was still far too close, the scent of her clinging to him. His body had been branded by her heat, her curves . . . every part of her that he needed far away from him.

He needed a bigger carriage, large enough that he would have to travel a good distance to reach her. A mile, perhaps. Instead, he knew all too well that all he'd have to do was reach out and . . .

He shook his head and swallowed thickly. "I didn't save you from that twisted trap to have you for myself."

She was quiet for a long moment and he glanced over. Her eyes were on him, her lips plump and red from his kiss, her hair in a tumble of disheveled dark curls, and he wanted nothing more than to finish what they'd started.

Instead, he reached over and pulled the hem of her dress down to cover the few inches of stocking-clad shapely calves he could see.

"Do you think your uncle had been attempting to catch me alone? That he might have tried to"—she shuddered—"kiss me?"

There was enough trepidation and tension knitting her brow to let him know that she wasn't that naive. But those troubled eyes also told him that she hoped she was wrong.

Jasper refused to conceal the harsh truth with honey. It was better that she understood. "Much worse."

Her head moved in a small nod as she smoothed her hands down her skirts. "I suspected his intentions might have been worse, but I convinced myself that I was being foolish. That, with Lady Abernathy there, nothing would happen. Then I heard his voice in the maze and I knew."

"Always trust yourself." He pulled her against his side, his hand drifting along her arm to warm her as she drew her knees up under her and curled into him. He wished he could tuck her inside his pocket and keep her there. "You were right to be wary. Lady Abernathy wasn't even there to watch over you."

"She wasn't?"

"No. She is in a carriage on her way home."

Her head lifted from his shoulder, her eyes wide. "Did you send her home or did he?"

"I did. She had taken ill. And now I'm taking you home as well."

She shook her head. "If she is so ill, then I should go to her and not back to the townhouse. I wasn't even aware that she was feeling unwell."

"I'm certain her ladyship was perfectly hale until Redcliffe slipped a purgative into her tea."

"Surely not."

"This wouldn't be the first time." Jasper gritted his teeth, hatred for that vile blackguard sluicing through his veins. "In fact, that is how I knew the most effective method to inconvenience him at the Leighton Ball. I merely gave him a taste of his own medicine."

"Is that the reason he didn't dance with Miss Handscombe?"

"Aye. I know what kind of monster he is, so I do my best to him from as many debutantes as I can. But I failed this time."

Her hand covered the tortured beating of his heart. "No, you didn't. I'm here. I'm safe. Though, I cannot say the same for poor Lady Abernathy. Even so, it isn't your fault."

"You don't understand," he said. "I made a mistake at the Leighton Ball, dancing with you. It wasn't until I read the scandal sheets that I realized my actions might lead him to you. So, I made sure to stay away. But, clearly, it was too late."

"The only thing you're right about is that I don't understand," she said. "Why should you dancing with me matter to him?"

"Because I know the truth about him. I know that he sent his first wife to an asylum because he'd wanted to marry another. I know that it wasn't a tumble down the stairs that had left my mother bloodied and broken. I know about the other debutantes who've toured that maze and what happened while I was away at school, foolishly believing his only crimes were malicious cruelty and abhorrence for weakness."

"Good heavens!" she gasped, appalled.

"I think you mean hell. That is what spawned him."

"Why is such a man not in gaol?"

Why, indeed. "Because he has honed his practice of deception like an artist wields a brush. Believe me, I've tried. For years. But because of the lisp I had when I was a child and the awkwardness that accompanied my youth, it was an easy matter for him to label me as a simpleton. The bruises I bore from his attacks were explained as my clumsiness. At least, until I grew taller, then he never dared raise his fists to me again. And after he'd woven his lies to tutors and schoolmasters, ensuring that they had his permission to use a firm hand in my education, no one believed me."

"You were just a child! Was there no one to protect you?"

After seeing what he'd done to his mother, Jasper had had no doubt that he would have hurt anyone who dared to stand up for him. In fact, he'd often wondered if his uncle Jacob's financial troubles had occurred because he'd guessed the truth and Redcliffe had used his many connections to ruin him. Because of that, Jasper had known, even as a young boy, that it was better to stay silent.

When he didn't answer, Althea apparently saw the truth for herself. Her delicate hand balled into a fist over his heart, her voice shaking with vehemence. "I hate that you suffered, especially at the hands of your own uncle. I want to skin him alive for his crimes against you."

Angry tears shone in her eyes. Something about the sight of this fierce little goddess wanting to commit heinous acts for his sake tugged at his heart and at the corners of his mouth.

He rubbed the pad of his thumb along her lower lashes, wiping away the wetness. "I don't think you'd have the stomach for that particular task."

"And I don't think you know me very well. Give me a knife and I'll prove it."

She was a marvel to him, some rare, precious thing sent down from the heavens that he couldn't seem to stay away from, no matter how hard he tried. Though, to be honest, he hadn't tried all that hard. He was drawn to her like a plant to the sun.

"No need, my little warrior. I believe you." He pressed his lips to hers.

Her bloodthirsty nature momentarily placated, she settled against the crook of his shoulder once more. "I still don't understand the reason for your disguise, or why you haven't just proven everyone wrong. You are a grown man, intelligent, strong and capable. Anyone who knows you can see it."

"The situation is more difficult than that," he said. "He has too much power and wealth not to use it. When I was young and accused him of murdering my mother, he beat me with his walking stick, then claimed that I'd fallen from a tree. When I tried to tell the surgeon the truth, the man gave an alarmed glance over his shoulder to my uncle in the doorway. Then he straightened, his features a pitying mask I'd seen all too often. His diagnosis was *delusional*. 'A likely candidate for the asylum, should his head not heal properly,' he'd said. And my uncle paid him handsomely."

At the memory, Jasper let his head fall back against the squabs and expelled a long breath. "I knew then what I had to do. If I wanted a chance at any life at all, I would have to convince my uncle that I didn't remember. That the purported fall from the tree left me without my wits. Though, oddly enough, I never pretended to be dimwitted. I only started lisping again, and listened more than I spoke. Redcliffe's tales of my ineptitude had done the rest. At least, until one of my schoolmasters saw the truth in my marks and spoke to my uncle. I was summarily moved to a new school where money had greater influence."

"I'm surprised Redcliffe didn't try to kill you." She huffed.

"Oh, he did. When I was old enough, he purchased a commission for me, likely hoping that I would be killed in action," he said wryly. "But even he is intelligent enough to know that another death, of his heir no less, would draw suspicion. Besides, there is a twisted part of him that enjoys having the sympathy he gains from having a half-wit nephew."

"But when you reached your majority, surely someone from the courts . . ." Her words trailed off when he turned his head to look at her. "It's the money, isn't it? His fortune purchases favors."

Seeing her distress, he hated to confirm her suspicion, but he nodded. "Redcliffe buys debt to keep people under his control. Then he presents that control in such a way that those people are grateful to him for coming to their aid. They are seldom aware of how he manipulates them with subtle reminders of the way he'd kept them from debtors' prison, telling them over and over again that they cannot manage their lives without his assistance. And, before long, they believe him."

"He sounds like someone else I know," she said on a heavy breath. "Men in a position of authority and skill for persuasion know precisely how to lure you in with favors and pretty compliments. They study the way you respond to certain comments, and their praise becomes more specific. You feel seen, understood as no one has ever done before. So you give him your manuscript. Then it starts, those well-intentioned words of advice. He offers you ways to improve. It would be such a small thing to change, you tell yourself, and in doing so you've regained his esteem. This begins a habitual cycle—his praise, his disappointment, your desire to improve, to please—and before you know it, you're not really thinking for yourself. You've ignored the warning voice in the back of your mind for so long that you no longer trust it."

Jasper growled, pulling her closer. "I want to murder that playwright."

"He would love the attention of a grisly demise too much. The only way to hurt a narcissist is to take away the one thing he loves most."

"Money and prestige," he said, thinking of his uncle.

"No," she said. "You said it yourself—a narcissistic man like your uncle loves control. He loves the infallible image he has created of himself, and his ability to manipulate others gives him that sense of power."

Jasper blinked. *Damn.* At her words, something clicked into place. It was like discovering the key to a map and, all at once, he realized he'd been looking at it upside down.

But now, the world was laid out before him, waiting for his next step.

Redcliffe wasn't driven by money and prestige, even

though he certainly liked to lord it over people often enough. However, if all that wealth were stripped away, he would doubtless be the same monster.

"The problem is," she continued, "men like that have had so many people completely in their thrall for so long that it would be impossible to change the collective opinion."

"Not impossible," he said, his thoughts turning as a new strategy took shape. "Difficult, but not impossible."

And for the first time in a very long time, Jasper felt a spark of hope.

Chapter Twenty-Two

THE CARRIAGE STOPPED in front of Lady Abernathy's terrace house. A light drizzle was falling as Thea peered past the window shade.

She thought about what she'd endured with Kellum and how he'd made her feel worthless and lose sight of who she was. Even though her experiences hadn't been anywhere near the horrors that Jasper had suffered, she could see the similarities in the ways abusive men liked to isolate their victims. To make them feel separate and alone.

It was fortunate that things had ended when they did. She could see that now.

But what about a child who was forced to live beneath the roof of a monster, day in and day out? A child who had known that there was no one who could protect him?

The trials he must have endured broke her heart and made her furious. She wished she could travel back in time and protect him from that horrible man.

Turning back to Jasper, she slipped her hand into his. "What will Redcliffe do, now that he knows that both Lady Abernathy and I have gone? Will he come after you for intervening?"

"He wouldn't have seen me."

"Not see . . . you?" she asked with a dubious arch of her brow.

The corner of his mouth twitched. "I have a secret path in and out of the maze. Only the groundskeeper knows about it and he keeps the hedge gate concealed. He is one of the few servants loyal to me, who've been there long enough to have witnessed the truth. And by the time Redcliffe returned to the house after not locating you in the maze, a groomsman would have informed him that Lady Abernathy had become unexpectedly ill and asked for a carriage to take her and Miss Hartley home. Then, to keep Redcliffe's temper in check, the groomsman and a parlor maid would also relay her ladyship's regret at being unable to linger long enough to thank him for his generous hospitality."

Seeing a muscle tick along Jasper's jaw, she knew he must have hated always keeping the ego of man like Redcliffe pampered and petted and well fed. But after he'd told her about the circumstances of his aunt and cousins, she also knew that he did what he had to do for those he cared about.

"And this will placate him?" she asked. "What I mean is, he'll leave Lady Abernathy to recover on her own without paying a call?"

He brought her hand to his lips and pressed a kiss against her knuckles. "I'll ensure that you are safe by keeping watch close by. However, I don't think he'll come here at all. He believes he's infallible and that no one is as clever as he is. So, he will accept the fiction and start to plot again."

"I don't like the sound of that."

"Redcliffe sees any evasion as a game of sorts."

"Cat and mouse," she said on a shiver. "He said that in the maze."

"I heard him." Jasper pulled her close one more time, his hand skimming down her back in soothing passes. "You should know that he may attempt to court you."

"*Court* me?"

"He is looking for a new wife. An heir. While he typically marries to increase his wealth, he may decide that your hand would be the greater triumph, especially after the Leighton Ball."

"Because you danced with me?"

His shoulders lifted. "In part, but also because—"

"Lady Broadbent gave him the cut direct, didn't she?" Thea interjected in shock, only now realizing that the earl had been the man the countess had turned her back on. Seeing Jasper nod only confirmed it. "I wish I could tell her about you. No, don't think I would ever betray your trust. But I do wish that she wasn't quite so determined to guard me against you."

"I wonder if she might have the right of it after all." When she tensed, he pressed his lips to her temple. "But it's too late for that now."

Drawing back, she searched his gaze, unsure of what he actually meant. Was she just one more person he decided to protect out of obligation? Or did she mean more to him?

Since past experience hadn't been overly kind to her, she decided for him. "You are correct, St. James. It is too late because I'm never going to let you go."

Stalling any argument he might utter, Thea pressed her lips to his one more time, then dashed out of the carriage and up to Lady Abernathy's door.

❧

EARLY THAT EVENING, Thea sat with Lady Broadbent in her bedchamber. The countess was feeling better and had moved from her bed to the chaise longue by the fire, her gaze staring unreadably at the flames as Thea recounted the events of the afternoon.

She didn't tell the truth about the maze and what part Jasper had played. Instead, she kept to the fiction that the servant had relayed to Redcliffe—that Lady Abernathy had taken ill and they'd left, borrowing a carriage from the stables.

"And where was Redcliffe?"

"I believe he was in his gardens. There was no time to wait upon his return." *Not a single second to spare*, Thea thought.

Lady Broadbent's gaze drifted to Thea's hem and slippers, but she'd changed since returning from Lady Abernathy's.

"And Beatrice?"

"Much better now. In fact, she said she would rather forget the entire afternoon."

That statement was unfortunately true. Thea had attempted to tell Lady Abernathy that Redcliffe had orchestrated events for some ungentlemanly purpose, but the dowager viscountess only glared at her.

"Poppycock. The very idea is a slander to a fine man's character. You will speak to no one of this." Color had blotched her papery cheeks. "For if there is even a whisper, you would be ruined and I doubt the earl would marry you in order to save your reputation."

"I would never marry that—"

"We will forget this entire afternoon. Do you understand, Miss Hartley?"

Until that moment, she hadn't been convinced that Jasper was right about being unable to expose Redcliffe. But the earl was highly respected among his peers. He wielded his influence as easily as Kellum wielded a pen to entertain and enthrall.

Lady Broadbent coughed into her handkerchief and Thea stood to bring her a glass of water. When she held it out, the countess put her own hand around Thea's, staying her. A pair of dove gray brows knitted. "And you are unharmed?"

Thea swallowed. Apparently, her chaperone was able to read between the lines of the fiction she'd created. "I am unharmed."

"And you will never be in his company again."

It wasn't a question, but she nodded.

After the countess drank her fill, Thea returned the glass to the table. Without turning around, she asked, "Why did you give Redcliffe the cut direct at the Leighton Ball?"

A moment passed before the countess expelled a breath, the sound merging with the crackle of the fire. But when she finally spoke, it wasn't in answer to her question.

"One of my dearest friends, whom I had known since girlhood, married during one of the Seasons she and I shared together. She had a daughter and named her after me. Olympia and my daughter, Geraldine, grew up together. I was blessed to watch both of them blossom into bright and beautiful women."

Thea listened as she returned to her chair, watching the flicker of firelight over the countess's features.

"When my dear friend passed away, Olympia came to live with me for a time," she continued. "That was when I learned she had a special gift for writing poetry. Beautiful passages. Evocative images you could become lost in." A soft smile rested on her lips, but it vanished in the next moment. "Then she was courted by a man who pretended to admire her gift, her passion. Yet, as soon as they married, he made her feel less for wanting to *waste her time on such frivolity.*

"This man began demanding more and more of her attention. He even went so far as to keep her from reading in the parlor, unless it was to entertain him. He began inspecting all her correspondence, but made a show of doing so in order to admire her penmanship and her cleverness with words. Then he said that it was only necessary for her to write to his family. That her friends surely didn't want her to prattle on and on, wasting paper and ink. A wife, after all, had duties to her husband. She should obey him in all things."

A chill prickled over Thea's skin and she chafed her hands against her arms to warm them.

"When she was enceinte, she asked to have a ledger to write down her thoughts to give her child, his future heir. But he refused, telling her that sons do not grow into men who want to read the silly thoughts of their mothers. When she lost the child, her husband claimed she'd gone mad from grief. That she was hurting herself." Lady Broadbent swallowed, incipient tears shining in her eyes. "She died in an asylum. No one will ever know how brilliant she was, and it breaks my heart every single day."

Thea recalled Jasper's words.

I know that he sent his first wife to an asylum because he'd wanted to marry another.

"Was she Lady Redcliffe?"

The countess's mouth flattened into a grim line as she dashed away her tears. "She was. And I hate that I did not see the man he was until it was too late. I couldn't save her. But I will be damned if I'll let him near you."

Thea didn't know what shocked her more—the unbridled contempt in every syllable or the fact that the countess cursed in front of her. Either way, she had even more respect for her than before.

"Go to the top drawer of my bureau," Lady Broadbent said, gesturing with a flick of her handkerchief, and Thea stood, crossing the room. "Inside you'll find an old ledger wrapped in cambric. Take it out. I would like you to have it."

She did as instructed, carefully unwrapping the tome before closing the drawer again. Curious, she opened the worn cloth cover.

Inside were rows of figures, payments to the draper, the milliner, the stationer and so on. But in between this household's list of accounts were lines written in a small, tidy script. And not just words . . . poetry.

"It's my belief that she found a discarded accounting ledger and secretly recorded her thoughts," the countess explained when Thea sank down onto the foot of the chaise longue.

"How did you come by this?" she asked.

The countess held out her hand for it, pressing her palm against the cover. "She begged her maid to send it to me after she lost the child."

"Then she must have known what the earl intended to do."

"Perhaps."

As she handed back the book, something occurred to Thea. "I haven't thanked you for never making me feel like I was engaging in a silly pastime with my plays, and for giving me the freedom to write whenever and wherever I needed to."

"I still don't agree that ball gowns should have pockets."

Thea smiled. "But you've indulged me in my dream of becoming a playwright, nonetheless. Aside from my parents, I cannot think of anyone else who would have done the same. So, I thank you"—her voice broke on emotion—"for your unflagging support. I adore you, Lady Broadbent."

"Do not make me weep," she ordered, her own voice cracking. "I can hardly breathe through my nose as it is."

"Then I shall leave you to rest." She stood and pressed a kiss to her cheek.

When she reached the door, the countess left her with one parting thought. "You have a gift that not all of us have. You have talent and a voice that deserves to be heard, no matter what some peewit little playwright might have told you."

Sometimes, Thea thought as she sat at her desk later that night, it only took one person to believe in you that made all the difference.

Chapter Twenty-Three

❧

$\mathcal{I}$T WAS A commonly held belief that the best way to fell a large structure was with a seismic shift in the foundation beneath it. Then it would all come crumbling down.

It was with this thought in mind that Jasper's new strategy took shape.

He was going to make society question Redcliffe's word and his version of the truth. He knew that, once the first seed was planted, people would begin to wonder about everything he proclaimed, even Jasper's mental competence. This would be the only way to increase his chances of having the court rule in his favor when they convened again on his twenty-fifth birthday.

He had eighteen days and it wasn't going to be easy.

Telling an unwanted truth, which made the person hearing it feel foolish or flawed for not noticing it themselves, never worked in a society obsessed with vanity. Offering them this same truth as scintillating gossip, however, always did.

He began with one of his uncle's most cherished fictions—his honorable lineage.

Jasper selected the men to deliver these truths with careful precision. After all, not all the men indebted to Redcliffe were loyal to him. Some had grown too worn and weary from having to do the earl's bidding when he asked for a favor. Some were tired of barely scraping by because the remunerations for their debts kept increasing, leaving them forever at the earl's mercy and teetering on the verge of begging him for a loan.

Redcliffe liked when someone was close to the edge, a desperate breath away from falling into the abyss. That way he would be deemed a hero by offering a pittance.

Baron Reginald Woodthorpe was one of those men. He had two daughters just out in society, then a year of heavy rain had flooded his crops and he was unable to pay the debts accrued from the London Season. That was when Redcliffe had offered to purchase his debt, with interest. Unfortunately, a hard winter had wiped out another crop.

Redcliffe had paid these debts for him, then quadrupled the interest.

Woodthorpe had been overheard at a tavern, drunkenly declaring that he was being squeezed like a turnip and couldn't see any end in sight. He was a desperate man. And when he awoke the following morning with his head pounding from drink, he likely wouldn't remember having a conversation with a stranger who'd sat at a table in the shadows, telling him of the infamous history of the second Earl of Redcliffe.

But the following evening, when Woodthorpe attended a small gathering on Redcliffe's estate, that vague recollection was sure to float to the surface. And that was where the plan would begin.

⚊⟜

THAT NIGHT, JASPER concealed himself in the darkness, making sure that no one saw him in the garden where the torchlight didn't reach.

Redcliffe strutted around on his terrace, a veritable peacock showing off his plumage. He enjoyed putting on an ostentatious display for his guests.

As the gentlemen milled around, enjoying their port

and cigars, the earl gestured broadly to his grand house. "I am fortunate to come from such a long line of honorable men. The first Redcliffe had been bequeathed an earldom after service to King Charles II for heroism in battle. The second earl also proved his loyalty to crown and country. And the—"

"Didn't the second earl bankrupt the estate from gambling debts?"

Redcliffe lowered his cigar and scrutinized the man who'd dared interrupt. But he was good about controlling his temper in public, so he chuckled. "Who doesn't have a skeleton in the cupboard, eh, Woodthorpe? Correct me if I'm wrong, but don't you have a poor country relation in Fleet as we speak?" Redcliffe clapped him on the shoulder. "Fear not, old chap, even I have an idiot nephew."

Jasper had anticipated this. His uncle had a practiced way of sounding as though he were humbling himself while being condescending at the same time. The supreme self-assuredness in his own magnificence made other men tend to agree, nodding or laughing along with him without question.

At least, until someone did question.

Which happened at White's later that week as the second part of the strategy began to unfold.

Jasper was fortunate to have had a handful of professors who'd looked at his work before they'd cast judgment over his intellect or listened to his uncle. Of course, he'd had plenty of the other sort who were more apt to believe that good marks from the likes of him had meant he cheated. In the former category, however, he had attained respect and made a few friends.

One such friend did him a favor quite recently.

While dining with the Duke of Sherborne one evening, a former professor happened to mention Jasper in passing.

So when someone at the club repeated the comment regarding the second earl, Redcliffe again chose evasion by way of the "idiot nephew."

Hearing this, Sherborne folded his newspaper. "That's peculiar. I'd heard that St. James actually made good marks in school."

"Wherever did you hear such nonsense, Sherborne?" Redcliffe laughed and received an arched eyebrow.

No one ever laughed at the venerable Sherborne. "From one of his professors. And before you find fault either with that man's recollection or his honor, know that I hold him in great esteem and would take any insult personally."

If a pin had dropped in the room in that moment, it would have echoed like thunder.

Though, in such a group of men, there was always a devil's advocate, and always a fool. It was the latter who made a quip to break the tension and soon the incident was forgotten.

But not entirely.

Then, a few days later at Tattersall's, someone questioned a story that Redcliffe often told about how his father amassed his fortune. "Wasn't it because he'd sent his brother to war in order to marry the man's betrothed?"

Redcliffe had chortled. "Nothing more than a transfer of affections. Women are forever changing their minds."

That earned a laugh. Until another man mentioned that, when the first wife died in childbed, he'd taken his other brother's betrothed and made her his second wife.

Redcliffe waved that off, declaring that, clearly, women couldn't resist his ancestor. This earned another laugh. Upon hearing this, Jasper imagined that his uncle had nearly reached his limit of having his word questioned.

The earl proceeded to weave in a new thread of the story, of how beneficent his ancestor had been by marrying her after that brother had abandoned her. *The poor little heiress.*

Redcliffe was skilled at twisting facts. He could wind conversation into so many turns and loops that it resembled a coiled serpent with the head indiscernible from the tail. And while he may have been able to convince many of *his* truth, the seeds of doubt had been planted all the same.

Whispers had already begun. Just how noble and honorable was the great Earl of Redcliffe?

By the end of the week, Jasper started to dream of his own future for the first time in his life.

IT WASN'T UNTIL Redcliffe went away to his hunting cabin that Jasper felt it was safe enough to head to the tavern. He didn't like being a long distance away from Althea when he knew his uncle was in town.

As he stepped out of the carriage, he breathed in deeply, enjoying the fresh pine-scented air.

It reminded him of home. Even though he'd been just a boy the last time he'd lived on the St. James demesne, he remembered sitting on his father's shoulders as they walked the land. He'd felt like he was a hundred feet tall and able to touch the clouds with his fingertips.

Tucking the memory away, he turned around and held out his hands for Roly in the driver's perch. The boy had wanted to sit with the dog, believing it was unfair that he wasn't allowed to ride inside. But Jasper wasn't about to let Garmr shed all over his carriage if Althea was going to spend any time inside.

Not that he planned she would. But he wasn't *not* planning on it either.

Roly leapt down like a squirrel flying from one branch to another, arms and legs splayed. Jasper caught him and swung him around in circles as giggles erupted.

Once on his feet, Roly teetered drunkenly, grinning as Garmr licked him from chin to cowlick.

"Are you going to marry Miss Hartley?"

The question knocked the breath out of Jasper, taking him unawares. "What makes you ask that question?"

The boy shrugged. "You've been different, sort of happy like. Pitt says it's because you're in love."

Jasper shot a glare over his shoulder to his bald-pated driver, who started whistling and pretended to be incredibly busy brushing down the horses. "I could go back to being a surly ogre, I suppose."

"No. It's just . . . I think Thumper liked having her around. She's real nice. And pretty. And . . . if you married her we'd all be . . . sort of . . . a family."

"We already are a family," he said, ignoring the sudden jolt that shook him to the soles of his feet.

. . . if you married her . . .

"A family needs someone softer, don't it? Someone who smells nice and knows things. And we're all rough and tumble and hard around the edges, even Thumper . . ." Roly paused and thoughtfully stroked his dirty chin as if he were an old philosopher contemplating the wisdom of the ages. "But I ain't sure he's a man like us, since he lost his bollocks and his leg in that trap. Barrett says that's what marriage did to him."

Unfortunately for Barrett, at the same time that the boy said those words, both he and Nan emerged through the back door.

"Did he now?" Nan asked with one hand on her hip and a laundry basket on the other, her foot tapping like a death knell on the hard-packed earth.

Barrett shook his head. "Of course, I didn't, my sweet angel. My bride. The love of my life. Marriage to you has been a dream."

"While you're dreaming, just don't forget that I'm the

one who sleeps next to you and I can make sure you never wake up." She stormed off to hang the wet clothes.

Barrett blew out a breath. "Thanks for that, Roly."

"You're welcome," he said in singsong as he bounded after Garmr.

Jasper laughed. It took a moment to realize his friend was staring at him. "What?"

"You were laughing."

"*And?*"

Barrett shrugged as he walked back into the tavern. "And that isn't like you. It's just different."

"Bloody hell," he muttered and followed him. "Can a man laugh without everyone thinking the sky is falling?"

"I'm not saying it's terrible. I'm actually glad that you're happy for once in your life," he said, ladling up two bowls of porridge from the black pot hanging by the fire. Then he slid one across the trestle table to him. "And I think a certain Miss Hartley might have something to do with that."

Jasper feigned aloofness as he stirred his porridge, ignoring the fact that anytime someone mentioned her name a bolt of lightning zinged through him.

"I've begun a new strategy," he said, redirecting the conversation.

"To do what, exactly?"

The tip of his spoon dragged through the gray mush in a figure that strongly resembled the letter *A*. "To strip away Redcliffe's power and influence bit by bit."

Barrett slapped his hand down on the table, jostling the bowls, his mouth agape. When he recovered, he said, "Tell me everything."

So, he did. Jasper revealed all that had happened over the week, what he'd witnessed for himself and what he'd overheard from servants. There were similar episodes in store for his uncle in the coming weeks as well.

"I've been playing his game for far too long," he said at

the conclusion. "It needs to end. I'm not going to continue this way."

Barrett's mouth split into a grin and he slapped the table again. "You're going to give up the disguise and marry the girl, aren't you?"

"You're taking a gigantic leap from one thing to another."

"But you didn't deny it."

Heart lodged in his throat with the last bite of porridge, he said, "I'm not required to deny such a ludicrous idea."

Marry Althea? *Him?*

She deserved a husband who could be gentle with her on their wedding night, to treat her with the care she deserved. His own experience had taught him that he was, most assuredly, not the man for her.

His first encounter with a woman had been at the age of fifteen. It had been another one of Redcliffe's lessons in humiliation. He'd taken Jasper to a brothel and locked him in a room with the proprietress, an aging woman with heavily kohled eyes, few teeth and rouge on the nipples of her sagging breasts.

She'd cackled when she saw him. "My, but ain't you a big boy. Come 'ere and give us a tickle."

When he remained by the door, she'd come to him, naked, hips and breasts swaying. Then she'd touched him through his breeches, her skillful hands summoning a reaction against his will.

He'd apologized for it even as she'd fumbled with his front fall and cooed over the size of him. Though he'd tried to will himself not to respond, not to let his uncle win, when she'd turned and bent over in front of him, reaching through her legs to guide him in, his body had other ideas.

The entire encounter had ended with embarrassing swiftness, her cackling laugh ringing through the room.

"Big boy, indeed," she'd said, rapping twice on the door

to signal for it to be unlocked. "If you ever learn to use that monster, you'll likely split a woman in 'alf."

Sitting at the kitchen table, Jasper thought again of Althea, how soft, graceful and delicate she was . . . and how he was the exact opposite.

Of course, that hadn't stopped his imagination from conjuring all sorts of fantasies about her during these weeks. But that's all they could ever be—fantasies. Only a fool would ever dream that a woman like her could be with a man like him.

Which meant that he was a fool.

Until he'd met Althea, he'd never felt so drawn to another person. She had something that seemed to wrap around his soul like a rope that tethered him to her. No matter where she was, or how far apart, he felt that internal tug toward her, a constant sort of gravitational pull as if they were destined to orbit each other. And without that orbit, the world would fall into chaos.

"I don't see what's so ludicrous about it," Barrett said, breaking into his thoughts. "You're a gentleman and she's a gentleman's daughter. And she clearly likes you."

His heart started thumping erratically, and his lungs felt like he accidentally inhaled a hummingbird. And all from the idea that she liked him.

Pathetic.

Frowning, he shoved the porridge away. "There are stages to this plan. On my birthday, the court will meet and decide on my competence. With Redcliffe's word in question, I stand a greater chance of gaining control of my own estate holdings, minimal though they are. Then, if all goes to plan, I will invest to earn more money. Within a year's time, I might be able to build a house. Once I have a house, I can move Aunt Clara, Tempest and Iris out from under Redcliffe's thumb. After that, I will gradually begin revealing my true self to society. And, perhaps, within five years, I will be able to think of marriage."

Five years. Althea would be married by then. Perhaps have a child or two . . . with another man.

Then again, if she were married, she would be out of Redcliffe's reach, he reminded himself. But the thought did not console him.

"As you see," he continued, "any future with Miss Hartley would be a nearly hopeless endeavor."

Barrett wagged a finger and had the audacity to grin. "You just said *nearly hopeless.* Which essentially means that you have hope. And that is definitely different for you."

Jasper threw a spoon at him.

~

LATER THAT DAY, Jasper rode out to survey the St. James lands, trying to escape that *nearly hopeless hope* that he couldn't shake from his mind. But in everything he saw from forest to field, he couldn't stop wondering what it would be like if she were there with him.

He had to put the idea far from his mind. She would likely marry this year, not in five. And the sooner she did, the better, he told himself.

But all those thoughts fled on Sunday morning when a messenger arrived, stating that Redcliffe was back in town.

Jasper raced to Lady Broadbent's townhouse. Keeping an inconspicuous distance, he watched as the servants and the countess filed out to attend services, one by one.

Yet, when he didn't see Althea emerge, alarm sprinted through him.

Chapter Twenty-Four

❧

$\mathcal{T}$HEA FELT LIKE a prisoner. If Lady Broadbent meant to sequester her in her bedchamber simply because she'd appeared feverish, she was going to need more sustenance than weak tea and broth. Besides, it was surely cruel and unfair treatment to leave the door cracked so she could smell the sweet aroma of freshly baked scones.

However, it wasn't a cold that plagued her. Last night, she'd drifted off while reading, then awoke with her heart pounding and her lungs panting for breath. But not from a nightmare. She'd had a lurid, scandalous dream about forbidden kisses inside a dark carriage with Jasper's hands holding her close on his lap, the carriage rocking beneath them.

She would have called it more of a memory than a dream . . . if not for the giant sock puppet.

Yet, there it was, Lord Turgid, larger than life and barely able to fit through the carriage door to join them. When he'd suddenly pushed into the interior, she'd awoken on a gasp.

And, apparently, left her looking feverish. Which had made her a prisoner. A ravenous prisoner.

She needed to sink her teeth into something.

Knowing that everyone had gone to church, Thea padded belowstairs.

Entering the kitchen, she spotted the scones laid out on a plate. Her stomach growled. Surely, nobody would miss one . . . or two.

The stone floor was cold beneath her bare feet, the soft cambric of her nightdress swishing against her calves. Tiptoeing over to the timeworn trestle table, she leaned across and plucked a scone from the top.

Her eyes closed on the first mouthful, all honey-sweet and buttery goodness. "Mmm-mmm . . ."

Swaying back and forth, she stuffed another bite into her mouth, glad that no one was around to see her make a pig of herself. There were just times when a woman needed a heaping plate of scones and an empty house. Perhaps she'd even eat three of them. After all, there wasn't anyone to stop—

A throat cleared behind her.

Her eyes flew open on a gasp—a gasp which, regrettably, contained half a scone. Or, at least, that's what her lungs thought as she started to cough.

St. James came to her side as she turned to the sink, coughing, doubled over, her eyes watering. Of all the ways that Althea had imagined a character's demise—or even her own when her eldest sister murdered her lines in a family play—death by scone wasn't one of them.

His big hand patted her on the back. Well, perhaps *patted* was too tame a word. If she were an infant and that *pat* had landed on her backside, she'd be bawling.

Nevertheless, it effectively dislodged a wet lump of dough.

After another minute, her coughs subsided and he held a glass of water in front of her. She drank gratefully as he rubbed her back in soothing passes.

Setting down the glass, she looked up at him. "What are you doing here?"

"Saving your life?" He shrugged, all innocence. "I didn't know I'd catch you having a dance with your scone. And do you always take such enormous bites of your food?"

At his amusement, the heat of embarrassment rose to

her cheeks. "You'd be surprised by how much I can cram into my mouth when no one is looking."

She didn't know why that made his eyes instantly go dark, but he removed his hand and stepped away at once.

From the other side of the flour-dusted worktable, he cleared his throat. "I'm here because I didn't see you leave with the others and I wanted to ensure that you were . . . well."

Safe was what he'd meant, she thought. He'd told her that he'd watch over her. And he'd been worried enough that he'd chanced encountering a servant who might have stayed behind.

She felt a warm flutter beneath her breast. And seeing him glance to the door, his feet shifting in the way that reminded her of that first day he came to call with those paper flowers, made her melt a little inside.

"Come to think of it," she began, padding barefooted around the table and trailing her fingertip through the flour dust. "I'm not certain if I am well. Lady Broadbent thought I might have a cold. Do I look like I have a cold?"

Even though he practically had one boot out the door, he became instantly alert at this question. Then he looked at her as if it were a matter of life and death, his intense concern making her melt even more.

His brow furrowed. "You do look flushed."

"Do you think I might be feverish?" she asked, stopping on his side of the worktable.

He closed the distance between them and tilted up her chin to scrutinize her face. "Your eyes are bright, but not glassy. However"—he swept away the errant tendrils from her forehead then gently laid the back of his hand there—"you are warm."

Curling her fingers over his wrist, she held him there and closed her eyes. "I do feel a bit weak. Perhaps you should carry me upstairs to my bedchamber and tuck me in."

He stripped his hand away and lifted her at once. Then, without ceremony, he plopped her bottom onto the table. Hard.

Her eyes flew open, ready to scold him. "How dare—"

"Stop," he interrupted, glowering down at her. "You're playing with fire."

She sniffed. Clearly, she would need to work on acting the part of a seductress.

"I cannot help it. I really like having the bashful St. James all to myself." She looked up at him through her lashes and reached out to curl her fingers around his lapels. "Won't you at least kiss me before you go?"

"No."

She noted that he didn't remove her hands or step out of her reach. She also noted that his gaze dipped briefly down to where her nightgown pooled in her lap. He swallowed thickly.

"It's for research, you know. For a play," she said, all innocence. "Surely, you wouldn't want another man to kiss me. Would you?"

His hard gaze flew up to hers. "Which man?"

"Oh, I don't know. Perhaps Captain Summerhayes?"

But her ploy to make him jealous backfired with his next words.

"You should consider Summerhayes."

Her face fell. "Why?"

"For all the reasons we've discussed before. As it stands, I can give you nothing that any proper gentleman could."

Drat this man! She knew what he was doing. "You're trying to distance yourself from me."

"I'm trying to protect you. Even if my plan worked, it would take years before society accepted me."

"One little gargantuan obstacle is no reason to give up!"

"Years before I could provide for you," he continued. "Years before we could be together. I won't do that to you.

I won't make you wait to live your life. You should marry another."

"But what if I don't want another man to kiss me?" she asked, coasting her hands up to his shoulders, feeling his hands flex on her hips. "Or another man to hold me close? What if I only want—"

His mouth crashed down on hers.

The hard searing pressure spoke for him. *She was his.* He didn't say the words aloud, but he was proving it all the same. Firm hands cradled her face, his tongue demanding entry. She welcomed him as he took possession of her in a thorough, demanding kiss.

Weren't kisses supposed to soothe? To placate? At least, that's what she thought. When her parents kissed in the foyer, they usually smiled afterward as if satisfied from that brief contact.

But this? It only intensified the need for more.

He crowded her, his warmth drifting around her like phantom fingers drawing her closer. She laid her hands on him, feeling the beat of his heart bumping against the palm she slipped beneath his coat.

It wasn't enough. She wanted more of his passion, his taste, his heat.

So she tugged him to her, slinking her arms around his neck. A mewl of longing purred in her throat as their bodies collided and he growled in response. Rough hands traveled down her body as he pulled her hips to the edge of the table, cool air brushing her bare legs as the cambric drifted higher.

She didn't care. He'd done this to her. He'd given her back enough confidence to make sure she went after what she wanted.

"Do you know why Lady Broadbent thought I looked feverish? Because I'd been thinking of you. I'd been thinking of this," she said on a breath, her cheek pressed against his. Then she tilted her hips against him.

He groaned and captured her mouth again.

They were frenzied and reckless, kissing on the table in the broad light of day. But neither one of them cared.

He pulled at the drawstring around her neck and curled his fingers around the fabric of her robe and nightdress. Baring one shoulder, his mouth coasted down her throat, opening over her pulse. When he drew on her flesh with a gentle suction, she felt a thump deep inside her body, a tug that made her arch against him.

His hands were everywhere, anchoring her hips as he rocked—*once, twice*—against her, kneading the globes of her backside, skimming up her sides, charting a path along the underside of her breasts. She was so alive with tingles that by the time the pads of his thumbs rasped against the ruched flesh of her nipples, she thought she might fly apart into a thousand pieces.

He drew back, his gaze dark and intense as he wordlessly pushed her robe aside and shaped his hands around the swells of her breasts through the thin cambric. The way he touched her sent spirals of heat pooling low in her body. And that look in his eyes made her bolder than ever before.

She shrugged out of the robe, then slid one arm out of her nightdress, letting the fabric fall.

It hung, suspended, perched on the very edge of her nipple . . . until he traced a finger along her neckline in a slow downward sweep. Then the milky flesh was exposed to the morning light.

A breath stuttered out of him and he distractedly reached down to adjust the hard length behind the front fall of his black trousers. "Damn, Althea."

That husky tone and those hooded eyes made her feel beautiful in a way that no compliment ever had. His wasn't a flowery, practiced speech but raw, primal attraction. He desired her for who she was, and that was everything.

He crowded closer again, his mouth branding hers as

his hand cupped the weight of her breast, plucking and teasing the tip into an aching peak. Then her entire focus shifted to the path of his lips as they trailed hotly down her throat, the feel of his broad hands, and the warm liquid heat pulsing inside her.

Someone should write this down, she thought absently. It was excellent research. And when she was curious about something, she had to know everything about it. There was nothing for it except to keep . . . discovering . . .

She lost her train of thought when his mouth closed around her nipple, spurring the tip with a flick of his tongue, a gentle suck, sending a clenching sensation deep in her core. Her fingers threaded into his dark blond locks as her head fell back on a sigh. She never knew she was capable of feeling this way.

The heat of his hands burned through the thin layer of cambric as they coasted down her hips, her thighs. Then he was touching her skin.

Oh, the feel of those callused hands on her sent a siege of gooseflesh tingles over her. As he laved and worshipped her breasts, leaving the tips glossy and damp in the light, his touch skirted beneath her hem, almost tickling up along her inner thigh.

"Your skin is like the petal of a flower," he said thickly. "So delicate and"—he paused on a low groan as his finger brushed her nether curls—"wet . . . for me."

She felt her cheeks heat in embarrassment and she moved to close her thighs.

He shook his head. "Don't. Please. I promise I'll be gentle."

Did he think that she was worried about him hurting her? Nothing could be further from the truth. This was just all so new to her and, puppet play or not, she was feeling woefully uneducated.

Then she felt the slight tremor in his hand and the way he shifted awkwardly as if not entirely certain of the best approach, and she relaxed at once, knowing that this was not something either of them took lightly. She let her thighs fall open for him.

His shoulders shook beneath her hands on a shuddered breath as he slipped through the dewy folds. He touched her with gentle—almost reverent—passes as he soothed the thumping pulse in unhurried exploration.

"*Jasper,*" she gasped against the shell of his ear, eyes closed as she peppered frantic kisses over his face and jaw, his throat and lips. She was trembling so hard that it rattled the plate of scones.

"Shh . . . shh . . ." he crooned as he circled her entrance with the tip of one finger. "I won't hurt you. Just let me . . ."

He nudged inside, his finger thick and blunt. Then he cursed, accusing her of being too small, too tight. Spoken in a hungry growl, his voice tinged with primitive pleasure, she knew he wasn't criticizing her. He wanted her, and oh, how she wanted him to keep doing wicked things to her on that table.

"Does this"—he hooked his finger inside her, rubbing against some secret place that scrambled her wits—"feel good?"

"*Yes . . . there . . . don't stop . . . please . . . more,*" she said in a garbled rush, her eyes closed tight as the pleasure built, tingles dancing at the base of her spine. Blindly, her mouth opened against the skin between his earlobe and cravat.

She tasted the salt of him as his groan vibrated against her lips. A wash of warmth flooded down to the clench of her sex around his finger, her hips matching his rhythm, stroke for stroke. His head lowered, hunting for the aching peak of her breast, and when he drew her flesh into the heat of his mouth, she knew that nothing had ever felt this good before.

Then the pad of his thumb glanced across that taut bundle of nerves and her body hitched out of rhythm. He stilled for just a second as if deciphering her response. And then, he did it again, his thumb tracing a path that drew helpless whimpers from her.

Back arching, her fingernails bit into his scalp as she shamelessly held him to her breast. Then her hips hitched again—*once, twice*—before a choked cry tore from her throat.

She flew apart in an explosion of tingles that detonated from her core, rippling in outward waves. She curled into the sensation, hunching against the spasms, her face buried in the crook of his neck as he wrenched out every ounce of pleasure from her.

Still panting, she watched as he withdrew his hand and lifted his glistening fingers to his mouth. He closed his eyes on a quiet groan as he sampled her. It was such a primal thing to do. Seeing it made her stomach perform a little jig, her pulse quickening.

"What do I taste like?" she asked.

His eyes flew open and he lowered his hand like a boy caught stealing from the biscuit jar. He cleared his throat, his color high. But he must have seen the genuine curiosity in her gaze because he answered her. "Sweet and salty. Like ambrosia or something a man like me could only dream about."

Her heart quickened as his gaze skimmed over her once more. "Take me upstairs."

He bent to press his lips to hers, the hard heat beneath his trousers meeting her eagerly. Then he rested his forehead against hers and exhaled long and slow. It was a sound of resignation, and she didn't like it.

"If I take you upstairs, then I will *take* you upstairs."
He put her clothes in order with the quick efficiency of a
man smothering an ember that landed on the rug. "And
there will be no taking this morning, or ever."

Before she could form an argument, he walked stiffly
to the door, leaving without looking back.

Chapter Twenty-Five

IT TOOK TWO more days before Lady Broadbent was satisfied that Thea didn't have a cold. Then she took her out shopping. But Thea's first request after her release from bedchamber-gaol was to make a quick detour to Fife's Feathered Quill.

She'd done little more than write during her incarceration and wanted Mr. Fife to read it.

"What do you think?" she asked him as he turned over the last page and began to tap them against the glass case into a neat stack.

Instead of answering her straightaway, he pursed his lips then walked toward the wall of shelves. Climbing a rolling ladder, he withdrew a slender box. Then he returned and lifted the lid.

"What I think, Miss Hartley, is that this play deserves a proper home." His eyebrows lifted as he grinned at her. Then he opened a lovely leather portfolio and slid her pages inside.

She beamed. "So you like it? I mean, it's only the beginning of a play. There isn't an ending quite yet . . . But you like what I have done so far?"

He was already nodding before she finished speaking. "I especially enjoyed that handsome devil of a character who sells ledgers."

"Thought you might." She laughed.

The pads of his fingers drummed against the cover. "You thought all this up from our little conversation, hmm?"

"That conversation started it all," she said, without elaborating.

She'd believed it was good, too. But she didn't want to show it to Lady Broadbent for a couple of reasons. The first was that she would recognize the part about the highwayman. And second, she might begin to wonder how much of the tale was true.

There was probably too much truth, though she took care to make the highwayman with the dual identity not resemble St. James. She wanted to protect him. Yet, at the same time, she wanted to expose cowards and monsters like Lord Abernathy and Redcliffe. She wanted people to have their eyes opened.

"I think it's your best yet," he said. "Of course, this is unlike the other plays. Because there certainly wouldn't be a highwayman roaming around the *ton*, now would there?"

She issued a laugh. "No, indeed. The very idea is rather fantastic."

"Quite." He grinned in agreement and put the lid back on the box, his gaze full of mischief. "Although, speaking of the extraordinary, I've heard an interesting tidbit just this morning that might inspire a new character."

"Oh?"

He leaned across the glass case as if they weren't the only two in the shop. "I heard that the Duke of Sherborne invited that viscount to dine with him."

"What viscount?" she asked, only half listening as she smoothed her hands over the box.

Mr. Fife snapped his fingers, thinking. "You know the one. He's forever crashing into things. Oh, what's his name . . . Ah, yes, I've got it. St. James!"

Thea went still. Sherborne had invited Jasper to dinner? He hadn't said anything to her. Then again, they hadn't seen each other for two days. But she had to wonder if it was true. And, if it was, then what did that mean? "I had not heard."

"Perhaps you can write a character like him in your play, some clumsy fellow."

She frowned, sinking her teeth into her bottom lip. "Perhaps."

⚓

"I JUST CAUGHT the most peculiar bit of gossip at the tea shop," Lady Broadbent said the instant Thea entered the waiting carriage.

Or, at least, the second waiting carriage. The first carriage door she'd opened had belonged to someone else. She'd apologized profusely to the alarmed and vexed Lady Chetwynd but, honestly, all black carriages looked alike. She was surprised it didn't happen all the time.

Then again, she was distracted by the news from Mr. Fife.

"Woolgathering, Miss Hartley?"

"Hmm?" Dimly, Thea registered the beginnings of exasperation in her chaperon's cool, rounded tones. "Apologies. What were you saying?"

The countess was so eager to share that she didn't bother to be affronted. "You'll never guess. But the Duke of Sherborne has invited St. James to dine. Can you imagine?"

She punctuated the last three words by rapping the tip of her cane on the floor of the carriage.

So it was true. And the entire *ton* was likely all abuzz with the news.

"Whatever do you think it means?" she asked, telling herself not to speculate. Not to hope. *Not yet.*

"There is no way to know for certain. However, if St. James is able to win the support of Sherborne, he might come to have a welcome place in society."

Thea felt her heart rise higher in her chest, beating erratically. But she tried not to reveal her excitement. "How wonderful for him."

"Indeed." The countess pursed her lips in thought. "It does make one wonder how this will affect Redcliffe. He has never been kind to his nephew, and if St. James should win Sherborne's support then there would be many a critical eye cast in the earl's direction."

Which would make it possible for society to see Jasper in a new light. And that meant they might be able to be together sooner than either of them thought possible.

Dare she hope?

Lady Broadbent rubbed her hands together. "Oh, to be a fly on the wall at Sherborne's that night."

A fly? Thea was willing to be a mounted boar on the duke's wall if it meant she would be the first to know if she had a future with Jasper.

⟞

THE GOSSIPS AND scandal sheets had a banner day of speculation over the news of Sherborne's surprising invitation.

But the following day brought an entirely new scandal.

Thea heard a shout from Lady Broadbent's sitting room and went running.

She flung open the door to find the countess holding a magnifying glass to the morning's scandal sheet. "What is it?"

"My dear," she said, her face pale, her hand shaking as she laid the glass aside, the forgotten newspaper drifting to the Aubusson rug. "It's Lord Abernathy. He has returned from his hunting lodge."

Stepping into the room, she closed the door behind her, so the servants wouldn't overhear. "Well, I'm certain London doesn't need another cad in residence, but I don't understand what has you so distressed."

"He has told his tale about the highwayman and his wolf."

Thea stopped cold, her feet turning to lead. Her thoughts went back to that night, to what a sniveling cretin the viscount had been.

Then another thought had her heart thudding in a panic. If she had been able to discover the identity of the highwayman, she couldn't help but wonder if anyone else had . . . like Lord Abernathy.

But, surely, if he had even whispered a suspicion about Jasper, that would have been the first thing the scandal sheets printed. Wouldn't it?

Lady Broadbent gestured with a limp hand toward the escritoire. "I need my vinaigrette."

Forcing her feet into motion, she crossed the room to retrieve the small vile, then delivered it to her chaperone. "What all did he tell?"

"They are speculating"—the countess paused to take a wincing whiff—"that he wasn't alone in the carriage."

Suddenly, Thea understood why her chaperone was so alarmed.

Oh, this was not good. Not good at all. "And with my stories about the highwayman . . . specifically the one about Lord Zed . . ."

"Yes, my dear. We could very well be ruined."

Another Hartley scandal.

Blindly, Thea groped for the vile and inhaled, bracing herself for what was to come.

Chapter Twenty-Six

❧

*J*ASPER WAS USED to being noticed for his size, his manner of speaking and his carefully cultivated ineptitude. These characteristics typically meant that any gaze falling on him would swiftly turn to dismissal. In that regard, he was somewhat invisible and could attend to his own matters of business without being called upon to exchange pleasantries.

But one invitation from the Duke of Sherborne and his comfortable, inconspicuous life was over.

On his way to a wharf-side tavern to meet with one of the men who kept him abreast of his uncle's activities, he'd been hailed by three different gentlemen. Strangely, they'd all wanted to invite him to their gatherings.

Lord Bromley informed him of having a hunting box in Scotland and asked if he liked shooting quail. Caught off guard, he issued the first excuse he could think of, stating that he'd had a pet quail as a boy and found the very idea of shooting them a ghastly crime against the noblest of fowl.

It was a ludicrous response, but it managed to end the conversation.

He hadn't taken a dozen steps before he was hailed again. This time it was Lord Evans, who asked if he enjoyed cards. Jasper's reply to that was that he did enjoy cards and that he'd once built a house six stories tall before it collapsed. Lord Evans furrowed his brow, at a loss for words as Jasper took his leave.

But as he rounded the corner, the knighted Sir Reginald Wilton inquired if he wanted to be introduced to his cousin, who just so happened to also have a lisp. "You've so much in common already."

Jasper blinked owl-eyed behind his spectacles and spoke in a steady susurration, "*Also* has a lisp? I assuredly do not speak with a lisp, sir."

He'd left Wilton to puzzle that out.

Later that afternoon, he returned to his lodgings. But before he could climb the stairs to his flat, he was stopped by his landlord.

The scowling Mr. Remus unceremoniously deposited a heap of cards and invitations into Jasper's hands.

"I ain't your butler," the fractious man said, then turned on his heel and stalked to the kitchens.

Arriving at the door to his flat, Jasper saw another pile waiting on the floor and expelled a sigh. It was the worst possible time for Ansonby to be visiting his mother in Cheshire for a few days.

What was he supposed to do with all these?

He'd never had this problem before. When Jasper had asked his former professor for a favor and his subsequent conversation with Sherborne, he didn't expect it would lead to this.

But, because of Althea and the new strategy she'd inspired, his whole life was taking a turn.

It was clear that he'd been wasting years trying to defend against Redcliffe's type of warfare. He'd been on the receiving end of his attacks for so long that all he'd known was the necessity to shield and protect. In fact, that was still his first impulse.

This attention made him nervous. In the past, gaining attention—especially from his uncle—never boded well for him. So this collective interest from the *ton* was unsettling to say the least. It made him wonder what dark thing lurked on the horizon.

And yet, because of Althea, he was hoping to find a break in the clouds instead.

His dinner with Sherborne at the end of the week would be the deciding factor.

Jasper deposited the letters on the desk by the window, where he'd recently spent many an hour creating paper flowers.

Buried among the invitations, he saw a letter from his aunt. Breaking the seal, he skimmed the contents, grateful to learn that she had decided to stay with the busybody Lady Deardorff. Apparently, her sniveling son was off to Brighton and she would enjoy the company. With this news, even Tempest could have no arguments. Then again, knowing his cousin, she would find something to be querulous about. He felt a grin tug at his mouth.

He was glad that his aunt and cousins would have a house full of servants to watch over them and they could be at their ease for a time.

A sharp rap on the door reverberated through his flat and he exhaled through his teeth. If a constant siege of callers was a man's reward for being the latest *on dit*, then he wanted to remain a pariah.

As he strode back across the room, he was glad that he didn't have to hide the boy and Garmr. For the time, he thought it best to keep them at the tavern with Barrett and Nan.

Even so, he had to wonder why Mr. Remus hadn't disposed of this messenger. Perhaps, Jasper should have left word with his landlord that he wasn't at home.

When he opened the door, the last person he expected to see was Redcliffe. His surprise must have shown on his face because his uncle sneered with malevolent pleasure.

It was apparent at once that the furtive attack against his uncle's character was starting to take its toll. Whenever he reached a certain level of frustration, he looked for someone to crush beneath his boot. That someone was usually his addlepated nephew.

Jasper welcomed it. If his uncle was there, then he wasn't off hurting someone else.

"Have you read the latest scandal rag?" Redcliffe asked by way of greeting.

"No, Uncle."

"Of course, you wouldn't have done. There are too many words with more than one syllable. But I will leave my copy here, and perhaps you will be able to parse out a few of the less taxing words." He withdrew the folded pages tucked beneath his arm and dropped them on the writing desk, his gaze skimming the correspondence as well as the room around him. "Where is your manservant?"

"Out for the moment."

With the tip of his cane, he examined the threadbare draperies and issued a sniff as he let them fall. "I had the most interesting visit earlier."

Since it was clear that his uncle intended to linger until he'd said what he came to say, Jasper offered an "Oh?"

"With Lord Abernathy." He cut an unreadable glance to his nephew. "Did you know he was back in town?"

"And why would I know that?"

Redcliffe's brows inched higher with intrigue. "Why, indeed."

"Will that be all, then, Uncle?"

But Redcliffe was in no rush to respond. He was taking a leisurely tour of the room, his nose wrinkled in distaste.

When he meandered back to Jasper, the eyes that had once struck such terror in a little boy homed in sharply on him. "I heard you made quite a fool of yourself over Miss Hartley at the Leighton Ball."

Any mention of Althea raised his hackles and he didn't trust himself to respond.

"Pity I was not well enough to witness it," his uncle enunciated crisply as if he were chewing on glass.

Jasper held that gaze without flinching. "Indeed."

"You'll never have her, you know," Redcliffe proclaimed, his nostrils flared. Then he walked to the door. But before he left, he added, "And you should really have that chair repaired."

As he closed the door, Jasper let out a breath and threw the bolt.

Curious, he looked over his shoulder at the chair. Then he saw it . . . Garmr's teeth marks.

The weight of dread dropped to the pit of his stomach, and he wondered just what Lord Abernathy had said.

RUINATION WAS NOT on the minds of Lady Broadbent and Althea's callers the following afternoon. In fact, those who recalled Thea's attempted stories of the highwayman were titillated by the presumption that she had heard the rumor first.

To ensure that no one made the small hop in logic to suppose that she and the countess had been the ones in the carriage with Lord Abernathy, Thea and her chaperone had devised a plan to proclaim that the tale was, in fact, a play she was writing.

There were a few disappointed by this, but others who merely enjoyed the excitement of gossiping about something much more interesting than St. James.

This provided no small amount of relief for her. She'd been worried about him and what an accusation of highway robbery landing at his feet might do. In fact, she'd been much more concerned about him than her own reputation.

By the time her callers left the parlor, however, it seemed as though all worry was for naught.

"I'd say we performed splendidly, my dear," Lady Broadbent said as she ambled toward the hall, leaning on her cane a little heavier after coping with the strain of recent developments. "To celebrate, I think I shall rest and, later, have a tray sent to my rooms. It has been a rather eventful afternoon."

The countess presented her cheek and Thea dutifully bussed a kiss onto it. "I'll just put the parlor back to rights and read for a bit. Then I might retire early, as well."

When the maid left with the last of the teacups and saucers, and pillows were properly positioned in their places, Thea turned to go up to her rooms, thinking of continuing work on her play.

The instant she saw a familiar figure framed in the parlor doorway, all thought fell out of her skull like pennies through a pocket hole.

Kellum.

Well, perhaps not *all* thought. Unfortunately, her mind was completely capable of summoning the last things he'd said to her a year ago.

You, a playwright? . . . You are not even worthy of a footnote.

"Miss Hartley," he said with a grin as if they were just old friends meeting by chance.

Ever needful of acknowledgment, he let the stunned silence drag on, waiting for her to greet him in return. "Sir Archer."

"I remember when it used to be *Kellum*." He stepped into the room, his direct path to her forcing her back a step. "Do you?"

"What"—she swallowed—"are you doing here?"

He moved between two bronze chairs and casually laid his hat and gloves on the low table. "Surely, it isn't criminal to pay a call on an old acquaintance. Then again, we were more than that at one time, were we not?"

The smugness curling his lip as he let his gaze roam down her body snapped her out of her fugue state and she stiffened.

"It is late and I have other obligations. So, if you have nothing in particular to say, then I beg you would excuse me. I will have my butler show you out." Even as she spoke the words, she was surprised by her own mettle and felt quite proud of herself for walking to the doorway and sweeping her arm toward the corridor.

He seemed more amused than impressed, but he did pick up his hat.

Without hurry, he ambled toward her. "I had a pleasant little chat with our favorite stationer."

Instant dread filled her. *Mr. Fife! You lovable little gossipmonger, what have you done?*

"It seems you've managed to write a portion of a play involving, of all things, a highwayman. Really, Thea, do you have to read the scandal sheets for *all* your inspiration? That is old news. By the time you finish, *if* you finish, no audience would even be interested." His gaze dipped to her throat when she swallowed, then his eyes brightened in triumph. "Still hanging onto someone else's coattails, aren't you? Such a pity."

He tsked, lingering long enough to sniff in her direction as if testing the air for the aroma of cabbages.

She tried to think of the perfect reply that would take him down a notch or two. Something. Anything. But the words refused to form.

He smirked at her and left.

Thea looked over her shoulder to see if any of the servants had witnessed that encounter. She felt exposed and vulnerable, as if everyone could see her flaws. The voice of her not-so-distant insecurities resurfaced, making her wonder if he was right, after all.

She wanted to hide. She wanted to go home. But home was no longer a place of refuge.

There was only one place that made her feel as if she belonged—in the arms of the one person who made her feel whole. Who made her feel safe, accepted and cherished for who she was.

Don't ever let anyone make you doubt yourself, for they cannot fathom all the greatness that resides inside of you.

Thinking of St. James, her heart filled with so much warmth that it overflowed, rushing through her veins, uplifting her. And, suddenly, she thought of the perfect thing to say to Kellum.

Holding her head high, she stalked to the foyer, past the butler, and threw open the door.

"Beware of the ivy on your way out, you arse. I'd hate for you to trip," she called out.

Regrettably, Kellum was nowhere in sight . . . and she had to apologize profusely to their neighbor, Lord Morely.

Even so, she considered it a victory that the perfect setdown came to her within minutes. Usually, she had to wait until replaying the episode in the bath before winning an argument.

Chapter Twenty-Seven

꙳ꙮ

AT NIGHTFALL, JASPER relieved the man he had watching over Lady Broadbent's townhouse and took over. After Redcliffe's unsettling visit, he wasn't about to take any chances.

To make matters worse, the *ton* was all abuzz with the similarities of Althea's highwayman tale to that of Abernathy's. It took no great leap to imagine that some might speculate over those details and call her reputation into question.

Was that why she hadn't attended any parties that evening? Or why he still saw a light burning in her window, long after midnight?

From the constant shift of the shadows from the room within, he knew she wasn't seated at her desk. Was she pacing the floor with worry?

He knew that finding a place of acceptance in society was like trying to walk a tightrope during a squall with the wind buffeting from either side, forever keeping you off balance. And that was if society approved of you. But for those on the outside, it seemed impossible to reach the tightrope at all. He didn't want her to suffer such a fate, especially because of him.

Which was an excellent reason for him to stay in the shadows. An excellent reason not to throw a pebble at her window just to have a glimpse of her face and to tell her that he would do whatever he could to protect her. Even if that meant he would need to create a scandal to put the *ton*'s focus back on him. He would do anything—risk everything—for her.

In the end, it was the last thought that made the decision for him.

Bending down, he retrieved a small white pebble from the garden path and tossed it toward her window. As it struck the glass with a ping before pattering to the sill, he told himself that all he needed was to see her face. That would be enough. He just had to make certain she was safe and well.

Then the light extinguished from the room without even the faintest movement of the curtains. He frowned, not only disappointed but with worry gnawing at the center of his gut. So, he sent another pebble sailing. Like before, there was no face at the window.

For a moment, he debated over stealing in through the back door. But it was too much of a risk. Hadn't he already taken too many with her?

Resigned, he decided to send her a missive in the morning, along with the flower he'd brought with him. That way she would know he was thinking about her. And she would know he was watching over her, as well.

With one last glance at the darkened window, he turned away . . .

Just as a shadow sprinted across the garden.

Instantly on guard, he prepared to launch himself at this intruder and give him the pummeling of his life.

Then, much to his surprise, the intruder launched *herself* at him.

The hood of Althea's dark cloak flew from her hair as he caught her, and she pressed her head against his chest, wrapping her arms around him. "I'm so glad you're here."

He held her, searching her features and finding worry notched in the lines between her brows. "What has happened?"

"So much, I wouldn't even know where to begin."

He made a swift decision and took her by the hand. "You're coming with me."

~~~

THE INSTANT JASPER led her inside his flat, he regretted his decision.

With a glance around the space, all he could see were the imperfections—the frayed threads, patches of exposed webbing on the rug, mismatched furniture with more than a few nicks and gouges. He hadn't cared a whit about what his home looked like when his uncle had been here. But with her it was different.

She was too fine a creation to be in such squalor. Even standing there in a black woolen cloak, dark hair escaping her plait to frame her face in a disorder of curls, she was all grace and perfection.

When she absently picked up a broken bookend, it made him all the more aware that they were from two different worlds.

"I've never been in a gentleman's flat before," Althea said, her eyes wide as she took in the ramshackle surroundings of his hovel.

"I should hope not." He came up behind her and slid the cloak from her shoulders. He did have manners, after all. But when he saw her, he quickly put the garment back on her body. "Do you ever wear anything other than your nightclothes?"

Was she trying to test his self-restraint?

"Perhaps if someone hadn't ruined three of my gowns . . ."

"And all for naught, it seems. I should have tried harder to keep Lord Abernathy quiet instead." Taking long strides to the other side of the room, he busied himself with pouring her a glass of whisky.

Then he stopped. *Whisky?*

What the devil was he thinking? He didn't want her drunk, tipsy or even sleepy. Because then the seldom-inhibited Althea would only want to curl her soft, warm and enticing body against his.

No. No. Definitely not a good plan.

So he downed the whisky himself and poured water for her.

"Not to mention, if you had ever let me finish my tale, I could have relayed that the man in the story, which I supposedly only heard"—she cleared her throat—"had cried like an infant and soiled himself. I'm certain Abernathy would not have wanted that version linked with him."

"Now I'm regretting that I stopped you."

He turned, water glass in hand to find her perusing the room, her fingertips reaching through the part in her cloak to trail lightly over the fluted edge of a creamware dish that he'd never paid much attention to before. Ansonby had likely acquired it at some point. By way of an excuse for wasting good coin on bric-a-brac at market, his manservant was forever citing that even a viscount without means needn't reside in such squalid surroundings without an occasional reprieve for the eye.

But the dish wasn't what captured his attention. It was her. *Always her.* She made everything beautiful and elegant just by being near it. Which was further proof that he never should have brought her here.

She cast a dubious glance over her shoulder on her way toward the mantel as she continued her exploration of the room. "As it stands, my days of telling tales of highwaymen are over. I've decided to retire the play. Not that it would have ever made it to the stage, as Sir Archer so kindly reminded me this afternoon."

Jasper tensed, trying to rein in a surge of anger at the reminder of what she'd told him in the carriage about her unwelcome visitor. It bothered him that the man had showed up on her doorstep without warning. In his opinion, unannounced visitors usually had an agenda. So what was Archer's?

"What I cannot fathom is why he felt compelled to pay a call on me?" she asked, mirroring Jasper's thoughts as she distractedly opened the glass face of the rosewood clock. "One would think a cat would tire of toying with a mouse he'd left for dead a year ago. What did he hope to gain? A final twitch? A death rattle?" She shook her head and snapped closed the oculus door. "It doesn't matter. I am wholly unaffected by the entire encounter. I've put it completely behind me."

What a lovely little liar.

Crossing the room, he abandoned her glass on the water-ringed surface of a wobbly table and went to her. He enfolded her in his embrace, ignoring the warning bell that clanged in the back of his mind as she settled perfectly against him.

"Don't listen to him. If you want to write that play, then you shouldn't let anyone stop you." He pressed a kiss to the top of her head. "Besides, Archer is a self-important little man, threatened by those who have seen him for what he is, because he knows that you can shatter the illusion he has created for himself."

"I appreciate your support, more than you'll ever know," she said with her cheek resting against his chest. "However, the bigger reason I've given it up is that I don't want to endanger you."

A wry grin tugged at the corner of his mouth. "I can take care of myself."

Even though he knew her play was about a highwayman, he was more concerned with someone daring to tell her that she wasn't good enough to write it than about any trouble it might cause him if it were performed for an audience.

Jasper would be her champion, her protector. No matter what it cost him.

"That may be true, but I'll protect you, all the same." She plucked at a loose thread on one of his waistcoat buttons. "That's what people do when they love each other."

His breath caught. The reliable gears that had kept his cynical heart ticking all his life suddenly ground to a halt, quaking the floor beneath his feet. His pulse raced through his veins, rushing in his ears so loudly that he was sure he hadn't heard her correctly.

Then she stepped out of his stunned embrace, blinking up at him, owl-eyed. "That was . . . unexpected."

Right, he thought. It had been a mistake. Of course it had. After all, for most of his life the idea of what he should expect, what he deserved—and, more importantly, what he did not—had been pummeled into him.

"A slip of the tongue. Easily forgotten," he managed.

She didn't seem to hear him, but began to pace back and forth from one side of the worn rug to the other. "I'm usually quite observant. Then, one minute I was just talking and the next . . . *love* came out. Is that how it happens? But no, that cannot be true."

"You don't need to explain."

"I have to write this down. Something this monumental is vital for future character development," she said to herself as she pivoted on her heel and whisked past him on her way to his cluttered desk.

Without pausing in her one-sided conversation, she uncapped the ink, grabbed the first quill she could find, then began to write on the backs of his discarded invitations. "I supposed that I've been carrying around an empty husk for so long now that I didn't realize what was happening. But I think it must have started with your lisp."

"My . . . lisp?"

"Mmm-hmm," she murmured absently, quill scratching over the paper. "There was just something about the way your tongue touched the edge of your teeth that had me enthralled. I couldn't look away. The very sight of it made me all flustered and warm. That warmth transformed into a peculiar fluttery feeling of unknown origin. Then it happened again when you first paid a call, looking all bashful and adorable. I'd wanted to throw my arms around you, right then and there. And, honestly, the very fact that I could so easily forgive you for ruining the gown with the velvet pockets should have told me everything. It seems so obvious now. I've been in love with you for weeks and I didn't even know it . . ."

Jasper wasn't sure what was happening to him. All he knew was that he couldn't draw in a single breath. The more she talked, the harder it was to breathe.

"The stealthy beginnings of this love have been coming on so gradually that I didn't really know until I'd just blurted it out. But what an abominable trick for it to happen at Nell's soiree, of all places!" She laughed, shaking her head. As she dipped into the ink, she glanced over her shoulder. "Your lips are starting to turn blue around the edges. Better take a breath, St. James. If you decide to faint or have a fit of apoplexy, just wait until I'm finished, hmm? Now, where was I . . . Oh yes, the paper flowers . . ."

She turned her attention back to the hasty scrawls while Jasper was slowly asphyxiating. He needed her to stop talking. Just . . . stop.

He felt as though he were standing in the center of a storm with the wind sweeping and swirling all around him, blowing with such force that it left an absence of air where he was. And her words were a cacophony of wind chimes, ringing all at once.

"Those blossoms are the last things I see every night before I close my eyes, and the first when I open them each morning. Is it any wonder that I fell in love with you?"

"Stop," he rasped, his throat dry as dust.

He needed air. He needed quiet to think.

She continued to scratch the tip of the quill. "That's a peculiar thing to say. 'Stop.' As if I had a choice in the matter. Besides, it's your own fault. That night in Abernathy's carriage, you claimed that you didn't take from women. But that was an unmitigated lie, because you clearly stole my heart."

She was relentless. Absolutely relentless! Couldn't she see that he was on the brink of death? And when she laughed, the music of it was too much to bear.

His steps toward her were heavy, sluggish as if he were ripping away roots that anchored him. "Stop. I mean it, Althea. You don't know what you're saying."

"What? That I'm in *lo*—"

He didn't give her a chance to finish.

Taking her by the shoulders, he lowered his head and crushed his mouth to hers.

It was only meant to stop her. To give him a moment to gather his thoughts, to formulate a concise argument that explained all the reasons it was impossible that she could love him. Not him. Not the awkward gangly boy he'd once been, and certainly not the behemoth viscount without two shillings to rub together that he'd become.

And yet, as her arms twined around his neck and her mouth surrendered sweetly beneath his, he started to want the impossible.

Chapter Twenty-Eight

THEA DIDN'T UNDERSTAND why Jasper was so determined to silence her, but she didn't mind his method. Not a single bit.

His mouth tasted like whisky, the burn setting her blood on fire in a kiss so intense that her bones incinerated. He kissed her like he wanted to devour her, his mouth hungry and searching. Anything less wouldn't have been enough.

This was what she needed. This kiss. This heat. This embrace.

Though, in actuality, he was still holding her shoulders. But the promise of his embrace was so close that she could feel her body melting into the only place that made the world right again after such an abysmal day.

Then, all at once, he withdrew. And cursed.

Stalking over to the window, he threw up the sash and leaned out to draw in a ragged breath, leaving her on legs as insubstantial as ribbons. She staggered to find her footing. Reaching out, she gripped the desk for support and struggled to find her own breath.

"Well," she panted, "when you want a girl to stop talking, you certainly have an interesting method."

"You didn't know what you were saying."

And she didn't need air in her lungs to become instantly offended by that.

He'd said it before and she hadn't had time to become properly vexed. But now, with all the blood simmering through her body with no ready outlet, her temper was quick to ignite. "I beg your pardon? Are you accusing me of not understanding the words exiting my own mouth like some empty-headed nitwit?"

"Of course not. But you are a romantic," he accused.

"And just what does that have to do with anything?"

Curls of steam were surely escaping her ears as she glared at his back. *You don't know what you're saying* was a line Kellum might have used. Never would she have expected Jasper to do the same.

Hands on hips, she narrowed her eyes as Jasper shut the window and turned. If he so much as attempted to placate her with pretty words, she was going to throw the inkwell at him.

It would be David—no, *Davinia*—taking down Goliath.

As the curtains closed behind him, she caught a glimpse of hunger in his gaze before he scrubbed a hand over his face.

"I am a penniless viscount."

"So? I don't care about that."

"Damn it all, Althea! I rob men under the cloak of darkness. I make them fear for their lives."

"You have your reasons," she fired back.

He growled in frustration and shoved a hand through his hair, leaving the short layers in disorder. "You've cast me as some sort of romantic hero, when that couldn't be further from the truth."

The vehemence in his tone crackled like cinders shooting from a roaring fire, each trying to set a path of destruction in their wake.

She felt one of those flames ignite inside her, seething. "You think I've just conjured these feelings from the ether, don't you? That my foolish romantic heart has simply attached itself to you for no reason at all."

"You may not see it now but, come morning, you will

regret all you've said. You will see that I am unworthy of
your regard." As he spoke the last sentence, his voice went
quiet, almost apologetic as if he were taking all the blame.
As if he, and he alone, must bear the burden of every mistake ever made.

But it was at the subtle break on the word *unworthy* that
Thea knew the real issue at hand.

No matter how far he'd come in his life, no matter how
much good he'd done for the sake of others, there was still
the boy who'd been told he was undeserving of basic kindness and decency—not to mention love—that still resided
in him.

Oh, Jasper, she thought, the freshly beating organ beneath her breast breaking for him.

"Rest assured," he continued, "I won't think less of you
for any alteration that the brightness of day will bring."

In that moment, all her vexation fell away like a layer of
bark burning off a log in the grate. The warmth left behind
emboldened her to shrug out of her cloak and drape it over
the back of the desk chair.

"Wh-what are you doing?"

"I won't regret a single thing come morning," she said,
knowing with complete and utter certainty that she wasn't
leaving before dawn.

He eyed her warily as one would a torch bearer beside a
barrel of gunpowder. "The hour grows late."

She took a step toward him. "It was already late when
you brought me here."

"Regardless"—above the open neck of his black shirtsleeves, his throat worked on a swallow—"I should take
you home."

She couldn't help but notice that he didn't move from
the spot as she neared. Nor did he make any gesture to
hold her. Clearly, she needed to take matters into her own
hands.

Closing the distance, she stood on tiptoe to loop her arms around his neck. His hands found her hips, though more as if to steady her than to encourage her. Even so, his grip tightened, fingers splaying beneath the small of her back as she pulled herself up high enough to press her lips to his throat, to the tempting shadow beneath his Adam's apple, tasting the salt on his skin.

His scent curled warmly inside her as she breathed him in, nuzzling beneath his open collar. Her parted lips opened over the corded muscles of his throat, finding the galloping pulse that told her he wasn't unaffected by her nearness.

"Kiss me," she whispered, trailing her lips along the silken rasp of stubble emerging along his jaw. "If you kiss me, I'll consider allowing you to take me home."

Liar, her Greek chorus chimed in.

Thankfully, St. James was a bit more trusting. He lowered his head just enough for her to lift her mouth under his. The pressure was light, his lips dusting gently over hers, tenderly as if she might break.

This would not do. She wanted his unbridled passion. Wanted him to feel the same uninhibited joy and love that were building inside her as if she were a cannon ready to explode. So, as he started to withdraw, she caught his lower lip, raking her teeth over it.

He growled, his arms tightening. His breath staggered between her parted lips. "You said one kiss."

"Actually, I never specified a number," she countered, nibbling at his mouth.

When she threaded her fingers through his hair and suckled the tip of his tongue, a low, hungry sound vibrated in his throat and he lifted her off her feet. Rough hands burned a path along her back and down over the curve of her bottom, gripping fistfuls of her nightdress.

On a ragged breath, he said, "Tell me to stop."

Even as he spoke, she could feel the heat from the intriguing hardness against her stomach. It tunneled through her, setting her pulse to a quick canter. *Stop?* The word was missing from her lexicon.

"Only if you do something I don't like. But I should warn you . . ." She brushed her tender lips against his. "I like everything you do. Although, I'm completely willing to let you try new things. Is that your bedchamber?"

He followed her gesture toward the closed door on the adjacent wall and swallowed thickly. She took that as affirmation.

Wiggling down his body, and delighted when he sucked in a breath during her progress, she stood in front of him. "I'd like to see where you sleep."

He was quicker to react this time, attempting to stop her, but she ducked under his arm, grabbed a chamberstick and made for the door.

The instant she curled her fingers around the knob, he covered her hand. "We should be married before we cross this threshold."

"Is that a proposal?" She beamed up at him and he groaned in agony.

He pressed his forehead to hers. "You cannot smile at me like that. When you do, it opens up everything inside me and it's nearly impossible to resist you. But I must resist you."

Unrepentant, Thea smiled again.

Chapter Twenty-Nine

✌️

"I'M THINKING OF a new play," Thea said as she opened the door to Jasper's bedchamber. A brief glance over her shoulder revealed a rumpled bed as massive as a barge on the Thames taking up most of the room. Stepping backward, she gripped a fistful of his black shirt and tugged the big man across the threshold. "Picture the curtains opening to a carriage, racing toward Gretna Green. A pair of lovers embrace in the dark confines, making the most of their time."

"But he has nothing," Jasper said, his voice pained as he staggered inside.

"Not true. He has land. Additionally, she has a small dowry, but enough to build a cottage with room for them, his aunt and cousins, along with Roly and Thumper."

"Garmr," he corrected, his lungs pushing against her hands as he watched her smooth the wrinkles she'd just made in the fabric of his shirt. It was impossible not to notice that there wasn't any give in the muscular torso beneath her hands.

"If you say so," she said, briefly leaning one-footed to slide the chamberstick onto the mantel. "The curtain closes then opens again on Act Two with the arrival of their first child . . . born scandalously premature."

She looked up at him through her lashes and smiled again.

His eyes glazed over as if entranced and she knew she had him. Her very own rapt audience.

He swallowed. "Then what happens?"

"Well, every good play requires a conflict."

He tensed, his hands finding her waist as if to shield her.

"Theirs is that they cannot seem to stay out of each other's arms," she clarified and felt his chest rise and fall in relief. "They mortify their children with their affection."

At last, Thea understood her parents. If they felt even a portion of the passion and yearning that she had for Jasper, she couldn't blame them.

Standing there, with the heat of his body warming her through the layers that separated them, she wondered what he'd do if she untied the cord of her nightdress and let it fall to the floor, right then and there. And yet, she wanted to explore him first.

So, she continued her leisurely perusal, tracing the open V that revealed a triangle of dark blond hair. It was crisp and curling, tickling her fingertips. His grip on her waist went slack as she charted a path lower still, roaming down the ridges of his abdomen to the waist of his black trousers.

He stilled her hands. "I wouldn't want to hurt you. You're too . . . delicate for the likes of me."

Delicate? She wanted to laugh until she saw the worry etched between his brows. "I'm hardly made of glass. Besides, you've always been careful with me, when we waltzed and . . . when you had me on the trestle table."

She lifted her face in a silent query. He stared back at her with dark, hooded eyes and a breath shuddered out of him. She interpreted that as permission.

His head fell back on a groan as the flat of her hand traveled down the considerable length of him, the thick column positioned at an angle. It was only when she'd traversed from the taut base and all the way to the tip that she felt her first stirring of trepidation.

"Shakespeare's soliloquies!" She gasped. "Are all men . . . made like you?"

A muscle ticked along his jaw as he took his time in answering. Then he offered a hesitant "Yes."

Thea wasn't entirely convinced. Truth be told, she'd assumed her mother had been exaggerating the size of Lord Turgid for shock value. Now she wondered if she'd minimized it to spare her daughters from the truth.

Drawing her hand away from her explorations, he took her mouth again, the scorching pressure of his lips obliterating all traces of uncertainty. She wanted him. And she wasn't going to leave this bedchamber without having him.

He lifted her off her feet, his large hands gripping the globes of her bottom, gliding her center against his length. "You can still change your mind," he said against her throat, his tongue laving the thrumming pulse.

Her fingers twined in his hair. "I won't."

"But you can."

She knew this already. But even the fact that he said it—cemented it—made her heart flutter.

"You're smiling again, aren't you," he accused, nipping her collarbone through the thin cambric.

"No," she lied, smiling wider.

When he raised his head and caught her, he groaned. Sliding a hand to her nape, he took her mouth again. His kiss was feral. Gone was the patient man, still holding on to control. Taking his place was the unrestrained Jasper, who was finally willing to seize what he wanted. And she thrilled at the knowledge that she'd made him this way.

Never leaving her lips, he walked her deeper into the room until the backs of her calves brushed the black-lacquered footboard. After setting her down on a velvety soft coverlet the color of midnight, he briefly drew away to reach back with both hands and pull his shirtsleeves over his head, tossing them carelessly to the floor. Then he was back again, licking into her mouth.

She barely had time to marvel at his body as she shifted

up to her knees. But, oh, when she laid her hands on him, skin to skin, exploring the muscles along his arms and chest with greedy fascination, she could scarcely catch her breath.

Her overeager examination caused her fingernails to accidentally bite into the thick cording of his broad shoulders. An apology was on the tip of her tongue. But before she could draw back to utter it, he issued a low animal purr of pleasure, his grip tightening on her, encouraging her.

"I love your hands on me," he said, his voice rough against her throat. "And your scent . . . I want it all over me."

In that moment she understood when she'd started to fall in love with him. From the very beginning, he made her feel wanted and desired for who she was. He didn't see her as lacking some fundamental quality. Instead, he shined a light on all the parts of her that she thought were either deficient or flawed and he made her see herself as whole. As if she'd never been lacking in the first place.

She wanted to be the person who did the same for him.

"Tell me what you like," she said, peppering kisses against his hair, his temple, his brow. "I need to know how to please you."

"You already are. Just by being you. Just by being here." His big hands traveled up from her waist to the warm space beneath the curve of her breasts as his open mouth followed the line of her clavicle. And when he reached the cord that held her nightdress in place, he freed the knot with his teeth.

She felt the tug of it all the way to her core. And when he found her breast, she gasped, her fingers flying to his hair. The heat of his mouth engulfed her, the sweet suction almost too much.

"I cannot tell you how often I've thought of having you here," he said, his breath feathering over the damp, tender flesh, making it pucker in the cool air. Fiery licks of his tongue charted a path to the other side, where he plumped the swell in his hands like a ripe fruit ready for the feast. "All the wicked things I've dreamed of doing."

Her lips parted when he took her into his mouth but no sound emerged. The pleasure was too intense. Her insides went up in flames, burning everything down into a molten liquid that pooled between her thighs where her body pulsed in a wanton rhythm.

But she wanted more. Wanted to be closer. Even though her mother's play had been embarrassingly informative, there was one thing she'd neglected to mention. The ache. The yearning to be so close they would share the same skin.

Thea needed to feel his flesh on hers. Now. This instant.

Drawing his mouth up to hers, she shucked out of her nightdress, slipping her arms free and letting the cambric pool around her bent knees on the mattress. She felt the hitch in his breath, the tremor in his hands as he touched the bare skin of her waist, her hips, skimming fingers down her thighs and up along the inner softness. Her breath caught as he cupped her, a bold, possessive gesture.

"You're wet. For me," he growled, nipping along her jaw as a flush of heat suffused her skin. "I still think about the taste of you. All the time. And I just need you to let me . . ."

She wasn't sure she was completely in control as she nodded without thinking. Before any trepidations could form in her mind, she let him tip her backward on the bed and strip away the nightdress, tossing it aside.

A low, guttural sound left him as he gazed at her body, the greedy intensity making her squirm.

Something had changed in him. The bashful man who was all apologetic and reluctant to have her in his flat now looked at her as if he was half feral, half starved, and she was the meal he intended to devour.

A shiver rolled over her, gooseflesh prickling her skin.

"You cold?" he asked, his voice husky.

She had no doubt that he would stop to light a fire in the hearth if she asked. But stopping was the last thing she wanted to do.

Mutely, she shook her head.

His attention never wavered. Even in only the faint flicker of a single candle flame, he was wholly attuned to her. He missed no detail, not her ticklish response to the graze of his knuckles along her insteps or the catch in her breath as he encircled her ankles.

Modesty might have bade any number of young women to try to shield themselves. But curiosity had always ruled her actions. And in that moment, she couldn't stop staring at him.

Her gaze roamed over those broad shoulders, along the fleece of dark tawny curls covering his brawny chest that tapered to a line down the ladder of his abdomen, disappearing beneath the waist of his trousers to the thick shape—

"The way you look at me . . . it takes every ounce of restraint not to . . ." He swallowed and gripped himself through the fabric, the corded muscles of his forearm flexing. The sight caused a corresponding clench deep inside her.

She licked her lips. "I want to see you. All of you."

He didn't heed her request. Instead, he leaned down and pressed a kiss to the top of her foot, then the other, his open mouth burning a path along the inside of her calf. "After."

"After what?"

"After I've tasted you," he said. "*All* of you."

His hands drifted along the underside of her knees, the light stroke of his fingertips sending a jolt of sensation between her thighs. But it wasn't until he urged her legs wider and his kisses roved ever higher that the previously absent modesty rushed in all at once.

Surely, he wasn't intending to . . .

She covered her sex with both hands. Then she gasped

as he tugged her lower on the bed, draping her knees over his shoulders in one motion.

He looked up at her, his eyes forest-dark, his wicked intentions clear as he began to kiss the top of her hand, every knuckle, even the delicate webbing in between. Taking a finger into his mouth, he gently tugged that hand out of the way. He offered the same ministrations to the other hand, his gaze on hers all the while.

Thea knew that it would only take one word to stop him. Just one. And yet, when she opened her mouth, not a single objection rushed forth.

Jasper pressed another kiss to her inner thigh as if in reward.

Hands cupping her bottom, he drew her closer, nuzzling into the dark thatch of curls. He breathed in deeply, nostrils flaring.

Then his mouth—his *entire* mouth—opened over her, his hot breath steaming her fevered flesh.

A choked gasp left her throat, her hands flying to his head. Surely, she should push him away. Surely, this wasn't part of it. She'd seen the play, after all!

Then he licked her in a hot . . . slow . . . wet slide.

He exhaled a deep hum of pleasure, the vibration so lovely that it made her toes curl. And that was when she wondered if stopping him was a tad shortsighted. This would make excellent research . . . just in case she'd ever want to write a very, *very* naughty play.

"So sweet," he murmured, his eyes drifting closed, and added as if to himself, "*all mine.*"

Lifting her bottom off the bed, he ate into her flesh with the determination of a man licking melting ices on the hottest day of the year and refusing to let even a single drop go to waste.

He tasted her from bottom to top, his tongue spearing

into her honied center, circling the taut bundle of nerves. He left no part of her unsampled or unstirred.

With eager growls of satisfaction, he seemed to revel in his feast and her responses. When he found a place that elicited a gasp, he lingered. Each time her hips hitched, he explored, drawing out garbled sounds from her throat.

Molten heat pulsed through her, quickening deep, driving her to madness. Her fingers were tangled in his hair, her body arching to push against his mouth. She was lost in the enthralling flicks of his tongue, her head thrashing from side to side.

This, she thought. This was how she was going to die. From too much pleasure.

"Not yet," he rasped as if he'd deciphered the incoherent ramblings between her supplicant chants of *yes* and *please*. "Let me . . . a bit longer. I've thought about this . . . so many times and I just need . . . more . . ."

He urged her knees wider, higher, opening her as the blunt tip of his finger teased inside the swollen cleft. As he edged inside, her body clenched around him and she squeezed her eyes shut. He cursed and withdrew, his finger nectar-slick. Then he dipped in again and again until the heat and tingling were all-consuming. Nothing else mattered. And when he opened his mouth over her, suckling the thrumming bud, she felt as if lightning lanced through her body.

Her back bowed off the bed, mouth opening on a soundless cry as her world exploded in a cataclysm of sparks.

He ate at her greedily, chasing every spasm and quake until she was left boneless and panting and unsure of her own name.

By the time she was able to see anything other than stars, she was gathered in Jasper's arms, lying beside him on the bed. He held her limp body and kissed her slowly, deeply, feeding her the taste of her own pleasure.

This seemed even more wicked than what he'd actually done. And yet, as his mouth ardently moved over hers, his hands caressing, massaging and kneading her body until her pulse was simmering again, her opinions regarding a possible overabundance of wickedness swung wildly in favor of it.

As her senses stirred, she became more aware of him, the feel of his crisp hair and hard muscles against her soft skin. Tingles! So many tingles! Greedy, her hands explored his shoulders and chest. She followed the line of hair farther down, past his navel and then . . .

He covered her hand, stalling her examination.

"I need to touch you," she said, her body clenching on the emptiness where his finger had been.

He pressed his forehead to hers, the warmth of his breath teasing into her mouth. "I think that's enough for tonight."

"Don't you"—she swallowed down a sudden rise of fragility—"want me?"

"More than I can bear. But I don't want to hurt you."

If it wasn't for the tremor in his hand as he tucked a stray curl behind her ear and the intense desire burning in his eyes as he looked down at her, she might have assumed he was trying to placate her. "I understand that a degree of discomfort is expected the first time. But I know you'll be gentle."

"I haven't done this . . . in a long while. And I want it to be good for you. I just don't know if I—"

A choked sound left him as her fingers slipped beneath the waist of his trousers.

"Let me?" she asked when his hand shot down to encircle her wrist.

He sucked in a breath, his nod almost imperceptible. She brushed a kiss to his jaw in reward. And then she explored, grasping him tentatively.

His hard flesh branded her palm. He was so intriguingly hot and thick, but marble smooth with a jagged vein running down the length. It came as a tremendous surprise that she wanted to explore Lord Turgid for hours.

Through the fabric, Jasper's hand curled over hers, urging her to grip him tighter as he drew her up then down the considerable length, his teeth gritted all the while. He looked to be in pain.

"Am I doing something wrong?"

"No," he groaned.

She wasn't convinced. "Because if I am, perhaps I could use my mouth like you—"

He bolted off the bed. Apparently, that was the wrong thing to say. And she feared he'd reached his limit.

Then he surprised her by shucking out of his trousers. But she was barely able to catch a glimpse of formidable flesh before he returned to her.

Then the world seemed to grow quiet as he moved over her. So quiet that she could hear the bed ropes creak beneath his weight, the soft crunch of the horsehair mattress as he braced his hands on either side of her, and the combined shudder of their breaths as skin connected with skin.

"Am I too heavy?" he asked as he lowered down to his elbows, his fingertips gingerly smoothing away a sable curl from her scarlet cheek.

Thea could hardly respond. Her senses became almost painfully acute. A heady scent of musk and spice filled her nostrils, making her lightheaded. Every place they touched sparked to flame as if she had a layer of gunpowder directly beneath her skin. She was overwhelmed by the heat of him, by the feel of the crisp furring on his chest that rasped against her breasts, drawing her nipples to aching peaks. He had coarse hair on his legs, too, tickling along the insides of her calves and thighs. And between them was the heavy, searing weight of his flesh.

A small degree of trepidation dropped into the pit of her stomach, a tremor shivering down her legs.

She licked her dry lips. "No. I . . . like the weight of you."

A boyish grin lifted his cheeks, his eyes glowing with unabashed pleasure at her answer. There was an excited eagerness to his kiss, as if suddenly free of the shackles that had been holding him back. Loving him as she did, she couldn't help but become caught up in his enthusiasm.

But then his kiss slowed as she wrapped her arms around him. She felt as if he wanted to savor every moment, his hips rocking languidly against hers, coaxing heavy liquid pulses from her body.

His mouth never left hers as he shifted to reach down between them. A series of sparks ignited inside her as he glided the thick mushroomed head along her slick folds, his thighs urging hers wider so that she needed to bend her knees and brace her feet on the mattress.

"Are you certain?" he asked, a flush of color across the crests of his cheeks.

Her chin jerked in a nod. Then she felt him nudge her entrance.

But he didn't push inside. It was just a test, it seemed, something of a brief handshake between body parts.

How good it is to meet you, sir.

The pleasure is all mine.

At the thought, a bubble of nervous laughter nearly escaped before she pressed her lips together.

His gaze darkened. "You're smiling again. And you know what that does to me."

Unfortunately, knowing what it did to him only made her smile in earnest. He growled, taking her lips again, the intensity of the kiss leaving her breathless and her flesh pleasure-stung.

As his open mouth coasted down her throat to claim her breast, his body bowed over hers and she felt the handshake

come again. This time it was a *rap, rap* on the door before
he nudged inside. Her flesh burned from the stretch. Then
he withdrew, but nudged back inside at once, like someone
who'd forgotten their umbrella. Then he was gone again.

These short visits had them both panting as if they'd
endured a trial of sorts. And yet, every time he nudged,
she received a lovely tug to that bundle of nerves, a jolt of
promise spearing through her.

When her legs started to quiver, he guided them to his
waist. The position pulled more of his weight down on top
of her, anchoring her to the bed. It was unexpectedly perfect. And when he nudged again, he lingered, hips flexing
in a series of shallow thrusts that dragged against some new
part of her that had her nails digging into his shoulders.

"You're so bloody tight," he groaned against her temple,
his words more like a prayer than a chastisement. "I don't
want to hurt you. Tell me . . . if I am and I'll . . . stop."

She felt as though she were melting from the inside out,
her body turning liquid and malleable. "I like this."

"This?" He rocked his hips, the shallow thrust meeting
with hot honey.

A zing of pleasure rippled through her, so lovely that she
had to close her eyes. Turning her head into his neck, she
hummed, "Mmm-hmm."

Chasing that sensation, she arched her hips to meet his.
But her actions made his breath catch, his carefully mea-
sured strokes stuttering out of rhythm.

What followed was like learning the steps of a new
dance, neither of them sure-footed, body parts bumping
together in a way that should have been nothing more than
awkward. And yet, with each clumsy collision a new thrill
rifled through her.

At least, until he drove in, deep, rending her flesh in a
sharp bite of pain.

A strangled gasp left her throat. For an instant, they

both went still, assessing. Her first impulse was to squirm away to ease the ache. But then he began to apologize, his voice so stricken and shredded, that she felt the need to comfort him.

"No, you're not a monster and you haven't torn me in half, you silly man," she said, rasping the half-truth against his cheek, hoping he took the breathless quality of her voice as passion. "I was told that the first time would bring some pain, but that it would be fleeting."

Oh, please let it be fleeting.

He nodded jerkily with relief. "I won't go in any farther. But I don't think I can move yet. I just . . . need to stay still for two more seconds before I die."

His morbid prediction pulled a reluctant grin to her lips despite the discomfort, and she turned her head to press a kiss to his cheek. The words *any farther*, however, caused a tiny jolt of alarm. Surely, there wasn't *more* of him. Was there?

As if arming against a supplementary invasion, her body clenched reflexively.

He cursed and abruptly withdrew, his hand gripping the base of his cock. When she reached up to smooth the damp hair from his brow, he shook his head. "Don't touch me just yet. If you do . . . I might lose . . . the last remnants . . . of my restraint."

"But that's what I want." She propped herself up on her elbows, his heavily lidded gaze drawn to her breasts. "I want you to feel safe with me as I do with you. I want you to lose yourself inside—"

His mouth collided with hers, swallowing down the rest of her plea on a groan of surrender. The kiss was almost bruising, his passion all-consuming as his body moved over hers. This, at last, was him giving himself to her, holding nothing back.

His hand roamed between them, scouting the hooded

flesh that guarded the little bundle of nerves, the blunt tip of his finger moving in heavy rotations.

"There?" he asked on a ragged breath, his hand trembling.

The pleasure that swelled inside her was almost too much, too fast. But after another rotation, she was already there with him, blood simmering, her hips hitching eagerly. "Yes. There."

His open mouth dragged along her throat, until he took the tender peak of her breast in his mouth, his skillful flicks making her arch beneath him as his finger slipped inside her, sinking to the hilt.

"Yes. There," she said again. Feeling drunk on pleasure, she clutched at his shoulders, shamelessly riding the hand between her thighs.

"Can I . . ." Without finishing the question, his head dipped between her legs once more, hands on her bottom, lifting her to his mouth.

He feasted on her, his lips vibrating on a low, hungry growl, laving and licking until—Heaven help her—she gripped his head and began to move herself against him. She was truly wanton now. Wanton and needy. Willing to do anything to feel that bright explosion of ecstasy.

But just as the fuse was lit, he stopped, leaving her body to smolder without detonating. "Wait . . . I haven't . . ."

He came back to her, his mouth greedy on hers, a faint coppery flavor lingering on his tongue. And then his hips pressed against hers, the heavy weight of his length rocking against her slick folds.

This time when he nudged her entrance she was ready, bracing herself for the invasion. But the pain never came.

He entered her in a hot, slow slide that sent starbursts of sensation shooting through her. It was different this time. The stretch not unbearable. In fact, it felt good when her swollen flesh closed around him, welcoming the fullness, the sure, thick thrust.

"This . . . good?" he asked hoarsely, the two syllables reduced to rubble.

Unable to form words as tingles collected at the base of her spine, she nodded. Her legs wrapped around his hips, their bodies grinding together, the friction making her womb quicken, her sheath squeezing around him.

His hips hitched out of rhythm, and the drag of his flesh inside the tight constriction buzzed through her. Her nails bit into his shoulder as she arched her back, undulating on a tidal swell of pleasure as needy mewls wrenched out of her throat.

He cursed, sinking deeper. "You cannot make those sounds . . . It makes me . . . I'm going to . . ."

His next words were choked as he withdrew then thrust in again as he lost himself in a frenzy.

Thea was caught up in it, too, unable to bear the pleasure of holding on to his big body, skin to skin, his flesh driving in and in, sensation building to a pinnacle that seemed to have no end, no limit, and if she didn't go over the edge soon, she was sure to lose her mi—

She came apart on a cry, sparks exploding behind her eyes and scattering in showers of tingles beneath her skin as she tumbled over the edge, taking him with her as he buried himself three times deep, the guttural shout of his release against her neck as he filled her with rivers of molten heat.

And when she could catch her breath, she finally understood why Lady Content was so willing to be ravished.

Chapter Thirty

JASPER STARED UP at the gamboling firelight on the ceiling as Althea dozed softly beside him, her head resting in the crook of his shoulder. He tried not to think about the warm press of her body, the way she nestled perfectly against him, her limbs trustingly curled around him as if contentedly resigned to the fact that she was his, and his alone.

But she wasn't his. Not yet. Not in the way that would protect her in the event that all his plans fell to ruin.

If he'd been thinking clearly, instead of abandoning all reason, he would have waited to bed her. Or rather . . . he might have waited.

Damn it all. What was the point in lying to himself? There wasn't any force on earth that could have helped him resist her. And he didn't regret a single blistering moment.

Perhaps that was the problem. Because he knew that an invitation to dine with the Duke of Sherborne might open many doors, but society's acceptance wasn't guaranteed. The court's ruling wasn't guaranteed either.

Even if Jasper met with the best of possible outcomes, earning a reputation worthy of being considered marriageable would still take time.

And then there was the matter of Redcliffe.

Without a doubt, his uncle would try to thwart whatever progress he might make. For every inch he advanced, Redcliffe wouldn't rest until he'd stripped away the ground beneath his feet. It was in his ruthless nature to take and take until there was nothing left.

Because of that, Jasper would always have to be on his guard.

This was especially true now that he was on the precipice of having everything he ever wanted. But he was afraid of losing it all. In his experience, something was bound to go wrong.

"You have your thinking face on," Althea said sleepily, interrupting his thoughts.

He cut a glance down to the top of her head. "You cannot even see my face from your position. How would you know my expression?"

"The same way you know whenever I'm smiling," she said, clearly smiling with erudite smugness. "I can just feel it. Those little furrows form a pair of Vs, one stacked on top of the other. And when you wear your spectacles they make you look like a professor before delivering a stern lecture."

"Consider them kindling for the fire."

"No, don't." She turned to look up at him. "I'm rather fond of Professor St. James. He has recently starred in a number of salacious dreams. And his assignments are always . . . well . . . rather inventive. Would you like to hear one?"

The instant her lips curved in a slow grin, Jasper's body temperature rose, his mind caught in a mirage of haze and heat. From the impish tilt of her sooty lashes, she knew precisely what she was doing to him.

He blinked, trying not to be distracted by the temptress again. He had a strategy to form, after all.

But thinking was rather difficult with her beside him, so uninhibited with her affection, skating her fingertips in his chest hair in swirling patterns as if her only concern was carving magical runes into his soul.

Even after their lovemaking, when he'd padded naked across the room to light a fire, she hadn't been shy with him. In fact, she'd openly admired his body, giggling when her brazen comments about his backside made him blush. The intimacy of it was foreign territory for him. And, in that regard, she seemed the one with far more experience.

However, when he saw the pink tinge of her blood as he'd bathed her tender flesh with a cloth in water heated by the fire, all his discomfiture fell away under a tidal wave of violent protectiveness. He felt at once a combination of fierce male pride over having claimed her as his own, but also mortification over his roughness and utter abandon. The conflicting emotions left him with the perverse desire to bolt the door and keep her inside with him for the next twenty to seventy years.

He'd settled for tucking the coverlet high around her shoulders as a reminder to avoid further temptation.

But when she stretched beside him, the coverlet lowered an inch or two. Unconcerned by the fact that her bare breasts were tantalizingly pressed against him, she bent her arm over his chest and rested her chin on her hand. Her glorious hair was in a tumble, her cheeks rosy and her lips bee-stung from his kisses . . . and it took every ounce of control not to ask about those dreams.

"I should take you home," he said with a laughable lack of conviction.

He didn't move a muscle. In fact, the arm holding her against the crook of his body might have tightened reflexively, tucking her hips against him. And from the amusement glowing in her eyes, the action didn't escape her notice.

"Or we could hie off to Gretna Green," she offered with a lift of her dark brows.

He reached up to sweep a curl behind her ear. "As much as it pains me to say this, it's too soon. If I abscond with you to Gretna Green now, the Duke of Sherborne will surely rescind his invitation. Then any plan for the future would be for naught. This isn't the time to put the cart before the horse."

"Says the man who just spent a glorious hour divesting an innocent of her maidenhead and introducing her to all manner of carnal delights."

His heart stopped and he felt all the color drain from his face. "Althea, I hope you know that, when I brought you here, I never intended to—"

"I'm only having a go with you," she chided tenderly, her fingers resting against his lips. "Besides, I am the one who seduced you, knowing full well what was at stake. However long it takes, I can wait. In the meantime," she continued, dragging one fingertip down his throat, over the center of his chest and to the edge of the coverlet, "we will have our nights together. And, during the days, jaunts through the park and . . . Why are you shaking your head?"

"Because we cannot be seen together. Not yet," he said, lowering her hand and threading their fingers together. "One hint of our relationship would ruin you and your family. Redcliffe would see to it."

"He hasn't even approached me since the maze."

He knew this already from the reports he'd received, but that didn't put him at ease. "Redcliffe's pride doesn't permit him any personal failings, especially where the fairer sex is concerned."

She issued a dry laugh. "Then I find myself grateful that his ego is so easily wounded."

"But if he knows you are important to me, he will devise a way to have you at his mercy. I cannot risk that. I *will not* risk that."

"If it were up to me, I would expose him for the villain he is."

"He still has far too much influence," Jasper warned. Cupping her cheek, he held her gaze. "You must promise me you won't draw attention to yourself by mentioning what you know of him. Not even to Lady Broadbent."

After a moment of consideration, she sighed, her mouth turning sullen. "Fine. But the Duke of Sherborne had better do his part. If he doesn't profess to the entire *ton* that you are absolutely magnificent and that you've been grossly underestimated all your life, then I shall be quite cross."

A peculiar sensation rattled awkwardly inside his chest. It felt like a cliff face giving way, an avalanche of rocks tumbling into a dark abyss. He slid his hand to her nape as if to hold on, to keep them both away from the edge.

"We cannot take any chances," he said, his voice rough with emotion. "Which means pretending indifference to each other during the days. And"—he drew in a breath and forced out the words—"no more nights."

"None? For how long?"

"At least a fortnight."

"A *fortnight*?"

"By then, the court will rule. I'll have a better idea of what I'm facing. Then, if all goes to plan, I can begin to pay calls on you," he said. "In the meantime, you should act as though nothing has changed and continue on with your usual engagements."

"Such as tours through the park with other men? Dancing with other men? Receiving flowers from other men? *Those* usual engagements?"

He heard the grinding of his back molars. "Aye."

"And if I were to tell you that Lady Broadbent has already hinted that I should accept Captain Summerhayes's invitation to the opera at the end of the week? What would you say to that?"

"I would tell you to go," he articulated carefully through clenched teeth.

She growled and rolled away from him. Wrapping a

sheet around her, she glared from the other side of the rumpled bed, a dark gulf between them.

"Ooh! You are such a stubborn, infuriating man! Haven't you spent enough of your life looking at the world through Redcliffe's eyes? Not everyone is like him, you know. You'll have to trust someone at some point. You'll have to take a chance on seizing the life you want."

He sat up against the bolster, his spine ramrod straight. "That's what I'm trying to do. But one cannot simply launch oneself toward the future, eyes closed, and hope that everything will turn out for the best. It's better to be prepared for the worst."

"Safer, you mean," she argued.

"Fine. Call it safer, if you must. Because I don't know how I can keep you safe if my reputation is good for nothing."

At his declaration, her thunder faded as swiftly as a summer storm—all wind and bluster one minute, all soft air and sighs the next.

"Oh, Jasper," she breathed, her heart in her eyes. Slowly, she hiked up the sheet and crawled over to him, her hands cupping the sides of his face. "I love you so much. But preparing for the worst doesn't alter the outcome. It only takes away the wonder in every moment we spend together. And if you walk into Sherborne's dinner, waiting for an attack, you'll never let down your guard and he'll never meet the real Jasper Trueblood, Viscount St. James. And that would be a detriment to you both."

His hand covered hers, his gaze imploring. "I cannot lower my guard with people I don't know."

"You did with me."

"Only because you cast some sort of spell on me," he grumbled.

"Well, I will tell you this. The Duke of Sherborne was one of the few gentlemen who remained friends with my father after the scandal. I think that speaks well of his character. And if you are nervous about your dinner with him, perhaps an evening at the opera . . ." As soon as he opened his mouth to object to escorting her to the opera for all the reasons he already mentioned, she pressed a finger to his lips. "Not to attend with me. But the Earl of Dovermere has a box beside Lady Broadbent's. He was also a friend to my father, and his daughter was a friend to me in our first Season. I could ask for an invitation."

"It just so happens that Dovermere has already issued an invitation. It sits among the mountain atop my desk—a mountain I have no intention of scaling."

"You are such a curmudgeon when you want to be," she groused, crossing her arms beneath her breasts. "You've relied on David and Nan, Roly and Mr. Pitt, and a number of others who've kept your secret. I don't understand why you're so determined to stay away from me for an entire fortnight when it might benefit your standing with the courts if they see that you desire to settle down with a wife."

His shoulders relaxed marginally on an exhale. "So that's what all this is about."

"It just doesn't make sense that, after tonight, you wouldn't want to see me."

Not want to see her? He wanted her with an intensity that frightened him. He didn't know what to do with the feelings storming his defenses as if with a thousand battering rams and a legion of trebuchets hurling boulders.

She was his, damn it all! His to kiss. His to pleasure. His to protect. But how could he keep her safe while society still thought of him as an ape and buffoon?

Pulling her onto his lap, he lowered his forehead to hers. "I'm asking you to trust me until I establish my reputation. A fortnight of indifference should keep you safe from"— Redcliffe, he thought—"wagging tongues."

"I don't care about any of that. All I want is you, just as you are."

She was asking him to try, to give his trust to a man he didn't know. To put his fate in someone else's hands. But he couldn't.

Althea pressed her lips to his, soft, beseeching. The warmth of her kiss lingered long after she eased back, as if she'd left a hot ember in his mouth. He swallowed it down, feeling it scorch a path along the tissue of his throat to the center of his chest, setting fire to the toughened walls that surrounded his heart.

He feared that it wouldn't stop until every layer burned away and left him exposed. Vulnerable in a way he hadn't been in a very long time. And with a man like Redcliffe standing in the way of everything Jasper wanted, he couldn't afford to be vulnerable.

"It has to be this way," he said.

She sighed. "And it won't bother you at all to see me with Summerhayes?"

Actually, it was killing him. But admitting to that would hardly help the situation. After tonight both his life, and hers, depended upon him making a favorable impression.

He crooked a finger beneath her chin. "Just don't run off to Gretna Green with him, hmm?"

She pursed her lips as if thinking about it. Then the imp looked up at him through the veil of those sooty lashes. "I won't . . . However, if I'm not going to see you for all that time, then I want something in return."

"I would give you anything," he said without hesitation.

She grinned, her teeth sinking into her bottom lip. "Then I want to explore."

"What do you mean?" He eyed her warily.

Instead of responding, she wiggled down his body, lowering the coverlet inch by inch, pressing kisses long the way.

"I don't think that's a good—" His words stalled when she unleashed her weapon, beaming up at him. "You're not playing fair."

Staring holes through the ceiling, he ordered his body not to respond. Nothing would come of her exploration. He certainly wasn't a cad who would use her delicate flesh again so soon.

"You're ticklish," she declared with bright triumph as if she'd discovered a pot of gold at the end of a rainbow when his stomach twitched beneath the tingling caress of her fingertip.

"Apparently."

"And you have a good deal of hair. But it's very soft. I like the way it feels against my skin," she said as she dusted her lips along the trail beneath his navel.

He gripped fistfuls of the coverlet. *I am a statue*, he said to himself. *I will not respond and lose all control because I am a statue.*

"Aww, just look at him. He's like a little bird in a nest. Not at all frightful."

Jasper made the mistake of glancing down to see her admiring his flaccid cock, which wasn't going to remain that way for long with her lips an enticing breath away.

"And you called him a monster. Shame on you," she chided, clucking her tongue. Then she turned her full crooning attention back to his cock. "Don't listen to him. You're absolutely adorable."

Then she pressed a tender kiss to the head.

"Now you've done it," he groaned when his flesh bobbed up as if to kiss her back. He quickly lost his battle in restraint.

"Oh!" she said with a start as his flesh began to unfurl. She watched with engrossed fascination, then swallowed audibly. "Well, he is a rather . . . large fellow, is he not?"

"Just give me a minute, so that I can think of . . . something else."

She blinked up at him. "Why would you want to do that?"

"So that I'm not like this when I take you home." He

gestured broadly to his turgid flesh and wished she wasn't so close. "Perhaps you should move to the other side of the bed."

She shook her head. "After."

"After what?" he asked warily, already regretting the question when a slow, impish grin curved her lips.

"After I've tasted you."

Chapter Thirty-One

꧁

Thea had known what to expect for the days that followed. Jasper had said they were to pretend indifference to each other. But never before had her acting skills been so challenged by a role.

Whenever she saw him at a party, or by chance while passing the shops on Bond Street, or touring the park with a gentleman caller and Lady Broadbent, her heart spun in Catherine wheels, sparks fairly shooting out of her. And all she wanted to do was go to him and remove the distance between them.

But, apparently, he didn't experience the same struggle when seeing her. In fact, he seemed to look straight through her as if she wasn't there at all. There was no warmth in his gaze. No grin on his lips. He did not so much as wave.

The opera tonight had been the worst of all. She didn't know he'd been planning to accept the Earl of Dovermere's invitation. So it came as a surprise to see him standing just outside the earl's box.

Dovermere had greeted her, Lady Broadbent and Captain Summerhayes warmly, then proceeded to introduce them to his son, Jack, and his wife, Lilah. After which, he turned to Jasper. "And I believe you are already acquainted with my esteemed guest, Viscount St. James."

Esteemed guest! Thea was thrilled. All this and he hadn't even had his dinner with Sherborne yet. Everything was falling into place.

But when her gaze shifted from the earl to Jasper and she held out her hand in greeting, all she received was a stony expression as he inclined his head, offering a bland "Miss Hartley."

He never took her hand.

As embarrassment swiftly climbed to her cheeks, Captain Summerhayes came to her rescue by setting her glove on his sleeve. "Forgive me, Miss Hartley, but I do believe I hear the first strains of the orchestra. May I escort you to your seat?"

She swallowed, then smiled up at him. "Thank you, Captain. I would like that very much."

As she'd kept her gaze on the stage for the remainder of the opera, Thea repeatedly told herself that it meant nothing. Jasper was likely nervous, that's all. And he wasn't the type of man to allow himself to appear vulnerable. So, he kept himself distant, aloof.

Yet, she never imagined he would be that way with her, when he never was before.

It hurt more than she cared to think about. She supposed there was enough of the wounded uncertainty from the past year still left inside her, like a bruise that refused to heal.

She'd expected her relationship with Jasper to change after they'd made love. What she hadn't expected was that, instead of holding fast to each other and facing whatever challenges the future posed together, they were now more apart than ever.

"That was a splendid outing," Lady Broadbent said as they moved through the foyer of the townhouse, leaving their wraps with the butler. "Although, I shall not forgive St. James for his abominable manners. Imagine refusing to take your hand. I wanted to throw my fan at him."

"Please, don't judge him too harshly. He was likely nervous," she said, hiding her own misgivings.

The countess stopped at the foot of the stairs and

searched her gaze. Then she offered a resigned nod. "Very well. But I will expect more from him in the future, should our paths cross again."

So will I, Thea thought.

"My dear," the countess continued, her tone edged with soft concern, "is something amiss? I only ask because you haven't seemed yourself of late."

"Is my ennui showing?"

"You could say that."

When her attempt at lightening the mood with a teasing quip fell flat, she expelled a breath. "I think I'm simply tired. This week has been inordinately long, and I fear the next will be the same."

"Yes, the London Season can be taxing," she said, setting a hand on the railing and the other on Thea's arm as they ascended the stairs together. "I had to wait three years before Pomeroy finally proposed. He only did so after another man's pursuit made him inordinately jealous. And do you know what? Throughout our entire marriage, I never admitted that I'd struck a bargain with that other man. Who, by the by, had absolutely no interest in me, but wanted to make another girl jealous."

Thea laughed. Her first genuine laugh in days. "You are positively diabolical and I am in awe of you."

"We all do what we must for the sake of our heart's desire," she said with a shrug as they reached the top. Then she presented her cheek for a kiss. "Now then, off with you to bed. After a good night's rest, I imagine that tomorrow will feel much brighter."

Bidding the countess a good night at her door, Thea turned and went down the hall to her own bedchamber. Tally was just coming down from the servant's stairs and greeted her with a smile.

"I saw the carriage arrive from the dormer window, miss," she said. "I imagine you're eager to step out of that dress. As fancy as it is with all those tiers of ruffles, it cannot be comfortable with such a cinched waist."

Thea opened the door, the room only lit by a single log burning in the grate. The flames illuminated the cream-colored upholstered chair and the wine table on the rug but left the rest of the room in shadow.

Stepping inside and walking toward the dressing screen in the corner, she said, "Madame LeBlanc insists that smaller waists create a more attractive silhouette. But I do miss breathing. And eating."

"Shall I fetch a plate from the kitchen after you're all settled, then?" Tally asked from the hearth, pausing to light a chamberstick.

It wasn't until she turned with the lamp in hand that Thea saw the large figure move deeper into the shadows. A gasp stalled in her throat as she saw Jasper lift a hand to his lips.

Turning swiftly, she intercepted her maid. "Actually, Tally, I have a mind to write for a bit. And I don't want to lose the inspiration. So I'll send you off to bed and see you in the morning."

"But . . . your dress? Don't you want to remove it?"

Thea steered her to the door, walking with her. "Actually, I haven't been eating much lately and the waist isn't all that tight. If it weren't for all the ruffles, I could likely climb a tree in this. It's so comfortable."

And the award for least believable performance goes to . . . the chorus said.

Tally's brow scrunched. "If you're certain."

"I am. Absolutely. Have a good night. And thank you for understanding." She took the chamberstick and summarily closed the door.

Thea waited a few seconds before she dared to turn the lock. Then, setting down the chamberstick on the demilune table by the door, she whirled around and stalked to Jasper.

"What do you think you're doing, stealing into my bedchamber?" she hissed as he came out from behind the screen. "And how did you get in here without being seen?"

He didn't answer, but glanced toward the window. Only then did she notice the drapes flutter in the breeze.

"You climbed through the window?" she asked inanely, an unwelcome flood of worry rising inside her. He could have been hurt. He could have been seen. And, she reminded herself, he had no intention of marrying her. Not yet. Suddenly every ounce of hurt she'd felt over these past few days rushed through her. "I think you should leave."

He took a step forward, his face still in shadow. "Don't you want to know why I'm here?"

"I imagine it's because you wish to continue being a complete arse to me as you did at the opera."

"The opera. That was a mistake."

She stiffened. "So you admit that you were horrible to me, then? You could have at least taken my hand."

"If I would have touched you, I don't think I could have let go. Seeing you with Summerhayes, it was . . . unpleasant."

"Is this some sort of exhibit of male pride? A threat to your manhood?" She set her hands on her hips, reveling in righteous indignation. Albeit whispered righteous indignation. "Need I remind you that you told me to go out with him."

"Then you smiled at him and I—" He raked a hand through his hair, gripping the short layers. Then he turned toward the fire, muttering to himself, "Madness. This is madness. I cannot afford to be plagued like this."

And that was when she understood.

This was all new to him. This big, strong man who'd spent most of his life trying to protect the people he cared about had never allowed himself the chance to feel. He was able to keep himself apart, to distance himself from whatever methods he had to employ in order to keep them safe.

At least, until now.

Of course, climbing through her window wasn't a proposal of marriage or romantic declaration. But that's what she wanted. She wanted him to admit how he felt about her, and to trust her enough to give her every part of him.

And if she had to goad it out of him, she would.

"You should leave. I need my rest," she said. "But, before you go, could you help me with my fastenings?"

He glowered at her over his shoulder and growled.

She took that as a promising sign.

"Fine then. I'll just ring for my maid." Turning away from him, she slowly sauntered to the bed. Pausing to grip the carved post and step out of her slippers. "After all, I forgot to tell Tally that I'd like to wear my blue dress tomorrow for when Captain Summerhayes arrives. At least, he isn't afraid to pay a ca— *Ah!*" Her taunt ended on a squeak of surprise when she turned to see Jasper standing directly behind her, his eyes blazing. "You frightened me. I didn't hear you approach."

"What are you doing to me?" he asked miserably.

Instead of confessing his undying love, he took her by the shoulders and claimed her mouth. The kiss was hard and lewd, scrambling her wits as he licked into her mouth, his hands raking over her body, gripping and kneading until she had to cling to him or else melt into a puddle at his feet.

"I don't know what you mean. I'm not doing anything," she panted as his mouth trailed down her throat.

"Watching you in that box, all I could think about was what I wanted to do to you." He gripped the satin perched on her shoulders, then tugged down her sleeves and bodice in one motion, exposing the swells of her breasts. He closed his mouth over the ruched peaks, every flick and pull making her body clench and quake, her hips hitching toward his. His grip tightened, steering her back against the bedpost as he lifted her hands over her head to grab hold.

Then he jerked up her skirts, cupped her through the damp saturation of her drawers and growled. "You're wet."

She closed her eyes as he coasted a finger along the swollen seam. "It's your fault. You make me wanton."

"I've thought about this. Being here, in your bedchamber," he rasped as he sank to his knees, tugged the drawstring free and let her drawers fall around her ankles, his breath hot on those private curls. "And I thought about tasting you at the opera. About kneeling down in front of you, lifting your skirts and making you come apart with my mouth in front of the entire *ton*. I wanted them all to hear you gasp my name as you shuddered."

"I wouldn't have let you," she said, still trying to goad him into telling her how he felt.

But then he proceeded to prove her wrong.

Taking her off balance, he lifted her knees to his shoulders, forcing her to hold on to the bedpost for support. Then he opened his mouth over her center and ate into her flesh, groaning with abandon in a way that quickly took her to the edge.

She bit into the back of her hand to keep from crying out in pleasure. And he was relentless. She had no hope of resisting.

Spasms arced through her like lightning, bowing her body as she came apart against his mouth, her throat hoarse as she gasped his name, over and over again.

Then he set her down on wobbly legs and stood, jerking at the fastenings of his trousers, his mouth glistening damp, his eyes greedy on her exposed breasts.

Then he stopped. He just . . . stopped.

Cursing under his breath, he stalked across the room. Slumping into the chair, he lowered his head in his hands. "What is happening to me? I cannot control myself. I thought that after we were together, I would be able to think clearly. But this want, this ache is worse than ever."

Even though her legs were barely more stable than molded gelatin, she made her way to him and laid her hands over his, easing them away. "Why are you resisting this so much?"

"Because I need to be in control of myself. That's all I have."

"You're wrong," she said softly. Drawing his hands away, she pressed her lips to his for every point she made. "You have your friends." *Kiss*. "You have your aunt and your cousins." *Kiss*. "You have Roly and Garmr." *Kiss*. "You have me." *Kiss*. "And no one can ever make us stop loving you." *Kiss*.

He surrendered on a groan, pulling her off her feet and onto his lap, his mouth greedy on hers. The kiss was desperate and seeking as if he was afraid to believe her and needed proof.

She fed him the answer, straddling his hips and grinding herself against him. Then, reaching down, she freed him from his unfastened trousers and gripped him the way he showed her, earning a growl of approval. But soon his rough hands were groping under her skirts, lifting her by the hips as she positioned him at her center. And then he was inside of her, his breath rushing into her open mouth as she lowered down and down and down, slick flesh cinching around him as she sank all the way to the hilt.

This time, a breath shuddered out of *her* at his size, at the fullness. It was clear that he hadn't given her all of him before. But she was taking all of him now.

His head fell back on a curse, his throat tight above the shirt points and cravat. "You're . . . perfect. So bloody perfect."

In that moment, she felt perfect, and powerful as she rocked her hips, a spear of pleasure sprinting through her. Then their mouths met again, his hands guiding, his fingers digging into the cushion of her backside, spreading her open to take more of him.

Within seconds she was arching over him, undulating, chasing that sensation. The room filled with the sounds of their breaths, ragged, gasping and pleading as they clutched at each other, shuddering toward ecstasy, then plummeting over the edge together.

She collapsed against his chest, his flesh still wedged inside her. "Now do you see . . ." she panted, "how good it would be . . . if we didn't avoid each other."

"You certainly present . . . a valid argument," he said, equally winded, his hands still roaming over her bare hips, bottom and thighs, as if he couldn't get enough of touching her.

It was only then that she fully realized that they were both completely—well, mostly—dressed. And there was something exciting about that. Just imagine what it would have been like if they had met in a darkened box at the opera . . .

Her body clenched, approving of the idea.

His hips arched reflexively and a choked sound escaped him. "Don't do that. Not yet."

"What? This?" She focused on her inner muscles and clenched again. Hearing his groan, she giggled.

His mouth curved against her temple. "Shhh . . . If we get caught, I won't be able to linger."

"You're going to stay?" Now she was grinning.

"I don't think I can stay away. You've done something to me." Then he lifted her face, wonder in his expression as he searched her gaze. "Is this what happiness feels like?"

She swallowed, trying to keep a tidal wave of hope from pouring out of her. "I think so."

"I like it," he said and brushed his lips over hers. "And I like seeing you happy, too."

Draping her arms around his shoulders, she said, "Well, it would make me extraordinarily happy if you came to tea tomorrow."

He cringed. "Anything but that."

Chapter Thirty-Two

*J*ASPER HAD NO intention of paying a call the following afternoon. He had never sat in a ladies' parlor over tea and cakes in his life. There was no need to start now, and he'd fully meant it when he'd told Althea precisely that.

But then she'd smiled at him, in that impish way she had of looking up at him through her lashes, as she'd buttoned up his waistcoat before dawn. "Fine. I'm sure Captain Summerhayes won't mind your absence."

Which was the very reason he was standing on the step outside of Countess Broadbent's townhouse.

He blew out a hard breath that puffed his cheeks, then knocked.

In short order, the butler opened the door and escorted him to the parlor. Through the archway, he saw Althea and the countess sitting amidst the upholstered furniture and a sea of hothouse flowers, chatting amiably with Summerhayes.

In the instant before he was announced, he thought of how much better the captain fit into her life. After all, Summerhayes was well established. The men of the *ton* admired him. He had wealth and status. Jasper had nothing.

Even if his plans proved successful, and he regained control over his own land, what would he have to offer her? A plot of earth where a house had once stood? Would they live in his flat with the boy and the dog and Ansonby? Or in a room at the tavern?

She'd talked about a dowry, about a cottage and a happy life, but there was no guarantee. She'd talked about love surmounting any obstacle. He wanted to believe her, but that was harder now when he had so much more to lose.

"Viscount St. James," the butler announced.

Body tense, Jasper nearly tripped on the way inside. And it wasn't on purpose.

Were his feet always this large? Then he looked down at his boot, belatedly remembering Garmr's teeth marks. Bloody hell.

"Countess Broadbent," he said with a bow, and if she noticed he no longer spoke with a lisp or a higher-pitched voice, she revealed nothing in her countenance. Then he handed her the violets he'd purchased.

Accepting them, she inclined her head. "You are welcome here, St. James."

He turned to greet Althea, and she did him no favors by unleashing that heart-stopping smile. He nearly forgot his own name, let alone the flowers he was holding for her.

"Are those for me?" she asked impishly.

Just like the first time, he awkwardly thrust them forward. But she was better prepared and even brushed her fingers against his.

After gathering his composure, he turned to Summerhayes in acknowledgment.

He was glad that there was no posturing and that their handshake was firm and genuine. And as they exchanged a few pleasantries, he could say that everything he'd heard about the captain being an agreeable fellow was correct.

Then tea arrived. And the cups were small. Quite small.

He already felt ungainly and unkempt in his baggy coat. To make matters worse, he accidentally snapped off the handle of the teacup when he pinched it between his thumb and forefinger. He darted a glance around the room, hoping no one saw. Then he surreptitiously slid the handle into his pocket.

Having no practice at making small talk, his answers to questions were limited to one or two words, just enough to deliver information and no more.

Summerhayes, however, excelled at carrying a conversation and redirecting his responses to include everyone. It was clear that the captain was better than him at everything.

Well, after last night, perhaps not *everything*.

An urgent knocking sounded from the front of the house. For a moment, Jasper wondered if a siege of new callers had arrived, each gentleman better suited than he.

But he was surprised to see Barrett appear in the doorway, hard-eyed and out of breath.

Jasper stood at once. He knew that look. Something had happened.

Althea crossed the parlor, deftly removing the untended teacup and saucer from his hand as he joined Barrett in the corridor.

"It's Tempest," Barrett said in a low voice. "A missive arrived, supposedly from the doctor about the medicine for your aunt. He didn't have time to make the drive to Lady Deardorff's and asked to meet Tempest at the house. But it wasn't the doctor. It was—"

"Redcliffe," Jasper growled, fury and dread roiling inside of him. "What has he done?"

"Not the worst," he assured. "At least, that's what Tempest says. And I believe her. Roly saw a fancy carriage with a gold crest when he was out playing with the dog. I had him describe the crest and I rode off at once. There wasn't time. There couldn't have been. And she gave back as good as she got. I found her crouched in the corner armed with a fire poker. There was blood on it." He scrubbed a hand over his face and blew out a breath. "She's safe. She's with Nan now."

As it sank in, only then did he see that the taunt Redcliffe delivered at his flat had been a distraction to keep Jasper focused on Althea, leaving his aunt and cousins unguarded.

Why hadn't he seen this before it was too late? How could he have let this happen?

But he knew. He'd taken his focus off his uncle and allowed himself to be caught up in fanciful ideas about a contented life. A future.

Fool!

"You should go to her," Althea said, bringing him back into this moment. "Redcliffe can wait."

He nodded. But he knew that there was only one way to truly protect his family and everyone he loved, and that was to rid the world of his uncle.

It was something he should have done long ago.

Knowing what he must do, he allowed himself to look at Althea one last time. Allowed himself to brush an errant wisp of silken dark hair from her cheek and tuck it behind her ear.

Her eyes flared with alarm as if she could read his thoughts.

"St. James. Think about this. Your family needs you." She searched his gaze, her hand covering his. "I need you."

Jasper didn't answer. He dropped his hand, then walked away without looking back.

Chapter Thirty-Three

❧

As soon as Thea saw that look in Jasper's eyes, she knew she had to stop him before he did something he'd regret.

Returning to the parlor, she saw Captain Summerhayes standing and went to him. Without even waiting for an explanation, he offered his services and the use of his carriage. Apparently, he'd heard some of the conversation. And when she saw that Lady Broadbent's complexion had gone pale, she knew that she had heard as well.

"Go, my dear," the countess said stoically, then turned to the captain. "Summerhayes, this is a matter of great delicacy. May I depend upon you?"

He'd bowed. "You have my word."

Within half the hour, Thea and Captain Summerhayes arrived at the tavern.

Along the way, he'd told her that he would do whatever was necessary for her sake. And she was grateful that he was so matter-of-fact and didn't try to distract her with meaningless conversation.

When they drove into the stable yard, she breathed a sigh of relief at the sight of Jasper's carriage. If he was here, she thought, then there was still time to convince him to let the authorities deal with the matter. What was more important was seeing to the well-being of his family.

Thea was greeted excitedly by the huge Garmr, his red fur resembling gamboling firelight as he awkwardly hopped from his forelegs to his single back leg. She paused long enough to pet him. And when he growled at the captain who'd come up behind her, she ruffled his thick hide and introduced Summerhayes as a friend. It took a moment, but the wolf accepted this with a sniff of the captain's hand.

Then Roly raced outside and threw his arms around her waist. "Miss Hartley, you're here! I knew you'd come. I told Nan you couldn't stay away." Then he looked up and his smile fell. "But Miss Trueblood . . ."

"I know," she said, leaning down. "I wonder if you would do me a favor, Roland the Brave."

"A course."

"This is my friend, Captain Summerhayes. And I'm sure that he's never met a dog as smart as Garmr—Thumper, I mean. Do you think you could show him a trick or two?"

Roly stood taller, beaming. "You can count on me, Miss Hartley."

She pressed a kiss to his cheek before looking over her shoulder. Summerhayes offered a nod of understanding.

Squaring her shoulders, she walked in through the kitchen door of the tavern. There were fires burning beneath two large pots of water on the stove, the air hot and humid. Seeing Nan and David in conversation through the archway leading to the taproom, she waved but didn't interrupt. And when she reached the base of the narrow stairs, she could hear the low murmur of voices.

By the time she reached the partially open door of the lodging room, she overheard the tail end of Miss Trueblood's account.

". . . and when I spat in his face, he hit me with the back of his hand. I fell, hard against the hearth. Everything went black and then . . ." She drew in a shaky breath. "The next thing I knew, I had the fire poker in my hand. I swung out and struck him on the side of the head. He bellowed and came at me again. And I stabbed him in the eye."

When Thea knocked lightly and no one answered, she took the chance of pushing open the door.

Jasper turned at once, bracing as if for an attack. His eyes were hard with rage, but cold, too. "You shouldn't have come."

She chose to ignore that for the moment and stepped around him. "I apologize for the intrusion. I'm Althea Hartley. You must be Miss Trueblood."

The young woman assessed her warily. She had a mass of hair the color of flames in a tumble around her head and shoulders. But even it could not disguise the bruising along the left side of her face, the blackened eye, or the split lip. She wore a rough woolen blanket draped over her shoulders, the opening revealing evidence of her torn dress, speckled with blood.

"Tempest," she corrected.

"I don't know if Jasper has mentioned me, but—"

"He has." Tempest glanced wryly at her cousin. "Said your beauty was otherworldly and that your eyes were like jewels."

Thea smiled. "He can be quite a romantic when he wants to be. But he can also be a bit abrasive at times." In response, a huff left his cousin. "Therefore, I wanted to offer my assistance, in whatever fashion. I imagine you would like to change your clothes, and Nan is preparing water for a bath."

Tempest swallowed, but hiked her chin. Then she nodded stiffly. "I would appreciate that. Thank you."

Even though Thea didn't know her yet, she already admired her determination and unwillingness to let what happened take away her pride.

"Miss Hartley," Jasper said sharply from the door. "May I have a word with you?"

Thea didn't like the sound of that. Seeing a water pitcher on the side table, she poured a glass and took it to Tempest. "I'll return shortly."

Jasper didn't wait for her at the door, so she walked downstairs and saw him pass by the kitchen window outside. She rushed to catch up with him.

He stopped without turning to face her. Instead, he looked toward the low stone fence in the distance, where Captain Summerhayes and Roly were playing fetch with Garmr.

"Whatever you're thinking of doing, please don't," she said, curling her hand over his sleeve.

He blew out a lengthy breath. "You should marry Summerhayes. He is a good man."

"This again. How many times do I have to tell you, I'm not going to marry Summerhayes?"

"You may need to." He glanced down to her midriff before looking away again. "I was careless. Twice."

She flushed crimson. "Stop it. You're only behaving this way because you've had a fright, and rightfully so. I know how much loss you've endured and what it has cost you. But you've battled this on your own long enough. You are not alone any longer."

"You knew where this would lead," he said. "I told you from the beginning, but you kept pushing. And now, our affair has reached its natural conclusion. There is nothing more to say."

"*Affair?*" She swallowed down her rising dread. "You're just trying to distance yourself from me. It's difficult for you to trust. I understand that about you. But you must know that you did all you could. You even had men watching him."

"It wasn't enough. I allowed myself to become distracted."

"This isn't your fault, Jasper. And when this is over, because it will be over if you allow the proper authorities to—"

"*Proper authorities?* Where were they when Redcliffe

beat my mother then shoved her down the stairs? Where were they when he turned my uncle Jacob into a beggar? Or all the times that he has dismissed a physician from tending to my aunt in the hopes that she would be desperate enough to ask him for help?" He threw his arm out in a wild gesture. "I'll tell you where they were, in his pocket. And without money, no man can stand against him unless he's willing to—"

Even though he stopped himself, she knew what he'd been about to say. The unspoken words sent a chill to her bones.

"Unless he's willing to do the unthinkable? No, Jasper. That is not the man you are."

"Then you don't really know me at all," he said, his voice tight. "Marry Summerhayes, Miss Hartley."

He walked away.

Panicked, she chased after him, gripping his hand. He tried to shake her off like a pesky fly, but she wouldn't budge.

"You're wrong. I do know you," she said, tears stinging the backs of her eyes, clogging her throat. "I know that you don't want to rely on anyone because you've been let down so many times in your life. I know that the only people you trust are those you've helped because you think you've earned their loyalty by doing something for them. But I'm going to tell you something you don't know about yourself. You believe that you don't deserve love and affection on your own merit, but you do. You don't have to earn it. And you don't have to go after Redcliffe to prove yourself worthy."

"Stop." He turned, wrenching free of her hold, his face lit with fury. "This is something I have to do."

"Please don't, Jasper. We can face this together. I'm only asking for a chance to have a life with you, and I'm afraid that if you leave—"

"And how are we to live, hmm? Shall I make a house out of paper? Or will you write a script that we can live in, where our characters have a happy ending? Wait. You have a dowry. Enough for a small cottage," he said, his tone dripping with mockery. "And I am your muse. That's how I'll put bread on the table. I'll just trail after you like a lost puppy while you scribble in your little ledgers and Redcliffe destroys everything around us." He threw up his hands. "You're not thinking like a grown woman. This isn't one of your foolish plays."

She flinched as if he'd struck her, the wetness along her lower lids spilling in two hot trails down her cheeks. The look in his eyes told her that this was no slip of the tongue. He'd wanted to hurt her.

Then he stood there, hands fisted at his sides, bracing himself as if he imagined that she would attack him in return, or plead with him again.

Had she been the same person she was a year ago, a month ago, she might have begged him not to break the fragile thing between them. But she was different now. She had more self-respect.

Roughly, she swiped away the tears. "This isn't who you are."

"You're wrong. This is who I've been from the very beginning."

Her mind flashed to the first night he'd brought her to the tavern, and to those precious stolen moments in the early hours when everything had changed for her.

Althea, I won't allow myself to fall in love with you.

She'd been a fool not to believe him.

And when he chose to walk away, she didn't stop him.

Chapter Thirty-Four

𝒯N THE TAPROOM, Thea poured three glasses of brandy with a surprisingly steady hand.

At some point in the last few minutes, she'd decided to be strong. With all that was occurring, it would only be selfish to fall apart. Besides, her heart had been broken before and she'd lived through it. She would simply do it again.

Though, part of her suspected there was nothing *simple* about this time. And that once she finally allowed herself to break, there might not be anything left of her to put back together.

But she didn't want to think about that.

So instead, she carried the glasses into the kitchen and handed one to Nan. "I hope you don't mind. But I thought we could all use something a bit stronger than tea."

Pausing to knead a fist into her lower back, Nan nodded gratefully. "I just finished filling the tub. My husband sent that missive to Lady Broadbent, and went off to fetch Mrs. Trueblood and Miss Iris. And I'm about to start readying another room."

"I'd be glad to help. I'm not much use in the kitchen, un-less it's toasting bread. But when a girl grows up smuggling animals into the drawing room, she becomes surprisingly adept at cleaning up a mess before anyone notices."

Nan offered a smile despite the gravity of the situation. Then she looked down into her glass and let out a breath, the air settling heavily around them. "It was good of you to send Captain Summerhayes after him. St. James is lucky to have you."

Thea lifted her own glass instead of responding. Taking a sip, she let the brandy burn away the devastation trying to claw out of her throat.

Without another word, she turned and headed up the stairs.

In the muted light filtering in through tea-stained curtains, Tempest sat huddled in the tub, hugging her knees to her chest. The curling tendrils of her fiery hair spilled from a haphazard topknot as she stared, unseeing, at the milky surface of the water.

"I thought you could do with a brandy," Thea said, holding the glass over the lip of the tub. "And then I'll wash your hair, if you like. Nan has made some lovely lavender soap."

Tempest took the glass without releasing her hold on her knees. "He didn't, you know."

"Who, St. James?"

"No."

"Oh . . . *him*." The instant Thea thought of Redcliffe, her stomach turned, fury roiling inside her. She tasted bitterness and bile on the back of her tongue. "You were brave to fight back and hit him with the fire poker."

She nodded, but the hands cupping the glass of brandy started to tremble.

"Don't think about him. He doesn't deserve your thoughts a moment longer." Leaning forward, Thea guided the glass to the other woman's lips. "Drink this. It will soothe you."

Tempest gulped down the amber liquor as if she'd been in the desert for a month. She hissed in a breath. "It burns . . . Do you have any more?"

"Here."

Thea offered her own glass and watched as it was gulped down even faster than the first.

"He didn't, you know," Tempest repeated. But this time her voice cracked.

Thea put her arms around her as this brave woman buried her face in her neck and broke down in sobs.

JASPER RODE HIS destrier as if they were flying into hell together. In a way, they were. One final ride.

He only slowed to turn onto the road leading to Redcliffe Court. Then, out of the corner of his eye, he caught sight of a gray stallion charging up alongside him.

He tensed in recognition. "Summerhayes, stay away from me."

"I'm here to stop you from making a mistake."

"Ever the hero, is that right? Well, you're too late," he sneered, jaw clenched, his hands gripping the reins tighter. "I already made a mistake by not killing that bastard after he beat my mother with his fists and his boots then claimed she fell down the stairs. It was a mistake to let him live after he'd sent her to a disease-riddled asylum to die. A mistake to let him live after he'd committed a dozen more atrocities. And now this?"

Rage roiled inside him, burning like ice in his veins. Rage and hate . . . and blame.

Because he could never forgive himself for not protecting his cousin, for not seeing Redcliffe's plan all along.

He *should* have seen it, damn it all. Only he knew what that monster was capable of.

But Jasper had failed. And while he could never undo what had already been done, he'd be damned if he was going to stand by and let anyone else suffer when he could stop it.

"I didn't know about your mother," Summerhayes said,

his tone somber. "And you have my deepest condolences. But if you do this, you will hang."

"At least they'd finally be safe." Jasper kept his eyes focused straight ahead. There would be no diverting from this path. "I had it all wrong, you see. I'd thought that I could protect them. In actuality that was my own arrogance in believing that I could make a difference. The truth is, only his death and mine will stop this."

A sense of cold finality fell over him as he thought about all the other avenues he'd tried throughout his life, to no avail. He knew down to his bones that this was the only way.

As they neared the grand gated entrance, Jasper felt the old walls surround him, blocking out the world.

Through all the beatings he'd endured as a child, he'd learned to close himself off. To shut out the pain and distance his mind. It had comforted him to think of strategies, of what to do and what not to do, in order to keep his uncle from losing his temper.

As he'd grown older *and* larger, those strategies had helped him maneuver in the world that his uncle had created. Jasper had made plans. *I'll show them*, he'd thought long ago. He'd show all the people who'd never believed him or bothered to see him, and they would finally understand. Someday.

Only, that *someday* never happened.

Then, Althea had appeared in his life. A ray of light shining through black storm clouds. She was all warmth, tenderness and beauty—everything he never dared to dream was possible. And for a time, she had been his.

Althea and her smiles, he mused wistfully. He'd never deserved them. She should be with a man who could protect her. A man who would never hurt her.

"You should marry Miss Hartley," he said to the naval hero, swallowing down the bile of self-abhorrence.

Summerhayes reached out across the space between

them, trying to grip his arm. "Stop being such a pigheaded fool! I won't let you do th—"

Jasper watched his fist connect with the captain's chin. Saw the man's eyes roll back.

Before Summerhayes toppled to the ground, he grabbed him by the waistcoat and folded his limp body over the saddle. "You'll have a headache and a good deal of wounded pride when you awaken, but you'll thank me for this one day."

Jasper refused to think about the captain's bright and blissful future.

Instead, he let the black sludge of hatred fill his veins as he spurred his horse and rode through the gates of hell.

He saw his uncle standing beneath the portico, a blood-soaked wrapping of muslin angled over one eye. The sight was jarring. His uncle's vanity never allowed for imperfections.

The shock of it only reminded Jasper of what Redcliffe had done to deserve it.

Spurring his horse, he rode at a full gallop. Without stopping, he swung his leg over his mount and leapt off, landing with a spray of gravel beneath his boots.

In a flash, he had his uncle by the throat, his fist raised. It would only take one blow to end him. One blow to the nose to ram the bone into his uncle's twisted brain. And the world would be rid of him.

But something stopped him.

Jasper heard his mother's voice break through the darkness in his mind, making him promise not to hurt others the way they'd hurt him . . . He heard Althea's voice, pleading with him to stop before he did something he would regret . . .

"Do it, you worthless buffoon," Redcliffe sneered. "Go on and unleash that rage. I've seen it there, every time you look at me. But you've always been too much of a coward to unleash it. A sniveling coward like your father."

He shoved his uncle back, pinning him against one of the columns. "My father was more of a man than you'll ever be."

"If that was true, then why was your mother whoring herself out, looking for a new husband with your father barely cold in his grave?"

"You lie."

"Do I? Ask Sherborne if you don't believe me." He bared his teeth in a grin at Jasper's confusion. "Surely, you didn't think his little invitation to dinner was because he was interested in conversing with you? Or that he might actually help you find a place in society?" His biting laugh echoed around them. "Such an ignorant fool! He only wanted to find out what you knew, and to ensure that his name was never associated with that whore."

Jasper shoved him again. "Stop saying that!"

"Ah. There it is." That grin dripped with malevolence, a trickle of blood running down his cheek from beneath his bandage. "Am I finally making a man out of you? Or perhaps you need another push. Shall I tell you what I did to your cousin? How much she begged me to—"

Jasper reared back. But he didn't want it to end quickly. No, his uncle needed to suffer.

Striking the solar plexus forced the air out of Redcliffe's lungs in a guttural rush. His body hunched forward, but Jasper held him upright, delivering blow after blow, feeling the satisfaction of fists sinking into flesh, of ribs cracking under the force.

He was so blinded by fury that he didn't see the guards approach. Didn't feel them try to pry him off. And didn't notice the butt of a rifle coming down on the back of his head until pain lanced through his skull and everything went black.

⟿

AN EERIE HOWL sent a shiver over Thea as she stepped outside. The boy and wolf sat by the fence, their silhouettes limned by the waning afternoon light that bled through the canopy of trees overhead.

Leaving Tempest with her mother and sister upstairs, she closed the door behind her and walked across the back garden.

When a twig snapped under her foot, Roland surreptitiously swiped an arm beneath his nose and sniffed before he faced her. "I think Thumper's scared. But I keep telling him that there's nothing to be afeared of."

"You are a good friend to him," she said, kneeling down beside Roly to comb her fingers through his tangled curls. "Sometimes all we need is a bit of reassurance."

"That's what I'm doing then, giving him lots of"—he hesitated, uncertain—"'surance."

She bit the inside of her cheek to keep from smiling at his sage nod, his face adorably smeared with all manner of mud and filth. Withdrawing a handkerchief from her sleeve, she licked one corner and began to set him back to rights. But her hand stilled when Garmr lifted his head and howled again, the sound so low and mournful that she felt the sting of incipient tears.

"Oh, Miss Hartley." Roly threw his scrawny arms around her neck and choked back a sob as he climbed onto her lap. "Thumper wanted us to be a family. Wanted it more than anything. That's why he's so sad. He's afeared that St. James won't come back to us."

Her arms snaked around him and she held tight, swaying back and forth. Though she wasn't entirely sure if it was to soothe him or to keep herself from falling apart. Because when she closed her eyes, she could still picture that cottage where they were all supposed to live . . .

No, she told herself firmly. She wouldn't allow herself to break. Not this time. She'd done that once for a man who didn't love her and she refused to be that stupid again.

"Fear not, my brave boy. I sent Captain Summerhayes to look after St. James and—" She stopped short as the thunder of horse hooves sounded on the hard-packed lane. A sigh that she refused to call relief slipped out of her lungs. "See? I bet that's the gentlemen returning now."

And she was about to give St. James a piece of her mind. He had some nerve, saying those awful things and then leaving. If anyone was going to walk away, it was going to be her with her head held high.

The wolf stood at attention, ears perked and nose twitching as he scented the air. Then he whined deep in his throat and sank back on his haunches in disappointment.

An instant later, she heard the jangle of rigging and realized that the new arrival couldn't have been St. James or Summerhayes since neither of them had left in a carriage.

She stood in time to see the black-lacquered coach and Lady Broadbent's troubled face peering through the window.

"You'd best hold on to Thumper for now," she said, pressing a kiss to the top of Roland's puppy-scented head, then stroking a hand over Garmr's. "I'm not certain how her ladyship will react to our large companion."

Though she needn't have worried that the wolf would have frightened anyone. At the moment, he just let out a weary sigh as he slumped to the ground, resting his head on his forepaws as if waiting for St. James had become too much to bear.

Holding a tight fist around her heart, Thea turned away and dashed over to the carriage. As Lady Broadbent found her feet, she leaned in and pressed a kiss to her cheek. "When I sent word, I didn't expect you to come. But would it be terrible if I say that I'm glad you did?"

"I would have come regardless," the countess said, patting her hand with affection. Then she inhaled deeply and exhaled heavily, the sound far too ominous. "I have news, my dear. Which will wait until I am seated and, preferably, by a fire."

"The kitchen is rather cozy. However, there is a sitting room upstairs—"

"I've always liked the atmosphere of a kitchen," Lady Broadbent interjected. Though, considering how she leaned upon her cane and on Thea's arm, her preference likely had more to do with stairs than atmosphere.

After a careful trek across the uneven ground, they stepped through the kitchen door, welcomed by the sweet, yeasty aroma of freshly baking bread.

Nan's eyes went wide at the sight of the regal countess in her lavender velvet traveling costume and she nervously wiped her hands on her apron, bobbing a curtsy as Thea made the introductions. "Lady Broadbent. It is a great honor, but I humbly beg your pardon for the dreadful state of my kitchen just now, with all this flour and bits of what-not for lamb pie on my worktable."

"A woman should never apologize for her labors, my dear Mrs. Barrett. Men often make the worst messes of everything and hardly bother with a by-your-leave. Therefore, I see no reason why we should," Lady Broadbent said easily.

Nan smiled, her shoulders relaxing. "Shall I put the kettle on, my lady?"

"That would be lovely. Thank you." Then the countess sighed with relief as she sank down onto the wooden chair by the fire. "Ah. Much better. One learns to appreciate a moment of stillness the more one travels."

Anticipation spread like a cold inside Thea. She just wished she could sneeze it out and be done with it. And as Lady Broadbent rested her bones and her eyes, she tried not to press her for the conversation she'd begun outside, but she failed. "You said you have news?"

"I do, indeed. However, I am summoning my courage to tell the last of it," her chaperone said, stopping Thea's heart. "Therefore, I shall convey the first and tell you that I've sent a messenger to your parents, my dear. Tally and Beth are packing our trunks and will be on their way to Addlewick shortly."

"We're going home? But why?"

When Lady Broadbent opened her eyes, it suddenly became clear that her exhaustion wasn't entirely from the short carriage ride here, but from something far worse. "Viscount St. James has been arrested."

Nan's rolling pin clattered to the floor.

Thea gripped the fabric of her bodice in her fist as if trying to hold her heart together. "For murder?"

It seemed to take a lifetime before the answer came. Her entire life . . . and his . . .

"No," the countess said. "There were guards waiting at Redcliffe's estate. Apparently, the earl knew that St. James would come. Lord Abernathy was there, too. He identified St. James as the highwayman."

Chapter Thirty-Five

ॐ

*L*ADY BROADBENT UTTERED no qualms over Thea taking control of their cold and rainy trek to Addlewick. The countess seemed to understand that her charge needed an occupation to distract herself from her thoughts and readily relinquished the lead role during every change of horses.

Having learned much from her no-nonsense chaperone, as well as her own mother, Thea ensured that everyone was well fed and that there was a hot brick placed in the foot warmer.

She was glad that those small comforts allowed Clara time to focus on her daughters. Especially when the rumors regarding the arrest of the viscount highwayman spread faster than ale sloshed from a drunkard's pint.

For that reason, they had collectively decided to push on through to Lincolnshire without taking rooms at a coaching inn.

Yet, even with the frequent stops to change horses and fitful naps in the bouncing carriage, exhaustion took its toll.

By the time they reached Hartley Hall, her body ached as though she'd been dragged by the carriage the entire way. The feeling of relief that swelled inside of Thea was akin to agony. It was so intense that she struggled not to weep when her mother rushed out and enfolded her in a familiar lilac-scented embrace.

It must have been the stuttered breath that escaped that, which caused Roxana Hartley to withdraw a lace handkerchief from her sleeve. But when she drew back to blot her daughter's cheeks, there were no tears. She lowered her hand, her gaze searching for a fraction of a second before she nodded.

Thea didn't know what she saw. Her mother had always possessed an uncanny knack for looking at her children like a scholar reading the last page of a book. Even so, Thea put on a good show of pretending there was nothing at all wrong. She was a Hartley, after all.

In turn, her mother pretended to believe her, directing her attention to the other arrivals.

It had always been a point of pride for Baron and Baroness Hartley to offer a home to friends in need, and the Truebloods were no exception. In fact, Roxana remembered Clara from their days as debutantes. Even though much had changed in the years since, they soon spoke with the familiarity of longtime friends.

In the weeks that followed, Addlewick's local doctor became a regular guest of Hartley Hall, seeing first to Tempest's wounds and then to Clara's health, which began a remarkable improvement. In fact, on the day she was able to walk through the garden without having a coughing fit, she was so grateful and overcome with emotion that she turned to the doctor and began to cry.

The doctor, who'd proven himself to be aloof and analytical on the best of occasions, let the woman sob all over his lapels, patting her back in comfort.

Thea saw this play out from the terrace of the dower house during one of her daily visits with Tempest. Her health had made improvements as well. The bruises had faded, along with the cuts and scrapes. And over the course of these weeks a friendship had formed.

It had begun with Thea merely trying to distract her from her memories. She'd sit at Tempest's bedside, either recounting stories of the local villagers and the myriad of outlandish stunts they'd pulled over the years to "audition" for one of her father's plays, or she'd simply read to her. Although, since she had no enthusiasm for plays and maudlin poetry didn't appeal to either of them, she'd read aloud from a book on horticulture.

It was surprising how much one could latch on to a discussion regarding indigenous trees and herbaceous plants when there were other topics one was trying to avoid.

Thea admired her new friend. Everything about her screamed strength and vitality. She was the wildflower that broke through the snow, bright, determined and audacious. And where it had always been Thea's own habit to seek isolation when mired in self-doubt and worry, Tempest faced each obstacle as if on a mission to conquer it.

Proof of that was how aggressively she deadheaded the flowering shrubs that bordered the stone terrace, a carnage of white and pink petals at her feet.

"Rumor has it that those blossoms fall to the ground on their own," Thea quipped over the staccato snick of the sheers.

Tempest paused long enough to shove a hank of auburn hair away from her forehead with the back of her hand then immediately went back to snipping. "Just helping nature along."

Or perhaps, Thea mused, taking out her anger on an unsuspecting plant after the news arrived this morning about Redcliffe.

Apparently, the earl was using his connections to ensure that Clara's widow's pension went unpaid. Therefore, the Truebloods had no money of their own. No freedom to do as they pleased.

After having lost their own fortune due to the scandal years ago, the Hartleys understood that no one wanted to feel as though they were living on the charity of others. So Roxana had put it to Clara that she would be doing them a favor by staying on.

Ben Lawson had been living at the dower house for years, but primarily as caretaker. He never sat in the parlors or took up residence in any of the bedchambers. He lived in an apartment above the stables and saw to the horses. But the dower house needed a woman's touch. And ever since Mother had begun painting again, she didn't have time to ensure the drapes and linens were in good condition, not to mention the furniture.

It was all true, for the most part. And Clara was grateful to be of service to her friend.

Tempest, on the other hand, didn't take the alteration in their circumstances well. But Thea couldn't fault her.

Though, thankfully, before every single blossom in the garden met an early demise, Iris emerged onto the terrace and offered a welcome distraction.

"Good morning, Thea," Iris said with an ear-to-ear grin, practically bursting from her skin with excitement. "I'm ready for my first riding lesson. What do you think?"

She twirled, testing out the flare of the riding costume that Tally had altered from among those in the attic trunks. The maid had been more than willing to volunteer for the responsibility of adding to her duties by seeing to Thea and the Truebloods, especially since that provided her the opportunity to see Mr. Lawson more often.

"I think you look the very picture of a riding master," Thea offered.

There was no mistaking that Iris had blossomed during her time with them. Gone was the shy girl she'd been four weeks ago, and in stepped a vibrant young woman, eager to fill each and every moment with something new and thrilling.

"Mother is worried that I will fall, but then Tally assured her that Mr. Lawson would never let that happen."

Thea didn't bother to mention that Tally was a bit biased when it came to matters of Mr. Lawson's magnificence.

"Mr. Lawson is quite skilled with the horses. He gave me my first riding lesson, too."

After the scandal, hiring a riding master had been a luxury the Hartleys hadn't been able to afford. In Thea's opinion, this further cemented the sense of kinship she'd found with the sisters. Which helped to lessen the feeling of how pathetic she was for desperately hoping to hear their stories and shared memories of Jasper whenever she popped in for a visit.

Masochist, thy name is Althea, the chorus taunted.

They weren't wrong.

Iris gave another twirl, losing her hat in the process. Tempest was there to pick it up and carefully brushed the dust from the crown and brim. Then she perched the hat on her sister's head.

"You need to be more careful," she said, anchoring the hat with a sturdy pin. "Mother is right to be worried."

Iris rolled her eyes as her sister fussed with errant pale blond curls, tucking them in place. "If you're finished, Mother Hen . . ."

"Just be—"

"Careful. I know," Iris said with exasperation. She paused long enough to buss her sister's cheek and wave at Thea before she gamboled off toward the stables.

In an effort to reassure Tempest, Thea turned to her. "Mr. Lawson truly is an exceptional teacher. He won't let anything happen to her."

"He's still a stranger to me, so I'll reserve the right to decide for myself, if it's all the same to you," she shot back. Then, almost at once, she sighed. "My apologies. I don't mean to be so testy. My anger is a pot that boils over when I least expect it. And after the letters this morning, there seems to be no turning down the flame."

Thea held her breath. *Letters* meant that there was more

than just the one from their solicitor. "You had news from your cousin?"

Tempest slid her a pitying glance. "He still hasn't asked about you. I'm sorry."

"It doesn't matter," she said, ignoring the crack in her voice. "He made himself perfectly clear when he told me to marry another man. I suspect he wanted me to be certain of his utter lack of regard."

"My cousin has a peculiar way of trying to protect himself. He closes himself off and refuses to feel anything."

Thea nodded in a spectacular display of understanding when, in actuality, nothing made sense anymore. She loved him and she thought she'd meant something to him as well. But what if all of it was just a fiction she'd created?

The tide of emotions she repeatedly tamped down threatened to rise up again, her throat raw and tight around the swell. It was happening more frequently of late, and the effort to restrain it was taking a toll. She felt as though she were choking, and a strangled cough seized her then.

"What is it? Are you unwell?" Tempest laid a hand on her shoulder.

It took a moment, but Thea forced herself to drag in a steadying breath. "Just swallowed an insect. I'll be fine."

That made Tempest laugh and she went back to pruning. And as Thea returned to the main house, she wondered how many times people lied to each other and to themselves when they said everything was fine.

―❦―

IT WAS A warm spring afternoon, the sky dotted with cotton fluff when Thea's sisters arrived. First came Verity with her husband, Magnus, and their rambunctious two-year-old son, Alexander, in tow. Followed shortly by Honoria with her husband, Oscar, and her hugely swollen belly.

The following day, as was the habit when they'd all lived beneath the same roof, they gathered in the morning room for tea.

"I'm positively enormous, not to mention hot all of the time," Honoria said, wisps of pale blond hair clinging to her cheeks as she lowered herself down onto the cream-colored settee. "Oscar says I'm glowing, but I'm sure he actually means that I'm the size of the sun. Soon, planets will begin to orbit me."

"I remember comparing myself to an elephant when I was carrying you and"—Mother paused, a wan smile on her lips—"your brother."

Honoria reached out and clasped her hand. "If it's a boy, we'd like to name him after Ernest . . . unless that would be too painful."

"No. I think that is a wonderful way to remember him," Mother said with tears shimmering in her eyes. "I'd like that."

Verity smiled softly as she poured the tea. Her dark blond hair was in a haphazard twist at the nape of her neck ever since she and Magnus had returned from their *walk* by the river. "I remember when Ernest used to smuggle toads into the nursery."

"And Grandmother pinching one by the foot as she carried it down the stairs, regal as a queen," Honoria added with a laugh, absently rubbing a hand over her midriff.

As they continued to speak of their memories of the brother and grandparents that Thea had never known, her thoughts drifted to the play she'd tried to write last year, when no words would come.

It was to have been about a ghost of a girl who had never been born because of the brother who had lived. Unwanted, her spirit had been cursed to wander in the ether surrounding the family, existing as a shadow that watched the parents live happily with the four children that they'd always wanted.

Your doldrums are showing, her chorus chided.

Thea took a sip of tepid tea, hoping it would numb everything inside her.

She loved her parents and siblings dearly, and would always cherish the memories she had of growing up in this house. But this house wasn't the same.

The feeling inside her was like a wound scabbing over, not yet a scar. It pulled at the skin around the edges. Not unbearable, just tight and itchy with a sense that, underneath, a different skin would emerge.

She wondered how long it would take to finally heal. Wondered when the wound would no longer be red and sore to the touch, the ache underneath too raw and tender to be exposed.

The only thing she knew for certain was that she couldn't heal at Hartley Hall when her thoughts were still tethered to a dream of a cottage with the man she loved.

But that life she'd imagined was a fool's fancy.

Regardless, she would have to find somewhere to belong, and the sooner the better. Because her courses were late. A fortnight late, in fact. And because it had been a month to the day since she'd last been with Jasper, she was fairly certain that she was with child.

Thankfully, no one knew. Yet.

Tally hadn't even noticed. She'd had her head in the clouds from the first moment that she saw Mr. Lawson wave at her from down the hill at the stables upon her return. Thea even saw them walking together after church, Mr. Lawson bending to adjust her shawl when it slipped from her shoulder.

She hoped it would end well for them. *Someone* deserved a happy ending.

"Thea, I'm surprised you aren't writing all this

down," Verity said, her violet eyes bright with amusement. "Having all these embarrassing details from our childhood written in a play would make for excellent blackmail one day."

Apparently, it escaped their notice that none of the stories were from her childhood.

"I regret to say that I cannot blackmail you. It seems I left my ledgers in London," she lied but with a careless shrug in the tried-and-true Hartley fashion.

She'd told a similar lie yesterday in the foyer, just after Magnus had caught Alexander sliding down the banister. When Thea picked up and returned the wooden sword that her nephew had dropped through the gallery railing, he held it up and shouted, "Pie! Pie!" then growled, "Arrgh!"

"Ah. So you're a pirate, hmm?" she'd said with quick understanding and ruffled his dark head.

Magnus arched one disapproving brow at the boy on his hip. "Perhaps Auntie Thea could write a play about a naughty little pirate who was sent to the nursery without any biscuits because he slid down the banister, which is very dangerous."

"Pie! Pie!" Alexander cheered, unmoved by his father's plight, and summarily wiggled down to the floor in search of new adventures.

Then she'd told her lie about the ledgers to her brother-in-law before he went off in pursuit of the little brigand. Though, not for the first time, she wondered if being a playwright was the only way she'd ever fit in with her family. The only way she'd found acceptance.

But if she never wrote again, then where would that leave her?

"Dearest," Honoria began, pulling her back into the morning room. Seeing her sister's all-too perceptive gaze studying her from across the low table, Thea went still, sure that every emotion she'd been trying to subdue was on display. "If you're not going to eat that cake, I'll take it off your hands."

A breath of relief left her.

"Of course. I'm not even hungry." Standing, she passed the plate to her sister. "And I promised to visit Tempest, so I'll just walk to the dower house."

She left without another word, knowing that they didn't need her to continue on with their reminiscences.

As she stepped out onto the back terrace, her gaze settled on the family stage.

The Pit, as they called it, was an amphitheater that Truman had designed to blend perfectly with the natural landscape of rock and hill. It had demilune tiers carved into the escarpment for seating across from a stage, which was inlaid with stone in a pattern that resembled a great eye.

For most of her life, it had been a place of plays and family laughter. But now it seemed nothing more than a painful reminder of her failings.

Her father was currently holding a rehearsal for *Twelfth Night*, the villagers garbed in various gowns and pantaloons. Upon seeing her, he raised his hand and waved. "Care to join in, poppet?"

Thea shook her head and pointed toward the dower house.

After passing through the budding rose garden, she climbed the hill, walking beneath the canopy of a shade tree, the leaves rustling in a warm breeze that promised summer. As the path took her down beyond the stables, her thoughts drifted to Jasper.

She knew the post had come today, just as she knew that there'd been nothing for her. He never responded to the letters she sent.

Perhaps one of the reasons she visited the Truebloods so often was a way to cling to the last threads of what she'd had with Jasper. But she needed something to hold on to, just one little thing.

The white glazed door of the dower house stood ajar as the servants carried out the rugs for beating, so Thea let herself in.

Knowing that Clara favored the west parlor so that she could watch Iris's riding lessons, Thea moved down the hall in that direction. As she neared, she overheard the murmurings of a conversation.

"According to Jasper, the date of the trial has not been set," Clara said with the same hope that Thea clung to threaded through her voice. "I have a good feeling about this barrister of his."

A frustrated feminine growl answered. "The only reason he hasn't stood trial is likely because that bastard earl is compiling evidence against him!"

"Tempest!"

Her hollow laugh echoed out of the room. "You're reprimanding me for my language? I've a mind to call him far worse."

"Just put him out of your mind."

"How can I when it's my fault that Jasper is facing transportation . . . or worse?"

Thea's step faltered, her lungs constricting as her hand flew to her throat. She didn't want to think about the *or worse*. She'd spent weeks swallowing down the fear of *or worse*.

"But it isn't your fault, my dear. Jasper made a choice. He only wanted to protect you. To protect us all. That's what he does for those he loves."

"I know that," Tempest said, her voice rising. "But I thought Thea would have talked sense into him. I thought he would have stayed for her sake. I thought that he loved her enough to—" She broke off at the creak of the floorboard and turned to the doorway. Then her face lost all color. "Thea, I didn't know you were there."

Wanting to be anywhere else, Thea shook her head and backed away, her vision blurring around the edges.

As she ran out of the dower house, choking on devastation, the final but most fragile thing she'd been holding on to fractured.

Chapter Thirty-Six

🙟

JASPER STOOD IN the shadows of his cell, avoiding the bleak rectangle of light bleeding in through a high window in the stone wall. Every time he felt the warmth on his skin, it reminded him of Althea.

Althea and her smiles. He would go to his grave thinking about them.

Redcliffe had known exactly what he'd do. He'd counted on his nephew driving to his estate to kill him. But Jasper had been too angry to see his uncle's ultimate plan to get him out of the way. To teach him one final lesson on which one of them was superior.

He wished he'd understood before it was too late to protect any of them.

Though, it should offer him some semblance of consolation to know that Summerhayes would shield Althea with his name. And she would be with a man better suited to her than Jasper ever was.

He also knew from his aunt's and cousins' letters that they were safe and living with Baron and Baroness Hartley.

The Barretts agreed to take Roly and Garmr. The boy would finally have the family he'd always wanted. Though, perhaps not the one he'd imagined.

Jasper rubbed at an ache in the center of his chest, reminding himself that David and Nan were good people. They would take care of him and, in a year or two, Roly might even become a big brother when they have a child of their own . . .

A child. He wondered if—

He stopped himself from finishing the thought. She would marry Summerhayes and that was that.

A hard banging sounded on the rough wood of his cell door, followed by the jangle of keys. Then the guard announced, "You've got a visitor."

Even though Jasper had requested no visitors for the past month, the gaoler had been making a pretty penny on those who wanted to take a gander at society's buffoon. It didn't matter that he'd kept his back turned to them.

The typical insults he heard were in the vein of "Calls himself a highwayman. Doubt he even knows which end of the horse is what" as they snickered.

Then there were others who weren't quite so cordial. And others still who felt sorry for the dimwitted fool and brought him food. He didn't mind those visits as much. Prison rations didn't quell the hunger pangs.

"See 'ere! Face front! I said ye've got a visitor," the guard shouted as if Jasper were hard of hearing before addressing the unwelcome guest. "Don't think he knows what a door is, sir. Spends all day staring at the wall. Doesn't talk neither."

"Leave us," a man said with authority, his familiar tone causing Jasper to turn.

That was when he saw the Duke of Sherborne, his aristocratic features austere beneath a distinguished cap of silvered hair.

Jasper bent his head. "Your Grace."

"I only have one question for you, St. James," the older man said in his infamously no-nonsense manner. "Are you guilty of the crime of which you are accused?"

Jasper met his gaze and made no excuses for his actions. "I am. I have been a highwayman these past two years."

Sherborne nodded, his expression inscrutable. Then he turned to walk away.

"If I may ask a question, Your Grace?" Jasper said, staying him for one moment more.

"Very well."

Remembering all that Redcliffe had said, he swallowed. How did one ask a duke if he'd had an affair with one's mother? Lacking many social graces, he decided to be direct. "Did you know my mother?"

"I did," Sherborne answered. "Lady St. James was a fine woman and a great source of comfort to my sister when she was ill. I am very sorry that neither of them are with us today."

A breath left Jasper. He'd known all along that Redcliffe was despicable. He would say and do anything to wound someone. But it was still a relief to hear the truth.

"Thank you," he said.

Perhaps it was those two words that made the duke linger a moment longer. He paused on the threshold, his gaze quizzical. "St. James, are you aware that the Earl of Redcliffe is looking for other men to testify against you? That he wants to ensure you hang?"

"I would expect nothing less."

Though, in truth, Jasper had expected his uncle to hire an assassin to steal into the prison and slit his throat while he slept. But, apparently, he preferred the idea of his nephew's body swinging from a rope for all to see.

Sherborne turned away.

"But if I may ask a favor of you, Your Grace," Jasper said quickly. The duke didn't respond, but waited. "Do you have any daughters?"

He slid him a curious look. "I do."

"The favor that I would ask is to keep them far away from Redcliffe. Please."

❦

THEA DIDN'T KNOW that she was running toward Swan-scott Manor until she found herself staring at the winged swan doorknocker. Perhaps she came because Lady Broadbent was such a stickler for composure and that was just the prodding she needed in order to put herself back together.

After she dragged her sleeve across her cheeks, she knocked.

The stoic butler was good enough not to look surprised by the sight of her, all red-nosed and perspiring, her hair in disarray, and her words coming out in hiccups as she asked to see her ladyship.

After being shown into the parlor, Thea couldn't bear to look at the cheerful surroundings, the walls papered in bright flowers. So she stood at the window instead.

"What a lovely surprise," Lady Broadbent said, the steady clip of her cane muffled as she stepped onto the Aubusson rug. "I've already rung for tea. Why, my dear, your hair appears quite disheveled. Did you walk all the way from Hartley Hall?"

Thea nodded jerkily, unsure if she could speak without opening the floodgates she was barely holding back.

"Then you must have some important news. Come, my dear, and sit with me while we await our libations," the countess said in a genial manner.

Anyone who didn't know her well might think her tone perfectly normal and not at all tinged with concern. But Thea knew her better than most and she dared not turn around to see that same concern in her gaze.

"No?" she continued. "Well then, perhaps you wouldn't mind if I'd hazard a guess or two. Hmm. Let me see. Could it be concerning a certain captain of our acquaintance? I have it under good authority that Summerhayes has written to you. And more than once."

It was true. Thea had corresponded with Captain Summerhayes. Or rather, *he* corresponded with her. Their letters were not evenly matched. She had only sent him two responses to his eight.

"He has been most kind," she said to the window.

"Ah. I see. Poor Summerhayes," the countess tutted. "Though, I suspected as much when I saw you with St. James. The way your eyes lit up reminded me of the way your parents still look at each other. Even so, I held on to the hope that I was wrong. And that you would not have such a rough road ahead of you."

Those words, spoken with sympathetic gloom, reminded Thea of the night Jasper kidnapped her. "Insurmountable obstacles."

"Quite. And he'll never be accepted in society, even if the trial ends in his favor. That blackguard Redcliffe will make certain of it." Her cane thwapped sharply in disgruntlement against the floor. "I heard the earl wears an eyepatch now, and has been behaving erratically, shouting at his steward in the street. He has lost some favor among the members of the *ton*. So, perhaps . . ."

Lady Broadbent let the thought dangle in the air as if there was still hope.

Thea sniffed and smoothed a hand down her midriff. "St. James has washed his hands of me. He wants me to marry Summerhayes."

"Men." The countess issued a growl of exasperation. "Why don't they listen? No other creature is so determined to do things the hardest way possible." She tapped her fan thoughtfully. "My husband was like you. Pomeroy could get lost in the bathtub. He frequently became turned around on our walks. I simply had to march off in the right direction and hope he would follow. That's the way it is with men, my dear. Sometimes when they cannot see a solution, we have to lead them to it."

The old Thea likely would have become inspired by this speech and moved by the unflagging support of the countess. Yet, in that moment, she felt shattered instead. Because she had tried to lead him and he'd refused to follow.

Even if the trial went in his favor, he wasn't ever going to ask for her. Because he didn't love her.

As the realization hit her full force, it seemed as if her body would split in half. Skin and tissue, bones and beating heart all ripped apart. The ache was too much to bear.

A cry broke out of her, her knees buckling. As her vision wavered, she staggered, hand outstretched toward the settee. Then she collapsed, doubled over as a raw, choking sob clogged her throat.

She couldn't breathe. Grief was drowning her, the tears building and building. But nothing would come out.

"Oh, my sweet Althea. It is a burden to hold the pieces of a broken heart together for so long."

Chapter Thirty-Seven

꙳

THEA DIDN'T KNOW how long she blubbered all over Lady Broadbent. But, apparently, it was long enough for her to send a messenger to Hartley Hall.

The next thing she knew, she was enveloped in Roxana Hartley's sweetly perfumed embrace. "What is it, my darling? You can tell me."

The instant she buried her wet face in the crook of her mother's neck, Thea felt about four years old, watching from the nursery window as her brother and sisters went off on an adventure without her. And some of the anguish she'd been suppressing for so long just slipped out. "Sir Kellum Archer told me that I wasn't worthy of a footnote. He called me small and insignificant, and said that my plays would bore a dullard to his grave."

"That arse! He wouldn't know a good script if it bit him in the bollocks!"

Thea wasn't certain if it was her mother's vehemence or her unconditional, unflinching support, but it opened the floodgates.

Then everything poured out of her at once.

"That horrible Nell Hunnicutt had a party and I told a story about a highwayman. The next thing I knew I was covered in punch and in the arms of an actual highwayman . . ."

Even feeling her mother stiffen at the news, and likely casting a pointed look at the countess, Thea still couldn't stop. She told her all about that night and how she'd been inspired to write for the first time in a year. About Redcliffe and Lady Abernathy and the maze. And about how she'd figured out that Jasper was the highwayman.

Though, by some miracle, she managed to edit out the part about being kidnapped in the middle of the night, as well as all the other scandalous bits.

"I fell in love with Jasper, but he doesn't"—she sucked in a soggy, staggered breath—"he doesn't love me. Even Tempest knows it."

Mother drew back to smooth the damp, straggling hair from her cheeks. "Tempest doesn't believe that for a moment. She came by to apologize and was positively devastated that you overheard her angry tirade."

"But I know the truth," Thea lamented. "You didn't see him. His eyes were so cold and stony. It was as though he'd closed himself off from me irrevocably. And the things he said . . ."

The memory lodged in her throat like thorns digging into the tender lining, refusing to let her finish.

Lady Broadbent handed her a cup of tea, a soft smile on her lips. "Surely, you understand a nature that bends toward isolation."

Taking the saucer, Thea gazed pensively down into the dark amber liquid. "It's true. He does have a tendency to handle matters on his own. But if you knew the terrible treatment he has endured, then you would see that he had no other choice."

"No, my dear. I was referring to you."

"To me?"

The countess shared a look with Roxana and, this time, it was her mother who smiled. "Yes, my darling daughter. Apparently you have that trait in common with him. And," she added more somberly, "with me.

"When I was a girl, my parents demanded perfection in all things. Mistakes were never forgiven, not even something as insignificant as spilling milk onto the nursery table or wobbling when I curtsied for their guests. It made me feel angry and sad and so many other emotions that I could never express. So, I learned to sequester myself. If they couldn't see me, then they couldn't find fault with me." A rueful puff of amusement left her. "Then I turned fifteen and their friends started to comment on my beauty. So I was sent to a Paris finishing school, where I learned how one should behave in society. But more importantly, that is where I learned how to paint and how to put all the things I couldn't say onto the canvas. It was liberating. My parents hated it, and were greatly disappointed in my unseemly display of independence."

Thea shook her head with sympathy. "I didn't know. That sounds dreadful."

"Yes, well, that is one of the reasons I never took any of my children to Surrey to meet them. The other reason, I believe you know, is that they cut me off when I eloped with your father." Her eyes glowed at the memory. "And our life together has been everything my heart had yearned for, even when I didn't know such happiness could exist."

Then her gaze turned distant, the light in her eyes dimming. "But no life is filled with constant gaiety. And when sorrow came, I withdrew into my old ways. I could no longer join your father on the stage. Sewing costumes held no appeal. And I couldn't paint. The palette of watercolors seemed to mock me. My world was oil black and void of emotion."

Thea felt the fresh sting of tears along the rims of her eyes. She imagined the empty void inside herself, a black and swirling mass, sucking in every ounce of feeling and leaving her as nothing more than a husk. She couldn't see a way around it. But when she met her mother's gaze, she saw complete understanding.

"How did you get beyond it?"

"When all the color had faded from my life," her mother said, "I thought it was because my heart had shattered and everything inside of it was just . . . gone." She drew in a careful breath that seemed to have taken years to master. "It wasn't until later that I realized I had buried my heart instead, in a box under earth and stone. And I think you have done the same. Buried the things that are, perhaps, too overwhelming to speak aloud."

Thea swallowed thickly as the truth of those words sank in.

"But know this, my darling," Mother continued, brushing a final tear from her cheek, "time and again, you have proven yourself brave enough to give voice to those feelings. Trust yourself to open your heart to whatever this life may bring, and I promise you that the words will come." She settled the crook of her finger beneath Thea's chin and held her gaze. "After all, you are a Hartley. We are made of ether and iron, the heavens and earth. Everything you need is already inside of you. And it is infinite."

At that, Thea ended up blubbering again like a broken faucet.

By the time her eyes were dry, she felt as if a weight had been lifted from her chest. The heartache remained, but she believed she knew precisely what to do with it.

Apparently, so did Lady Broadbent, because she slid a ribbon-wrapped parcel of new ledgers onto Thea's lap. "I've had a maid prepare a room upstairs, with plenty of ink at the writing desk. Just in case."

She turned to her mother, her brows lifting in a silent query.

"Well? What are you waiting for?" Roxana Hartley asked with a smile.

Thea only paused to press a kiss to her cheek and then to Lady Broadbent's. Then she dashed upstairs as tingles of inspiration tightened her scalp and sprinted down to the tips of her fingers.

———

THEA SPENT THE following week writing. The idea for the play—and for a plan to help Jasper—came to her, like a gift. A gift she wasn't about to question.

Would her plan work? She had no idea. All she knew was that Jasper needed to know that he could rely on other people to help him. So it had to work.

She wrote all throughout the days and long into the nights until she was finished. Only then did she return to Hartley Hall.

Now she was ink-stained, exhausted, pacing the floor outside her father's study, and gnawing on her thumb's cuticle. He was inside with her script as the longcase clock ticked loudly from the foyer, the sound reverberating inside her skull and needlessly reminding her that time was running out.

After an hour, Conchobar Hartley emerged and simply stared at her, his expression inscrutable. And in that moment, her heart sank.

"It's terrible, isn't it?"

Her father surprised her by wrapping his arms around her and hauling her close. "It's the best play you've ever written, and one of the best I've ever read."

She pulled back, uncertain. "Truly? You're not just saying that because you're my father and you've taught me far too much about theatrical poisons and fear that I will put that knowledge to use?"

"No." He held her face in his hands. "You, my daughter, are a brilliant playwright."

She took a moment to soak that in. It had felt good when she'd written it. "Thank you."

"You never have to thank me," he said, standing apart to chafe his hands together. "All you have to do is tell me what we're going to do with this gem. I know I've offered before and you've refused my help, breaking my heart in the process," he added with his signature flair for dramatics. "But I still have a few friends in the playhouses of London . . ."

In the past, she'd had something to prove to herself. So she'd refused to let anyone in her family help her. Now that decision reminded her a great deal of the way Jasper refused to let anyone assist him. She knew firsthand how frustrating it must have been for those who cared about her.

This time, she didn't hesitate. "I accept."

THEA NEVER EXPECTED an answer to arrive within two days.

She was certain that it would be a rejection. After all, who could decide on something so quickly?

So it came as an immense surprise when her father gave her the news that her play—*her play!*—was on the schedule at the playhouse. His friend was already printing bulletins to paste on brick walls and lampposts. The only drawback was she had to be ready in a fortnight.

"A fortnight?" She gawped. There were sets to build, backdrops to paint, actors to be hired and rehearsals . . .

"That is all he has open. And he loves your play. He thinks it's timely and he has every confidence that an audience will storm the doors."

She was nodding even before she had any inkling on how she would manage it in such a short time. "When do we leave?"

Chapter Thirty-Eight

᠔᠊ᡐ

AFTER SPENDING OVER a week in London, Thea believed they were making progress and it filled her with hope.

At least, until all the actors quit four days before the performance.

"You cannot leave. Look how far we've come! Don't give up," she called out from the stage one morning as they began to file out of the theatre.

One straggler appeared from stage left and he eyed her guiltily.

"Mr. Samson, please. Won't you stay?"

He worried the brim of his felt hat and looked toward the door. "I wish I could, Miss Hartley. But, and I shouldn't be telling you this, we've all been offered parts in one of Sir Archer's plays. There's fame in that. Immortality. And, frankly, better pay."

She growled. Of course it was Kellum's fault. What was wrong with that man? Why wasn't he happy unless he took everything from her?

Well, she had ether and iron inside of her, the heavens and the earth. And she was done with his games. This was going to end, once and for all.

"My apologies. But he already offered me the part of Mr. Bumbleton in his new play," Samson said from beside her as she marched down the center aisle.

She stopped in her tracks. "Did you just say . . . *Bumbleton*?"

"Oh, yes. He's a dance instructor, a right solid comedic character. The play is sure to be a smash."

It didn't make sense. She'd written a comedy featuring Mr. Bumbleton and Kellum had told her it was rubbish. The play had been in the ledger that had accidentally slipped out of her pocket last Season.

Unless . . . it hadn't been an accident.

Suspicions wove like a spider's web inside her mind all the way out the door as she took her father's carriage to Haymarket. It was high time she confronted Kellum.

She stole in through the back door of the theatre. The familiar path was the same that he'd shown her when he'd said that he never revealed his private lair to anyone, and that she was special. Pretty words without substance.

But she didn't find Kellum in his office. She did find the pages of his script, however. At first glance, she saw the list of characters that *she'd* created. Reading further, she noted that he'd altered the script somewhat—a word here or there—but everything else was hers.

That arse had stolen her play!

She slammed the portfolio shut, the papers on his desk fluttering. And then she saw it: her lost ledger. Of all the despicable, loathsome—

"What the devil are you doing here?" Kellum demanded from behind her.

She whirled on him, smacking the pages of his pilfered script against his chest. "I could ask the same of you. You stole from me!"

Her accusation grabbed the attention of a handful of the stage crew.

"Lower your voice, Miss Hartley. It's just as annoyingly shrill as ever," he said crowding closer, forcing her back a step.

Was he trying to intimidate her?

Well, her temper was beyond intimidation. She shoved

at him to get away and moved around him. And she was ready to storm off, but then something occurred to her.

That was precisely what he wanted. Just like before.

"You came to see me at Lady Broadbent's because you wanted to send me away from London, to make me feel worthless again. You didn't want me to hear about this play."

"You are delusional," he said with a laugh, ensuring that his voice carried to the onlookers.

Thea knew she wasn't. She might have been for a time, but not any longer.

She wished it hadn't taken her this long to figure it out. But when one's sense of self-worth was constantly under siege, it was difficult to see the truth. She could forgive herself for that, and be grateful that her eyes were finally open.

"I see you for who you are," she said, squaring her shoulders. "You are nothing. A void. You feed on the light and passion in others until you drain them. And even that isn't enough. It will never be enough for you. Because, every time you look at your own reflection, you see it, too. The darkness. The void. Because you know you are nothing. Now I know it, too."

With her head held high, she strode off and let the stage door slam shut behind her. She walked down the stairs like a queen . . . then accidentally approached the wrong carriage.

"Apologies," she said, closing the door. Drat! Why did they all have to look the same?

※

UNFORTUNATELY, HER CONFRONTATION with Kellum didn't solve her problem.

"I don't know what I'm going to do," Thea lamented to her father later that week. "I've been trying for two days to find replacements, but that villain has threatened that any actor who assists me would never work in theatre again."

"It will all work out as it ought," Father said, unconcerned as he continued to paint the backdrop. "Pick up a brush. The solution will come."

Thea looked at him and wondered why she was the only one panicking. The play was in two days. Two! Even if she managed to find one or two actors, they would still need time to learn the lines.

But it had to work. It *had* to! There was too much at stake.

"Your mother was always so much better at this part than I," he said, painting a sky with swirls of blue. "Give me a sword-fighting scene any day."

Perhaps he was right, she thought. What could she do about it in this moment? And the scenery still needed to be finished.

So, she picked up a brush. "Until recently, I didn't even know Mother painted. I had seen her sketches, but none of the landscapes or portraits."

"Mmm . . ." he murmured in agreement. "It was especially difficult for her, losing our boy. She'd lost herself in grief. And, in turn, we had almost lost her."

Thea had never experienced that kind of pain. But when she thought of the life growing inside of her—a life that she dearly loved already—she had a better understanding.

"When I returned home from my first Season, all her paintings were hanging in the house. And I want to say that, first of all, I'm glad they are. I think it's important for us to keep the ones we love close in our hearts and never forgotten." She swallowed, feeling emotion tighten her throat. "I wish I had known them—Ernest and my grandparents. I wish that I could take part in the conversations that you have with Truman, Verity and Honoria. But I cannot and I feel . . . like I've been left out."

From the corner of her eye, she saw that her father stopped painting. But she wanted to say all the things she'd bottled up over the past few years, before she lost her courage.

"I realize now that the reason I first began writing plays was to feel like I was part of the family. I suppose I wanted to prove that I truly did belong. And I know it sounds self-ish and perhaps infantile, but I've often wondered if you and Mother only had me to replace the child you lost." Her breath stuttered and the sting of incipient tears burned the backs of her eyes. "And with all that has changed of late, I don't really belong anywhere."

His heavy breath came out in a gust, then he went to her, brushing a blue hair away from her face. "Don't you know, my sweet daughter? You were made from enduring love and hope. Every part of you is filled with it, shining out like a beacon. The warmth of your light has always brought this family together and always will."

Her tears spilled over and she embraced her father.

When the doors of the playhouse burst open, she didn't know what to expect. Was it someone coming on Kellum's orders to shut down her play?

"What now?" Turning, she faced this new obstacle with dread.

Then she gasped. Her hand flew to her mouth as she saw her entire family and half of Addlewick flood in through the doors.

They were there for her. Because they were a family. She felt the truth of it swimming inside of her. And she would always find a place of belonging, no matter what the future held.

❧

THE NIGHT OF the play, all of Thea's hopes depended upon the Duke of Sherborne. She knew that if he saw it, he would understand that Jasper didn't deserve to hang for his crimes.

But when she peered through the tormentor curtain, she saw that the duke wasn't in his box.

"I thought you said he would be here," she said to her father.

"'Time goes on crutches till love have all his rites,'" Father said, quoting Shakespeare as he always did when giving advice.

She threw one of the bard's quotes back to him. "'Better three hours too soon than a minute too late.'"

Father grinned and held up a finger. "'Make use of time, let not advantage slip.'"

"'I wasted time, and now doth time waste me,'" she groaned.

What if this was all for nothing? This was her only chance to expose Redcliffe—or *Redstone* in her play—for the villain he truly was.

But all she could do was hope, because it was time.

Chapter Thirty-Nine

꩜

$\mathcal{D}$UE TO BARON Hartley's connections, along with the rumor that the Duke of Sherborne was to be in attendance, the playhouse was brimming full, the patrons eager to be entertained by *The Knight of the Road*.

The curtain opened to the scene of a carriage bumping down a shadowy forest lane.

Father played the part of Lord Flabbernatty. Mother played The Debutante. Verity, who was never comfortable on stage, agreed to play The Silent Chaperone. And her husband, Magnus, played The Driver while four Addlewick villagers dressed up as the pair of horses pulling the carriage.

And Honoria's husband, Oscar, played The Highwayman.

Thea kept the script as close to the truth as possible. That was the only way to articulate the nobility of The Highwayman and the reason he'd been forced to resort to thievery in order to save his family from Redstone's vile clutches.

Act I went off without a hitch. The audience laughed and cheered at all the right lines. They booed Lord Flabbernatty when he said to *take the women and do whatever you want with them.*

Then the curtain closed.

The villagers, who were used to performing in The Pit, were exceptional at changing stage dressing from one scene to the next. Even Percival, Peter and Carlton Culpepper were there to help.

In Act II, to ensure that Lady Abernathy's unfortunate illness was never revealed, Thea didn't name a character Lady Flabbernatty. Instead, she chose the name Lady Oblivious.

Honoria wanted to play this part because it required dramatic retching. Which, she claimed, she had become an expert at in her condition. And she was quite good.

In fact, she was putting on such an exceptional performance, moaning as though she were in agony—while the lecherous Redstone chafed his hands together and ventured to the maze—that no one realized that she'd gone into labor.

Not until her water broke. On. The. Stage.

When the curtain closed on Act II, chaos ensued.

"Should we take her to hospital?" Mrs. Horncastle asked, holding the horse's head beneath her arm.

"I'm afraid there won't be time," Honoria said with a sheepish grimace as she clutched her middle and doubled over. "You see, I think this actually started yesterday. I just wasn't sure until now."

"Signore," Oscar said, sweeping her up into his arms. "Why didn't you tell me?"

"Because I knew you'd stop me from making my debut as a London stage actress."

He leaned down and pressed a kiss to her lips. "If I didn't love you so much, I'd throttle you."

"I've no qualms against throttling my sister now," Truman offered, his brow furrowed with worry.

"Let's take her to that cot, behind the stage dressing," Mother ordered. She was exceptional at managing a production. "We need clean blankets. Truman, hand over your flask of whisky. Verity, give me your petticoat. And Thea, get ready for the next scene."

She started to shake her head in response. After all, they were a family. They needed to stick together. And besides, her family made up the entire cast.

But Mother stopped her argument before she could speak. "There's nothing you can do. This is Honoria's path. You have your own, and we'll be right here, cheering you on."

"She's absolutely right," Honoria groaned through another birthing pain. "And if you don't finish this play, I'll never forgive you."

Verity huffed, wagging her finger, but there was a smile tucked into the corner of her mouth. "Nor will I. And if you think I endured the horror of that stage for nothing, then think again."

"You're doing swimmingly, my dear. I've no doubt you'll think of something," Mother said and pressed a kiss to her cheek. "Now go. Off with you."

Thea, feeling as though the floor were crumbling beneath her feet, looked to her brother-in-law. "You're on. Act Three is your big reveal."

Oscar shook his head. "Apologies, Thea, but I'm not leaving my wife's side."

She wouldn't force the issue. After all, he did take part in creating the child that was on the way.

The problem was, this was the pivotal moment when Redstone and Lord Flabbernatty cornered The Highwayman and carted him off to gaol. Without The Highwayman, the scene wouldn't work. And the entire point of her play would be for naught.

Hearing the drag of the ropes, she turned to see that Addlewick's baker, Mr. Brown, was on the other side of the stage, parting the grand drapes.

No! They weren't ready. She waved her hands, trying to get him to stop, but he didn't see her.

Her father, playing Lord Flabbernatty, and Truman, playing Redstone, began their lines while she was left to watch from backstage, knowing full well that The Highwayman would never enter stage right.

There was nothing she could do. Unless . . .

She frantically began searching for props. Perhaps if she could find a black hat and a cape, then she might be able to—

The sound of a howl pierced the air.

The hair at Thea's nape lifted and she whipped around to peer through the side curtain just as the theatre doors swung open. The light from the torches outside shone down on the wolf and the boy standing beside him.

She clutched her heart at the sight of Roland the Brave and his faithful Garmr. And she was just about to rush down from the stage and greet them when something else filled the doorway. Something large and dark.

Then, much to the audience's delight and her utter shock, a horse and rider came down the center aisle.

The rider was all disguised in black, from his hat to his boots, right down to the mask he wore. But Thea would recognize that hulking figure anywhere.

Jasper! Her heart nearly sprang out of her chest.

She was too stunned to move, to even speak as she watched him swing a leg over his mount and vault onto the stage.

Then he whipped off his hat and his mask, and his deep voice rang out. "I do not deny it, Uncle. I *am* the highwayman."

The audience gasped.

Thea just gaped at St. James standing there. He cast one look to her, his expression unreadable. Then he turned as Redstone ordered the guards to haul him away.

The audience booed Redstone and Flabbernatty.

The curtain closed. And, she had to admit, the abridged scene worked.

But she was still in shock when he came to her. So much so that she reached out and pinched him. He laughed, flooring her with a broad smile that made a dimple appear in his cheek. She didn't even know he had a dimple.

"Is it really you?"

That dimple winked at her. "Who else would I be?"

"I don't know." Her voice was breathy as she dazedly shook her head. "I suspect I have an excellent imagination. Even better than I thought."

"The Duke of Sherborne certainly seemed intrigued by your script."

"The Duke . . . but how?"

"Apparently, someone sent him a copy." He looked over his shoulder to her father and Truman, who both sketched a bow from the other side of the stage as the crew carried scenery on and off. "Then Sherborne spoke with Abernathy—or should I say, Flabbernatty—and asked if he wanted to ally himself with a man like Redcliffe."

"And?" she said, poking him in the center of the chest just to be completely sure this wasn't a dream.

He took hold of her hand and brought it to his lips. "Abernathy recused his claim. And, without any accusers willing to aid Redcliffe, I was released. However, because I'd told Sherborne the truth, he made me promise to give up my disguise and my nights as a highwayman."

"So, you're . . . free?"

"I am."

She wrapped her arms around him. Then, remembering how angry she was at him, she pulled back and swatted him in the chest. "You broke my heart. You told me to marry Summerhayes because you didn't love me."

"I never said that I—" He scrubbed a hand over his face. "I'm mucking all this up. Let me be clear, I only told you to marry Summerhayes if the need arose."

She huffed and set her hands on her hips. Did he actually think that he could make an amendment, after the fact, that would rewrite history and erase her heartbreak? Men! "Well, it just so happens that—"

Her sister shouted a string of curses from backstage. A moment later, a baby cried.

Thea shot her arm out to point toward the sound. "That."

Jasper blinked, brow furrowed. Then his jaw dropped. "Do you mean to tell me—"

"Argh! What the blazes? Confound you, Oscar!" Honoria shouted before her curses changed to Italian.

Mother called out, "Twins!" And it wasn't long before another baby cried.

With the curtain still closed, Father dashed across the stage, his blue eyes shimmering. But before he went to meet his new grandchildren, he paused to kiss Thea on the cheek. "Remember: a Hartley never leaves her audience waiting."

Tears were glistening in her own eyes. She couldn't wait to meet her new nephews or nieces, or whoever they were. But she shook her head, needing to focus on the task at hand.

The next scene was between The Highwayman and The Debutante with the bars of his gaol cell between them. Her mother was supposed to play The Debutante.

"Drat! You and I will have to go on stage together." Irritated by the fact, she looked up at St. James to see that he was still staring at her, his mouth agape. She snapped her fingers. "Jasper, I need you to focus. I know I did all this in order to have the duke see it and free you from gaol, but just because you're standing here doesn't mean I'm willing to leave my audience without the final tear-rending scene."

When he didn't respond, she took him by the hand, dragged him on stage, and put him behind the bars.

"The script is pasted to that fake rock," she whispered.

Then she signaled Mr. Brown to open the curtain.

This was the part when the audience would cry. At least,

Thea had been crying when she'd written the debutante walking into the gaol to say one last farewell to her love.

Thea said her lines flawlessly, taking inspiration from the day she'd said them in the stable yard. She even heard several sniffles and whimpers from the audience. Excellent!

"Read your lines," she mouthed to him and was thankful when he finally glanced down to the rock.

Then he frowned . . . and the highwayman went off script.

The Highwayman was supposed to stoically tell her to marry another. Instead, Jasper stood and began to pace in his cell. "I've heard news that my uncle has gone quite mad. In fact, a physician has said that his brain has become infected. This evening, the court has ruled that he is no longer capable of managing his own estate and are sending him to an asylum."

A murmur traveled through the audience. It rolled in wave after wave that caused Thea to sway on her feet. "Is this true?"

Jasper—her Jasper and not The Highwayman—held her gaze and nodded. "This same ruling declared that I, being of sound mind, would inherit the earldom without delay."

"You have just inherited an . . ." She couldn't finish. Honestly, this was a much better ending than she'd written. Gathering her composure, she couldn't stop herself from asking, "So Redcliffe Court is yours?"

"I'll never live there. I couldn't," he said. "But it occurred to me that the house and grounds would make for a nice hospital. After all the pain he has caused, it seems right that his palace would be turned into a place of healing."

Thea felt tears swimming in her eyes. "I think that's a lovely plan."

"And there's one more thing," he said. Reaching through the bars, he cradled her face. "I want to thank you. For years, I remained in the shadows, believing that I had to bear the burden of what I knew on my own. But you showed me that I wasn't alone. You gave a voice to the part of me that I shut away." He paused to wipe the hot tears that spilled down her cheeks. "Though I never told you, I've loved you from the very first moment we met. You were in Regent's Park and had lost your parasol on that windy afternoon."

Wait a moment. "But that was over . . . two years ago."

"It was your smile," he said. "It has always been your smile, Althea Hartley. Somehow you opened my heart and I've never been the same." Lowering his head, he delivered his next line only a breath away from her lips. "And if I have to break through these bars to keep you from marrying another man, then I'll do it."

Much to the audience's delighted cheers, he pulled the bars apart, stepped through, and swept her into his embrace.

She gasped and threw her arms around his neck. "Where are you taking me, highwayman?"

"To Gretna Green."

Then the audience shot to their feet, applauding uproariously.

But there was no curtain call. Most of the actors were busy backstage, especially The Highwayman and The Debutante.

They were barely behind the drapes when his mouth found hers, their kiss greedy and yearning. The only reason they stopped was because Roly bounded over to them, Garmr following at his heels, tail wagging.

"Miss Hartley! Miss Hartley! Did he tell you? We're going to be a family, all of us, even Thumper!"

Thea waited for Jasper to correct him as he always did.

Jasper searched her gaze and when she nodded eagerly, he said, "Even Thumper."

Then he spun her around in a circle, laughing.

"I hope you know that you went completely off script

and stole the scene right out from under me," she chided breathlessly.

That dimple flashed again. "Is there anything I can do to earn your forgiveness, madam playwright?"

"Well, you could repeat your line. I'm not certain the audience was entirely convinced."

"And which line would that be?"

"Oh, I think you know."

He nipped on her bottom lip. "I love you, Althea. My heart has been yours from the very first moment and it always will be."

She beamed up at him. "You certainly have a way with words."

Acknowledgments

Writers tend to be solitary creatures, holing up in our caves. But we couldn't do it without the support of our favorite people. With that said, there are a few that I'd like to thank.

To my readers, thank you for all these years of welcoming my books into your hearts and homes. I hope you've enjoyed the journey as much as I have.

To all the editors I've had over these years at Avon Books—Chelsey, Nicole, Sylvan, and Shannon—thank you. I've learned so much from each of you.

To my agent Stefanie Lieberman, thank you for having my back and for the support you've given. You are truly appreciated.

I also want to thank the supporters of the Richardson Adult Learning Center (RALC) for all you've done to help people reach their goals and realize their dreams. The world is better because of people like you.

And special thanks to Vickie, who named the dog in this book. Your Thumper has found a place in all our hearts.

Warm wishes and happy reading,
Viv

Discover more from *USA Today* bestselling author

VIVIENNE LORRET

The Liars' Club

The Mating Habits of Scoundrels

Misadventures in Matchmaking